THE
LAST GOOD
SUMMER

J. J. GREEN

The Book Guild Ltd

First published in Great Britain in 2023 by
The Book Guild Ltd
Unit E2 Airfield Business Park,
Harrison Road, Market Harborough,
Leicestershire. LE16 7UL
Tel: 0116 2792299
www.bookguild.co.uk
Email: info@bookguild.co.uk
Twitter: @bookguild

Typeset in 11pt Minion Pro

Printed and bound in the UK by TJ Books LTD, Padstow, Cornwall

ISBN 978 1915352 712

British Library Cataloguing in Publication Data.
A catalogue record for this book is available from the British Library.

To my parents, Charlie and Mary R Meehan

1
DONEGAL, 1986

The day Fionn Power arrived started out like any other day. Belle McGee was in her favourite place, perched in the boughs of an ancient sycamore at the edge of the field behind the barns, reading the Agatha Christie novel she had got for her birthday the day before.

'Belle!' her mother's distant voice called. 'Belle, you're wanted in the house.'

She tutted but closed her book and, with the agility of a spider monkey, clambered to the ground. She hoped that whatever her mother wanted wouldn't keep her away from Poirot and all the mysterious carry-on in King's Abbot for too long.

Running into the courtyard at the back of the farmhouse, she noticed a strange car with a Northern reg parked next to her father's car. A man she'd never seen before got into the driver's side and drove off down the lane. Belle's parents stood at the back door, watching the car disappear round the side of the house. Her mother looked up, spotting Belle. She smiled and waved her over.

'What were you calling me for?' Belle asked.

From inside, she could hear her older sister, Maeveen, laughing and giggling.

'Come into the house, Belle,' her mother said, 'we want to talk to you and your sister about something.'

Belle followed her parents into the kitchen where Maeveen was filling the teapot from a boiling kettle on the range. There, sitting at the end of their long, thin kitchen table was a boy – no, not a boy, a man, but not a man like her father; he was younger, maybe a little older than the eighteen-year-old Maeveen.

Belle stopped in the middle of the kitchen floor, the oddest feeling coursing through her, starting in her stomach and, like a wave, washing up into her chest before going back to her stomach. Her heart beat erratically against her ribcage, the way it would if she'd run the hundred-metre sprint on school sports day.

She was transfixed by the exotic boy-man, scarcely able to describe him or understand why merely looking at him caused such a reaction in her body. He was tall; even in a sitting position, she could see that. He wore a black muscle shirt, tight-fitting and revealing tanned arms and muscles, and curiously he had a gold stud in his right ear – Belle had never seen a boy wearing an earring before. His hair was shoulder-length and the colour of dripping honey and his eyes were the shimmering blue of flowering flax. He was... he was gorgeous, though she'd never thought of a boy as being gorgeous before. It had never occurred to her.

He looked up and when his eyes met hers, he smiled with a smile that stretched for a mile and lit up his face like a sunrise over a mountaintop. Only then did Belle notice her mouth was hanging open.

'Are you asleep, Belle?' her mother said.

'What?'

'Didn't you hear me? Go and close the door.'

'Oh, right.' She came out of her stupor and did as she was asked.

Maeveen put a cup of tea in front of the boy-man, spilling a drop or two and grinning at him, and plopped herself on the chair nearest his.

'Everybody, gather round,' their father said. 'Take a seat at the table.'

When they were settled, he cleared his throat and began to talk.

'Girls,' he started, 'this is Fionn. He's going to be staying with us for a while. Fionn, these are my girls, Maeveen and Belle, the baby of the family.'

'We call her Baby Belle,' Maeveen said, giggling.

Belle threw Maeveen the most evil look she could muster. She wasn't a baby. Fionn flashed that mesmerising smile again and Belle noticed the cutest space between his front teeth. Out of nowhere, Belle suddenly wished her long brown hair wasn't tied up in its usual untidy ponytail. She felt all the more dowdy beside her good-looking sister who had lovely swarthy skin and long silky hair that shimmered when it swung from side to side.

'How's it going?' Fionn said. He gave Belle a quick glance and then turned to Maeveen. 'Nice to meet yous.'

'Fionn, here, is your cousin,' their father said.

The grin on Maeveen's face dropped faster than a dead bird from the sky.

Belle wasn't far behind. 'Our cousin?' she said. 'But I know all my cousins.'

'You mean first cousins, love,' her mother said, giving their father a sideways glance. 'Fionn's a second cousin, the son of one of my cousins from County Derry – you've never met her.'

Belle thought about it a while.

'I didn't know you had a cousin living in County Derry,' Maeveen said. 'I know our relatives that live in Derry City but you never mentioned County Derry before.'

'Probably not,' her mother said. 'We were never close to that side of the family.'

'But how's your cousin connected to us?' Maeveen went on. 'Who are her parents? Does she have brothers and sisters? Are—'

'I'll explain later on,' their mother said.

'Why not now?'

'Maeveen,' their father said, with a cross look, 'leave it.'

Maeveen frowned and folded her arms.

'Anyway,' Belle's mother said, 'Fionn's going to be here a while.'

'Helping Daddy on the farm?' Belle asked.

'Probably not,' her mother said, not looking entirely sure.

'Is Fionn on holiday then?' Maeveen asked.

'I suppose that's one way of putting it,' her mother said.

'He can come with me and my friends to Buncrana,' Maeveen said. 'We can go to the disco and the amusements.'

'No,' their father said, raising his voice, 'no way.'

Belle jumped, startled by the unusual agitation in his voice.

'Keep your hair on,' Maeveen said.

'Have some manners, lady,' their mother said. 'Your father's right. Fionn won't be going to Buncrana or anywhere else with you.'

'Why can't he, if he's on holiday?'

'He's not on holiday as such, more like a rest. He's been, um, sick and he needs rest.'

'Oh, sorry,' Maeveen said, 'that's different. What were you sick with, Fionn?'

A red dot flared up on each of Fionn's cheeks and he began to fidget with the stud in his ear. 'Ah, I, well—'

'Maeveen, mind your manners,' their mother said. 'Fionn, you've no need to answer.'

'The main thing is this,' their father said, 'Fionn has to get peace and quiet. He doesn't need us or anybody else annoying him.'

'We won't annoy him,' Belle said. She turned to Fionn, who was still fussing with his stud. 'We definitely won't.'

'That's as it may be, Belle,' their father said, 'but we have other people, outside of us, to keep in mind, too. So, and this is very important, you can't mention he's here, not to a single soul – not your school friends, not your cousins, nobody. And Belle, not Hunter Campbell. Is that clear?'

Maeveen nodded and Belle mirrored her, but she couldn't help wondering why her father singled Hunter out.

'Speak up. What can't you do?'

'Tell anybody Fionn's here,' the girls chorused.

'Good.'

'It's like we're hiding him,' Belle said.

'Listen to me, now,' their father said, his voice serious – a voice he didn't use often, but when he did, they knew he meant no nonsense. 'Fionn is not hiding – never say that.'

Belle gazed at the floor, feeling small and reprimanded.

'What happens when we get a visitor?' Maeveen asked.

'Fionn'll just keep upstairs if anybody's in,' their mother said, 'and we'll not say a word about him.'

Fionn stayed quiet all the while, Belle noticed, his eyes following whoever was speaking. He didn't seem to mind a bit that they were talking about him like he wasn't there. A ray of the sun streaked across his face. In the golden light, he was like something painted rather than human, flawless, breathtaking. What was it her new favourite author called men like that? That's right. Greek gods. Fionn was like a Greek god.

'And if somebody comes to buy spuds or something like that,' Maeveen went on, 'what then? We get people calling all the time, even Fr O'Kane and Sergeant Buckley.'

'Maeveen, for God's sake,' their mother said. 'No matter who it is, we do the same thing.'

'Can Fionn leave the house?' Belle asked. 'To go for a walk or sit in the rose garden or something?'

Her parents looked at each other.

'You can hardly expect him to stay in all the time,' Maeveen said. 'He has to get a bit of fresh air sometimes.'

'We'll see how that goes,' their father said. 'It'll depend on how he's feeling.'

'Is he going to stay in the spare room?' asked Maeveen.

'No, he's going to be in the cubbyhole—'

'The cubbyhole?' Belle said. 'That's mad! You can't make him stay in there.'

Their house was old – really old – maybe a couple of hundred years or more. For some reason that no one seemed to know, it had a secret room at the end of the landing. The room was about the size of a prison cell and had a door that merged seamlessly with the wall. They used it as a storeroom and the door was wallpapered over, so that when it was closed, it was practically invisible to the casual observer. In front of the papered-over door – obscuring it even further – was a sideboard.

Belle loved the idea that their house had this mysterious, hidden place that no other house she knew of had. But it wasn't exactly a nice place to spend a lot of time. She couldn't believe Fionn would want to sleep there and she wondered if it had something to do with his illness.

'He's sleeping in the cubbyhole,' their father said. 'It's where he wants to stay. Your mother's clearing it out today and making up a mattress on the floor.'

'We'll make it cosy,' their mother said.

Maeveen had a look of disgusted incredulity on her face.

'If we all stick to these few ground rules,' their father said, 'we'll get on grand and won't have any bother. Can we depend on the two of you to do that?'

He looked at Belle and then her sister.

'You can depend on me,' Belle said.

'Me too, I'll not let you down,' Maeveen replied.

'Good, that's good, daughters,' their father said, 'I'm trusting the both of you.'

Belle's father seemed content. Her mother did, too. But Belle couldn't help thinking the whole thing was all a bit weird.

2

DUBLIN, PRESENT DAY

'Attention!' a voice came over the microphone as the music faded into silence. 'Can I get your attention?'

The crowded function room fell quiet except for a howl of boisterous laughter from a group in the corner, who realised after everyone else that Alma Travers, Belle McGee's boss and editor, had called for hush.

Good old Alma never missed an opportunity to take to the stage, Belle thought, as she nodded to the barman and raised her empty glass.

'Another Morgan and coke, thanks,' she said, 'and a pint of Harp.'

She licked her lips, tasting the sweetness of the coke, and waited impatiently for the barman to return with her order. The night was proceeding along nicely and she was enjoying the fuzziness brought on by early drunkenness. Pity she'd opted to go all out with getting dressed up for the occasion because she was starting to feel less and less steady in her high heels, and her up-do hairstyle was wobbling a bit. Slacks or jeans and her hair tied in a ponytail were much more comfortable but she supposed it was nice to make an effort now and again. And the dress was flattering – it was a perfect fit for her tall, athletic frame, long legs and square shoulders.

'I won't interrupt the party for long but it's time for the draw,' Alma continued. 'Get your tickets out.'

Belle's colleagues began rummaging in their pockets and bags for the free draw tickets they had been given on the way in. Belle didn't bother looking for hers.

The barman arrived with the drinks and Belle paid him, just as her date returned from the loos. Shane Reilly, her moderately handsome co-worker and drinking buddy, was also her part-time boyfriend and all-round nice guy.

'What's Alma doing?' he asked.

'The draw... there's your pint.'

'I was worried she was going to start singing.'

'Don't speak too soon. The night's still young.'

Shane dug into this trouser pocket and pulled out a ticket. 'Maybe I'll win the weekend for two to Paris.' He grinned.

Belle faked a smile back. *You'll not be going with me*, she thought. She lifted her phone from the counter and checked for messages. There were none, only another missed call from Maeveen. Damn. That was twice she'd called that day. Belle had meant to ring her back but, with one thing and another, had forgotten.

'So good to have you here tonight for the *Spectator's* summer blowout,' Alma said. 'The newspaper's way of saying thanks for your hard work and dedication during the year.'

'Here, here,' someone shouted from the crowd.

'Before I get on with the draw,' Alma went on, 'I wanted to give a special mention to our star reporter, Belle McGee. Belle, where are you? Can anybody see where she is?'

'She's at the bar!' Lisa from advertising shouted. Lisa waved to Belle.

'Where else?' another voice called out, though Belle couldn't see who it was.

'Ah, I have you now,' Alma said, her face beaming with pride. 'Belle's been with us for nearly two decades – where does the time go? – and this year, again, she's been a winner at the National Journalism Awards. *Investigation of the Year*, no less. Can I get a round of applause for Belle?'

The room exploded with clapping and cheering.

Belle cringed, wishing the party would just move on. She loved her job, loved it to the point of being obsessed, but she hated this sort of attention. Alma knew that and yet, there she was, creating attention. Belle bore a smile until the racket died down, wishing she could drag Alma away from the mic. As much as Belle respected and liked her, there were times she wanted to strangle her, too.

'Okay, now it's prize time,' Alma said. 'Can I get a volunteer to draw the tickets?'

Belle turned to her drink and threw it back in one go, skipping the mixer. The spicy vanilla liquid burned in her throat.

'Bit early to forgo the coke, isn't it?' Shane said.

'I'm congratulating myself,' she said, her tone sardonic, 'not that it's any of your business.' She checked herself. 'That wasn't nice, sorry.'

He shrugged and turned his attention to the draw.

Belle ordered another drink, a double. She was tired, dog-tired, the way you get when you've worked too many weekends and late nights. Her last assignment had been intense. Come first thing Monday, she would ask Alma for a couple of weeks' leave.

Her phone lit up and she checked the display. Maeveen again. Belle made a move to answer but decided it could wait 'til morning.

*

Belle stepped out of the taxi and into the gentle night air. She swayed on her damned high heels, cursing herself again for wearing them.

'Shane, do you mind if I don't ask you in?' she said, leaning into the back of the car. 'I've a lot on tomorrow and, well, why don't I

9

give you a ring and we'll arrange something for tomorrow night, something subdued.'

Shane was drunk but not drunk enough to hide the disappointment in his eyes.

'Oh right,' he said, 'whatever you say. Sure, you're the boss.'

'Thanks, Shane, I knew you'd understand.' She patted him on the cheek like a pet dog.

'Would you care if I didn't?'

'Don't be a nag. You know I like to keep things light.'

'You can take that too far, Belle.'

'Think so?' She chuckled. 'This is all getting very serious. Look, we'll have a nice time tomorrow night, just the two of us, no mad drinking, no crowd from work. Now, go home and get some sleep.'

Belle closed the taxi door as Shane's huffed face turned away. The car drove off and she watched until the tail lights vanished at the bottom of the street. She inhaled slowly, turning her head to the heavens. The moon gazed down, a shiny orb floating in the vast blackness of the sky.

'Aren't you beautiful tonight?' she said. She thought of home and of the same moon high above there, too, above the sea and the hills and the woods – more deserving than this dirty town. *Stop*, she scolded, *this dirty town is where you live now and where you'll stay.*

For the most part, she was content with that arrangement. Just sometimes, like after she'd had a skinful, did she dare to wish it could be different.

She stumbled up the path like a pony, her clip-clopping heels the only other sound apart from the low throb of the city in the distance.

'Shush,' she said, stifling a giggle. Amazing what you could find funny after a few too many.

Rummaging in her bag, she found what she was looking for. 'There you are,' she said, dangling her keys in the air with a smile.

'Which one am I looking for here? Hmm, a-ha, in you go.'

The keys scratched against the lock a few times before finally finding home. Belle unlocked the door and stepped inside, pushing it closed with her back. She rested against it as her eyes adjusted to the gloom.

Silence leaned in on her, the kind of silence special to a house with a sole occupant – the kind that wasn't merely the absence of noise. She observed a patch of silver light growing out of the shadows, the moon seeping through the casement window at the end of the hallway.

It was then she saw him.

Right there, by the window, indistinct at first but developing form and shape as her vision sharpened through the darkness: arms and shoulders; standing tall; his hair grey and no longer like honey; his eyes, still that shimmering blue. They stared past her, fixed on something only he could see.

'Fionn?' she whispered. 'Is that you?' She tried to swallow but her throat was too dry. She wrestled with the implausibility of his being there. She was suddenly sober, the silliness from earlier gone like a trail of smoke on the wind.

He didn't move.

She shivered as the air around her turned cold, and stood motionless, waiting, for what she didn't know.

'Yes, it is you.' A salty bead of moisture splashed onto her cheek.

Still not a move from him. No glance, no word, no indication he was even aware of her presence.

'I'm sorry, Fionn.' An awful pressure bore down on her chest, making it hard to breathe. She groaned. 'I'm sorry for how it all ended up.'

The pressure on her chest became suffocating. She couldn't bear another second.

She flicked on the light, banishing the darkness.

Banishing Fionn right along with it.

Though he could never have been there in the first place. She'd imagined him, her eyes playing tricks at this late hour and with a night of hard liquor behind her, not to mention all the extra hours she'd been working lately. Because it couldn't actually have been him, right? Because if she'd seen what she thought was him, it could mean one thing and one thing only—

Maeveen. Maeveen calling her all day.

Belle felt in her bag for her phone, hands trembling, heart as cold as a corpse.

An eternity passed before her sister answered.

'Maeveen?'

'Belle?' Maeveen's voice sounded thick.

'Sorry for calling so late. Sounds like I woke you up. It's just you were ringing earlier and – and I...'

She stopped, willing Maeveen to jump in with a cross word about disturbing her sleep and saying it could wait 'til morning. The other end was quiet.

'I'll let you get back to sleep because there's nothing that can't wait—'

'I – I've got some news to tell you.'

'No, no, don't tell me.'

Maeveen's voice cracked at the other end. 'I have to tell you.'

'I can't hear it.'

'It's about—'

'Fionn, it's about Fionn Power, isn't it?'

Maeveen began sobbing. 'Oh, Belle, he's been murdered.'

3

DONEGAL, PRESENT DAY

Belle rounded the corner and, at last, the five-hour drive from Dublin to her childhood home was almost at an end. She clicked off the radio and smiled. Alma had happily approved time off, as much as Belle needed she'd said, and Belle wasted no time packing and getting on the road. She hadn't bothered to tell Shane her plans until she was an hour into the trip. Of course, he'd complained that she never considered him in any of her decisions and had been brazen enough to suggest she invite him to join her. She told him she'd think about it – though, knowing him, he wouldn't have the wit to realise that was code for no chance. She preferred to keep life in Dublin separate from life at home.

Stretched before her was half a mile of causeway road connecting the island to the mainland at the spot where the sea was shallowest. Sturdy stone walls bordered each side, buffers against the waves in stormy weather.

Belle drove across, the water shimmering crystals, the sky above a hazy azure, the island itself a riot of green. A breeze whipped through the open window, tangling with her hair and filling her nostrils with briny seaweed air.

Reaching the end of the causeway, she took a right and followed a narrow bending road. Hawthorn hedgerows ran right and left, overshadowed by ancient beech, ash and oak, all in full summer dress. Glittering sunlight dripped through the foliage, sprinkling the shaded route with pools of gold.

She kept a low speed, ready to slow down for any oncoming car. Noting the houses she passed here and there along the way, she automatically recalled the family name of every dwelling, deliberately ignoring the Campbell homestead where she knew Hunter Campbell still lived. She cautiously passed a man strolling with his dog – one of the old Craigs from the far side of the island. They stopped, man and dog both, and gave her a long stare, the man lifting his walking stick in acknowledgement. She waved back.

The hedgerows gave way to open fields and there, up ahead, was the shimmering silver-blue of the wide Lough Swilly drifting towards the North Atlantic. Belle's stomach somersaulted.

In minutes, she was turning up the lane to her family home. The dirt track was only wide enough for traffic going one way. Grass grew in the middle and burgeoning hedges of pink-and-yellow-speckled brambles gently brushed against the paintwork of her car as she crept along. Rounding the final bend, the house came into view – a place that couldn't be more different from the cosmopolitan life she had in Dublin, but a place as rooted in her as her DNA.

Two border collies bounded out, raising the intruder alarm with urgent barks. The bigger one Belle recognised as Jess – she'd been around for years. The smaller one was new, little more than a pup. She drove through to the cobbled courtyard at the back of the house and her childhood years exploded in her mind like fireworks. The past was in front of her eyes, as real and as present as the here and now. Her parents and grandparents, all passed away; her cousins and her old friend, Hunter; her reading tree and the cherry orchard; the woods and the river – they all called it the 'burn'. And Fionn, of course. Fionn and the summer of 1986, when he came to stay. She pictured him on his first day, sitting in their kitchen, her Greek god.

Her chest tightened, that pressure again, and she tried to catch her breath. She didn't often let her thoughts meander back to 1986 if she could help it, but after Friday night, after seeing Fionn – she couldn't really have seen him – and after what Maeveen had told her, she could do little else but remember.

Belle drew to a halt as a couple of geese and a handful of half-grown goslings scattered in a flutter, honking disapproval at being disturbed. Jess and her new friend caught up with the car. They bounced and leapt and barked while a small brown hen by the barn fixed a beady eye on them . Black-grey granite outhouses, two hundred years old or more, cast shadows across the cobbles and, by contrast, the whitewashed walls of the house virtually glowed in the sunlight.

She stepped out of the car and stretched her legs.

'You're actually here.'

Belle turned to see Maeveen standing with a wry grin on her face.

'Sorry it's been a while,' Belle said.

'Well, at least you're here now and that's the main thing. Give us a hug then, Baby Belle.'

*

Belle sat down at the end of the table by the bay window in the kitchen. This was the place at the table she liked best, always had been, where she had eaten countless breakfasts and dinners and whiled away wet afternoons reading and drinking tea.

From her vantage point, she had full view of the woodland in front of the house and a rose garden that had seen better days.

'There's your green tea – always keep some for you.' Maeveen put a mug on top of a coaster.

Belle dunked the teabag a couple of times. 'Thanks... Mammy's roses aren't doing the best.'

'They only need a bit of pruning. You're always welcome to come up and tend to them yourself.'

Belle knew Maeveen didn't mean that as a friendly invitation; she'd touched a nerve.

'I was just saying. Mammy loved that garden.'

'I know and I've been looking after it rightly, along with everything else.'

Belle got the message. 'Here, tell me how you've been getting on. You look good. Healthy.' So she did, her swarthy skin had a vibrant glow – Maeveen took after their mother's family who were brown-eyed, dark, small and stocky, while Belle had the blue-grey eyes of her father's side of the house and was like a tall glass of milk.

'That's all the outdoor work, and look at this,' she pulled up the sleeve of her T-shirt to reveal a tattoo of a delicate blue feather on her toned, muscular arm.

Belle smiled. One of Maeveen's biggest regrets from her wayward younger days was getting a tattoo with the name of some waster boyfriend. A permanent reminder of a time long since gone; she refused to wear short sleeves for fear of it being seen.

'That's cool,' Belle said.

'They were able to put this little baby over the top of that other disaster. I got it done a few weeks ago.'

'Good for you.'

Maeveen beamed with a smile that reached her eyes. 'I love your hair, by the way.'

'Yeah, I decided to go for the purple platinum look.' Belle flicked a few locks of shoulder-length hair away from her face. 'I like yours, too. You've cut it shorter.'

'It's a pixie style – low-maintenance – and the colour's darker. Mahogany brown, they call it.'

Belle nodded. She paused a moment, wondering when it would be a good time to mention Fionn. A heavy sick feeling rose from her stomach as she decided not yet. She needed more chit-chat. Did Maeveen feel the same?

'How's things on the farm, anyway?' she said.

'Grand. It's not too busy this time of year, you know the craic.'

'Cillian's still working for you?'

'Aye,' Maeveen blushed.

'What's that about?'

'Nothing.'

'It's definitely not nothing. Come on, fess up.'

'Me and Cillian…'

'You're not!'

Maeveen tried to stop her full lips curling up into a smile.

'How long?'

'Since St Patrick's Day.'

'You kept that quiet, sneaky. We've talked on the phone a couple of times since then.'

'I know but I wanted to let it breathe a bit before putting it out there.'

'It's serious then?'

Maeveen shrugged and sipped her tea.

'Does it complicate things, you know, with him working for you?'

'Naw, that side of it's all grand, and he's got his cleaning business, too, so he doesn't totally depend on the work here. It feels like we've been together for years.'

'Well, you sort of have – you've known him your whole life. Will I get a chance to catch up with him?'

'You should do. He's here most nights.'

'It *is* serious then.'

Maeveen looked away.

'I'm glad, honestly,' Belle said. 'You deserve happiness.' Belle lifted her tea and blew cold on the steaming liquid. 'If it's all right, I was planning to hang around for a few days, maybe more.'

Maeveen raised her eyebrows. 'Really? That'd be nice. Stay as long as you like; your old room's always waiting.' She bit her lip. 'You'll be staying for Fionn's funeral, won't you?'

Belle breathed relief. Maeveen had mentioned him first.

'Goes without saying.'

'You said you saw him,' Maeveen said.

An image popped into Belle's head: Fionn as still as a frozen lake, with his faraway eyes and strangely serene countenance. She rubbed her cold arms. 'I was pissed and I probably imagined it.'

Maeveen turned up her snub nose. 'Well, I'm sort of shocked you're dismissing it so easily. It's not like that kind of thing hasn't happened before.'

'I don't really believe in that stuff anymore. It's fanciful.'

Belle thought back to her college days where she'd learned the hard way that seeing apparitions was irrational bullshit. Even though she was brought up to think it was totally normal, fellow students in college had laughed at such things.

'Sure, leave the fanciful stuff to the rest of us crazies,' Maeveen said.

'That's not what I meant.'

'No? Subtle, sensitive Belle would never say anything hurtful.'

Belle counted to ten. 'Let's try not to have a row until I've been here at least a day.'

'Whether you saw him or you thought you saw him, you can't deny it was uncanny.'

Belle took a breath. 'Tell me how... how he died.'

Maeveen slumped in her chair. 'You already know; I told you on the phone.'

'Tell me again.'

Maeveen sighed, long and heavy. Her face was strained. 'He

was beaten to death.' She covered her mouth with her hand. Belle saw it was shaking. 'I heard he was beaten so b-badly that they had to use dental records to formally ID him.'

'Jesus. Poor Fionn.' A lump pressed into Belle's throat.

'He'd been drinking in his flat, not on his own. The police know another man was with him. They don't know who yet. Though, whoever he is, he's the main suspect. Mostly because the flat wasn't broken into so the scumbag that killed him had to be somebody Fionn knew – somebody already in the flat, probably.'

'It's like the kind of thing you read in the papers – a fight in a drinking den gone awry. I can't imagine Fionn fitting that picture.'

'But don't you remember me telling you before? He'd started drinking a lot in recent years,' Maeveen wiped her eyes. 'Even so, it makes me want to scream, him dying like that, so violently, in his own home.' Tears rolled down her face. 'He... me and him... it could've been so different.'

Belle couldn't look. Maeveen had no idea how different it could have been.

'If it hadn't been for that fucking Hunter Campbell,' Maeveen wept. 'The pain he caused – him and all belonging to him.'

Maeveen was on the verge of going into a rant about the Campbells, which was one of her favourite pastimes. Was she ever going to tire of it? Belle knew the answer. She wanted to put her arms round her sister, wanted to tell her how much she loved her and how sorry she was. She didn't. Too much had happened for something so paltry as a hug to do any good. Instead, Belle let her gaze wander to the garden again, taking comfort from the softness of the evening air through the open window, and left Maeveen to cry uncomforted.

'Did you talk to any of Fionn's family?' Belle said, when Maeveen's sobs subsided.

'His sister, Chrissie,' Maeveen's voice was muffled. 'She still lives in that same house in Derry. I called her; she was destroyed.

She mentioned you, funnily enough. Said Fionn was on about contacting you before it all happened.'

Belle straightened in her chair. 'What about?'

'She didn't say. I didn't ask.'

Belle pursed her lips.

'I gave her your number,' Maeveen said. 'I'll go visit. I'll go tomorrow.'

*

Belle dropped her bags on the floor and threw herself on the double bed in her old bedroom. The smallest of the four bedrooms in the farmhouse, her room faced the front and had a view of the woods that bordered both sides of the lane. The room was clean, spacious, with plain sage wallpaper and a polished wooden floor. Apart from a musical box that sat atop a large chest of drawers, no evidence existed that the room had ever been hers. In spite of that, it felt like home, even more than her bedroom in Dublin, which was full of her things and decorated exactly as she wanted.

She stared up at the ceiling, same as she had done when she was a girl, and thought of how much had changed. In 1986, a family had lived in this house: Mr and Mrs McGee and their two daughters. And Fionn, too, for a while. Had that been the last happy time, the last truly happy time? That was the tragedy about life. You never knew when you were living your happiest time; you never knew to savour it and make the most of it.

She wondered if it were possible to be too broken to cry.

Her phone pinged, distracting her from her maudlin thoughts. A text from Shane. She'd answer that later. Probably.

'Fuck this,' she said, sitting up and reaching for her laptop bag.

There was only one thing she knew to do when her head was in such a scramble. She took out her Dictaphone. She switched it on and began talking.

'Fionn had wanted to contact me. Why? Tomorrow, I'll visit Chrissie. My plan is to stay until Fionn's funeral and go back to Dublin soon after. Reminder: invite Maeveen and Cillian to come and stay for a weekend.'

She stopped recording and tapped the little device against her forehead, deep in thought. She pressed the record button again.

'What the fuck am I even doing?'

4

DONEGAL, 1986

The morning after the Greek god arrived at the McGee home, Maeveen came into Belle's room early and woke her up.

'Get up, Belle,' she whispered.

Belle turned over and pushed Maeveen's hand away. 'Leave me alone; I'm tired.'

'He's downstairs eating breakfast,' Maeveen whispered.

'Fionn?'

Maeveen nodded with the vigour of an excited pup, her eyes dancing.

All at once, Belle was wide awake. She jumped out of bed and grabbed the powder-blue shorts off the bedroom floor from where she'd thrown them the night before. She was about to put them on when she changed her mind. She had a really cool denim dress that might be nice to wear for a change and she grabbed it from the wardrobe.

'What're you doing?' Maeveen asked.

'Getting dressed.'

'Why're you putting on that dress? You need to be blackmailed into wearing dresses or skirts.'

'No, not all the time,' she lied. 'I like this dress. I wear it plenty, you just never notice.'

'Bullshit.'

Belle rolled her eyes. 'Bullshit' was Maeveen's new word; she loved using it every chance she got, pronouncing it as two separate words and stretching out the second one as though she was saying 'sheet'.

'I can't remember the last time you wore it,' Maeveen said, 'or any dress.'

'Shut up and leave me alone.'

Maeveen giggled. 'I know you fancy Fionn, that's it, isn't it?'

'Now who's talking bullshit... anyway, take a look at yourself. You're supposed to be helping Daddy clean up the yard. You're hardly going to do that with your Sunday shoes on and that stupid skirt.'

'I'm going into the town with Mammy to get some shopping before I help Daddy. You want me wearing my wellies into town?' Maeveen's cheeks flared red.

Belle shrugged and slipped on the denim dress anyway, along with a pair of pumps.

'He's our cousin, don't forget.'

'Shut up, Maeveen. Anyway, I don't think I believe he's our cousin. I know Mammy said so but...' Belle had been giving the matter quite a bit of thought and had come to the conclusion that it didn't make sense.

Maeveen pursed her lips. 'For once, I agree with you. We know all Mammy's relatives and there was never a mention of family in County Derry.'

'Why would she make up something like that?'

'Dunno, but we'll say nothing and just go along with it 'til they tell us otherwise.' Maeveen laughed. 'Race you to the kitchen.'

Belle thumped her arm and ran for the door. Maeveen closed in quickly and overtook her on the stairs.

'Slowcoach,' Maeveen leapt the last three stairs in one go and dashed down the hall towards the kitchen.

*

Maeveen was already settling down at the table, along with Belle's parents and Fionn, when Belle came through the door. A country and western song played almost inaudibly from the radio perched on the windowsill.

'You're up, too,' her mother said. 'Usually don't expect to see you 'til the morning's well behind us. Put out some scrambled egg for yourself and make a slice of toast.'

'How's it going, Fionn?' Belle said, in her sweetest, butter-wouldn't-melt voice.

'What about ye, Belle?' he said, with a smile that made her feel she was the only person in the whole world.

'Hi, Fionn,' Maeveen said, 'did you sleep all right in that cubbyhole?'

'Like a baby in a blanket,' he said, taking a bite of toast. 'It's a grand spot.'

'Were you warm enough?' their mother asked.

'Perfect, Mrs McGee, thanks.'

'Agh, call me Kitty. No need for the formalities.'

'Well, sure, you can tell us if there's any problem,' their father said.

'Appreciate that, Mr McGee.'

'Like Kitty said, no need for formalities. Michael will do.'

Fionn nodded and Belle watched as he manoeuvred a forkful of scrambled egg into his mouth. She caught his eye.

'Can you play Cluedo?' she asked, slightly turning her head away from his gaze.

'What?'

'Or draughts?' Maeveen said.

'Everybody can play draughts, Maeveen,' Belle said, wondering why her sister had to butt in.

'Not necessarily… what about Monopoly?'

'Or Scrabble?' Belle asked.

'And Trivial Pursuit?'

'Othello?'

'That's boring; do you know any card games?' asked Maeveen.

'For pity's sake,' their mother said, 'give the man peace.'

'Sorry,' the girls chorused.

'Naw, they're grand,' Fionn said. 'I know draughts and Monopoly and if you have a deck of cards, there's a few games I could show you.'

'Can you play poker?' Maeveen said, and she threw him a coy smile.

He smiled back and now Maeveen was the only person in the whole world. Belle felt a resentful little knot in her stomach.

'He can show me first,' Belle said. 'You've got stuff to do today. And anyway, you don't want to play with her, Fionn, she cheats.'

'How dare you—'

'That's enough out of you two,' their father said, standing up and pushing his chair away from the table. 'I'm going to get to work. Maeveen, when you're ready, I'll see you out there.'

With their father gone, it was quiet at the table for a moment or two.

'You better move yourself, Maeveen,' their mother said. 'Your Daddy could do with the help.'

'I'm nearly finished,' she said, scooping up a forkful of egg.

'But isn't Maeveen going into town with you?' Belle asked.

Her mother threw her a quizzical look. 'Where're you getting that idea?'

Belle turned to Maeveen. 'You'll probably need to change out of those good clothes you've got on, Maeveen.'

Maeveen mumbled something and kicked Belle under the table.

'Can I show Fionn the orchard?' Belle asked.

'Belle, we've already explained,' said her mother, 'Fionn's got to rest.'

Belle didn't think he looked in need of any rest at all. 'But a walk as far as the orchard's not going to kill him.'

'Maybe some other time,' Fionn said.

Before Belle could say another word, the jarring trumpeting theme tune of the news came on the radio.

'Quiet now,' Belle's mother said, turning up the volume.

Belle rolled her eyes as everybody stopped to listen to the newscaster's solemn voice. "... *Deputy Leader of the Democratic Unionist Party, Peter Robinson MP, was arrested and charged with illegal assembly after a loyalist mob took over a village in County Monaghan...*"

Fionn sniggered.

'He's some craic,' Belle's mother said. 'The sectarian bigot – who does he think he is?'

'They think they're above the law, that crowd,' Maeveen said. 'It's good to see him put in his place.'

'I doubt getting arrested will put any manners in him,' Fionn said.

The newscaster went to the next news story. "... *An on-the-run IRA man was arrested last night from a safe house in County Louth. The man, believed to be from West Belfast...*"

Fionn coughed. Belle's mother turned down the radio.

'On the run,' Belle said. 'I know what that means.'

'Shush, Belle,' her mother said. 'Never you mind.'

'But—'

'Enough.'

Maeveen gathered her breakfast things and took them to the sink in the pantry.

'So, could you show me how to play poker then, Fionn?' Belle asked.

'Fit you better, Belle, if you helped Mammy out around the

house,' Maeveen said, glaring, as she passed on her way upstairs.

'Now, Belle, I don't want you pestering Fionn,' said her mother. 'He doesn't need you hanging off him every day.'

'Naw, it's no bother,' Fionn said. 'Go and get the cards.'

Fionn looked right at her and there it was again, that smile of his. Belle thought she was going to melt and it occurred to her that she might do just about anything to have that smile fall on her and her alone.

5

DERRY, PRESENT DAY

Belle knocked on Chrissie Power's door. Hers was a terraced house in the Brandywell, a tucked-away part of Derry. The sun blazed, melting soft patches of tar on the road and bouncing an uncomfortable glare off the hard, concrete surrounds. A couple of kids played a lethargic game of kick-about. The place looked like any other built-up urban area – a far cry from the war zone it had been during the decades of the conflict.

The door opened.

'Chrissie?'

She was barely recognisable. She was older, much older, fatter, hair short and unkempt, deep wrinkles around her mouth, and eyes so dull they could've belonged to a dead person.

'Sorry I—'

'I'm Belle McGee, Maeveen's sister.'

'Really? Belle? Aw, what about ye, love?' Chrissie's eyes widened for a second before drooping again. 'What's the chances? I was going to give you a ring. Maeveen probably said to you. Are you coming in?'

Belle followed her, welcoming the cool of the interior, and took a high chair at the breakfast bar in the kitchen. The air hinted of cigarette smoke.

'I was about to stick on the kettle,' Chrissie said. 'Want a cup of something?'

'Nothing for me, thanks, Chrissie.'

'Do you want some water or mineral – I've lemonade?'

Belle put her hand up. 'I'm grand.'

Chrissie filled the kettle and lit a cigarette.

'I… I was shocked to hear about Fionn. I'm so sorry for your loss.' Belle bit her lip, regretting what she had said. 'Sorry for your loss' was what you said to somebody you didn't know about some dead person you also didn't know. They weren't the words you used on the sister of a man who was once your whole world.

'Thanks, love.' Chrissie's voice trembled. She pulled long on her cigarette. Belle noticed the strain on her face. 'I still can't really believe he's gone…' She pushed the cigarette packet across the breakfast bar towards Belle.

Belle shook her head. 'Do the police have any idea who did it or why?'

'If they do, they haven't told me. Not that I'd expect the PSNI to tell me anything – no love lost there.'

The PSNI, the police service in the warped little state that was the North, had replaced the previous police service who were a sectarian militia called the RUC. No, definitely no love lost there.

'I knew it'd come to a bad end,' Chrissie was saying. 'I told Fionn all the time he was flying close to the flame.' Belle heard resentment in her voice. 'I told him.'

'How do you mean?'

'He'd been hitting the bottle hard these last few years, was drinking far too much. He'd started a habit of bringing people back to his flat for all-night drinking sessions and he wasn't too fussy what kind of characters they were. I told him it wasn't safe but he always laughed it off and said there was no harm in it.'

29

Belle struggled to imagine the Fionn she knew living in such a way. Her heart weighed heavy like a lump of granite. 'So, you think it was one of these… *acquaintances* that muh… that did it?' She didn't want to use the word 'murder' in front of Chrissie.

'Has to be, aye?' Chrissie poured boiling water into a mug, spilling some on the worktop. The steam wavered in the air before vanishing. 'Maybe they'll get some answers from the post-mortem – they haven't released his body yet, you know. Said it'll be another week at least before they let us have him back. All that time before we can lay him to rest.' She flicked her cigarette, missing the ashtray, and put a splash of milk in the cup that still had the teabag floating. 'Has this actually happened? I keep thinking I'm going to wake up sometime.'

'I understand,' Belle said, softly.

'He always had a great word on you.'

Belle flinched, uncomfortable with the praise.

'He followed all your stories, 'specially that last one on the care home scam. He was a big fan. He said he hadn't seen you in about twelve, thirteen years—'

'I think the last time I saw him was about twelve years ago. I bumped into him going up Waterloo Street.' Of course, that wasn't strictly the last time she had seen Fionn. There was that – whatever it was – in Dublin just days ago.

'Waterloo Street? That'd be about right.' Chrissie sucked on her cigarette. 'His favourite watering holes were on that street.' She shuddered and heaved a deep, sorrowful sigh.

Belle touched her hand. She was no stranger to grieving family members – in her work, she often had to interview them. Their sorrow was always the same regardless of the circumstances and, over the years, she'd developed a way of being that respected what they were going through but still got the story from them. It allowed her to empathise but not get sucked in. This occasion was different. Her techniques were useless. She was already sucked in and swimming around in the pain right alongside Chrissie.

'He was talking about you, you know,' Chrissie said, sniffing and rubbing her nose with the back of her hand. 'Only a week ago. Did Maeveen tell you?'

'She did.'

'He said he was going to get in touch with you.'

'Did he happen to say why?'

'Naw but what I do know is he had a story he was sure you'd be interested in.'

'A story?' Belle tried to wade out of her emotions. 'And you've no idea what it might've been about?'

'Not a notion.' Chrissie took another drag from her cigarette and a long cylinder of ash dropped onto the countertop. 'But if anybody knows, it'll be my cousin, Dermot. Him and Fionn were best muckers, lived in each other's pockets. Dermot enjoys a drink, too, but I prayed every day they'd keep each other safe. The two of them even work – worked – together, some waste company out near Greysteel. It'll be a while before I forgive Dermot for not being with Fionn that night.'

'Do you have an address for him?'

'Um, he lives off William Street, Brewster's Close... can't remember the door number, but, here, I've his mobile number.' She lifted her phone out of an otherwise empty fruit bowl and dabbed the display a few times. 'There you go.'

Belle recorded the number. 'And he's Dermot Power?'

'No, he's from the other side of the house. He's McDermott.'

Belle did a double take. 'Dermot Mc—'

'I know, say nothing. My aunt and uncle must've been on something the day they named him.'

Belle stood up. 'I should go; leave you in peace.'

Chrissie discarded what was left of her cigarette into the ashtray and gave Belle a hug.

'Will you be here for the funeral?' Chrissie said.

'I wouldn't be anywhere else.'

Belle started the car and drove back along the Lecky Road towards William Street and Dermot's house. Her brain clicked and whirred as she tried to put order on Chrissie's scraps of information. So, Fionn had had a story he wanted her to look into. She couldn't help but be intrigued. Her journalist's nose was on the trail. Though it was more than idle curiosity, of course. After the impossible encounter in her house that night, she felt an obligation to him, like she was honouring a dying wish.

Her next step was to talk to this Dermot guy and find out what he knew. Of course, there was a good chance Fionn's story was nothing – not worthy of investigation. On the other hand, there was a sliver of a chance it could be something. If it was the former, then no harm done; if the latter, she'd have to make an assessment about how to proceed. A short extended stay up North might be necessary – a very short one. No harm in that; she didn't exactly have to rush back to Dublin, not right away. She imagined Shane might be pissed off with those plans but Shane could like it or lump it.

There was another thing. She hadn't liked to raise this possibility with Chrissie, but her suspicious mind couldn't help thinking that if there was something to Fionn's story, perhaps it could be linked to his murder? If Dermot was as close to Fionn as Chrissie said he was, he might be useful on that score, too.

*

Dermot McDermott's house was not the kind of place you got too cosy in. Although clean, it was also sparse and functional, with bland marigold walls, vinyl flooring, a basic suite – well-cared for but not new – a coffee table, a bookcase crammed with political and historical texts, and a TV in the corner. There were no ornaments or unnecessary extras, just a few family photos hanging from the walls and a framed charcoal sketch of *Free Derry Corner*. Belle's gaze lingered on it for a moment. Two casement windows looked out onto the street, both shut tight and serving to mute the steady rhythmic swish of traffic on nearby William Street. A thin layer of blue-grey cloud hovered near the ceiling. From the smell, Belle could tell it was the lingering trace of a cigarette – yet another smoker.

'Thanks for inviting me in,' Belle said, perching herself on the edge of the sofa.

'No bother.' Dermot leaned forward in the armchair nearest the TV and began rolling tobacco. 'So you're the famous Belle McGee,' he said, lifting his head to look directly at her.

Belle gasped. His eyes, though sad, were the shimmering blue of a flowering flax plant. Instantly mesmerising. Exactly like Fionn's. She could nearly believe he was sitting there instead of his cousin.

Of course, Dermot didn't look like Fionn in any other way. She guessed he was in his late forties, medium height and skinny as a whippet. He was light-featured, had high cheekbones, dusty-brown hair speckled with grey and cut into a flattop, and a long, narrow nose that hooked and flattened slightly at the tip – like Bob Dylan's. It was a shape she found oddly appealing. For no reason, Belle felt nervous flutters in her gut.

'Belle McGee... the journalist... Maeveen's sister. She's a dote, Maeveen. I know her well.' He finished rolling his cigarette, a perfect shape and size. 'You smoke?' He reached it out.

'No thanks,' she said, 'don't touch the things.'

'Wanna cup of tea?'

'Not for me.'

'Um, maybe just as well, I don't think I've any milk. Too much else going on to worry about getting the shopping in.' He lit up and sat back, placing a metal ashtray on the arm of his chair. 'Fionn always talked about your family, specially Maeveen, and about the time he stayed with yous back in the eighties.'

'Summer of '86.'

'The summer when all shit broke loose. You know, for a long time, I wanted to murder those Campbells for what they did. I nearly did, too, only I was persuaded to change my mind, but that's a story for another day.'

Belle squirmed. The conversation was flying too close to somewhere she didn't want to go. 'The first day we met him,' she said, changing the flow of their exchange slightly, 'my parents told us he was our second cousin from County Derry, though we never really believed it.'

Dermot laughed ruefully. 'Gave him a cover story. Didn't you used to have a wee thing for him?'

Belle worried that her face might combust. 'Thu... I... it's...'

Dermot managed a giggle. 'Don't have a seizure; I'm carrying on with you.'

'I was only turned thirteen,' Belle said, the power of speech resumed. 'We've all had crushes on people that were too old for us.'

'Fionn thought it was cute. He thought you were funny, smart, when you weren't in a huff.'

Belle frowned. 'He said that?' Maybe she had been a bit huffy in those days.

'He was seriously impressed with where you ended up and it didn't surprise him you were winning awards.'

The frown fell away and her mind went to the place where memories of Fionn were stored, a secluded place that wasn't easy to visit. She felt undeserving of his admiration.

'I keep expecting him to show up anytime,' Dermot said. 'I can't believe I'm never going to see him again. Every day I wake up I've to remind myself he's gone.' Dermot dabbed the end of the cigarette against the ashtray.

'It's... hard to believe, and the way it happened,' Belle said.

'That'll stay with me 'til the day I die.'

'Do you know anything about the night he was...' Belle hesitated, 'you know, the night it happened?'

Dermot choked on his cigarette. 'What do you mean?'

'Just that you two were close, Chrissie said, so I wondered if you'd seen him at any point that night.'

'Nuh, not when it happened. I wasn't there. I was at home.'

Belle noticed he seemed uneasy. 'Okay,' she said, her voice deliberately comforting, 'I understand. You weren't with him. Had you seen him earlier in the day?'

'Um, aye, at work. Then after work, we went for a few drinks.' Dermot coughed but his agitation was gone. 'Me and Fionn have a drink most weekends – you know, a few pints on a Thursday or Friday night, maybe a Saturday night. Eleven, half eleven sort of time, we get a carryout and head home, before the bars close and the whole town shites itself.'

'Was that what happened that night?'

'More or less. Our last stop was Tracey's Bar, you know it?'

'At the bottom of Waterloo Street. What time was that?'

'Ten or thereabouts. We had a drink there and bought a carryout. The plan was to go back to Fionn's.'

'But you didn't go to Fionn's.'

'I wasn't anywhere near his place that night – that's a bona fide fact.' Dermot was uneasy again. 'Me and him left Tracey's and whatever way the air hit me when I got outside, I nearly boked my ring up.'

'The air caused that? Not the alcohol?'

'Right, the air, and the burger I ate earlier on. I've ulcers – aw, bastards, they play me like a fiddle if I go near greasy food. I tough it out most times but not that night.'

Spoken like a true drinker, Belle thought but didn't say out loud. 'So you went home instead of going to Fionn's?'

'Spot on and I said to Fionn, well, I said I'd see him the next day.'

'And that was the last time you saw him?'

Dermot rubbed his chin and Belle noticed Indian ink dots on his knuckles. He took a long, unsteady breath.

'The last time. It's hard to think about. Jesus, if only I'd known I'd never have left him on his own.'

'You can't blame yourself.'

'I do though, I do.'

Dermot's face turned ashen and his eyes – those gorgeous, irresistible eyes – swirled as though he was seeing the whole grisly event unfold before him. His anguish was undeniable. Much to her shock, Belle had an overwhelming urge to reach out and hold him, and more shocking, she imagined herself kissing him. She blinked away the image.

'I heard he wasn't on his own in the flat that night,' she said.

'I heard the same.'

Dermot looked away and Belle noted it.

'Do you have any idea who might've been with him? Were there any others who were in the habit of joining the two of you?'

Dermot took a last drag on his cigarette and decisively stubbed it to death in the ashtray. 'Fionn was well known and plenty of times he'd bring people back after the pub.'

'Would it be likely he met somebody after he left you and asked them back for a drink?'

'That's one hundred per cent likely – I'd say that's what happened. His flat's close to Waterloo Street and there's any number of people he could've met going home.'

'Um, do any of the regulars stand out as particularly rowdy or likely to start a fight?'

He stared at her with those eyes of his. 'The police asked me a lot of the same questions when they interviewed me. You know, you're starting to sound very like a peeler; a peeler interrogating a suspect.'

'My bad, force of habit. Investigative journalists can come across that way.'

'And there was me thinking you were here as Fionn's friend.'

Dermot's words stung. 'I am,' she said, 'but it's just Chrissie said Fionn wanted to contact me about a possible story and, I dunno, now he's dead and… and it makes me wonder—'

'That they could be connected. The thought did cross my mind.'

'So you know what Fionn was onto?'

Dermot shook his head and began rolling another cigarette. 'All I know is that it had something to do with the place me and him worked, Evergreen Waste Resources. I wouldn't put anything past them. They're bastards. They play dirty to win the big waste contracts from the councils. I think they've about seven council contracts on the go at the minute and that's big, big money. They undercut their competitors, grease more than a few palms along the way, and they've eyes and ears in all the councils – elected councillors, council staff, all getting backhanders to make sure Evergreen has the advantage for any contract they go for.'

'How do you know all this?'

'The dogs in the street know,' Dermot said. 'Fionn had suspicions that something more was going on, though he didn't say much other than he had to keep it quiet 'cos it might not be safe knowing what he knew.'

Belle tingled – that tingle she got when she was on the scent of an exciting new story.

'He would've bet his last shirt they were following him,' Dermot went on.

'Who?'

'Evergreen. We started to notice their two security men in the bars all the time. Tony and Dessie or something like that – we just called them Beavis and Butthead.'

'Nothing out of the ordinary in seeing somebody you know in a bar in Derry, like bumping into somebody called Doherty.' Doherty was so common a name, there were jokes about it.

'There's a limit and you'd get paranoid, even in this town, if you kept seeing the same two people nearly everywhere you went.' Dermot pulled on his cigarette, taking in a mouthful of smoke, before holding it and slowly blowing it out in wide perfect rings that wafted lazily upwards until they disappeared.

'Um, maybe that is a bit much.'

'So, the only thing I know for definite is Fionn was gathering up evidence, enough for you to write a story he said, and he was keeping it hidden away.'

'You know where?'

'At Chrissie's.'

'She didn't mention it.'

'She doesn't know she has it. Fionn keeps a few things in the shed in her backyard.'

'Why Chrissie's?' Belle asked.

'Keeping it at his own place would be too obvious.'

'Now I'm even more intrigued to know what was going on.'

'Are you going to follow it up?'

'It can do no harm to have a look,' Belle said. 'Would you mind if I called with you again, if I have more questions?'

'A good-looker like you, naw, I wouldn't mind one bit.'

'I didn't mean—'

'I know what you meant. I'm only joking with you.' Dermot grinned.

Belle wanted to show indignance, but instead her stomach gave another flutter – that grin of his was irresistible. 'So, that's you trying to be funny?'

'Aw, come on, I saw you smile.'

She stood up. 'Well, thanks for your time, Dermot, I appreciate it.'

Dermot got up, too. 'Ah, I nearly forgot.' He opened a small drawer in the coffee table and lifted out a pair of keys on a green plastic keyring. 'You might find these useful. Keys to Fionn's flat, if you wanted to look round. There's a key for the outside door and one for the flat door, number twenty-six, though the outside door's off the latch most of the time. The cops did their forensics on the place so they're all finished with it.'

'Thanks,' Belle said, taking the keys and making her exit.

'It was nice meeting you, Belle.'

'Call me McGee. I prefer being called McGee.'

'Really? I use surnames on people I don't like much.'

'It's my professional name, the one I introduce myself as. McGee's a better name for a no-nonsense journalist than Belle, do you not think?'

'Or Baby Belle,' Dermot said, and his irresistible grin appeared again. 'Wasn't that your pet name when you were a kid?'

'Oh God, Fionn told you that, too.'

'Don't worry, your secret's safe with me. I'll call you McGee, if that's what you want.'

'Thanks. Well, I'll be in touch.'

'I hope so, McGee.'

*

For the second time in the same day, Belle found herself at Chrissie Power's house. The sun was sliding low in the pink-vanilla sky and a group of youths stood at the street corner, horsing around and smoking, their laughs and shouts lingering on the still evening air.

'Belle?' Chrissie said, on opening the door.

'Sorry to barge in on you again, Chrissie, but I have a strange request.'

'Okay?'

'I've just been to see Dermot. He told me Fionn had some stuff stored in the shed out your back, to do with that story he wanted me to cover. Would you let me have a look?'

A surprised look animated Chrissie's face for a moment. 'He's got bits and pieces out there but I've no clue what. Come on ahead, I'll show you where.'

They walked through the house to get to the yard, which was little more than a patch of green with a huddle of flowers, a clothesline and a small apex shed.

Chrissie opened the shed and pointed inside. 'I'll leave you to it.'

'You don't want to come in with me?' Belle said, surprised Chrissie wasn't curious about what might be hidden in her own shed.

Chrissie just shrugged. 'You go ahead. Just come back into the house when you're finished.'

The interior of the shed was darker than the inside of a coal bucket. Giving her eyes a few seconds to adjust, Belle was soon on the hunt for Fionn's evidence.

The shed had the pleasant aroma of planed wood and was littered with the usual things: a coil of hosepipe, a grass strimmer, a rusty bucket, a watering can, a shovel, some plastic storage containers. A sturdy shelf ran the length of the shed, its surface covered with old pots of paint and brushes, more tools and a broken mirror.

She saw no sign of any paperwork but guessed the containers were her best bet. She searched them, going through each one methodically, carefully. She struck gold on the third. Under an assortment of knick-knacks and jumble was a box file with a faded-black exterior. A mere glance at the documents inside confirmed she had what she needed: ordnance survey maps, and lists of names and placenames, none of which she recognised. She even saw her own name written in a couple of places.

With the box file tucked under her arm, she returned to the house. Chrissie was standing at the cooker, stirring something in a saucepan. She looked up when Belle came in.

'Ah, you're back,' Chrissie asked, managing a feeble smile. 'Did you get what you were looking for?'

'Think so. Do you mind if I take this with me?' Belle pointed to the box file. 'It'll be easier for me to study at home.'

'Take anything you need.'

Chrissie opened a cupboard door and took out a bowl. 'I've heated some soup. Do you want some?'

'None for me, Chrissie, but thanks all the same.'

'So do you think that box is going to be any help?'

'I'm sure it's going to be a big help.'

'That's good.' Chrissie rubbed her eyes.

For a second time, Belle noticed her lack of curiosity. Poor Chrissie, it seemed, was too far gone to care much about anything.

Belle said her goodbyes and went to her car. A text came through on her phone as she set down the box file on the passenger seat. "R u comin home 4 dinner? Making pasta." Belle sent a quick reply and, giving the box a gentle tap, she set off on the short drive to Donegal. She couldn't wait to see what it had in store.

6

DONEGAL, 1986

The weeks passed and Belle and her family settled into a routine with their new addition. In the evenings, she and Maeveen spent most of their time with Fionn in the sitting room, just the three of them. If the family had a visitor, they moved upstairs where guests to the house never went. They amused themselves by watching TV and playing board games and cards – Snap, Strip Jack, Pontoon, Switch, sometimes even poker using matches for stakes. Fionn was nifty with origami, too. He showed Belle and her sister how to make all sorts: birds, fish, frogs, roses, boats, just about anything. Now and again, their parents would join them for a game of Monopoly or a film.

During the days, Belle and Maeveen tried to spend as much time inside with Fionn as they were allowed, interrupted only when Maeveen had to go to her part-time summer job in town and Belle was forced out the door to get some fresh air and exercise. The times Belle enjoyed most were the days she had Fionn all to herself.

*

'You win again,' Fionn said, throwing his hands in the air.

'You're letting me win,' Belle said.

'Not a chance, you're beating me hands down.'

He stretched his arms and yawned. Belle's eyes wandered towards him, soaking in a covetous look at the contours of his body under his T-shirt. She looked as long as she dared without getting caught.

'Your turn to deal,' she said.

'Right-oh,' he said.

Fionn shuffled the cards and dealt them with expert speed and they began another game of Strip Jack.

'You don't get much company,' Fionn said. 'You must get lonely.'

Belle threw down a king. 'Sometimes. I've loads of cousins, but most of them are a bit older and the ones my age are all boys and live too far away for me to visit on my own. I've friends from school, too, but they don't live nearby either.'

'So you end up stuck at home on your own.' Fionn followed her king with a three, a six and a queen.

'Mostly. Maeveen lets me go to town now and then when she's meeting her friends, but mostly she doesn't want me tagging along and cramping her style.' Belle played a four and an ace. 'That's what she's always saying anyway.'

Fionn smiled and flicked out three cards in a row: a five, a two and a king.

'I'm friends with a boy that lives not too far away. We usually run about together in the holidays.' Belle played another ace. 'He's called Hunter Campbell. Remember Daddy mentioned him on your first day here? He said I definitely wasn't to tell Hunter about you.'

Fionn nodded, slowly. 'I think I remember.'

'Why would he say that?'

'What?'

'About Hunter.'

Fionn's hand went to the stud in his ear and he began twisting it. 'I dunno; he might just want your family's business kept to your family.'

'Um,' Belle said, 'I suppose. I don't have to worry about it, though. I haven't seen him since before the summer break. His older brother moved to Australia so Hunter has to do more work on their farm – they have a dairy farm, so it's busy all year round.'

'And what do you and Hunter get up to, when he's not busy working on the farm?'

'Nothing much. Just exploring in the woods and the burn beside the house; going for big walks across the fields; the odd time, we go to the shore or up into the hills. There's the ruins of a castle up there – it's really old.'

'Sounds like good craic. You must miss him.'

'Kinda,' Belle said. Any other summer, she would've, but this year she didn't miss him at all. Not when she had Fionn.

Fionn took his turn and on the fourth card played a Jack.

'Oh, damn,' Belle said. She turned her next card. Another Jack. She giggled. 'I'm on thin ice… but it's not over 'til the fat lady sings, right, Fionn?'

'You're dead right.' He flicked his card – a nine. 'And there she sings! It's over now.'

Belle cheered. 'I won some good cards there.' She pulled the stack of cards towards her.

Belle's luck stayed on the up and up and in another few rounds she'd all but won the game. Fionn had a handful of cards, none of them face cards.

'I'm beat,' he said, 'you're unstoppable today.'

'Want to play again?'

'Maybe later; Maeveen's going to be back soon.'

Belle's stomach knotted. She hated when he mentioned Maeveen.

'It'll be a while yet. She doesn't get out of work 'til half one and then she has to get the bus home.'

Fionn nodded and yawned again. 'I'm so tired, I don't know why. This sitting about, all day, every day, isn't doing me any favours.'

Belle thought his being tired had something to do with the illness he was recovering from. She didn't want to bring it up; it might make him feel bad to be reminded. 'I suppose when you're at home, you're out all the time,' she said, instead.

'Aye, pretty much.'

'You've probably got a lot of work to do on your family's farm.'

'What? Aw, right, our farm, aye, that keeps me busy.'

'Do you have a dairy farm or one like ours – arable?'

'Um, both.' He twisted the gold stud in his ear.

'Both? That must be one busy farm.'

'Mad busy.'

'Do you—'

'What about another game, after all? See if I can beat you this time, Baby Belle.' He tapped her gently on the nose.

Belle smiled. 'You don't see me as a baby, do you? I'm grown up, you know.'

'Sure, I know you're not a baby, but it's nice to have a nickname, isn't it?'

She beamed. So, he knew she wasn't some silly little child. She reached for the pack of cards and started shuffling.

'Give them a good shuffle now. No cheating.'

Belle dealt the cards, trying to throw them out fast and cool the way Fionn did, but they went everywhere and Fionn had to tidy them up as she went along.

'Do you miss home a lot?' she said, lifting her cards.

'Miss it something terrible,' he said. 'Miss me Ma the most – it's hard, you know.'

'Why can't you just go back then?' Belle said.

'I wish I could but it's not that simple.' His beautiful smile was gone and his eyes were wet, like he was holding back from crying.

Belle's heart tightened as though someone had squeezed it in their fist. She didn't want to see him sad, especially when he wanted to be somewhere else instead of with her.

'My Mammy can look after you.' She played on the cousin story. 'We're family, sure.'

'Ach, Belle, you've got a big heart and you've all done so much for me already.'

Belle was about to say something but was interrupted. Her mother popped her head round the door. Dinner was ready and their conversation was over.

7

DONEGAL, PRESENT DAY

'How did it go today?' Maeveen was draining a pot of tagliatelle into a colander. The steam enveloped her in a mist, drifting through the kitchen and leaving the windows cloudy with condensation.

'All right,' Belle said. She tore off a piece of garlic bread, just out of the oven, and bit into the soft buttery centre. 'It was tough seeing Chrissie.'

'Poor Chrissie; did she recognise you?'

'No, I had to tell her who I was, though she remembered me then. I stayed with her a while. And I talked to a cousin of theirs, Dermot McDermott. Do you know him?'

'I know Dermot,' Maeveen said.

'He's a character and a half.'

'He's that all right, but he has a good heart, and you'd hardly believe that behind the wisecracking is a conscientious, hard-working guy. Smart, too.'

Belle was surprised, pleasantly.

'His eyes are just like Fionn's, don't you think?' Maeveen went on. 'Not bad-looking either.'

'Yeah, he's got a Bob Dylan nose.'

'Last time you said that about somebody, you ended up engaged.'

'Well, not this time.' Belle sliced the garlic bread and put the pieces into a wooden bowl, not wanting to think about that less-than-successful episode in her life. 'Anyway, turns out Fionn was planning to get in touch with me about some suspicious activity he was digging into.'

Maeveen set the colander of cooked pasta on the worktop. 'Really? Do you know what?'

'No, but I intend to find out. That box file there might have the answer.'

Maeveen shot a look at the box, as she stirred the pasta sauce. 'Think this is ready,' she said, tasting it.

Belle's stomach gurgled. 'It definitely smells ready. Can I help?'

'Take the salad and bread to the table and set three places, would you?'

'Three places?'

'Cillian comes round most nights. He practically lives here.'

'It'll be nice to see him,' Belle said, and began preparing the table.

Maeveen's old cat – no more than a ball of white fur with a sardonic face – arrived at the door and padded over the limestone tiles in Belle's direction.

'Shoo, cat,' she said, before it got close enough to curl itself around her leg.

'Auntie Belle's bad, isn't she, Snowball? My poor baby.'

'Don't encourage her. Me and that cat never hit it off.'

Maeveen laughed. 'So, do you think there's going to be something to write about in this box?'

'Dunno. There might be. Or maybe Fionn was away with the woodbine.'

'You don't believe that, do you?'

'No, of course I don't.'

Maeveen put three plates of piping hot food on the table. 'All cooked from fresh. Hope you like it,' she said, looking out the window.

A car was coming up the lane, its headlights bright against the fading purple-blue of the evening sky. The dogs barked from the courtyard.

'Cillian,' Maeveen said. 'Right on cue.'

The back door opened and Cillian stepped into the kitchen, a wide smile on his bearded face, his brown hair spotted with grey and tied in a ponytail, his eyes deep-set and dark. 'Hi, Maeveen. Hi, Belle, long time no see.' He gave Maeveen a peck on the cheek and stretched out his hand. Belle shook it.

'How're things?' Belle asked.

'Couldn't be better. How's the big smoke treating you?'

'Good, busy, you know.'

'Grab a seat,' Maeveen said. 'You at that one, Belle. This is yours, Cillian.'

They settled in and began eating.

'This is delicious,' Belle said, wrapping a few long strings of pasta and sauce around her fork.

'I'll second that,' Cillian said, giving Maeveen a lingering smile, which she returned.

Belle couldn't help thinking they were a well-matched pair. He was a good bit taller than Maeveen and his skin had that same healthy glow. A scar cut a jagged path down the right-hand side of his face. If memory served, he had got it when he was knocked down by a car as a child. He was the steady, reliable type; the kind of man you wanted to avoid in the wild abandon of youth, but who was exactly the kind of human being you'd want to get old with – exactly the kind of human being Maeveen deserved.

'I wondered when you two would finally get together,' Belle said.

Both their faces brightened.

'If it hadn't been for me making the first move,' Maeveen said, taking a sip of water, 'I'd still be waiting.'

'I'm not pushy,' Cillian said.

'There's pushy and then there's nearly comatose,' Maeveen said, laughing. 'We got there in the end though, right?'

'That we did, light of my life.'

They loved each other, Belle realised. She could never imagine sharing a tender moment like that with Shane. She could scarcely remember the last time they did something normal like have a civilised conversation over a home-cooked meal. Still, she didn't begrudge Maeveen her happiness just because she didn't have it.

Soon, they finished eating. Maeveen made a pot of coffee and some green tea for Belle. Cillian took a small cloth sack from the dresser drawer and brought it to the table. Inside was a lighter, a pouch of tobacco, cigarette papers and a bag of grass.

'I'll do the honours,' Cillian said.

Belle was surprised. 'Weren't you going to stop smoking?' she asked Maeveen.

'I did. I don't smoke cigarettes at all,' she said, 'and you know it's years since I touched any of that other shit I used to put in my system.' She came back to the table with the hot drinks. 'I'm able to keep it very tame now. I stick to a couple of joints some evenings and a few drinks.'

'Sorry, I suppose I can't help worrying.'

'I know but you shouldn't,' Maeveen said, sounding a tiny bit offended. 'You can't actually believe I'd start using again, the way I was before.'

'The temptation's always there.'

'That's not how it works – not for me, anyway. Back then, all I wanted to do was forget my horrible life. I'd nothing to live for. Now, I love the life I have. I've everything to live for.' She sneaked a glance at Cillian.

Belle could see it was true. For the first time ever, she envied her sister. 'I'm one to talk. You're living a healthier, happier life than I am.'

'What do you mean? You're a big success, you've a job you love, you don't have to worry about money and aren't you going out with, ah, what's-his-name, Shaun, no, Shane?'

'You've made it sound better than it is, and Shane's not exactly my soulmate.'

'Maybe you should come back home to live,' Cillian said, rolling a line of tobacco and grass into a joint. 'Be around places and people you know.'

'I haven't lived at home since I went to university. I'm not sure I know the place or the people, anymore.'

'You'll always know. You're connected to here,' Maeveen said.

Belle drank some tea. It was more complicated than either she or Cillian understood. Life was always more complicated. She couldn't just come home. She could never come home. She knew that when she had first left and she knew it still. After what happened, she didn't deserve to.

Maeveen lit the joint Cillian handed her. The earthy aroma of sweet tobacco and grass filled the space between them with curling, encroaching smoke.

'I'll wash up the dishes,' Belle said, 'and then I'll leave you two in peace.'

'You will not,' Maeveen said. 'The dishes are rinsed off and they'll be all right 'til tomorrow. Stay here with us a while. We'll watch something on Netflix.'

'I wanted to get a look at that box file.'

'The box file will still be there in the morning. Spend a bit of time with us – you're supposed to be on holidays, aren't you?'

Belle was swayed. She'd done enough today and a relaxing evening with Maeveen and Cillian was tempting. Besides, Maeveen was right. The box file wasn't going anywhere.

*

Belle slept late the next day and it was after ten before she stumbled downstairs dressed in a tracksuit and trainers. She found a note on the kitchen table: *"B, working in the shore fields. See you later, M."*

Belle went for a run to the end of the lane and back up again – she ran every weekday when in Dublin – and took a shower when she returned. She quickly whipped up some breakfast – scrambled egg on a couple of slices of sourdough, washed down with green tea. Snowball was curled up on an armchair by the unlit range, but the smell of food roused her. She hopped off the chair, tiptoed across the floor and stood beside Belle, meowing. Belle tossed her a morsel of egg. Snowball sniffed it but didn't eat it, meowed again, and trotted back to her armchair, a contemptuous tail in the air.

'Have it your way, cat,' Belle said.

When she finished breakfast, she washed the breakfast dishes, along with the dishes from the night before, and brushed the floor before finally taking the seat by the open window and settling down to the box file, a notepad and her trusted Dictaphone. Through the window came sounds blunted by the heat: a sheep bleating in a far-off field, a clucking hen scratching in the rose garden, a cooing wood pigeon somewhere in a nearby thicket of hazelnut trees.

'Let's see what you've got to tell me,' she said, opening the box.

On the inside lid, a small white sticker had *'Property of James Power'* written in black ink. Belle smiled. She'd almost forgotten that James was his actual name and Fionn was only a nickname.

The box itself was crammed with a jumble of papers and maps in no obvious order or organisation. Over the years, she'd developed a routine for putting order on chaos. She lifted each piece out and, one by one, arranged them methodically in rows and columns. She glanced at each item before placing it in a spot of its own. Very slowly, she began to build a picture.

By the time she'd emptied the box, the table was covered. She sat motionless for a moment, staring at Fionn's secret research. She felt a tingle.

Some of the materials on the table were written in Fionn's shorthand and would take some effort to decipher. Other materials were printed reports about waste management and the environmental risks of waste disposal. The maps – A3 print-outs of ordnance survey maps – were bunched into a single stack. She took them in her hand and examined them closely, noticing large Xs with names next to them. One of the Xs was located near the Glenshane Pass in the Sperrin Mountains. She remembered one of the pieces of paper had a reference to the Glenshane.

Her heart beat a little louder.

A quick search of the papers and she found what she wanted: a couple of pages containing handwritten lists of place names. She clicked on her Dictaphone.

'Glenshane – old quarry,' she said.

She checked another map, and matched its X against a location on the list.

'Plumb Bridge – abandoned mine,' she said.

One by one, she went through all the maps and compared them against the lists, pairing the Xs with locations. She found dozens of matches. In her mind, the fog was beginning to clear and definite shapes were forming. She breathed in sharply and her heart quickened.

'These locations are in some of the remotest parts of County Derry, County Tyrone and County Donegal. Most of them are old quarries and mines. What could they be used for?'

She scanned the lists and some of the other pages, looking for a clue. She read aloud some handwriting on one of the pages.

'Fionn's written: "*They've got waste contracts for more than one council – like winning the lottery. Creaming money off these contracts by using the sites to dispose of waste. Visited eleven of these sites. Followed the lorries going to five sites at different dates and times. Multiple lorries a night, carrying at full capacity. Got reg numbers.".'*

Now the tips of her fingers were tingling. She couldn't tell if it was from excitement or fear, or both. Her body tensed like a runner waiting for the starting pistol to fire.

'Jesus,' she said, stirring Snowball from her sleep, 'I think I know what this means. Fionn works for a waste management company. An old quarry would be the ideal place to do some illegal dumping. These Evergreen scumbags are burying waste in the ground, tonnes of it, instead of processing it safely. We could be talking about a multi-million-pound racket here, the kind of thing that can't happen without insider collaboration, and people turning a blind eye or actively playing a role. Big players must be involved – high-up officials, councillors. There's a lot at stake here, not just money but careers, reputations, status.'

Belle combed through the written pages, hoping to find more precise details about Fionn's visits to the sites. Those were the kind of details that helped build credible evidence and would help her to verify the facts.

'Damn, he doesn't provide any of the site names, dates, times, reg numbers,' she said to the Dictaphone. 'There's nothing.'

It was a setback but not one that could lessen her enthusiasm. She looked across the handwritten page again and was about to put it down, when she noticed a name scribbled at the bottom right-hand corner. *MaCcOoL.*

'MacCool,' she said, 'but with alternate letters in caps and lower case, which is a bit weird.'

Despite the gaps and missing information, Belle had enough to know there was a story worth following. She reached for her phone and rang Alma Travers.

'Belle?' Alma answered. 'I hope you're calling me from a beautiful beach in Donegal or some other equally relaxing place.'

'Alma, I've found something.' Her mouth was dry with nerves.

'What do you mean? I thought—'

'My friend, Fionn, well, seems he stumbled onto something serious, I'm not totally sure yet. He's left me with a treasure chest of evidence that I'm still trying to decipher.' Belle's mind flashed back to the night she – thought she – saw him in Dublin.

'That's a bit vague.'

'Can't be more definite at this stage.'

'What's the evidence like? Can you trust it?'

'Yes, I can trust it. I'm sitting here nearly about to explode.'

'You never cease to amaze me, Belle,' Alma said, chuckling. 'Who else would take off for a break and end up finding a new assignment?'

'I've got to go – got to get my thoughts in order. Just wanted to let you know.'

'Keep me posted and if you need anything, you know where I am.'

Belle ended the call. If she'd only suspected before now that Fionn's investigation might be linked to his murder, this made her pretty certain. And if she could get to the bottom of what Evergreen were up to, she might uncover who was responsible for his death at the same time. The police would be conducting a murder investigation, of course, but they didn't know what was going on with Evergreen or how that might be connected to Fionn. Nor would they know – not until she had more to give them.

She turned her attention to another page of notes and spoke into the Dictaphone.

'Two names here, written beside the words *"good info"*: *"Dr Rita Wilson and Dr Patricia Healy"*. Fionn says he plans to interview these women and he has phone numbers for them. He heard Healy talk on Radio Ulster about cancer rates in the northwest and her concerns about pollution. He doesn't say anything about Wilson. I also see the words *"dodgy / untrustworthy"* written next to the mysterious *"MaCcOoL"*. It's obvious this box of evidence is incomplete and only has part of the story. MacCool, whoever he or she is, is the key to finding more.'

Belle began to write in her notepad, setting out a loose plan of action and next steps. Top billing went to making contact with Healy and Wilson. Next would be to find who MacCool was. And a trip to one of the locations on the maps would be worthwhile. She needed to see for herself what these sites looked like. A search of Fionn's flat would do no harm either. Not that she expected it to yield any clues. Fionn wouldn't have stashed anything about his investigation there and the police would already have gone through it with a fine-tooth comb for forensics, but it would be good to see where he lived.

Her thoughts settled for a moment on Fionn. Was it strange that he was so entwined with her family, with everything that happened, that she thought of him as part of them and yet the truth was she knew very little about the man he'd become? Not so strange, though, as she'd kept him and pretty much everybody from home at arm's length. Guilt gnawed like a toothache. She sighed.

Reaching for her phone again, she thumbed in a number. After a few rings, someone picked up.

'Good afternoon, University of Ulster at Coleraine, Heather speaking. How can I help you?'

'Hello Heather, I was wondering if you could put me through to Dr Rita Wilson.'

'One moment,' Heather said, 'putting you through now.'

The line went quiet and then began ringing. Belle felt that tingle again as she prepared herself for a conversation with Wilson.

'Hello, you've reached Rita Wilson.'

An answering machine. The tingling stopped.

'I'm on leave at the moment and won't be back until the twenty-first. If it's urgent, you can contact my colleague, Rodney McGregor, extension 447. Otherwise, leave a message after the beep and I'll call you on my return. Thank you.'

After a few seconds' pause, there was an extended beep and then silence.

'Hello Dr Wilson, my name's Belle McGee and I'm a reporter with the *National Spectator* in Dublin. I'm researching a story about the dangers of landfill sites and was hoping I could interview you.'

She recited her mobile number and left a request for Dr Wilson to call her when she was back in the office, which wouldn't be for another week. Maybe she'd have better luck with Healy.

'Dr Healy's office, can I ask who's calling?' The voice sounded officious and slightly impatient.

'Hello, my name's Belle McGee, I'm a reporter with the *National Spectator* in Dublin. I'm researching a story about the links between cancer and pollution, and I was wondering if Dr Healy would be interested in an interview.'

'Dr Healy's in clinic today but I'll take your details and pass on your message.'

'That would be great.'

Belle repeated her name and job title and left her number. She was disappointed she'd have to wait longer than she wanted before talking to these leads. It came with the territory, though, and getting worked up about it was pointless. She made her next call to Dermot.

'Hey,' she said, 'it's McGee. I was talking to you yesterday—'

'Baby Belle McGee,' he said. She could tell he was smiling at the other end of the phone. 'You couldn't stay away.'

'Not quite,' she smiled, too, in spite of herself. 'And please, it's McGee. Look, I was wondering, what time do you usually get off work?'

'You just can't wait to see me again. I knock off at six, get home for about half past. Why?'

'Are you free this evening?'

'Not this evening; all the family's going round to Chrissie's. She has the priest coming to say a rosary and stuff for Fionn. Have to do something 'til we're able to have a funeral.'

'Sure,' Belle said, 'sure, of course, it's only right.' She paused. 'Well, what about tomorrow?'

'Tomorrow's Friday; I finish up at three on Fridays. I've nothing planned.'

'Fancy coming on a short road trip? I can pick you up from the house at half past three.'

'Only if you come out with me for a drink afterwards.'

'I thought you'd be happy to help me, without conditions.'

'Oh, you look like a girl who could do with a night out. And I could do with a few drinks meself. I'm going stir-crazy in this house; all I can think about is Fionn.'

'I dunno...'

'Come on.'

'One drink and that's all,' she said.

'One drink. It's a date.'

'It's not a date. Will I pick you up from your house at half three?'

'Grand, see you then.'

She pressed end call, wondering how she got coerced into having a drink with Dermot. She promised herself a drink was all it would be. If he made a move – a tad presumptuous on her part, wasn't it? – she'd bat him away. The problem was she liked him. The other problem was he was Fionn's cousin. It wouldn't be a good idea to let anything happen. Of course, there was Shane, too. Although, when it came down to it, Shane wasn't strictly a factor.

'What's my next move, Snowball?' Belle said.

Snowball sprang onto the floor, purring, and strutted over. Belle checked the time; it was close to one. Maeveen and Cillian would be back for lunch soon.

'I should get some sandwiches made, what do you reckon?'

Snowball meowed.

'And then I think I'll go take a look-see at Fionn's flat, find out something about him.' Truth was, she didn't know him, not really, the man he was before he died. What she knew of him was from a very long time ago. 'And maybe I didn't even know him then either, Snowball.'

Snowball gave her a haughty look that only cats can give.

'Yeah, I know, shut up and get on with lunch.'

8

DONEGAL, 1986

The family was in for the night and Belle was helping her mother in the kitchen when the weather took a sudden turn for the worse.

'Grab this,' her mother said, handing Belle a basket. 'Bring in the clothes before the rain starts.

Belle hurried to the washing line. The sky darkened over, bringing night sooner than it should have, and waves of black cloud rolled across the vast sky. The wind was picking up, too, soft like a piece of silk on Belle's skin, but getting strong enough to hint at worse to come. The branches in the trees creaked and shook, their leaves rustling like a thousand whispers.

As soon as Belle had the last piece of clothing unpegged, she lifted the basket and ran back to the house with the wind pushing into her back.

'It's got stormy out there,' she said, as she joined Fionn and Maeveen in the sitting room.

They'd both been sitting very close together on the sofa, but Maeveen leapt up like a startled cat as soon as Belle arrived.

'There you are,' she said, her face was flushed. 'You're just in time; *Blackadder's* about to start.'

She giggled and Fionn stifled a laugh.

'What's so funny?'

'Just thinking about *Blackadder*,' Fionn said.

'Aye, *Blackadder*,' Maeveen said.

Belle frowned and folded her arms. They were acting weird and she just knew it had nothing to do with *Blackadder*. Before she had a chance to question further, the opening credits were rolling and Maeveen was sitting on the sofa again, telling Belle to hurry up and get a seat.

Belle normally sat between Fionn and Maeveen – the sofa was big enough for the three of them – and she walked in that direction.

Maeveen put up her feet. 'Aw, Belle, sit on one of the chairs, I want to stretch out.'

Huffed, Belle took the armchair farthest from the TV so she could keep an eye on the other two. She noticed Maeveen's feet were almost touching Fionn and they were looking at each other, not the TV.

'You're missing the show,' Belle said, her words coming out like a slap.

Not that Belle understood the show, not really. She knew it was cool and clever, but she didn't quite get all the jokes. Most of the time she had to take her cue to laugh when Fionn and Maeveen laughed. Tonight, though, neither of them seemed to be that interested. Belle felt like she was watching it on her own.

The windowpane rattled. Belle looked over. Through the open curtains, she could see only darkness and one strip of half-light in the sky where there was a momentary gap in the clouds. A few raindrops hit the glass with muffled thuds, and the wind whooshed and whistled around the house.

The ads came on and Fionn stood up.

'Nature calls,' he said.

Maeveen followed him out the door. 'Going to put the kettle on – want tea, Belle?'

Belle shook her head.

She was alone. Her eyes wandered to the window, the ads too boring to watch. She thought she saw a flash of light outside, so quick she might not have seen it at all. Seconds later, the sky rumbled like an empty stomach waiting for its dinner.

Fionn and Maeveen came back and took their places on the sofa, even closer together this time.

'Where's your tea?' Belle asked.

'My tea? Um, changed my mind.'

'I think there's going to be a big storm,' Belle said. 'There was thunder and lightning when yous were out.'

'I'm scared of thunderstorms,' Maeveen said.

Belle was about to say 'Since when?' but Fionn spoke up before she got a chance.

'I'll look after ye.' He smiled at Maeveen.

Belle felt a twinge in her stomach. 'You—'

The TV flickered off and on and the lights wavered. The three of them looked up to the ceiling at the same time.

'Shit, what was that?' Fionn said.

'It's the storm,' Belle said.

The lights and the TV went again. Rain drummed against the window, the wind driving it all the faster.

'I'm going to tell Mammy and Daddy,' Maeveen said. 'They'll get the candles in case the lights go altogether.' She disappeared out the door.

'The lights won't really go out, will they?' Fionn said.

'They could,' Belle said. 'It happens sometimes where there's thunder.'

As if on cue, the house blinked into pitch-blackness, so black it was as though Belle was in a mine with her eyes shut tight. She heard a scream – Maeveen, caught in the limbo between the sitting room and the kitchen.

'We're going to get the candles,' their mother's voice called from the kitchen. 'Everybody just stay where you are.'

'Belle, I'm coming towards you,' Fionn whispered. 'Reach your hand out in my direction.'

Belle stood waiting for him, holding her arm out into the nothingness, hoping Fionn would find her. She felt his hand – sure, gentle – touch her.

'There you are,' he said.

He drew near and put his arm around her. Belle had never stood so near to Fionn, except in daydreams. His skin was hot and smelled of salty sweat. She was going to faint.

'Are you all right?'

She nodded, then realised he wouldn't see. 'I'm grand.'

She leaned close, breathing in his musky odour and feeling the heft of his body against her. She wanted to wrap her arms around his torso but didn't dare.

'Fuck, it's dark,' he said, with a nervous laugh.

'Are you afraid of the dark?' she said.

'I don't like it much, not this black anyway.'

'We'll get the candles soon. Mammy keeps them in a drawer in the pantry.'

The wind squealed through the trees and a crack of thunder invaded every particle of air.

'I think my eyes're starting to adjust,' Fionn said. 'I can see some shapes.'

'Same for me, over by the window mostly.'

Maeveen called out from her limbo. 'Hurry up and bring the candles, Mammy. I'm getting the creeps standing here on my own.'

'Will we try to make our way out to Maeveen?' Fionn said. 'I don't like her being stranded like that with nobody around her.'

'We'll trip over things and hurt ourselves. And Mammy told us to stay where we were.'

'We can give it a try. She's scared.'

Belle sighed, her moment alone with Fionn was over, stolen by Maeveen as usual. 'Suppose so.'

She was about to take a step towards the door when she felt Fionn squeeze her shoulder so hard it hurt.

'Wuh… what the fuck's thu… that?'

'What?'

'Do you see it, in that corner there…?'

Belle strained her eyes. At first, there was only a long shape barely visible in the silvery glow cast by the storm outside. Then, she saw.

'Stay still,' she said to Fionn. 'Stay still; he means no harm.'

'You can see him, too… but how did he get in here? Who is he?'

'Don't be afraid.'

The man by the window was motionless, silent. Belle felt his gaze on her.

'Granda?' she whispered, knowing she'd get no answer. A knot of anxiety tightened in the back of her skull. 'He's appeared like this before, Fionn,' she whispered. 'It usually means somebody's going to die.'

Fionn gasped, his breath loud in the silence. 'Thu-this… this can't be happening. I don't believe this.'

The figure turned and passed across the window, disappearing into the shadows of the room.

The lights suddenly flashed, glaring and shocking and painful to the eyes. They flickered rapidly two or three more times before stabilising. Belle's parents and Maeveen appeared at the sitting room door, her mother holding a lit candle.

'Got here a bit late,' she said, snuffing out the flame with her finger and thumb.

Belle and Fionn were still clinging to each other. Fionn's face was pale grey and he looked like he was going to throw up.

'What's going on here?' Belle's mother said, squinting her eyes. 'Surely you weren't afraid of the dark, the pair of you?'

'We saw Granda,' Belle said, 'didn't we, Fionn?'

'I don't know what I saw,' Fionn dropped to the sofa.

'Enough of that, now,' her mother said. 'Why don't I make us some tea and toast?'

The rest of the night passed uneventfully, with not a mention of what Belle and Fionn had seen, although Fionn was unusually quiet.

The next morning, they were having breakfast when the phone rang, cutting through the air and demanding attention. Belle's father went out to the hallway to answer it.

'Jesus, don't tell me that,' Belle heard him say, his voice alarmed.

Everyone fell silent, poised like deer in the woods, sensing danger. And then it came, the arrival of whatever it was they were waiting to hear.

'Aw, dear God,' Belle's father said. 'Well, sure, thanks for ringing me, Mickey.'

Belle heard the click of the handset going back on the hook and her father returned.

'That was bad news,' he said. 'Poor auld Peadar McDaid was knocked down and killed last night by a tree that fell on the road near the Post Office.'

Fionn's frightened eyes settled on Belle.

9

DERRY, PRESENT DAY

Belle jangled the keys to Fionn's flat as she stood outside his apartment block. Two stories high and painted cream and chocolate with a black double door for an entrance, the block was in the centre of town, just off Great James' Street and a few minutes' walk from Dermot's.

She approached the building and pushed the outer door. It opened with a creak – unlocked, as Dermot predicted. She stepped inside a poorly lit but clean foyer that smelled of bleach. A 'No Smoking' sign on the wall was marked with graffiti; some wag had drawn a stickman and a cloud of smoke coming out of the stick-cigarette in his mouth.

Belle took the staircase, two steps at a time, passing a young couple who were on the way down, holding hands and laughing. She climbed to the second floor where another wall sign read, 'Flats 21-40'.

A long dim corridor with fluorescent lights at intervals lay ahead. Belle gripped the key to the flat as she walked along, checking door numbers to her right and left. She needn't have bothered. Number twenty-six stood out like a neon light in a graveyard.

The door was criss-crossed with yellow police tape that repeated 'CRIME SCENE. DO NOT ENTER' in black capital letters.

Belle looked up and down the corridor and slipped the key into the mortice lock. Slowly, she turned it and heard the lock click. She pressed down on the handle and the door opened. Glancing around again to satisfy herself no one was in sight, she pulled away a few strips of tape to make room to squeeze through.

Once across the threshold, she closed the door behind her. She could get in a lot of trouble, breaking a police line, but she didn't care. All the forensics were done by now so she couldn't possibly destroy any evidence and she'd be sure to leave everything as she found it. Nothing would be disturbed.

Belle stood still, flicking on the light switch to find herself in a small entrance hall that gave her a choice of doors. She peeked quickly into each: bathroom, bedroom, living room. The living room was the best place to start.

The air was stifling, the way a place got when the weather was hot and the windows hadn't been opened in a while. She heard the muffled sounds of the city street outside, life going on oblivious to the death in here. The blinds were drawn, probably exactly as they had been on the night Fionn met his death. Luminous dust specks danced in a narrow beam of light that cut through an opening in the curtains.

She circled the living room, with deliberation, thoughtfulness. Family photos decorated the walls: a family wedding, a birthday party, a fun day at the beach. She recognised Chrissie and Dermot and Fionn, but no one else. She lingered a while on what seemed to be a recent picture of Fionn and surveyed the changes the years had made. Those eyes were still vibrant but he'd put on a little weight, had grown a goatee, and his once-golden hair was grey-speckled, cropped and receding in a widow's peak.

A bookcase, in a corner opposite a flat screen TV, stood lopsided and burgeoning with books on climate change, poverty, politics, history, the Northern Troubles. The Troubles, indeed;

something of an understatement for nearly thirty years of conflict against imperialism and oppression.

On top of an occasional table by the wall was a precarious tower of newspapers, a bundle of charcoal sticks and a couple of sketchpads. Fionn had had an artistic bent. Of course, he did. A memory of an origami lotus flower sneaked up on her.

Underfoot was a deep-pile fawn carpet, and a sofa and armchairs that didn't match were arranged in a wide arc in the general vicinity of the TV. In front of the sofa was a wooden coffee table, its smeared glass top barren, no doubt because whatever had been on it had been taken away for testing by the police.

Below the coffee table, and stretching under one of the armchairs, was a carmine stain. It didn't leave much to the imagination. The spot where Fionn lay in his last moments, where his life trickled away drop by drop. She wondered if he'd been in pain, if he'd had any notion what had been done to him, if he'd called out for his mother or his sister or somebody he loved and that loved him. Belle couldn't take her eyes away for the longest time.

She kneeled down and touched the stain. Feeling the hardened blood on her fingertips made his death suddenly, unbearably, real. A pang struck her, so tight it was as though her heart was being turned in a vice. Fionn was gone, forever, and she'd missed her chance to put things right. All these years, she'd chosen to say nothing and instead just carry the guilt around like some putrefying corpse that she kept hidden out of sight. Now, it was too late.

She pulled herself away and wandered into the kitchen, which she accessed via the living room. Yet more books and newspapers lay strewn on the table. A box crammed with used plastic and cardboard containers and packaging leaned against the wall by the fridge, which itself contained several microwavable meals – all spaghetti Bolognese, a carton of semi-skimmed milk and a tub of spreadable butter. A fridge magnet left explanations unnecessary, 'Many people have eaten in this kitchen and gone on to lead normal healthy lives'. She smiled, remembering Fionn's sense of humour back in the day.

She moved to the bedroom, a room that was trying to be untidy but didn't have enough clutter. A double bed with a black metal frame took up the space, next to an attractive bay window with a window seat. An array of medicines lay strewn on a small table by the bed. Belle scanned the labels on the boxes and recognised two of the names: fluoxetine – aka Prozac – and tramadol. An anti-depressant and a painkiller – high dosages, too. *Jesus, Fionn,* she thought, *what was going on with you?*

Belle opened a pine wardrobe near the door. A subtle whiff of aftershave met her nostrils, mingled with a musky odour so immediate she had to turn round to be sure Fionn wasn't standing beside her.

A couple of white shirts dangled from the rail along with one black tie and a well-worn dress jacket and matching trousers. The shelf space at the top stored two pairs of jeans, a half a dozen T-shirts and a charcoal fisherman-knit jumper. Not exactly John Paul Gaultier.

She went back to the living room. A deep breath escaped from inside her body, from the pit of her stomach or maybe her soul. She wished she hadn't come. Her visit achieved its goal but what she discovered left her wanting to rip her heart out so she couldn't feel anymore. The thought popped into her head; Fionn standing in her hallway in Dublin, not seeing her.

She had to get out of there, right away, and not breathe the stifling air for another second.

*

The corridor for all its dreariness was more welcome than a cold beer on a blistering hot day. Belle locked the door and exhaled slowly, taking a minute to calm her mind as it swirled with images from the flat all mixed up with memories of the past. She needed to get away, away from this building, the city. She needed to go back home to the clean open air. She needed a walk on the beach with her bare feet sinking into the warm sand and the sea breeze blowing in her hair.

The shrill ring of her phone interrupted her thoughts. She checked the display. Damn, it was Shane. She wanted to ignore him as she'd had before, but decided she shouldn't. She didn't have to be a bitch every day.

'Hi,' she said, 'what's up?' She leaned back on the corridor wall.

'Belle? Uh, um, you picked up,' Shane answered. 'Well, how're you getting on?'

'All good here, been busy, you know, catching up with folks.'

'That's good. It's nice to hear your voice. I've been worried about you.'

'No need for that. I can take care of myself. Anything new at the office?'

'No, just the usual. Oisin and Fintan had a bit of a set-to yesterday, highly entertaining, you know how they can be, but a storm in a teacup as always.'

Belle smiled. The normality of the goings-on at the office was comforting after her unsettling visit to Fionn's flat.

'I was thinking...' Shane was saying.

Belle's smiled disappeared. There was never a happy ending when Shane started a sentence with that.

'What if I took a few days off and came up to see you? Could be nice to spend some time together outside of Dublin, away from work. And I'd like to be there for you, when you're dealing with the loss of your friend.'

The phone almost fell out of her hand. Shane? Coming to her home in Donegal? That was never going to happen. She didn't like mixing her life in Dublin with her life at home. Easier, cleaner, to keep them separate.

'Shane, that's nice of you—'

'Don't say no. I've been thinking about it. I could stay in a hotel nearby so I wouldn't have to intrude on your family home and…'

A man appeared at the end of the corridor. He piqued her interest as she observed him walking at a painstakingly slow pace in her direction. He was in his late forties, she guessed, tall but hunched over slightly as though he was self-conscious about his height. He had a head as round as a football, a flat wide face and cherub cheeks. At first glance, his attire looked formal, but closer inspection revealed something off about the picture. His suit trousers and jacket were stained and shiny with wear; his white shirt was not so white, especially at the collar and cuffs; his tie was lopsided and clashed with the colour of the suit; and as for footwear, he wore a beaten-out pair of cheap trainers, minus laces.

She only half-listened as Shane rattled on.

'I've been looking up different places to go,' he was saying. 'You have a shitload of beaches up there…'

She decided she would let him say his piece before interjecting with 'Thanks, but no thanks' and ending the call. When she got back to Dublin, and that wouldn't be long, she'd have to end their relationship. She'd let it drag on and on for too long. Right now, though, ending the call would be enough, if only she could get a word in edgeways.

The curious man wasn't alone. He had a bedraggled black-and-brown Jack Russell terrier on a lead. He was talking to the dog, giving out to him, actually giving out to him and pointing his finger like the dog was another person, maybe a small child, who'd been bold.

'I told you, Spanner, didn't I?' he said, his voice grating, like he was hoarse but was straining to talk anyway. 'I told you never do that. Why don't you do what I tell you?'

The dog looked unperturbed, as though he'd seen and heard it all before.

'Are you listening to me, boy? You just wait 'til I get you home. It's the quiet room for you.'

The pair stopped opposite Fionn's door at number thirty-six and it was then that the man seemed to first notice Belle. He rooted around for his keys, all the while eyeing Belle with small eyes magnified behind thick glasses, looking her up and down with suspicion.

Belle caught his eye and waved. His gaze bounced away without acknowledging her, afraid to have been caught staring, no doubt. He opened his flat and he and the dog quickly disappeared behind the door. She made a mental note; he looked like a nosey neighbour, the type who noticed things. He might be worth calling upon, although it would do no harm to get a sounding from Dermot first.

'Can you hear me, Belle. Are you still there?'

She'd forgotten Shane was still on the call. 'Yeah, I'm here.'

'So, what do you think?'

'Think? I think it's a bad idea. I know you mean well, and thanks for that, but I just need space to deal with this myself.'

'But Belle—'

'I've got to go. Talk soon.'

10

DONEGAL, 1986

Belle's idyllic time alone with Fionn came to an abrupt end a few days after the night of the storm. They were watching an old black-and-white film on the TV when her mother came through to the sitting room.

'You have a visitor, Belle,' her mother said. 'Hunter Campbell. Go out now to see him.'

'Hunter?' Belle said. She wasn't pleased. 'Tell him to come in here.'

'Are you wise?' her mother said. 'What've we told you?'

'I forgot, we're not to be telling people Fionn's here. So, tell him I'm busy or something.'

'Get out, now, Belle, or you'll have your father to contend with.'

Belle puffed. 'It's not fair. I want to watch the film. Fionn says it's a noir.'

'Go on, Belle,' Fionn said. 'Do as your mother says. We'll have plenty of time this evening.'

'And remember, say nothing to him about Fionn,' her mother said. 'It's none of his business who we have staying with us.'

Belle threw a sulky pout and dragged herself to her feet. Hunter could be one serious pain in the neck.

*

'How's your holidays been going?' Hunter asked Belle, as they wandered down the lane towards the woods below the house.

'All quiet, taking it easy,' Belle said, careful not to mention Fionn – it wouldn't be easy when he was her whole world these days. 'What about you? I suppose you've been working with your Daddy the whole time?'

'Yup, this is my first day off,' he said, the brace on his front teeth making the words come out like he was sucking marbles. 'With our David being in Australia, more of the work's falling to me.'

'Um,' Belle said, glancing at Hunter as he walked by her side.

Compared to Fionn, he wasn't much to look at, not that she'd ever actually noticed before. He was a year younger and had always been slightly smaller than she was, until the last year or so when he seemed to shoot up like a magic beanstalk. The growth spurt left him looking gangly with limbs that were too long for the rest of him. He had creamy milk skin with ruddy cheeks and his hair was the colour of barley straw, which – for as long as she'd known him – was cut into the worst bowl haircut on the planet.

The chug-chug of a tractor engine came into earshot and rounding a corner was Belle's father. He stopped beside them and they waved.

'You two be careful, now, if you go near the burn, do you hear me?'

'We will,' Belle said.

He drove on and was soon gone.

'He tells us that every time he sees us,' Belle said.

'I know,' Hunter laughed. 'Daddy goes on about it, too. What age does he think I am? If he told me once, he told me a thousand times – it's got dangerous spots and when he was ten, a boy his age drowned.'

'I can swim anyway,' Belle said, 'so if I fell in, I could swim to safety.'

74

'Me too,' Hunter said, 'I could swim all the way across to Rathmullan and underwater, too.'

'No way, Rathmullan's at the other side of the lough.'

'But I could; I'm able to hold my breath for the longest time. My PE teacher even said so.'

At a large gap in the hedge, they stepped through into a wood of hazel and ash. The ground, soft and springy beneath Belle's feet, was wild green and dotted with buttercups and dog roses. They came to the burn and she plopped herself on a grassy slope. Hunter joined her and they chatted idly as they aimed stones at the other bank. The only sounds were the gentle trickle of the water and the occasional flapping of wings through the heavy foliage.

'How's your David getting on in Australia anyway?'

'Aw, he's mad about it. He's surfing and diving and everything and he says the Australians are the best of craic.'

'What's surfing?'

'David said you use a long board and you piggyback on the waves.'

'God, that's sounds like brilliant fun. Don't they have their Christmas dinner on the beach, too?'

'They do. David says it's so hot at Christmas you could fry sausages on the rocks.'

'That kind of heat would kill me.'

'He's made friends with some of the cyclists on the Australian team for the Commonwealth Games.'

Belle shrugged.

'Ireland's the only country in the British Isles that doesn't enter the commonwealth games.'

'That's 'cos we're not in the stupid commonwealth.'

'It's not stupid and it'd be nice if we were.'

'It would not. After the hundreds of years Ireland spent trying to get rid of the British, and sure we're still trying to get rid of them from the North, what would we want to be in the commonwealth for?'

'Speak for yourself. Daddy says the worst thing happened to us was leaving British rule.'

'Well, my Daddy says the worst thing happened to us was being colonised, and the second worst thing was Partition.'

'That's rubbish.'

Belle wanted to push Hunter into the river for saying what he said. Yet she should've known better than to talk to him about history or the British or the conflict in the North. His family were Protestants; they probably even came to Ireland during the Plantation of Ulster, when the English queen pushed the Irish off their land and gave it away like it was sweeties to her favoured gentry. The Campbells were openly pro-British and pro-empire. Not all Protestants were, that was true, but the Campbells made no secret of it. The McGees on the other hand made no secret of wanting an end to the British presence in Ireland and to the Partition that divided the country into the two jurisdictions of North and South. And yet, in spite of these differences, the two families were good neighbours and Belle and Hunter were the best of pals, for the most part.

'Let's go to the old hut for a while,' Belle said.

Hunter got up. 'Good idea.'

The old hut was a ramshackle outbuilding that no one went to much, except for Belle and Hunter. It was in an out-of-the-way spot at the end of the cherry orchard. A wooden pallet leaned against the gavel end and they used it as a ladder to climb to the roof, careful to avoid a bunch of nettles entangled around its slats. The corrugated tin roof rattled and creaked as Belle walked across to the middle. The rust-dappled surface was pleasantly warm and she stretched out like a cat basking in the sun.

Hunter settled next to her and breathed out a long, relaxed sigh. 'It's good here.'

'The best,' she said, not missing Fionn so much now.

The pair stayed quiet for a while. Belle followed the path of a fluffy cloud as it glided across the sun, blocking the rays for a minute before journeying on. An orange-and-black butterfly flapped past her nose and a ladybird landed on Hunter's arm for rest before taking off again.

'Did I tell you I've got the new Smiths album?' Hunter said, after a while.

'*The Queen is Dead*? Already have it – well, Maeveen has it. But I'm into LL Cool J and James Brown these days.'

'What? Since when?'

'Since…' Belle bit her lip before she said anymore. 'Since Fionn' was the answer but she couldn't say that to Hunter. 'I dunno,' she lied, 'I just started liking them this summer.'

'Are you still into our indie stuff?'

'I am but it doesn't mean I can't like other music. I'll make you a tape.'

'All right then.'

Belle closed her eyes, the sunshine making her drowsy.

'Aw, naw,' Hunter sprang up, 'look at the time. It's nearly five o'clock. I have to get back for milking time.'

'Five already?' Belle leaned up on her elbow.

'I better run. Don't want to be late.' He dashed across the roof. 'See ye… if I can get another day off soon.'

'See ye.'

Belle lay back down on the roof again, her hands cupped behind her head. She should probably get home, too, but with the air so warm and the evening so peaceful, she couldn't help but linger. She was in no rush. She could stay a while longer and let her thoughts dwell on Fionn. Her eyes drooped, then closed, as dreamy thoughts took hold.

Life was good with him around, exciting and fun. '*Play your card, Belle,*' she heard his voice whisper in her ear. '*Play your card, Belle,*' now Maeveen's voice. They were in the sitting room playing Texas Hold 'Em… Belle told them not to rush her as she strained with the choice of raising it or calling it…

Her eyes opened. She was still on the roof, not playing cards in the sitting room. Some time had passed, though, because the sun was lower in the raspberry-ripple sky. Her mouth was as dry as a desert wind and her head throbbed like a heartbeat. She sat up, feeling sick. She was sure she'd been playing poker with Fionn and Maeveen, playing for big money and she was wiping the floor with them, but it wasn't so. She'd been dreaming. Funny how it felt so real; she could hear them talking to her and everything. It couldn't be a dream...

Then she heard them again, Fionn and Maeveen, whispering and giggling. This was no dream. She really could hear them. Only they weren't talking about poker and they weren't talking to her.

'Want a cigarette?' Fionn said.

Belle's mind went into overdrive. How could Fionn possibly be outside? After all the warnings they got about him staying indoors.

'Light one for yourself,' Maeveen said, 'and I'll take a couple of drags.'

'Whatever you say.'

Belle eased across the roof, trying to be quiet so she could listen better to what they were saying, but the tin rattled loud enough for the sound to echo through the trees. Belle froze. Maeveen and Fionn went quiet. Not for long, though. They started talking again. Belle breathed out.

Her new position allowed her to look over the edge. The cherry orchard below was filled with deep shadows in the fading light, making it hard to see. The sharp, bitter smell of the nettles reached her nostrils. Belle searched between the trees, following the sound of the voices. Something was there. A flash of light green, the colour of the dress Maeveen put on that morning before going into town. Belle craned her neck lower to get a better vantage point. Now she saw a patch of blue beside the green. Fionn's T-shirt.

Clambering down silently, she just missed falling into the nettles. At ground level, Maeveen and Fionn came into full view.

Belle got on her hunkers to watch them. Maeveen was lolling back and forth on the swing their father made for them years ago out of an old car tyre and a rope secured to one of the low-hanging boughs. Fionn was beside her, lighting a cigarette. He handed it to her and she took a long pull before giving it back.

Something about them, the relaxed, familiar way they had with each other, made Belle think this wasn't the first time they'd sneaked out for a clandestine smoke by the swing. She felt a twinge in her heart and her stomach lunged as they laughed and talked like the closest of friends. Fionn wasn't that way around her but she couldn't quite work out what exactly was different. Was it how close he stood?

His hand went up to Maeveen's long, silky hair. Maeveen steadied the swing with her feet. They went quiet, not moving, not looking at anything but each other. As she watched what happened next, Belle's eyes widened and she blinked twice in the hope they were playing tricks on her. This couldn't be true. No, no, no, it couldn't. Spying on them from her hiding place, she saw them lean closer and kiss, and kiss, and kiss, until she couldn't bear to look any more.

Her hand flew up to her mouth to stop a scream. A whimper escaped, too tiny and faraway to be heard, and a tear rolled down her cheek. Another followed, and then another, until soon a steady stream ran in streaks across her face.

She got to her feet and, for a split second, she considered barging over there and telling them exactly what she thought of their carry-on. But she didn't. Instead, she ran, wanting to get away as quickly and as far from what she had seen and didn't want to believe. The undergrowth rustled as she fled, making noise that might betray her presence, but she was past caring. Nothing mattered anymore. Her life was as good as over.

11
DERRY, PRESENT DAY

Friday afternoon rolled round and Belle picked up Dermot outside his house.

'Where're we going on this mystery trip then?' Dermot asked, clicking in his seatbelt.

Belle drove across the top deck of the blue-and-white Craigavon Bridge, which crossed the River Foyle at a narrow point, and took a left at the other side. The sky above was dull; the sun, a shimmering disc behind a layer of hazy cloud.

'In the back seat,' Belle motioned with her left hand. 'And before I forget, I want to give these back.' She opened the glove compartment to reveal the keys to Fionn's apartment.

Dermot took them and put them in his pocket. He reached round and retrieved one of the maps from Fionn's box file. He studied it for a moment.

'Is this Fionn's? It's the Glenshane Pass. What's out there, apart from mountains and air that smells like cow shit?'

'I don't know but that's what we're going to find out.'

'Did you find out what Fionn was up to?'

'From what I've gleaned from his notes, it's about illegal dumping.'

'What? Fly-tipping? He was getting his knickers into a twist over fly-tipping?'

'I don't mean somebody throwing a bin bag into a ditch. This could possibly be thousands of tonnes of waste being buried in remote sites all over the place. Illegal dumping on this scale is a multi-million-pound racket; it's not selling jellybeans on a street corner.'

'Evergreen's behind it?'

'Seems so.'

'I shouldn't be surprised with all the other shit they're up to.'

'If Evergreen's as corrupt as you've said they are, I can see why Fionn was being cautious.'

They passed the hospital on the left, and leaving the city behind them, picked up the pace on the A6, which they'd have to follow for about twenty miles or more to get to their destination.

'They're supposed to recycle any waste they can,' Dermot said, 'and dispose of the rest safely. None of it should be winding up in the ground. But I suppose the less waste they have to process through proper channels, the less money they have to spend and the more they can siphon off.'

'They're in breach of their council contracts,' Belle said. 'Though that's only one side of their wrongdoing. This activity has huge environmental repercussions into the bargain.'

'They're scumbags. And they treat us workers like shit, too. The pay barely above minimum wage; we don't get company sick pay; they don't give us the right safety gear for handling some of the more toxic waste; and we're using machinery we're not even trained on.'

'Seems like they'd stoop to just about anything.'

'One of the workers was badly injured a couple of months ago when a bale of waste fell on him. They got the security guards to leave him off-site before they called the ambulance, and they let him go when he was still in hospital. He didn't get any compensation because they were able to deny anything happened on their premises.'

'Jesus,' Belle said.

'And you want to see how they treat the migrant workers. They've got Poles and Portuguese working and they keep them off the books. Never mind minimum wage. Half the time, these poor fuckers don't get any wage at all.'

Trees and hedgerows rushed by in a blur and the rolling hillocks of fields and heath created a collage of muted greens and yellows and browns.

Dermot extracted a crushed pouch of tobacco and a lighter from his front pocket. 'I'm gasping for a smoke, can I light up? I've a few rollies already made up so I won't get tobacco all over your car.'

Belle instinctively went to say no but changed her mind. 'Put your window down and let the smoke blow out your side. I don't want to breathe any of that crap.'

'You're a darling,' Dermot said, placing a cigarette between his lips and lighting up. He took a long, satisfying drag.

'Those things will kill you.' She cast him a sideways glance.

'Thing is, I know that,' he pointed to his temple with his free hand, 'up here. I've read all about how bad they are, full of poisons, even arsenic, and all the damage they can do. I get it. I do. But knowing it and doing something about it are two different things.'

'Maybe you need to get cancer first or a stroke.'

'You're a right ray of sunshine.'

'I am known for my glass-half-full attitude.'

'I bet.'

Belle smiled. 'Listen, I didn't mention it on the phone – 'cos I think we should be really careful how we deal with this – but I wanted to pick your brains.'

'Pick away.'

'Do you know anybody called Rita Wilson, Dr Rita Wilson?'

'Um, Wilson,' Dermot repeated. 'No, sorry, don't know her. Was she in Fionn's notes?'

'Yeah. What about Patricia Healy? She's a doctor, too.'

'Dr Healy?' Dermot pulled on his cigarette. 'Now, I do know her. She's one of the cancer doctors at Altnagelvin hospital; she was my ex-mother-in-law's consultant.'

'Okay, that's good to know,' Belle said. 'What about MacCool, do you know anybody called MacCool?'

'What's his first name?'

'Dunno; don't even know whether it is a he.'

'I know plenty of MacCools but unless I had more to go on, I wouldn't know where to start.'

'Shit, I—'

'Maybe I do know,' Dermot said, shaking his head slowly. 'It couldn't be, though; it's too fucking ridiculous.'

'Try me,' Belle said.

'Well, aw, okay, you know how Fionn wasn't his real name.'

'It was just a nickname.'

'Right, but do you know how he was given it?'

Belle shook her head.

'By the time he was twelve, he was very tall, like he was probably close to his full height by then, nearly six foot, and he had a rep for being afraid of nothing. Like at riots with the police and the Brits; he was legendary with his aim. And somebody, don't know who, said he was a warrior like Fionn MacCool.'

'Fionn MacCool from Irish mythology? So, that's how he got the name Fionn. But where does the MacCool bit come in?'

'MacCool was what he called me. He used to say me and him were two peas in a pod. He was Fionn; I was MacCool.'

'You're the MacCool from his notes. The problem is: you don't know anything about his investigation. What could I possibly find out from you?'

Dermot shrugged. 'I have no clue.'

'Did he ever say or do anything out of the ordinary recently? I'm grasping at straws here, but if he did, it might have meaning for the investigation.'

'Let me sleep on it.'

'Oh look, we're almost at the Glenshane Pass,' Belle said, 'I think the road we want could be the next right or maybe the one after.'

'From the map, it's the one after,' Dermot said, flicking the butt of his cigarette out the passenger window.

The car climbed ever upwards. The temperature dropped a degree or two, cooling the sultry air, and a spit of rain slapped off the windscreen. In a matter of minutes, they arrived at the turn-off they wanted, a narrow and winding country road that stretched for miles like a strip of liquorice unfolding before them.

They went higher and deeper into the Sperrin Mountains, flanked by undulating peaks and hollows of rushes and heather and white-beige mat-grass. Sheep grazed freely, each sheared and sprayed with a dot of colour, and small lively streams carved thin gulches into the marshy ground.

A farmhouse, small with whitewashed walls, came into view. An older man wearing a beanie hat and a dark boiler suit watched as they drove past and Belle waved. He nodded his head in acknowledgement.

The wind picked up, whistling softly against the wing mirror, and a ray of glorious sun finally broke through the veil of cloud. Soon, they came to an elevated plateau. The remote bog stretched as far as the eye could see, planted with managed forests of Lodgepole Pine and Sitka Spruce and scarred with overgrown turf banks. Distant blue-grey peaks floated on the horizon.

'This place's freaking me out,' Dermot said. 'It's like we're on the moon.'

'Said like a true city boy.'

'Give me the city any day.'

'See that turn-off up there, on the right?' Belle said. 'I think that's what we're looking for.'

A twisting track covered in light grey gravel disappeared into an expanse of forest.

'Aw, shit, this isn't even a road,' Dermot said. 'We could breakdown or anything here.'

'Keep quiet; you're making me nervous.'

Belle concentrated on her driving, following the track for about a mile before she came to the end of the forest. There, in front of them, hollowed out of a sheer incline was a decommissioned quarry the size of half a football field.

Belle brought the car to a stop and got out. Dermot followed. The wall of the quarry was sandy gravel rock, largely overgrown with moss, grass and willow saplings. A nearby stream gurgled and splashed on its flow downhill and a curious sparrow hawk circled overhead, emitting a harsh 'Kek-kek-kek' call and coming to rest on the bough of a nearby tree.

'I don't see any shite dumped here,' Dermot said, 'apart from the odd piece of rubbish and the plastic bag hanging off that bush over there. You'd see that anywhere. What were you expecting to find?'

Belle had her mobile phone in her hand, ready to record photographic evidence. She slowly scanned the site, careful to note the remarkable – and the unremarkable, for that matter. Anything could be a useful lead; an important clue.

'Let's check out that heavy machinery over there?'

She pointed to a yellow digger and a bulldozer, incongruous in such natural surroundings, parked a distance away at the far edge of the quarry. The bulldozer had lumps of soil stuck to its blade. At one side of the quarry floor, the sandy soil was freshly turned. At the other side was a quarry lake. Belle went towards the soil first, taking photos as she went. The soil was covered in tracks, from the digger and the bulldozer no doubt, and in parts, she could see tiny plumes of smoke hovering close to the surface.

Belle's hand shot to her face, covering her mouth and nose. 'Fuck, can you get that stink? It's like rotten eggs.'

'Aye,' Dermot said, coughing, 'I get it. It's burning the eyes out of my head. I'm used to rotten smells at work but this is taking the piss.'

'The soil's been disturbed here,' Belle said. 'Could be they're dumping waste and covering it over with topsoil. Let's take a look at the lake.'

As she drew nearer to the water, her nostrils were assaulted with yet stronger odours. She felt her stomach lurch and her hand involuntarily reached up to hold her nose. Behind her, she heard Dermot hurling up his lunch, breakfast and whatever else was in his stomach.

'God help us,' he mumbled.

'Do you want to go back to the car?'

'I'm okay,' Dermot said, breathless, 'there's nothing left to throw up at this stage. How're you able to stand it?'

'I'm holding my nose, though it's still awful.'

'It's like something went up this quarry's asshole and died.'

'That's exactly what it's like. I remember Daddy taking me to a meat factory when I was a kid – the stench would've floored an elephant. This is similar but worse, I think.'

She didn't dare go any closer. The water was deathly still, sludge-like and as black as a winter's night, and a tell-tale rainbow from an oil spill oozed across its surface. A spindly frog, dead and decaying, lay by the water's edge. Belle snapped some more photos.

'Let's get back to the car,' she said, hurrying to the safety of its confined space.

Dermot was at her heels. They jumped inside and closed the doors behind them. Belle breathed in a lungful of stuffy but mercifully odourless air.

'Can we taste smell?' Dermot said. 'I feel like I can taste it on my tongue, is that possible?'

'I'm able to taste it, too,' she rolled down the window to spit. 'If I ever doubted Fionn's file, here I've got incontrovertible truth.'

Dermot looked at her with bloodshot eyes. 'This is so fucked up.'

'And then some. Let's get out of here.'

'The sooner I get back to Derry, the better. We can have that drink you promised me.'

'I thought you might've forgotten.'

'No chance. Mind you, I'm not sure I can hold anything down after that.'

'All right, I'll keep my word, but I promised one drink and one drink it's going to be.'

*

Belle was soon out on the mountain road again and headed for Derry.

'I need another smoke,' Dermot said, clearing his throat, 'do you mind?'

'Keep the window down.'

They came to the farmhouse with the whitewashed walls and the man from before was still there, this time walking out of the gate.

Belle drove past and then stopped abruptly. 'Hang on,' she said.

She put the car into reverse, backtracking to where the man stood.

'Hello,' she said, 'how's it going?'

'What about ye?' Dermot said.

'How are yous?' the man said, casually.

He pulled off his beanie hat to reveal a shock of white hair that stood upright like stalks of grass. His skin was weather-beaten and he had a long sharp nose, the kind that could cut paper as Belle's mother would've said.

'Sorry to bother you,' Belle said, 'I was wondering if I could ask you something.'

The man jerked his head, indicating the affirmative.

'This might seem like a strange question, but have you seen much traffic going up into that old quarry back there?'

The man twisted the hat in his hand and turned to face the quarry as though looking at it was going to help him answer. 'I saw ye driving past a while ago. Ye went up into the quarry?'

'We had a look around.'

'Find what ye were looking for?'

'Maybe, so has there been much activity?'

The man sniffed and ran his hand across his hair. 'Activity, aye, ye could say that. What do they call ye, anyway?'

'My apologies, I should've introduced myself. I'm Belle McGee. I'm a reporter.'

'That's interesting now, Belle.'

'People just call me McGee.'

'I'm Martin Higgins. Martin'll do me fine.'

'Pleased to meet you, Martin.'

'Likewise. Are ye up here on business or pleasure?'

'Ah, business, I suppose.'

'Did somebody tell ye about the lorries then?'

'You've seen them?'

'Couldn't miss them. It's been going on a long while now. They rattle past the house in the middle of the night, a few nights a week, every week, up and down the road – or they did until very recently. Me and my son Paddy watched them from the living room window a few times and Paddy followed up as far as the turn-off there one time. That's where they're always headed.'

'What do you think they're doing?'

'Do ye not know? If ye were up there, ye wouldn't have to ask.'

'We didn't see anything.' Belle deliberately wasn't giving anything away. Best to have the information coming from Martin's side of the conversation.

'Ye have a nose, don't ye? Times ye couldn't miss the stink; depending on what way the wind's blowing, it could strip paint.

The burn that goes down the side of our house; it runs colours that water should never be, and sometimes big heaps of froth gather up at the river's edge. I've seen it with my own eyes. They're dumping stuff up there – Christ knows what. We get our drinking water from a well in one of our fields and we're worried it's been poisoned.'

'Did you report it?'

'We told Brendan Lynch from the council.'

Brendan Lynch. Belle made a mental note of the name; one to follow up, perhaps. 'And what happened?'

'Nothing, not one thing.'

Belle was about to ask another question when she heard a feeble shout.

'Granda,' a voice called. 'Granda, can I come with ye?'

'Go on into the house, Seanie. Ye can't be out here, son.'

Belle's eyes followed the voice. Her heart stopped in her chest. Seanie was a boy no more than six or seven. He wore a pair of baggy shorts and a T-shirt that hung off him like his body was a flimsy coat hanger. His head was as bald as a bowling ball and Belle could see he had no eyelashes or eyebrows. She turned to Martin and their eyes met, his scarred with sadness.

'But I wanna come with ye, Granda.'

'Sure I'm going nowhere, I'm coming back now.'

Seanie groaned, though he didn't go any further.

'Talk to Lynch,' Martin said. 'That's my advice to ye, and if ye can do something about what's going on, fair play to ye. I've to go, have to get the boy inside.'

Belle gave Seanie another glance. 'I'm sorry, Martin,' she said, 'about the boy.'

'Augh, cancer doesn't care what age ye are. He's getting treatment. It's sore on him, God help him. He got a bad infection last month so we've to keep him indoors, but he's like any youngster, he wants to be outside.'

'I wish him the best.'

'No bother, see ye now.' Martin stuck the beanie back on his head and walked away.

Belle started the car and began driving.

'The poor wean,' Dermot said, 'and his family.'

'I can't bear to think about it.'

Belle picked up speed, putting distance between them and the Higgins homestead. She thought about Seanie, the pitiful little figure he cut standing, sort of hunched, at the side of the road, calling to his grandfather.

'We've just come from an open-air cesspit,' Belle said, 'where downstream is a sick boy.' She glanced across at Dermot. 'And Fionn's evidence names a cancer specialist.'

12

Belle and Dermot were back on the main road. A road sign up ahead read '*Londonderry 25 miles*' – Londonderry, of course, being Derry's colonial name.

'Do you know much about the man living in the flat across from Fionn's, number thirty-six?' Belle asked.

'You mean Ed Ramsey? He's lost at sea. Me and Fionn called him Ed-the-ball, you know, instead of head-the-ball.'

'What a charming description of a fellow human being. So, what can you tell me about him?'

'Not that much,' Dermot said. 'He's smart, book-smart, so they say, was at Queen's and all, but he didn't finish his course.'

'Does he have any family, a wife?'

'No, he's not married and I've never seen him with any female companion, though I know he's got a few sisters living in Derry. He hated Fionn – and me, too, for that matter. Said we were out to do him harm, that we were talking about him all the time.'

'He sounds paranoid.'

'He is.'

'I'd like to get a chat with him.'

'What for?'

'He might know something about the night Fionn died.'

'Like what?'

'Like, I dunno, I just have a feeling he might've seen something. Maybe he saw whoever was with Fionn that night.'

'No way, he wouldn't know who or what he saw. He can't tell fact from fiction most of the time.'

'Still, he—'

'McGee, seriously, don't trust anything he says.'

She turned to see his eyes darken and his face become serious.

'Okay, if you say so,' Belle said.

She was a little surprised at Dermot's reaction and decided not to pursue the subject any further, but inwardly she planned to do her own thing regardless.

*

It was getting late as they neared the city, but Belle had one more stop to make.

'Do you mind if we make a quick visit to the Evergreen site?'

'What, now? Don't you think I've seen enough of that place for one week?'

'I only want to take a look, get a sense of it. We won't even have to get out of the car.'

'You owe me more than one drink for this.'

'Come on, this is investigative journalism in action. You're part of my team now.'

'Aye, right,' Dermot said, lighting another cigarette and opening his window a sliver to let the smoke escape.

'What's the fastest route to go?'

'There's a road to the right you can take, just before you get to the hospital. I'll show you where. It's a shortcut that'll bring you out onto the Clooney Road and Evergreen's a few miles out that way.'

Belle followed Dermot's directions. The sky above them began to clear of cloud and the sun dropped a little closer to the horizon.

'Take the next left,' Dermot said, 'into the industrial park there – that's the place you're looking for.'

Belle turned down a long, straight road and travelled for about half a mile, passing warehouses on either side until she saw a green and white sign with 'Evergreen' printed across it in big black letters. The Evergreen site was surrounded by high chain-link fences topped with barbed wire. Belle brought the car to a stop at a lay-by opposite. Inside was a tidy area with a grass verge and a gravel surface. A handful of cars were parked near the entrance and behind them was a sprawling warehouse, which had two red roller shutter doors along the side and another smaller door, labelled 'Reception', at the front.

'See that Merc?' Dermot said. 'That's the boss man's car.'

'Tom Sweet – he's earning a nice penny to afford wheels like that. What about the others?'

'The Saab convertible's the company accountant and that Astra belongs to Beavis or Butthead, I don't know which. The rest, I'm not sure.'

'Mm, I imagined it to be, I dunno, busier – more going on. It seems very clean and neat for a waste company.'

'All the waste gets brought into the warehouse – it's massive inside – and they make a point of keeping the outside spotless. It wasn't always like that; used to be a mess, but the tenants in the other units complained we were a breeding ground for rats. When Sweet took over, he put an end to that.'

'Probably worth his while making the outside look ship-shape. Lets them get up to all sorts without drawing unwanted attention. What goes on inside?'

'The lorries bringing waste drive in and there's different sections for recyclables, food waste, general waste. Us workers spend most of our time sorting out the recyclables, separating them into glass, plastics, cardboard, paper, that kind of thing. Most of the stuff's flattened or crushed, to make it as compact as possible, and then we put it into big square bales, which look like giant dice. The food waste gets put into holding tanks.'

'What happens then?'

'As far as I know, other lorries take away all the waste we process.'

'Where to?'

'You're going to think I'm a total dough-head, but I don't know where they take it. I couldn't care less; I just do the job I'm paid to do and watch the clock 'til home time.'

'You've never been curious?'

'Seriously? Maybe some people get a real hard-on for the world of waste but it does nothing for me.'

'Fionn took an interest.'

'That was Fionn for you. He was one of them conscientious types, always on a crusade for some cause or other, always trying to help people, fighting injustice. You know what he was like.'

Belle nodded. Even the Fionn she remembered from so long ago was like that. 'Come on,' she said, 'let's go. My stomach's had enough of this place for one day.'

13

'What's your poison?'

Belle stood at Dermot's side as he ordered their long-awaited drink. She thought for a second. Her car was parked in William Street and she had to drive home so it might be best to hold off on the alcohol. On the other hand, a stiff drink would be nice after her day's work. Not to mention it was Friday, or that Dermot would probably blow a fuse if she opted for a sparkling water.

'Morgan Spice and coke,' she said, deciding she could dilute it and drink it slowly, and still be just about safe to drive home.

'Nice one. Ah, Phil, Morgan Spice and coke and a pint of Harp.'

'No bother, Dermot,' the barman said. 'Jesus, shocking news about Fionn. Very sorry, man.'

Dermot shook his head, a grave look on his face. The barman went off to prepare their order. They were in the Dungloe Bar at the top of Waterloo Street – Dermot's choice.

Belle took a good look around. 'I can't remember the last time I was in here. I wouldn't recognise it.'

'The last time I was in here was with Fionn. The night...' Dermot looked down at the counter and scratched at a notch in the wood.

Phil arrived back with the drinks. Dermot went to pay, but Phil stopped him.

'This round's on the house.'

Dermot and Belle lifted their glasses and moved away.

'There's a corner over this way, off the beaten path,' Dermot said.

Belle followed. The bar was quiet with just a few barflies propping up the counter – every one of which Dermot knew – and a group of giggling, chattering girls taking up a table near the entrance. The lighting was low, casting a soft golden tone. The smell of stale beer and wood permeated the air, not unpleasant, especially after the olfactory assault of earlier.

Dermot plopped himself down on a small wooden stool. Belle took up position next to him.

'We'll drink to Fionn tonight, McGee,' he said, and held his glass in the air. 'To Fionn, the best there was.'

'To Fionn,' Belle said.

Dermot drank half his pint in one go. Belle consciously took a small sip.

'I don't know what life's going to be like from now on,' Dermot said. 'I'm lost without him.' He exhaled, puffing his cheeks. 'You know, it's funny, just sitting here having a drink with you. All the years of Fionn talking about the McGees and now here you are in the flesh, Baby Belle.'

Belle's cheeks felt warm. 'I'm hardly a baby anymore.'

'Oh, I can see that,' he said.

Belle caught his eye and a hot tingling rippled through her insides, uncomfortable and pleasant both at the same time.

'Right enough,' he went on, 'Maeveen was the one he talked about the most. If things had worked out different... but it's pointless going back over that old ground.'

Dermot didn't know how right he was. Belle had spent most of her life avoiding going back over that old ground. She lifted a beermat and tapped it against the table absently.

'They nearly did get together, you know,' Dermot said.

'I know all about it,' Belle sighed, 'back then—'

'Not back then. I'm talking about years later.'

Belle stopped tapping the beermat.

'They hooked up one night,' he said. 'Fionn said it was as if they picked up where they left off, even after all they'd been through.'

'She never told me. What happened? Did they start going out?'

'No, it was a one-night thing.'

'But why, if they were—'

'What I've told you is all Fionn told me. Trying to get any more out of him was as hard as getting a tenner off a Scot.'

Belle sipped her drink. The news left her feeling low, like her heart was somewhere in her gut.

'Maybe we should change the subject for a while,' Dermot said. 'What do you think, McGee?'

Belle half-heartedly smiled. 'Okay, why don't you tell me something about yourself?'

'Christ, where would I even start?'

'I'll help you. I'm a professional interviewer, after all.'

'Fire away then.'

'What age are you?'

'Forty-nine, five years younger than Fionn.'

'Were you born in Derry?'

'Born and raised. My mother and Fionn's mother were sisters. We grew up on the same street, went to the same schools. I was a bit wild in my youth, nothing serious, but I'm all sensible now.'

Belle laughed. 'I see that.'

He laughed, too, the heaviness of the previous conversation lifting a little, and his intense blue eyes lit up with mischief. Out of nowhere, Belle's stomach did a quick somersault.

'What about school?' she asked.

'I wasn't one for the books as a nipper. I hated school. I spent more of my days dobbing than in class.'

Belle grinned. It had been ages since she had heard anybody use the word 'dobbing' – which was Derry for 'bunking off'.

'I noticed you had an impressive selection of books in your living room,' Belle said, 'so something changed as you got older?'

'That was Fionn's influence. He was into Freire, education as a way for oppressed people to free themselves. Fionn helped me see the point in educating myself.' Dermot ran his finger along the side of his glass. 'I suppose you look down on somebody like that,' he said. 'You probably did well, went to university, the whole nine yards.'

'I did okay at school and, yeah, I went to university, but I don't look down on anybody who didn't take that route. I don't keep the score that way.'

Dermot nodded and drained his pint. Belle had hardly touched her drink.

'Let me get you another Harp,' she said.

'Naw, I dragged you out and I know you didn't want to come, so the least I can do is pay for my own pints.'

'Sit where you are,' Belle put her hand on his shoulder, the first time she'd physically touched him. He felt warm. 'I insist. And for the record, you didn't drag me out.'

She ordered another pint from Phil and was back at the table in no time.

'Sláinte,' he said.

'Sláinte.' Belle took a longer sip from her glass. 'So, tell me more. What happened after school? Did you move away, get a job?'

'I went to London for a year when I was seventeen, but I didn't like it much. I couldn't wait to get home. I'm one of them people that gets homesick in Bridgend.'

Belle found herself laughing again. Bridgend was a village about five miles outside Derry, just across the border in the South. She had to go through it every time she travelled between Derry and her island home. She took a swig from her Morgan and coke, noticing she hadn't much left.

'Eventually I trained as a welder and worked for a long while with an engineering outfit in County Tyrone. They went bust when the arse fell out of everything in 2008.' He swallowed down more lager. 'Since then, I've been in and out of work, mostly on contracts. The first permanent work I got was with Evergreen when Fionn hooked me up with them – it's a shite job, by the way, but better than nothing.'

'And are you married?' Belle's stomach somersaulted again.

'I was married. For fifteen years… we're separated now. I wasn't a model husband. I was an asshole, if I'm laying my cards on the table. Too much drinking, too much fucking about and not enough taking responsibility. She got pissed off and I don't blame her. I let her down – her and the kids.'

'You've got kids?'

'Two; a boy and a girl, nineteen and twenty-three.'

'Do you see them much?'

'Two or three times a week. I love them to bits in spite of being a crap Da. They're great, the pair of them, and no matter what else is going on, I keep Sundays for them. We go round to me Ma's for Sunday dinner and we go for a dander up the town or to the pictures or something.'

Belle found herself liking his devotion to his children. She found herself liking a lot of other things about him, too: his smile, his off-hand manner, his honesty, even the way he exhaled when he was smoking. She drank what was left in her glass, the Morgan Spice sending that warm fuzzy feeling through her chest and down into her tummy.

The lights in the bar dimmed further and Seventies rock music began playing in the background. By this time, something of a crowd was gathering and the tables were filling up, although the bunch of girls from earlier was gone. What looked like a live band was setting up for the night in the far corner.

'I'll get us another,' Dermot said, standing up.

'None for me,' Belle said, 'I've got the car. I can't drink anymore.'

'Ah, come on, you're hardly going to leave just before the band starts.'

'I can't stay.'

'There is no "can't" – you have to think positive.'

'I don't think the power of positive thinking applies in this context.'

'Well, you know what I mean. Come on, we did a good job today. We deserve this.'

Belle faltered. They had done a good job, he was right. And she was on holidays, or supposed to be... oh, to hell with it! She could get a taxi home and then get Maeveen to drop her back to Derry for the car in the morning. 'All right then, let's do it. Get me the same again... no, actually, get me a double.' She was in true weekend mode and she had catching up to do.

'That's more like it.'

While he was gone, Belle phoned Maeveen.

'Hi,' she said, when her sister answered, 'what's the craic?'

'All good,' Maeveen said. 'What about you, sounds like you're in a bar?'

'I'm in the Dungloe having a drink with Dermot.'

'Oh, a drink with Dermot.'

'It's a professional drink, nothing more, so don't go reading anything into it.'

'Right,' Maeveen said, 'a professional drink. So I take it you'll not be home tonight.'

'I'll be home, I'll get a taxi. And I won't be late either. What're you up to?'

'I'm just having a quiet night in with Cillian, the usual.'

'Good, that's good.'

Dermot arrived back with their drinks.

'Look, Maeveen, I better go, have a nice time and I'll see you when I get back.'

'I'll not wait up... be good.'

Belle hung up and put her phone away.

'Tell me something about you, then?' Dermot said. 'I know you're a hotshot reporter in a top paper in Dublin, but apart from that, you're a black box.'

'A black box? You're going to be sorely disappointed if you think this black box has anything exciting in it. Let me see: I grew up on our farm in Donegal, my parents are both passed away and I've one sister, Maeveen, who you know. I went to UCD after secondary school, did a degree in English Literature, then a post-grad in Journalism. I got my first job with a local paper in Kildare and after a couple of years there, I landed the job at the *National*, where I still work. I love my job; I'm very lucky.'

'I feel like a snotter hanging from the end of somebody's nose compared to that,' Dermot said. 'Though it was a bit like a CV. What about you, the person behind the job?'

Belle flicked her hair to the side. She rummaged her brain for anything more to say. Outside of her career, it was a struggle. 'What else? Um, I like nineteenth-century Russian literature and hate mundane daytime TV. I like to keep fit and stay in shape, so a normal day for me starts with an hour-long run. I enjoy socialising with my friends on the weekends, going to the theatre or out for a bite to eat or for a drink. There's a great bar near work called O'Sullivan's that we all go to – they'll all be there tonight, no doubt.' She paused. 'And here's a random fact: I hate my nose.'

'What's wrong with your nose?'

'Can't you see that bump in the middle?'

Dermot ran the index finger of his left hand down the bridge of her nose. Belle felt her cheeks blush.

'I like your nose,' he said, 'and your hair. And your eyes – they're blue-grey, like a squally sea.'

'I'm going to choke with embarrassment,' Belle said, enjoying the attention and, at the same time, uncomfortable with it. 'Here's some more random facts about me. I own a house in Dublin, I don't have any pets and my favourite show growing up was *The Incredible Hulk* – maybe because the reporter who was always stalking Banner was called McGee.' She polished off the remainder of her double Morgan.

'Thanks for sharing the random facts,' Dermot said. 'You didn't mention anything about a husband or kids – any of those in that Dublin house of yours?'

'No, I'm completely footloose and fancy-free,' she said. Which was true. Shane didn't really count. Did she just imagine the faintest smile on Dermot's lips? 'I don't have a lot of luck with men,' she paused, 'or maybe they don't have any luck with me. I've never wanted the things they wanted, like settling down and having children.'

'But isn't that the whole point, at least to settle down with somebody, kids or not?'

'I suppose so, but not all of us deserve a decent life like that.' *Especially not me*, she thought.

'What's that supposed to mean?'

'Nothing, absolutely nothing,' she said, rooting through her bag for her wallet. 'Want another drink? My round.'

Dermot put his hand on hers to stop her. His touch made her giddy. 'What about we get out of here and go on a pub crawl, just on Waterloo Street, starting up here at the top and rolling our way down?'

Belle knew it was a terrible idea but the brakes were off and she was blissfully freewheeling. Right now, it sounded like the best idea she'd ever heard – the best way to forget. 'Let's do it, as long as there're enough pubs.'

'I like your thinking, McGee.'

*

They left the Dungloe, the brightness of the open-air startling. Outside was still light, the day in no hurry to give in to the darkness for a while yet. Crowds of revellers were gathered in clusters on the pedestrian-only street, drinks and cigarettes in hand. Belle and Dermot crossed to a small bar called the Castle and had just the one round there before ambling down the street to the Gweedore. A kicking live rock band was bringing down the ceiling and vibrating the floorboards when they walked in. The place was packed, the air sweaty and hot, the light low. They had to fight their way to the bar like they were cutting a path through jungle undergrowth.

Drinks in hand, Dermot found them a spot where they had standing room and a ledge to set down their glasses, before he headed out for a smoke. Belle tipped a nip of coke into her Morgan double, barely enough to give the clear spirit some colour. Dermot reappeared but stood talking to a couple of men before making his way back. Watching him come closer made her stomach flutter as though electrically charged. She was like some lovestruck teenager and inwardly she scolded herself for getting so carried away. She had to be sensible and stop this silliness.

The band was so loud they gave up talking and instead went with the to-and-fro of the crowd that pushed them close enough to be almost in a clinch. Belle didn't try to pull away. She allowed her body to bump against his.

'It's mad in here,' Dermot shouted into her ear.

She could feel the warmth of his breath on the side of her face. 'Insane,' she shouted back, her lips touching his cheek as she spoke.

He leaned on her and his mouth brushed against her forehead. She felt a rush inside.

A couple of rounds later and Dermot pointed downwards in the direction of Peadar's, which was the next bar on the street. This time they didn't even have to leave the building for the two bars had an adjoining door. Peadar's was busier than the Gweedore, if that were possible, but here a traditional music band was belting out rebel songs. World flags adorned the ceiling, and the walls and wooden beams were covered in posters and paraphernalia of times gone by.

A man signalled to Dermot and they weaved amidst the crowd towards him. Another acquaintance of Dermot's; he was leaving the bar with his friend and offered them his seat. They settled into the space he had left for them, huddling together for lack of room, but pleased with the good fortune of having somewhere to sit. The crowd moved and cheered with the band, joining in with choruses and stamping their feet.

Belle's head was floating. She was drunk, really drunk, in the nicest way it is to be drunk, euphorically happy and completely at one with the world and everybody in it. Her cheeks felt flushed. She knew her face probably looked like a slapped arse. She didn't care.

'Enjoying yourself?' Dermot shouted over the music.

'Like there's no tomorrow,' she said, her voice hoarse.

He smiled and then, without warning, he kissed her. Belle pulled back, her eyes wide with surprise.

'Sorry,' he said, frowning.

'You will be if you don't kiss me again,' she said.

So he did and this time she was ready. Their mouths locked. Out of nowhere, she had a thought of Fionn and of never touching his mouth no matter how she'd wanted to, and then it was gone like a puff of smoke. In its place were thoughts only of the here and now, in Peadar's, with Dermot. And somehow, it felt right.

They held their kiss to the end of the song that was playing and then to the end of the next one, making it linger, their tongues exploring each other's mouths in that new first-time way, their lips pressed together. Eventually, they pulled away.

'I planned for us to get a last drink in Tracey's next door,' Dermot said. 'Do you want to do that… or do you want to go back to mine?'

'Back to yours.'

'Are you sure?'

'Let's go.'

*

Belle opened her eyes. She could only feel pain and discomfort. A bar of sunlight pierced through a gap in the curtains – curtains she didn't recognise – with the precision and intensity of a laser beam and her head lay directly in its path, marinating. A wall of agony crossed in front of her eyes, blurring her vision. She opened her mouth to groan but managed little more than a croak from a throat that was raw and a mouth that tasted of bananas, bizarrely, and the Oklahoma dustbowl at the same time.

'Jesus,' she rasped.

She rolled over to escape the relentless sun and, through eyes straining to focus, realised that nothing around her was familiar. She wasn't in her house in Dublin; she wasn't in Donegal.

'Where the fuck am I?'

'What?' a man's voice mumbled.

Her head shot to the left. Someone was in bed with her. Her heart dropped. She looked under the bed cover, fearing the worst. She was naked. The man was, too.

Ever so slowly, like sand passing through the neck of an hourglass, memories of the night before began trickling into consciousness: that first drink in the Dungloe, the pub crawl to the bottom of Waterloo Street, the crowds in Peadar's and that first kiss with… with Dermot. She tried to identify how she felt about that, about what had happened after they left Peadar's and came back to his house, but couldn't quite yet manage it.

'Hey you.' Dermot turned over and put his arm around her. He kissed her forehead and sighed. 'Christ, I feel like a pile of diarrhoea in a fishing net.'

'Don't get too descriptive,' Belle said, 'or I'll throw up.'

Dermot opened his eyes, their gorgeous blue no less mesmerising in spite of his condition. Belle got that tingling in her stomach, the one she remembered from the night before and, hangover or not, the fact of the matter was she liked him far more than she should.

'Last night was good,' he said, rubbing his nose against hers. 'Well worth the suffering this morning.'

She smiled, nestling closer. She took in the smell of his sweat mingled with stale aftershave and alcohol, and felt aroused. He kissed her gently on the forehead and she raised her face towards his, kissing him back.

'Wanna fool around?' he said, his voice thick.

They started kissing, deep and long.

Belle began to get lost in their embrace, falling into it like Alice falling into the rabbit hole. But something stopped her from going right in. Now that she was sober – well, at least not drunk – the voice of reason in her head admonished her. Dermot was Fionn's cousin and Fionn was... was lying in the morgue. This whole situation was wrong.

'No!' Belle pulled away. 'I can't do this.' She sat up slowly and began looking for her underwear.

'What's wrong? Did I do something?'

'Where's my clothes?' She couldn't see them.

'Calm down, McGee, they're around here somewhere. Are you going to tell me why you're freaking out?'

She got out of bed, a sheet wrapped around her, and went on a search of the room. Mercifully, she found what she was looking for.

'This is fucking weird,' Dermot said. 'Are you going to say something?'

Not until she was half-dressed did she feel able to answer. 'I'm sorry,' she said, 'but this was a terrible mistake. It should never have happened.'

She looked across at him. His usual cheerful countenance clouded over with hurt.

'I thought you liked me,' he said. 'I thought we clicked.'

She sat on a chair in the corner by the window. Her intestines churned and she felt faint. 'I do like you, I really do, but I came here for Fionn's funeral.' Her foggy mind flashed the image of Fionn standing at the end of her hallway. 'This,' she waved her hand, 'us, it can't happen.'

'But it has happened. You're overthinking things. Why not just go with the flow and see where it leads?'

'It wouldn't be right. It would disrespect Fionn.'

'How would it disrespect Fionn? If he was here, he'd be happy about us.'

'You don't know that,' she said. That wasn't all he didn't know. Things that if he did know, he'd hate her for.

'Why don't you come back over here and at least wait out that hangover? You look wrecked. I'll pick us up some breakfast from the bakery.'

Belle put her head in her hands. She felt so awful she wanted to put her head in a washing machine for relief. She was in no fit state to leave. Nor was it fair to walk out on him so abruptly. It was the kind of thing she did to the Shane's of this world, sure, but not to Dermot, not to Fionn's cousin. She could be a decent person for once instead of always being a bitch, leave on good terms and just keep her distance in future. She could do that, couldn't she?

'Okay, I'll wait a while. And if you go to the bakery, don't get me any food, just fruit juice.'

Dermot hopped out of bed, looking relieved.

'I still mean it about us not doing this again.'

'Not until the next time,' he said, managing a weak smile.

She didn't have the energy to reply.

They went into the living room and Dermot grabbed his coat and left. In ten minutes, he was back with a carton of orange juice and a bag of buns. Belle gulped a down a full glass in one go and then poured a second, while Dermot made tea.

'These are great, have one,' Dermot said, helping himself to a cream finger.

'Yuck!'

'You know, when I was out getting the buns there, I remembered something, something that might help figure out what Fionn meant by putting MacCool in his notes.'

Belle became alert, her journalistic instincts cutting through the haze of her hangover. 'Really? If you did, it would make my day.'

'I was thinking about what you said, about whether Fionn had done something out of the ordinary, and that's when I remembered.' Dermot walked over to where the charcoal sketch of *Free Derry Corner* hung. 'He gave me a present. We never gave each other presents so it wasn't the norm.' Dermot tapped on the sketch. 'He drew this. Good, wasn't he?'

Belle got up and went over to Dermot. The sketch was more than good, it was beautiful. 'I noticed it the first time I visited,' she said. Now, she examined it closely. Had Fionn written a clue of some sort into the picture? There was nothing.

'Do you think this means something?' Dermot asked.

'If it does, I don't know what. I...' She stopped. 'Hang on, can I check something?'

Dermot nodded. Belle gently lifted the frame off its hook. She turned it over in her hands to reveal the hardboard backing cover. Slowly, one by one, she prised up the little points that held the picture in place until she could finally remove the cover.

Dermot whistled when he saw it. Belle giggled with giddy excitement.

There, tucked into the bottom corner of the frame, was a small USB stick.

14

DONEGAL, 1986

Belle reached the cobbles of the courtyard. The image of her sister and Fionn under the cherry tree was so vivid they could still be standing in front of her. She'd never forget it for as long as she lived.

Fionn was supposed to be her special friend, hers, and she was his. They spent hours together without Maeveen or anybody else. She couldn't understand what he was doing.

'Mammy,' Belle shouted, as soon as she got into the house, wiping her face to hide her tears. 'Mammy, where are you?'

'Upstairs,' her mother's muffled voice came back. 'I left some sandwiches in the fridge for your tea.'

Belle didn't care about sandwiches. She took the stairs, two at a time, and found her mother folding clothes away in the hot press.

'I've something to tell you,' she said, panting.

'Steady yourself,' her mother said, 'you look like you're ready to bust. What's wrong? Are you all right?'

'Nothing's wrong, I—'

'Is it Hunter?'

'Hunter's gone home, it's—'

'So, what's the matter then?'

Belle went to speak and realised there was a lump in her throat. She was close to crying again, a proper bawling match, and had to swallow hard.

'Well?'

'It's Maeveen,' she said, 'and Fionn… they're outside.'

'What're you talking about?' Her mother threw her an impatient look. 'Maeveen's not even back from work yet and last I saw Fionn, he was in the sitting room.'

'I saw them out at the swing in the cherry orchard. Go there now and you'll see them yourself. I'm not making it up.'

Her mother stopped her task and breathed deeply. 'Hunter didn't see them, did he?'

'He was away before they showed up. But Fionn's not supposed to be out.'

'Belle, we've said to him he can go out once in a while, with Maeveen chaperoning.'

'Since when? I didn't know that. I'm never told anything. And why does Maeveen get to chaperone him? How come she's always the one to get picked?'

'Aw, give me head peace. Maeveen's older. And you shouldn't be telling tales, no one likes a tell-tit.' Her mother started folding clothes again.

Belle pouted. 'But are you not going to bring them in?'

'No, I am not. They haven't done anything they're not supposed to.'

Belle couldn't believe what she was hearing. She wanted to crawl into a hole and die. Her mother wasn't bothered one bit about Fionn and Maeveen being outside. They were out together, without Belle, having a great ol' time to themselves, and they were going to get away with it. It wasn't fair. She felt so weak, a puff of wind could've knocked her over.

But she wasn't beaten, not yet.

'Mammy, there's something else I didn't tell you.'

'Um-hum.' Her mother was nearly finished with the clothes.

'Do you know what they were doing?'

'Belle, I've heard enough of your nonsense?'

'What they were doing...' Belle felt herself choke up again, 'they were k-kissing each other.'

Her mother stopped and, this time, Belle could see a band of red flare up across her nose, a sure sign she was really angry but trying to hold it in.

'Even though they're cousins,' Belle added, not believing that to be true, but deciding to throw it into the mix anyway since it was what her mother expected her to believe.

'Stay here,' her mother said.

'Are you going to kill them?'

'Mind your business, daughter.'

Her mother disappeared down the stairs. Belle wondered if there was going to be war. She wanted it to be the case – that's what her turncoat sister deserved, and Fionn, too. Oh, and just wait 'til her father got home. He'd go through the two of them for a shortcut. They were so, so dead and she couldn't wait. Her vision blurred with tears that simply wouldn't be contained any longer and a ball of pain pushed against her chest.

'The fuckers,' she said. 'The lousy fuckers.'

15

DONEGAL, PRESENT DAY

By mid-afternoon, Belle was back on the island, with Fionn's USB stick carefully zipped up inside a pocket in her bag. She hadn't looked at it yet but she had high hopes it would fill in some of the missing pieces. Her hangover had subsided somewhat, although she felt tired and hungry and grimy. A hot shower followed by some food would be in order.

She came to a corner before the turn-off for the lane and almost collided with two people walking on the narrow road. She was going slowly enough for there to be no danger and instinctively raised her hand to wave, before she realised who she was waving to. Hunter Campbell and a small, sandy-haired boy she guessed must be his son. Belle knew Hunter was married and still lived on the island, working his father's farm. She stopped waving, though he never waved in the first place. Her eye caught his as she sailed past. No water under the bridge in that look – too much hurt and no hope of repair. One of the few good things about living in Dublin was that a random meeting like this could never happen.

Maeveen was out when Belle arrived home. Probably working in one of the fields. Belle went upstairs and hopped into the shower, savouring the warmth of the water as it soothed her aching joints.

Mercifully, her head no longer pounded like a bass drum and her stomach had settled a good bit. She wrapped herself in soft cotton pyjamas – it was early but she had no intention of leaving the house for the rest of the day – and made a quick meal: two chunky slices of French toast and a big mug of green tea.

Belle checked her phone as she ate and read through a string of emails and texts from the team at work. She was going to miss the surprise dinner planned for Siobhan's birthday that night. She'd make it up to her once she went back to Dublin.

Once breakfast was over and Belle felt human again, she sat down at her laptop.

'Now, let's see what you can tell me,' she said, slotting the USB stick into the port at the side of her machine.

She clicked open the USB drive as soon as it appeared on her screen to reveal just one Word document on the whole device. She double-clicked the document's icon. It was password-protected.

'Fuck,' she said.

She bit her lip, thinking for a minute, and then she had an idea. She typed in 'MacCool' and hit return. That didn't work.

'Bollocks, maybe it's his birthday or...'

Hang on, she remembered something. The strange way Fionn had written the name in his notes. Not 'MacCool' but 'MaCcOoL.'

She tried it. She was in. And finally, there it was, like the missing sock in a pair, the rest of the information that had only been alluded to by the box file evidence.

The Dictaphone was close to hand and Belle set it in motion.

'Several pages of numbers and dates here; a meticulous chronicle of every visit Fionn made to the dumpsites. Dates, times – all in the early hours of the morning – locations, number of lorries, vehicle reg plates, estimated tonnes of waste. My bet is these reg plates will match vehicles owned by Evergreen. Note: it might be worth staking out one of these midnight jaunts. By the looks of it, I could pick any random night and I'd be in luck.'

She scrolled to the bottom of the document.

'This is what I'm looking for. The dodgy untrustworthies. A few names are listed, along with job titles and telephone numbers. There's even one I recognise.'

She felt a rush of excitement.

'Brendan Lynch. Martin Higgins, the man we met near the dumpsite, mentioned him. According to Fionn's notes, he's a council officer. And two more names: Noel Kerrigan, Water Service, and Councillor Alan O'Dee. Next to O'Dee's name, he's written, 'O'Dee's a businessman; connected to businesses all over the show; his brother's an Evergreen director.' There's a last name with 'good friend' beside it: Sammy Alexander at the Environment Agency.'

Belle emailed Alma a quick update. She sat up and stretched. She now had several more leads, leads that might be dangerous. Those might have to wait until Monday right enough because she suspected the numbers were most likely work numbers, although she'd try them anyway on the off chance. And while she teed up meetings, she had plenty to keep her busy. A visit to Fionn's neighbour, Ed, could prove fruitful and it might do no harm to call back to Evergreen. It had to be said, though, finding out about MacCool had certainly been worth it.

*

Belle rapped three times on the door of number thirty-six, triggering the overexcited yapping of what she guessed was the Jack Russell she had seen before. In spite of the racket, she got no answer, so she knocked again, louder. This time, she got a result.

'Get to your bed, Spanner.' It was Ed, that grating voice of his unmistakable. 'Don't have me tell you again.'

Spanner growled but seemed to retreat. After some clicking and scraping of locks and bolts, the door opened just a crack, releasing a rush of hot, stale air.

'Who is it? What do you want?' Ed poked his head out the door as though he was a mole peeking from a hole in the ground.

'My name's McGee,' Belle said, flashing her press ID card. 'I'm a reporter. I was hoping I might talk to you about the murder that happened in number twenty-six.'

'I don't know anything about that. Lemme see that ID.'

He opened the door wider and Belle held her card closer.

'Um, you're with that big-deal Dublin paper, I see,' he said. 'Bit far from home.'

'No, actually, I'm from this part of the country. I'm visiting for a bit and thought I'd do a piece on Fionn Power's murder while I was here.'

'Well, you can't come in. I said the same thing to the police, nosey so-and-sos. You can't come in.'

'I'm not the police. I only want to do a good story. Please, I won't keep you long.'

'Doesn't mean they'll leave you alone though.'

'Sorry, who?'

'They're coming back to talk to me even though I don't want them to. All I was doing that night was watching season two of *Better Call Saul*. I love that show. Have you seen it?' He spoke slowly, like he was daydreaming aloud, and avoided all eye contact.

His internal thought patterns were scrambled eggs but Belle persevered. It was always the ones you least expected who had the best information.

'Yes, great show,' she said. 'So did you see or hear anything that night?'

'Did somebody tell you I did?' He jumped out of his dream state. His tone was sharp.

'No,' Belle said, treading carefully. 'No, I thought with you being right across the hall you might've noticed something nobody else did.'

'They were making a lot of noise. I hate noise.'

'Fionn, you mean?'

'He always had people round, drinking, loud music, and he knew I hated it. Noise gives me a headache.' He clasped his forehead with his hand in an exaggerated gesture. 'I knew it would all end in tears.'

'I understand how you feel,' Belle said. 'I don't like noise either. Did you see who it was making all the commotion? Somebody with Fionn?'

'Do you know his name's really Jimmy McGill and not Saul Goodman?'

'What?'

'Saul Goodman – *it's all good, man*. That's where he got it from.'

Jesus wept, Belle held in her frustration. Two conversations were going on; the one she was trying to have with him and the one he was having with himself.

'Clever, isn't it?' he said.

'Genius. So, did you see somebody with Fionn?'

'They were talking about me. They thought I didn't know, but I could hear them. Through the walls.'

'Shame on them. Who were they?'

'Fionn and his drinking buddies.'

'And did you see who those drinking buddies were?'

'You're making my head hurt with all your questions. You're worse than the police.'

'I'm sorry, I don't mean to – it's just I think you could be a big help. But, you know, I'm not the police; they don't understand that people like you are so important in these situations.'

'Um.' He suddenly smiled, revealing a row of small, sharp teeth.

'Could I come in, please? I think there's a lot you could tell me.'

Ed nodded and stepped back and Belle was finally in. He closed the door and Belle couldn't help observing it was secured with two locks and three bolts. In the corner was a baseball bat, leaning upright against the wall.

116

'Follow me,' he signalled and he shuffled off down the hall, dragging his feet in the same beat-out trainers he'd been wearing when she first saw him.

The stale odour she noticed at the entrance intensified to the power of ten, but was now fused with a few other unpleasant pongs that Belle guessed were a build-up of household waste and Spanner not being properly house-trained. She tried taking short breaths through her mouth to give her nose a chance to acclimatise. She passed a closed door and, behind it, heard Spanner whining and scratching the wood with his claws.

They reached the kitchen.

'Take a seat,' he said, pointing to a chair already taken up by a large cardboard box filled with clothes. 'You can put that box on the table.'

She did as instructed and sat down. 'So, you were telling me about Fionn's drinking buddies the night of the murder?'

'Aw, right.'

Belle took a jotter notebook and pen from her bag. 'Just going to take a few notes, if that's all right. Capture your words of wisdom.'

Ed seemed pleased. 'I didn't remember anything when the police interviewed me. My mind was a blank, you know, but it came back to me after they were gone and it's important. My information's important, like you said.'

Belle nodded patiently. 'That night—'

'Fionn moved in five years ago and since then, he's made my life hell. All I want is peace and quiet. I don't want to bother anybody and I don't want anybody to bother me. He made that impossible. We had words – I might as well come out with it. We had words, me and him, and plenty of times I was close to ringing the police with all his messing about.'

'I get that, a lot of people have problem neighbours. We all deserve our space to be respected.'

'Yes, yes, yes, you get it. See, that's what I used to tell him, but all he did was laugh. He had no respect for my space.'

Belle tried steering the conversation. 'Could I ask you about the night Fionn was murdered? You're the only person with any sense. No point talking to anybody else.'

'Well, I was having a nice wee night, just me and Spanner, and then them two came back from their gallivanting.'

'Fionn and somebody else?'

'Then the noise started up and that was the end of my fun.' He clenched his fists and breathed deeply through his nose.

'Who was Fionn with?'

'Dermot, who else?'

Belle went cold. She teetered on the stool and had to steady herself. That couldn't be right; Dermot wasn't there that night.

'Dermot and Fionn came in together as per usual about half eleven or so.' Ed's forehead crumpled into deep, trench-like lines. 'I heard them when they were trying to unlock the door to Fionn's flat.'

'But are you sure it was Dermot?'

'I'm very, very, very sure. I saw him with my own eyes. I was sneaking peeks through my door. And I'm gonna tell the police when they come back.'

He seemed adamant but he couldn't be right – that fried brain of his couldn't be right. Belle was overcome with an urge to run away from Ed and his voice and the suffocating sour air. She needed to talk to Dermot and find out if he'd really been at Fionn's that night.

'I think I have all I need,' she said, getting up. Her head spun for a couple of seconds. She gathered her things and made for the door.

'Where are you going? I'm not finished. I saw Dermot later on that night, too. He was running out of Fionn's like his behind was on fire. I saw him, it was definitely him, running away from his crime.'

Belle marched up the hall, Ed trailing behind, still rattling on.

'And Dermot must've still been there when the other two came along.'

Her head was swirling with thoughts of Dermot and she was only half-listening.

'I never saw them before. They looked like a pair of heavies. One of them was bald.'

In some recess of her brain, Belle took note of what Ed was saying, while at the same time, she struggled to open the door. With all the bolts and locks, she didn't know where to start.

'That's important information, isn't it?' Ed puffed his chest out, seemingly over his outburst.

'Can you let me out?'

Ed began the process of undoing the security on the door. 'D'you ever see somebody coming towards you on the street and think they're going to stab you?'

'What?' Belle was close to screaming.

'Maybe not,' Ed answered his own question, 'but it's something to think about. There's a lot of crazy bastards out there. If anybody came at me, I'd be ready for them. They'd get a surprise from me, I can tell you. I'm able to handle myself.'

The door finally opened, bringing a wave of fresh air that washed over Belle's face. She stepped out into corridor and was free.

16

DONEGAL, 1986

Belle was too annoyed to sleep. She turned on her side, then her other side, then back again. No good; she was wide awake.

The bedroom was dark save for a slice of golden light escaping through the crack in the door. Her parents were still up, their muffled voices from downstairs drifting on the silence of the house. She was dying to know what they were talking about. Fionn and Maeveen, she was sure.

For the life of her, she couldn't understand why they'd said nothing about what she witnessed that day. Her mother went out and brought the two wrongdoers in from the orchard, and all she did then was tell them to get their supper. Things went on as normal. Belle had hoped for a showdown once her father came home. But no, nothing happened then either. "We'll deal with it later" was all he said.

She considered going downstairs and making a cup of hot chocolate. That would help her nod off – plenty of warm milk with a few spoons of cocoa. Perfect. But she thought better of it. She knew her parents would only shoo her back to bed and tell her it was too late.

Belle lay for a while, still wide awake, ruminating about the hot chocolate and the creamy taste and the chocolaty smell and the steam coming off it and how the mug would be warm in her hands. Better fixing her mind on that than brooding over Fionn and Maeveen and the sight of them in the cherry orchard.

The problem was that the images of Fionn and Maeveen were stronger than the hot chocolate. It was useless. She gave up wrestling with her thoughts.

Throwing the blankets back, she got out of bed. On tip-toes, she opened her bedroom door and, with the stealth of a panther, crossed the landing. She stopped at the top of the stairs, listened and looked around, and then began a careful descent.

Halfway down, the voices below became more than mumbles. Belle found she was able to make out the words being spoken and the people speaking them.

'I'm disappointed in you, Fionn,' her father was saying. 'I expected more.'

Belle didn't go any farther. Jackpot. They were talking about it now. She squeezed herself to contain her glee. She wanted to hear it all. She sat down, wincing when the stair creaked with her weight. She leaned her head on the banister, resting it between two of the railings, and her hands gripped a rail on either side.

'You did so much that was wrong. I don't know where to start.' Her mother this time, her voice even and calm, but with emphasis on the last word of her sentences that betrayed her anger.

'You took a big chance,' her father said, 'wandering off like that. It could've ended very badly.'

Silence. Her father coughed.

'I was stupid,' Fionn said. His voice seemed different, not cheery the way he usually was. 'I thought it'd be safe, you know, after we agreed I could get out a bit.'

Belle shivered, the night air touching her bare arms and legs.

Her father spoke up. 'You're right enough; we did think you should get out of the house from time to time. But that didn't mean you and Maeveen could head off whenever you felt like it.'

'Don't blame Maeveen,' Fionn said. 'It's all my fault.'

'I wasn't a bit happy that Belle caught you,' her mother said. 'She was all confused.'

Belle held her breath at the mention of her name.

'I'm sure she was,' Belle's father said.

'But Michael,' her mother said, 'the Campbell boy was with Belle most of the day. Small mercies he was away home before all this nonsense happened.'

'You must have some idea how serious that could've been,' her father said. 'What a family like his would do if they put two and two together? Are you trying to get us all in bother?'

Belle frowned, having no clue what her father meant.

'Maybe you think we're being too cautious,' Belle's mother said. 'But let me tell you, Fionn, we can't be cautious enough. Country folk know who lives where and who's connected to who and they notice the slightest change. Sure, even the last day when I was in Porter's supermarket, Sarah made a craic about me buying enough groceries to feed an army.'

'Kitty's right. The Campbells are the very ones to be wary of with somebody new being about, the very ones to go straight to the Gards. Wouldn't be the first time the likes of them went to the Gards. Do you want that?'

Belle's eyes bugged out at the mention of the Gards. What were they on about? Why would they worry about the Gards? Was Fionn a criminal? No. Her parents would have nothing to do with a criminal. Maybe they had no choice, or did they feel sorry for him? She was being ridiculous. There had to be a sensible explanation.

'I'm sorry,' Fionn said and he sounded desperate, like he was pleading and afraid at the same time. 'I should've known better. I just got careless. It feels so safe here.'

'Well, it's not as safe as you think. The times we're in, and living along the border, there's a lot of suspicion,' Belle's mother said.

'But here, you got away with it,' her father said, 'so no harm done. This time. We'll have a yarn tomorrow when Maeveen's back from work, to see what we can arrange from here on. And say nothing to Belle, for the time being anyway.'

Belle squeezed the banister rails until her hands hurt. She was being left out again, being treated like a child, while Maeveen was going to be right in the middle of the action.

'Talking about Maeveen,' her mother went on, 'that's another thing I'm not happy about. I don't want you getting too close to her. She's only eighteen and you, well, with your situation, the last thing you need is to be carrying on with a girl and making things harder than they are.'

Her mother scolded Fionn but she wasn't necessarily getting worked up over Maeveen kissing her cousin. No one was. That only confirmed what Belle already knew. Fionn wasn't a relative from County Derry at all.

'I'm not carrying on with her, Kitty. I care about her. And she cares about me.'

Something cold touched Belle's heart and pressed hard. Fionn cared about Maeveen and Maeveen cared about Fionn. The words came out of his own mouth. She mightn't have believed them otherwise. She was special to him; they shared all those times together that meant so much, but Maeveen was the one he cared about.

'We want to be together,' Fionn went on. 'She wants to come with me once I'm settled down the country. They've said they're going to set me up in Limerick, but it doesn't have to be there.'

Belle's foot slipped and she nearly toppled off her perch. Since when was Fionn going to Limerick and who were the people who were setting him up? He couldn't go away.

'Jesus Christ,' Belle's mother said. 'Michael, say something.'

123

'Look, Fionn, you're a grand fella and Maeveen's eighteen – we can't stop her making up her own mind. But she only finished school this summer and she got accepted for Queen's in Belfast. That's a place where you can't live.'

'I know but we've thought it through. Maeveen got accepted in Galway, too, at UCG. She could go there instead and we could get married and I could get a job.'

Belle's world came crashing down around her. Her Greek god was on about marrying Maeveen… no, it couldn't be so.

'Enough, Fionn, that's enough.' Her father's voice was serious and Belle was glad. 'You'll not be marrying my daughter. That's an end to it. You've your own bothers; life's going to be hard for you. It's not fair to drag a young girl into that. She's just starting out.'

'I'd take care—'

'We want to help you – we're proud to. But Maeveen isn't going to be part of it. If you're not happy with that, Fionn, you can find another family to stay with 'til you move on.'

The talking stopped for a while. Belle gathered her thoughts. She felt empty. Fionn was lost to her, no matter which way she looked at it. Whether he was in trouble with the law or not, whether he stayed with them or left, he wasn't hers, he was Maeveen's. Her future wasn't worth living.

'All we're asking,' Belle's father said, 'is you stop this nonsense with Maeveen and stay out of sight.'

'Don't do anything to draw attention to us,' her mother said.

'Will you do that, Fionn, will you?'

'I definitely will, Kitty, Michael. You can rely on me. It's going to be hard telling Maeveen.'

'Don't worry about Maeveen,' Belle's father said. 'We'll have a word with her.'

'And maybe it would do no harm to spend less time with Belle while you're at it,' her mother said.

Belle breathed in sharply and held it, as though inhaling or exhaling was going to cause her to break. Her pulse throbbed in her ears.

'She was upset today when she told me about seeing you and Maeveen and, I dunno, it could've been the way she told me, but I got the feeling she has a bit of a thing for you, Fionn.'

'No way,' Fionn said, 'I think the world of her and we get on the best, but she's only a baby.'

'Exactly,' her mother said, 'she's only a baby and she shouldn't be entertaining silly notions about a grown man.'

'I never thought she was. I'll make sure she doesn't get the wrong idea from me.'

Belle's hand shot up to her mouth and her palm filled with the hot breath of a stifled scream.

'Well, you know the craic now,' Belle's mother said. 'We shouldn't have any more mishaps. Ah, I'm done in, I'm going to bed.'

'You go on, Kitty. I'll get myself a quick brandy and I'll be up soon.'

The sitting room door opened. Belle's mother was about to come into the hallway. Belle retreated from the banister as quickly as she could and, gathering her broken emotions, retraced her steps back to her room. She climbed into bed and curled into the foetal position, pulling the blankets over her head.

She was finally tired – maybe having your heart broken did that to a person. She closed her eyes and slowly drifted to sleep as though on a raft on the ebbing tide, thinking about Fionn and Maeveen and the cherry orchard and why Fionn was really staying with her family. And in the drowsy swirl of her pain, something took hold, like a seed taking root in the soil, only her roots weren't healthy and life-giving like a plant. They were twisted and sick and they'd grow into a festering sore.

17

DERRY, PRESENT DAY

Dermot's place was walking distance from Fionn's. Belle didn't know whether she should go straight there or just call him. She did both. She rang and rang as she stomped up the street but his phone kept going to answer machine. She cursed him. By the time she reached his house, she was homicidal.

She pounded on the door. 'Dermot?' she shouted. 'Let me in.'

She was in mid-pound when Dermot answered and she almost punched him in the face.

'Jesus, what the fuck's wrong?'

'I was calling you.'

'I was asleep, on the sofa. You're acting like a psycho.'

'Any wonder? You've some explaining to do,' she said, pushing past. 'Starting with what actually happened the night Fionn was murdered.'

'What do you mean? I told you the craic.'

'Like fuck you did. I've just been speaking to Ed Ramsey.'

'That headcase?'

'I'm giving you a chance now to come clean about what happened, or do you want me to tell you?'

'What did he say, exactly?'

'I suppose you'd like to hear what I've been told so you can recalibrate your version of events with a new set of lies.'

'Aw, don't be like that, Belle, I'm sorry—'

'Never mind your sorrys, and it's McGee, not Belle. What I want from you now is your side of the story, the truth. And if I think you're lying, I'll never break breath to you again.'

Dermot ran his hands through his spiky hair, his face like a chastised toddler. 'Okay, you deserve that much.'

He plopped down on the sofa and started rolling a cigarette. Belle saw his hands were shaking. She sat down, too, not on the sofa but on an armchair, a distance away.

'I'm waiting.'

'Okay,' he started, breathing out deeply. 'Me and Fionn were out having a drink, that's true. Only I didn't head home like I said. I did what me and him always did: got a carryout and headed to his. In no time, we were throwing back the beers, playing music off YouTube, shooting the breeze, the usual—'

'So how did it go from a genteel soiree to… to that awful end?'

He lit his cigarette and took a long drag. 'I ran out of tobacco so I needed to get stocked up. There's a twenty-four-hour shop on the Strand Road, not far from Fionn's. He put in an order for a packet of teacakes – me and him used to eat them like we hadn't been fed in a year – and I made tracks for the shop.'

He stopped and braced himself as though preparing for what came next.

'Keep going; don't get shy now,' Belle said.

'I got the bits from the shop and went back to the flat, tout suite, no dallying. I was away no more than twenty minutes. I… I had the keys so I let myself into the building and went up the stairs to Fionn's and, um, well, I could see his door was open, the closer I got. I knew there was something wrong with that picture 'cos I remembered closing the door, definitely. You have to pull it hard to make sure it closes right and we were in the habit of doing that. No way would I have left it lying open.'

He pulled on his cigarette but it had gone out and he relit it. 'I didn't go in right away. I listened for a while. There wasn't a sound, not a sound, and that made me even more suspicious. I went in, as quiet as I could. I went into the sitting room and there was no one, not even Fionn. But then I saw him…'

Dermot put his head in his hands. Belle's anger was gone. She felt a tug on her heart and thought about Fionn, about his grisly last night. She thought about that carmine stain on the carpet.

'I'm sorry,' she said, 'I'm so sorry, that must've been traumatic.'

She heard him sniff a couple of times before he lifted his head. When he did, his eyes were red, his face wet.

'What did you do after… after you…'

'After I saw Fionn? I went blank – I mean, brain-dead blank. I hadn't one thought in my head. I couldn't even remember my own name. I went over to him; there was no doubt he was… was gone. The carpet was mushy. I looked down and I was standing in his blood. In Fionn's blood. I should've been shouting or getting angry or something, but it was weird. I'd no feeling at all, like I'd been injected with that shit the dentist uses to freeze your mouth before a filling.

'I stood there in that one spot. I was stone-cold sober, staring at my boots stuck to the carpet, my hands covered in blood. I dunno know how long I stood – a minute, an hour – and then I ran. And I didn't stop 'til I got home.'

Belle's heart was heavy. 'Jesus, Dermot.'

Dermot leaned back and stretched his neck from side to side. 'I have to ask,' he said, 'do you think I did it?'

Belle met his eyes – it was like looking into Fionn's – and held the gaze. The fact was that she didn't know him at all, so it was possible he was guilty. But if she was made to swear on it, her gut told her that no, he didn't do it. It was obvious he loved Fionn. The way Fionn died, it was… so brutal. Whoever murdered him was full of rage and hate. 'No, I don't,' was all she said.

Belle went over to the sofa and sat beside Dermot. She touched his hand.

Dermot shook his head. 'The worst part was leaving Fionn lying there like he was roadkill. I fucking loathe myself for that. I'm ashamed. It's the most reprehensible thing I've ever done in my life – my family's going to hate me when they find out. It was a fella from one of the other flats that called the peelers the next morning. That shouldn't have happened.'

'Why didn't you report it that night, or tell the police when they interviewed you?'

Dermot looked away like a guilty schoolboy caught stealing from the tuckshop. 'Um… ah, it's tricky. I've a bit of… you know, previous with the peelers.'

'A bit of previous?'

'Nothing criminal. Everything I did was political.'

'Okay, but it's no excuse for lying, is it?'

'Is that a serious question? With my record? With my politics? And you know the score, too. In this state, the police haven't exactly been trustworthy – they were a brutal sectarian militia – and fair enough, they're not exactly the same today, but still, they're not going to be the first port of call for somebody like me. I honestly didn't think they'd believe that I nipped out to the shop and disaster struck when I was away. It sounds unlikely.'

What he said rang true for Belle. She had similar views about the police in the North and anywhere for that matter. Her job had forced her to ease up a bit, but her innate mistrust remained. In Dermot's case, however, coming clean was the best option. 'It does sound unlikely,' she said, 'but unlikely things happen in life. You need to tell them and it's better you do that than for them to find out through their investigation.'

Dermot shook his head. 'I'll take my chances. Are you going to grass me up?'

'Hardly. But it's only a matter of time before they come knocking.'

Belle slumped back on the sofa. It was then she remembered. 'Oh God, Dermot, when I was making my escape from Ed's, he was prattling away and he mentioned seeing somebody other than you.'

'Who?'

'I was too desperate to get away, too upset at what he'd told me, that I didn't ask him for details, but he described them as a pair of heavies. He said one of them was bald.'

'Fuck. He actually said that?'

'Why, do you know who he's talking about?'

'Remember I told you about the two security men from Evergreen, Beavis and Butthead? Me and Fionn clocked them that night, not just once but twice, in two different bars.'

'You think Beavis and Butthead got into his flat when you were away?'

'It's obvious, isn't it? Butthead's balder than Kojak.'

'Maybe. It definitely fits my theory that Evergreen were behind Fionn's murder.' She cupped her face in her hands. 'Talking of Evergreen, I'm going to pull an all-nighter and see if I can catch their lorries taking waste to the dumpsites. I want to go tomorrow night or Monday. You up for it?'

Dermot wrinkled his brow. 'Naw, those are my nights for staying with me Ma. Tuesday night I could do it.'

'Don't worry about it. I can go ahead myself.'

'I'd rather you wouldn't. It could be dangerous. Will you wait 'til Tuesday?'

Belle shrugged and Dermot seemed content. He stubbed out his cigarette.

'What a fucking day,' he said. 'I could do with a drink.'

'Urgh! I couldn't face a night out right now,' Belle said. She put her hand on his cheek. 'I'm hungry, though.'

'Will I get us a takeaway? There's a class Italian place at the bottom of the street.'

'That sounds good. Do you like wine?'

'What do you think?'

'We can get a couple of bottles to help wash down the food.'

Dermot leaned closer. 'We should get going then.'

He kissed her on the lips and she let him – in fact, she couldn't resist.

'You okay with this? You said this morning we were a terrible mistake.'

'We are a terrible mistake, but I don't want to think about that until tomorrow.'

18

Belle parked her car a couple hundred yards from the entrance to the industrial estate where Evergreen had their facility, making sure to park off the road and out of sight as much as possible. Tonight was the night she was going to experience one of the clandestine excursions Fionn had detailed in his notes.

A layer of cloud went almost imperceptibly over the dark sky, only noticeable as it drifted across the moon and stars. Thick hedgerows and towering trees on both sides of the road dripped shadowy foliage on the ground below. A hush surrounded her.

From her jacket pocket, she extracted her trusty Dictaphone.

'According to Fionn,' she said, quietly, 'this is the time – between two and three in the morning on any given night – that lorries leave Evergreen for the dumpsites.' She paused. 'For all I know, Fionn might've parked in this very same spot, waiting, like me, for the rumble of the engines and the first glimmerings of headlights.'

Belle set the Dictaphone on the passenger seat, wishing something would kick off soon. Her thoughts wandered. Today had been productive, though. She'd struck lucky and had managed to set up a couple of meetings with Tom Sweet, the Evergreen head cheese, and the council officer Brendan Lynch, spinning them a line about doing a story on zero waste and the environment. Tom Sweet had been particularly keen, much to her surprise, and his secretary had set up an appointment for the following morning.

Belle had used the bogus name of Gina Mullan. An Internet search of Belle McGee threw up details about her awards and high-profile features, all the wrong kind of information if she wanted things to stay on the down-low. Belle had a fake press ID card to go with her fake name. Alma Travers knew about it but pretended not to – 'I don't want to know what you do to get your stories, only that you get them' was the regular line she gave her team. Her blind eye approach suited Belle just fine.

She yawned and shivered against the coldness of the night air seeping through the windows, in spite of being wrapped in a padded softshell jacket, fleece-lined black leggings and DM boots.

Dermot wouldn't be happy she'd gone ahead with this outing on Monday night and hadn't waited for a night he was free. She was an experienced investigator; she didn't need him holding her hand every step of the way. She let herself think back to Saturday night and felt a warm glow in her chest. Dermot was growing on her and she was doing nothing to stop it. The sensible thing to do would be to end it before it went any further. There was a practical problem – she lived in Dublin, after all, so when would they even see each other once she resumed her life there? There were also more fundamental problems. She wasn't relationship material for a start; her track record was testament to that. And she couldn't forget that Dermot was Fionn's cousin. That alone doomed the whole venture to heartbreak. So yes, the sensible thing would be to end it. Only, she wasn't feeling very sensible.

'Fuck,' she exhaled, 'why am I finding it so hard to stay away from him?'

A sound in the distance interrupted her ruminations. She listened. Finally, something was astir. A spluttering engine dispelled the silence and a wedge of light splashed yellow across the road. A lorry appeared, turning in the direction opposite to Belle's car. Seconds later, another lorry appeared, and then a third and final one.

Belle started her engine and edged away from her hiding place. She was in no rush. With the darkness and the roads being pretty much deserted, the lorries would be easy to tail. By the same token, she'd be easy to spot so she needed to hang back.

She grabbed the Dictaphone.

'The time is two-forty-five-am, Monday 16th July. Three lorries have pulled out of the Evergreen Waste Resources industrial estate. I'm following at a discreet distance and can just make out the tail lights of the last lorry, several hundred yards up ahead.'

She switched off the Dictaphone. The car filled with emptiness again, leaving only the blackness outside and the bobbing red dots of the tail lights, a pair of eyes from something evil.

They drove for a couple of miles along the main road and took a left onto a by-road, the lorries maintaining a steady speed, Belle maintaining her distance. The road twisted and rolled, going deeper and deeper into the desolate hills.

After an hour or more, she rounded a corner and saw the convoy taking a right turn, their headlights cutting slices out of the night. Reaching the turn-off, she realised it must lead to the dumpsite because it was a dirt road that disappeared into the heart of a man-made spruce forest. The site she'd visited with Dermot had been similar. She drove about five hundred yards past the road before stopping the car. She switched on the Dictaphone again.

'I have only a vague idea of where I am right now,' she said to the Dictaphone, 'so I'll determine a precise location later when I'm looking at a map. The lorries have gone into the forest where I believe there's a dumpsite. I'm going on foot from here on to get as near as possible without being seen.'

Leaving the car, she backtracked to the dirt road, careful not to stumble as her eyes got used to the darkness. She wished she could use a flashlight but didn't dare.

An arctic-cold breeze whistled past her ear and spits of rain pattered intermittently off her jacket. The ground was uneven but mostly solid underfoot, hardened from the recent dry weather, with the odd stubborn moist patch here and there.

'I'm on the road leading to the dumpsite,' she told the Dictaphone. 'I can see lights in the distance, which means I'm not far. The forest's pressing in on either side and it's quiet enough that you could hear a pin drop, or in this case, a pine needle.'

Farther along the track, farther into the forest, she eventually heard the whine of machines at work.

'I've been walking for about a mile and it's only now the men's voices are within earshot. They're still a bit of a way off… and oh, I see something… dots of lights, shining like gems between the trees.'

She picked up her pace, encouraged to be nearing the site. The rain was falling in a steady mizzle and she lifted her hood over her head and tightened the pull cord.

She heard the rev of an engine, followed by the steady hum of a lorry on the move. She stood stupefied without breathing. The sound grew louder… it was coming her way. The first of the lorries, probably its payload discharged, was making its return journey. If she didn't get out of sight, it was going to go right past her and she'd be caught in the headlights, literally.

She snapped out of her daze and ran for the forest, tripping on a tangle of coarse undergrowth. She landed on her knees in a ditch, hitting one of them off a rock. The thorny shoot of a briar tore across her cheek and icy water soaked into her leggings. She had no time to nurse the pain. She had to hurry. The lorry was closing in.

Dragging herself to her feet, she managed to get to a ridge close to the trees and throw herself behind it just as the lorry appeared.

The noise of the engine filled the silence and the diesel fumes mingled with the fresh pine of the pure highland air.

Once the lorry was out of sight, Belle returned to the track and continued her journey in a hurry. She sensed she didn't have much time if she wanted to see first-hand what the drivers were doing.

Turning another corner, and ignoring the squelching in her boots and the pain in her knee, she spotted a clearing and the remaining two lorries. She scurried off the track and found a vantage point at the edge of the forest where she could spy on proceedings. Gasping as the stench wafted closer, she clicked the Dictaphone.

'The smell is suffocating, even in the mountain air,' she said, in a whisper so low she wasn't sure the Dictaphone would catch it. 'Putrefied food; chemicals, too, I think – so sharp I feel like the skin inside my nose is peeling away.' She breathed through her mouth. 'The trailer bed of one lorry is raised at a forty-five-degree angle. Its contents spewing out, they look like… like entrails from a slaughtered animal. The drivers are huddled round the tailgate with shovels in their hands. Nearby is a digger – there to dig holes for the waste, probably. The men are talking, joking about; they seem relaxed, surefooted, like they're well used to doing this.'

When the second lorry was unloaded, the men started on the last one. Belle was transfixed on the scene. This was it, the illegal dumping in action. She never doubted it was going on, she never doubted Fionn, but seeing it with her own eyes – well, that brought the picture into clear, Technicolour focus.

As the lorry emptied, Belle decided it was time to go. She'd seen enough and didn't think she should still be around when the men were ready to leave.

Putting the Dictaphone safely in her jacket pocket, she picked her way out of the undergrowth. Once her feet were on the firmness of the track again, she retraced her steps as quickly as the darkness and the bumpy ground allowed, keeping her gaze on the ground to avoid stumbling. She congratulated herself on a good night's work and began thinking about how she was going to handle her meeting with Sweet in the morning.

As she turned onto the road, the lights from another dumper lorry caught her in their beam, illuminating her like a spotlight on a stage. She'd been so focused on the path, so engrossed in her scheming and plotting, that she hadn't noticed its approach. Running for cover was pointless. The best she could do now was to go on walking towards the car. If the driver of the lorry stopped – and maybe he wouldn't – she'd play dumb. She was on a public road, after all. Her heart pulsed loudly in her ears as she willed the lorry to continue on its journey.

She lucked out. The lorry came to a halt just at the turn-off to the dirt track and a voice called out, 'You all right there?'

Belle detected a tone in his voice that suggested his question wasn't entirely one of concern. She turned to face him, only to be blinded by the glare from the headlights.

'How's it going?' She tried to sound nonchalant. 'Just got caught short and ducked in there to take care of business.'

'You sure you're okay? Where's your car?'

'Ah, up the road a few yards.'

'I'll follow you to it, light the way.'

'There's no need, honest, I can see grand. Bye now.'

She set off in the direction of her car, wishing he would fuck off. He didn't. He started up the lorry, his lights on full beam, and slowly rolled along behind her. Her heartbeat was deafening.

When she reached the car, he stopped.

'Is that you?'

'That's me,' she waved without looking back. 'Thanks for your help.'

She hopped into the car and turned the ignition. He was still waiting. Making sure she left, no doubt, and giving himself plenty of time, if he wanted, to take down her registration. She put the car into gear and, with a quick look in the rearview mirror, sped off. She had to drive forwards, she couldn't turn and go back the way she came because the lorry was the width of the entire road and blocked her way. And doing that would probably look very suspicious, too.

She drove into the unknown until the lorry was out of sight, until her heart stopped racing. She wondered what the driver had made of their encounter and whether he'd be telling his story to his boss at Evergreen. Nothing she could do about it now and, actually, she had a bigger problem. Where the fuck was she? As she drove, she tried not to panic. There had to be a road sign soon, something to hint at her location.

She breathed out a long sigh of relief when she eventually saw a sign. Four miles away was a village she'd never heard of and thirty miles away was 'Londonderry'.

'Londonderry, my fucking ass,' she said.

At least she was on the way home.

19

Next morning, Belle drove onto the Evergreen site a few minutes early for her appointment with Tom Sweet. She grabbed her bag and got out of the car, before crossing the car park. Making a beeline for reception, she fished out a small leather pouch from her bag where she kept the press ID card for Gina Mullan. A momentary thought crossed her mind. Dermot was probably around somewhere, hard at work. She hoped she wouldn't bump into him. She didn't want anybody at Evergreen making a connection between them both.

Belle stepped inside the office. The air smelled faintly musty and she noticed a streak of damp starting at one of the corners in the ceiling. A lanky potted plant wilted against the wall. The desk was cluttered with papers and files, and a half-eaten sausage roll lay abandoned on a plate.

The receptionist greeted her with a face that looked like it hadn't smiled in a decade.

'I'm Gina Mullan,' Belle said. 'I was talking to you yesterday, about an appointment with Mr Sweet.'

The receptionist got up. 'This way.'

She led Belle to a door near the desk and opened it. 'Take a seat in there. Mr Sweet will be with you in a minute.'

Belle did as instructed. She tried to calm the uncomfortable bubbling in her stomach as she prepared for his arrival. She couldn't help but feel nervous after last night. It was possible the driver had reported seeing a woman near the dumpsite and they might mark her visit as too much of a coincidence. That was a risk she was prepared to take; the investigation required it. She put her notebook on her lap and searched her bag for a pen.

The door opened.

A bulky man with a thick moustache and a stock of curly hair came into the office. 'You're Gina Mullan,' he said, settling himself into a rather grandiose leather swivel chair behind a desk, the only item of luxury anywhere in the office.

Belle held out her fake ID. 'That's me. As I told your secretary yesterday, I'm doing a story on zero waste management in Ireland, right across the island.'

'So she said.' His deep-set eyes locked on her. 'I notice your card doesn't mention any paper. Which one do you work for?'

'I'm freelance; it lets me do the work I want. I've provided features for nearly all the main papers.'

'I see. Your ID's for the press in the South. What brings you to this side of the border?'

'I want to do comprehensive research, get a sense of the industry across Ireland. We all live on the same island, after all.'

'But not the same jurisdiction. Northern Ireland and the Republic have different sets of laws and systems for collecting waste.'

'Different systems, but not such different laws. The EU directs most of the legislation dealing with waste.'

'Accepted... though with Brexit, Northern Ireland is leaving the EU. Might not be a bad thing. EU laws straitjacket businesses. We should be trusted to do the right thing with regard to the environment – which we certainly do here at Evergreen – instead of being regulated to death.'

'One person's straitjacket is another person's environmental responsibility.'

'That's not quite what I meant—'

'No, of course not.'

His eyes narrowed and he threw her a look that would cut steel. 'For someone looking for my help, you're not exactly scoring brownie points.'

'I hope I haven't offended you,' Belle said, admonishing herself. She wasn't there to get on a high horse about the environment. 'I'd value a half hour of your time for an interview and maybe a quick tour of your facility.'

'Why us, here at Evergreen, out of all the companies you could talk to?'

'I picked a half a dozen or so companies, one in each corner of the island and a couple in Dublin. Yours was the biggest in the northwest.'

Tom Sweet nodded slowly. 'Indeed,' he said.

'It could be a chance to get some free publicity for your company, show you in a good light.'

'So you're doing me a favour.'

His stare was beginning to feel uncomfortable. Belle pursed her lips.

'What I mean is,' she said, 'it can be a mutually beneficial situation.' She tried to smile, but it got stuck halfway.

'I don't quite agree.' He tapped the desk with a pencil. 'Tell you what, here's my card. It's got our web address on it. That'll give you plenty enough information about our outfit and what we do. No need for an interview.'

'An interview would be better.'

'Not going to happen.' His tone was final, his face stern.

Belle didn't care. An interview about the company wasn't

necessary. What she wanted was to spend some time with Sweet, to suss him out.

His eyes narrowed again in another intense stare. 'You've been getting about a bit, though, haven't you?' he said.

'What do you mean?'

'Come on, this is a small town.'

He was onto her, which probably explained why he'd been so keen to meet. He'd wanted to suss her out, too. She knew she was playing with fire, though not for the first time. Work assignments in the past had brought her up close and personal to very dangerous and desperate individuals.

The door opened and a man stepped into the office. He was smaller than Sweet with a body so top-heavy with muscles he was virtually tipping over. Belle guessed he was one of the security men Dermot had told her about, and judging by his bald bonce, he was most likely Butthead. A cold shiver went down her spine. Was she in the room with one of the men who had murdered Fionn?

'The Galway delivery's an hour away, boss,' Butthead said, speaking to Sweet but eyeing Belle.

'Good man,' Sweet said.

'Everything all right here?' Butthead asked.

'Everything's fine. This lady's just leaving, aren't you, Ms Mullan?'

The security guard didn't say anything but a look passed between him and Sweet that Belle didn't like. She got to her feet.

'Well, it was lovely meeting you, Mr Sweet,' Belle said, faking nonchalance.

'I don't expect to see or hear from you after this.' Sweet made it sound like an order, and a menace in his slow, grey eyes left her with no doubt he meant it that way.

Belle went outside, feeling their eyes following her, boring holes in her back. She strolled to the car, trying to look casual. She was about to open the door when a shadowy reflection appeared in the window. She spun round with a jump.

'Jesus,' she said, 'you scared the life out of me.'

Standing – closer than was appropriate – was Butthead, a mean-tempered expression on his face, like a bulldog chewing a wasp.

'Can I help you with something?' Belle asked.

He shrugged. 'Making sure you get off the property safely.'

'Very considerate.'

She pulled the handle on the door. 'Do you mind backing away so I can get into my car?'

His squat frame budged ever so slightly allowing her enough space and no more to squeeze into the driver's seat.

'I'm liable to knock you over,' she said, 'if you don't get out of the way.'

'Knock me over and it'll be the last thing you ever do.' He folded his thick arms over his chest.

Belle slammed the door shut and switched on the ignition, revving the engine unnecessarily. His face creased into a smile that was more like a grimace. Her whole body trembled as fear and adrenaline coursed through her. She thrust the gearstick into first and took off with enough speed to make the tyres screech against the tarmacked surface.

Shifting into second gear, third and lastly fourth, her eyes fell on the rearview mirror as she exited the main gates. Sweet had joined his guard dog, and standing side by side, the two of them kept their eyes on her. They were certainly making sure she got off the property.

Then, without a second thought, and acting on nothing but instinct, she slammed her foot on the brakes. The car stopped with a jolt. She grabbed her phone and hopped out of the car. Before she could say 'Jack Robinson', she snapped a photo of the loitering pair and jumped back into the car.

Belle cruised along at a steady sixty on the drive back to town. As she put distance between herself and Evergreen Waste

Resources, she mulled over her encounter. They didn't give any indication that they'd linked her to being at the dumpsite the night before, although they clearly knew she was up to something. But equally, she could tell they were people with something to hide. Why else would they be so guarded and hostile? Keeping such a big illegal operation under wraps took a lot of energy and time; they needed to be uber-vigilant round the clock. They, Sweet specifically, had to be feeling constant pressure. She managed to smile. People under constant pressure eventually made mistakes, if they got enough rope.

She hung a right onto the Foyle Bridge, a structure suspended hundreds of metres above the gold-and-blue glimmer of the expansive Lough Foyle.

Tomorrow she had Brendan Lynch lined up and there were a few more names from Fionn's USB stick that she wanted to chase up, too: Kerrigan, Alexander and Councillor O'Dee.

Her phone rang, giving her a start. Hooked up to Bluetooth, she answered hands-free.

'Maeveen?' she said.

'Hi, quick call. Chrissie Power just phoned.'

'Is she all right?'

'She wanted to tell us that Fionn's body's been released. He's going to be buried this Thursday.'

Belle's stomach sank. She couldn't understand why. Fionn was dead. She knew that. He had to be buried. She knew that, too, but hearing it out loud made it so... so final.

She pulled into a lay-by on the bridge and stopped the car and there, at the side of the road, she released a torrent of inconsolable sobs.

20

Brendan Lynch was in his mid-thirties, Belle estimated – younger than she'd imagined. He had a bulbous nose and a bouffant of shiny black hair, side-parted and swept across his head like a thick blanket. She eyed him from the counter as she waited for her coffee order. He shifted and squirmed like he was sitting on a thorn bush. She wondered if his disquiet had anything to do with her. How much did he know was the question? How deep in was he?

As her order arrived, the phone rang. It was Dermot. She answered.

'Hi,' she said, trapping the phone between her ear and her neck so her hands were free to pay for the coffees. 'I'm in the middle of something here, so can't speak long.'

'No bother, it's a quick call anyway. You know about Fionn's funeral, right?'

'Chrissie rang Maeveen yesterday.'

'Okay, will I see you there?'

'I'm going, but you'll want that time to be with family. I don't want to intrude.'

'I'd like to see you, though.'

'What about Friday night?'

'Okay.'

'I've gotta go; I'm about to do an interview here.'

'You making progress?'

'Some; I'll fill you in when I see you. Talk then.'

She returned to the table.

'Extra milk in yours, Brendan, like you wanted,' Belle said, setting down two small cappuccinos.

They occupied a snug beside the window in a cafe on William Street, thankfully quiet at this time of the day.

'Thanks,' he said, lifting two sugar cubes from a bowl on the table and dropping them into his coffee, where they sank without trace into the frothy liquid.

'It's good of you to meet me, Brendan.'

'Aye, no bother.' He stirred his coffee too vigorously. 'So, you're doing a story on waste. I don't know if I'll be much help. I don't deal directly with the waste section.'

'Well, I know you're an environmental health officer so I guess I wanted to get a sense of what you do, what kind of situations you might deal with. I'm being thorough in my research. You can't write about waste and not mention the environment, right?' Belle had her notebook and pen on the table. 'Mind if I take a few notes?'

He stared at the notebook like she was going to use it to record his innermost secrets. 'Um, ah, I suppose.'

'This is really informal,' Belle said, 'we're just two people shooting the breeze.' She smiled. 'Tell me, are you from Derry originally?' The question was posed as an icebreaker, to put him at his ease.

'Aye, born and bred.'

'And how long have you been in your job?'

'Ah, about five years, but I've been in council for nearly ten.'

Belle smiled. 'And what does being an environmental health officer entail?'

'My department's mostly concerned with things like air pollution, contaminated land, industrial pollution prevention, noise pollution, you know.' He slurped his coffee and wiped a line of froth off his upper lip. 'We monitor air quality and we investigate industrial noise and reports of fumes and odours from commercial premises. We'll also look into reports of soil and water contamination.'

'A lot of responsibility.'

'It is and I take it very seriously, so make sure you write that down. Environmental protection is number one on my priority list.'

Belle noted it. 'Done. And what's your role specifically?'

'I do fieldwork mostly. My department acts on complaints received from residents in the council area. When we get a complaint in, a fieldworker like me is assigned to investigate and to follow it through until it's resolved. There's a whole process we follow, everything's recorded, i's dotted, t's crossed. Make sure you write that down, too.'

'Of course.' Belle did so. 'What does the process look like? Take me through a hypothetical.' Belle thought about Martin Higgins – and tried not to think of wee Seanie. 'Say a man rings you up, he lives in a remote area, he complains about pungent odours and strange colours in the nearby river. What will you do there?'

Brendan shot her a wary glance. 'Are you talking about a specific case?'

Belle smiled. *Was that a flash of recognition?*

'No, nothing specific,' she said, in a reassuring tone, 'just hypothetical, like I said.'

He took another sip of coffee and Belle noticed a slight tremor in his hand.

'Well, my answer's going to be hypothetical, too,' he said.

Belle nodded.

'I'll interview the complainant first off,' Brendan said, putting his hand to his forehead. 'Then, I'll do a walkabout of the area and make observations, describe the scene. Depending on what's been reported, I'll take some samples for testing. So, in your example, I'd take leachate samples.'

'Leachate?'

'It's liquid that's passed through contaminated ground. Basically, it's dirty water. So, I'll take samples from a range of locations: river, soil, anywhere else catching my eye. Everything I do out there, I'll keep a meticulous record, as I said.'

'What happens after the field visit?'

'It's back to the office. I'll send samples off for testing, which usually takes a few weeks, and when they come back, I'll write up a report. The reports we write are standardised and adhere to regulations. The test results go into the report, as do my observations if there are any, and I'm expected to make some recommendations, too.'

'There's scope in there to make your own judgement then, to draw conclusions.'

'Aye, sure. Once the report's done, it goes up the chain to my manager.'

'What happens then?'

Brendan shifted in his seat. 'Um, I dunno, it's not my responsibility after that. I make the recommendations, nothing more. I don't have the authority to act on them. It's the higher-ups in council decide that.'

Belle thought she could hear an imperceptible edge in his voice, perhaps uncomfortable with the direction the conversation was taking. That pleased her because it invariably meant she was touching on something significant. He needed a nudge, here and there.

'You never follow up on any of your reports to see what's happened?' she said.

'I don't think you're getting it. That's outside my job remit. The people that make the complaints, they want something done about

their problem, but all I can do is make a record. I can't help them...
do you understand? I can't help them.' He turned away and looked
out the window.

'That upsets you, that you can't help them?'

He shrugged, still not looking at her. 'It doesn't matter if it
upsets me.'

'That the tests might uncover information,' Belle probed.
'Information about health and safety risks that people need to be
made aware of, but you can't tell them anything?'

His eyes darted from left to right. 'What is this? Who said
anything about risks? Are you talking about something in
particular?'

'No, no,' she said, 'I'm just saying it would upset me if I were so
powerless.'

'Listen,' he said, 'I'm no different from any other five-eight
working in council. We're all told what to do and mind our own
business and that's that. I don't give it a second thought.'

He leaned back in his seat and breathed out heavily. Sweat
beads dotted his forehead. Belle smiled inside. She pushed a little
more.

'There must be something you could do, surely? Rather than
do nothing at all, especially when people trusted you with their
complaint. Couldn't you alert the councillors, the local paper—?'

'Wise up,' he said, 'you don't know what you're talking about.
Some of the councillors...'

'What about the councillors?'

'Nothing – look, I need to go.' He grabbed his suit jacket and
stood up.

'I'm sorry if I upset you.'

'You're not one bit sorry.' He snapped the words out.

Suddenly he leaned in, close enough to kiss her.

'You should be careful, Gina. You don't know what you're
dealing with here; you don't know *who* you're dealing with.'

As quickly as he'd closed in on her, he was up and gone. The door of the cafe slowly closed behind him as Belle digested the contents of their meeting. She'd spooked him. But truth was, he'd spooked her, too, with his parting words. That, however, was an occupational hazard. She'd deal with it. She'd proceed with caution, sure, and she'd deal with it.

She gathered her things and left the cafe, heading straight for her car, which was parked nearby. With her head still ringing from her conversation with Brendan, she was barely half-aware something was off. Only when she pointed the key at the driver's door to unlock it, did she realise.

'Fuck me,' she said.

A massive scratch was etched into the paintwork on the driver's side, all the way from the boot to the bonnet. Her immediate thought was that some toerag had enjoyed a bit of random fun as they passed by. Her phone pinged with a message. She quickly checked. A withheld number. *This time it's the paint; next time, the brakes.*

Belle's throat tightened and the skin on her arms went cold. She glanced up and down the street. She was being watched. Of course, it had to be Evergreen and their cronies, probably Beavis and Butthead, but they were out of sight wherever they were. Maybe now they knew she'd been the person snooping around at the dumpsite. The stakes in this game just got higher.

21

DONEGAL, 1986

Belle looked down at her feet. Lying in the doorway of her bedroom was the cutest origami lotus flower. She picked it up. Written on one of the powder-blue petals was '*Mo chara, Baby Belle*'.

Mo chara? Irish for 'my friend'. Well, she wasn't his friend. Those days were over. The eavesdropped conversation with Fionn and her parents was three weeks previous. Since then, a handful of words, at most, had passed between her and Fionn. The same went for Maeveen, who complained about her being in a huff. But Belle got the message. She was a baby, while Maeveen was love and marriage material. If that's how he wanted it, that's how he'd get it.

Belle spent most of her days in her reading tree or with Hunter, whenever he had a free day, which was exactly how she would've spent her holidays if Fionn wasn't there. *If* Fionn wasn't there? For her, he wasn't.

In the evenings, the games they played together came to an end, too. Maeveen and Fionn still played while Belle stayed away, either up in her room listening to music and reading, or in the sitting room watching TV. Most times, they ignored her, other times they asked her to join in. Belle never relented. If anything, she got worse over time, her resentment growing. She wasn't repelled by that, she revelled in it, getting a perverse pleasure from feeling hard done-by.

She crumpled the lotus flower in her fist – Fionn's latest attempt to suck up to her – and stuffed it into the front pocket of her jeans. He was sorely mistaken if he thought she was so easily won over.

'Sit with us tonight, Belle,' Maeveen asked, when they were finishing their supper that evening. 'We'll play Cluedo.'

'You can't say no to that,' Fionn said. 'It's your favourite.'

'Oh, don't worry about me,' Belle said. 'Go on and play whatever you like. I've other stuff I want to do.'

'You have all day tomorrow to do your other stuff,' Maeveen said. 'Come on, one game of Cluedo. You'll be able to gloat when you win.'

'Ah, play with us. We miss you,' Fionn said and he ruffled her hair.

She pulled back, so she was out of his reach. 'I said, I've other stuff to do.'

Fionn looked hurt. She hoped he was.

'You don't have to be cheeky, Belle,' her mother said. 'Anyway, it's your turn to do the dishes, so go on with you and stop making the rest of us miserable.'

'Are you going to your sister's?' Belle's father asked.

'Aye, I told Fran I'd be round after teatime.'

'Will you get me some tobacco on the way home?'

'I need to pick up some milk, too. Anybody else want anything?'

Maeveen shrugged.

'No thanks, Kitty,' Fionn said.

'She didn't mean you,' Belle said, throwing him a defiant look.

Her father and sister stared wide-eyed, and Fionn had that hurt expression again, like his dog just died.

'Belle,' her mother said, with a raised voice, 'say you're sorry to Fionn.'

'Humph.'

'Right now, do you hear me?'

'Sorry,' the word left her mouth begrudgingly.

The family dispersed and Belle was left to the tedious chore of the washing up. She was filling the sink with water when Maeveen appeared at the doorway.

'Hope you're here to give me a hand,' Belle said, looking round.

'Give you a hand, my arse. I've been working all day – 'bout time you pulled your weight.'

'No need to be so hateful.'

Maeveen snorted. 'You're one to talk. I couldn't believe the way you spoke to Fionn.'

'So what? He needs to remember his place.'

'You are one right bitch,' Maeveen said. 'Remember his place, indeed, like you're lady of the manor and he's the hired help. I'm here to tell you this: you treat him with some respect. He's been good to you and he can't understand why you've turned on him. I can't either.'

'You can't? Want me to tell you?'

'What're you on about?'

'I saw you kissing him.'

Maeveen turned the colour of a blazing sunset, from her neck to the top of her head. 'Yuh… you… I… what—'

'I saw you and it made me sick.'

'Bullshit, you don't know what you're talking about.'

'I do so.'

'Wait a minute… you saw us… so that's how Mammy and Daddy found out.' The shock on Maeveen's face was almost alive. She ran from the door and, in one swoop, grabbed hold of Belle's hair. 'You horrible…'

Belle felt a stinging smack on her cheek and then another. Maeveen, who'd never as much as swatted a fly in her life, was slapping the face off her own sister.

'Leave me alone,' Belle squealed.

Maeveen flung her to the ground, letting go of her hair. Belle landed on the cold, hard linoleum floor, hurting her knees and her hands. Her head throbbed and her face smarted. She wanted to cry but stubbornly resisted.

'Why, Belle? Why'd you tell on us?' Maeveen's voice cracked, on the verge of tears.

Despite her wretchedness, Belle smiled. She was glad Maeveen was hurting; glad she was the one who'd made her sister hurt.

'Why did you have to ruin everything?' Maeveen said.

'I'm not taking the blame. You were the one doing something wrong.'

'I wasn't doing anything wrong, I...'

Belle staggered to her feet, holding the sink for support.

'Belle, I'm sorry, I should've done that.'

'You should be sorry.'

'I'm sorry.' Maeveen reached out to stroke her hair.

'I don't want you to touch me,' Belle said, pushing Maeveen's hand away. 'There was no call for hitting me.'

'I've said sorry. I won't do it again.'

'You think a pathetic sorry's good enough?'

'What?'

'It's not, I'm going to tell—'

'You are not, you tell-tit brat. Your big mouth's done enough damage.'

'Don't you call me a tell-tit.'

'What else would I call somebody that goes running to their Mammy and Daddy? You're a silly little child.'

'I'm not a child,' Belle shouted, rage swirling in her chest like a storm. 'I'm nearly a grown up like you.'

Maeveen eyed her with confusion.

'And I did the right thing telling Mammy and Daddy about you and Fionn.'

Maeveen shook her head. 'You don't know the full story.'

'What don't I know?'

'I can't tell you; I'm not even supposed to know. All I can say is it's not what you think.'

'Fionn's done something bad, hasn't he? He's a criminal or something.'

'He's nothing of the sort. You've got the wrong end of the stick.'

'Tell me then.'

'I can't.'

Belle breathed heavily through her nose. She glared at Maeveen with hatred.

'Belle, don't get so worked up. Seriously, you're freaking me out.'

'Why does he like you so much?' she said, using her words to release the venom inside her. 'Me and him got on the best. All the times you were away at work, it was just me and him, and we had great craic and he made me origami stuff and—'

'Christ, now I get it. You and him... you thought... aw, Belle, you're thirteen years old. He couldn't—'

'Stop it.' Hot, stinging tears spilled onto her eyelids. 'He liked me but 'cos of you, he doesn't anymore.'

'That's not true; he thinks you're brilliant.'

'He thinks I'm a child.'

'But you are.'

'It's not fair. I'm not that much younger than you.'

'Not much, but he's twenty-one – nearly ten years older than you, a man. If you can't see the problem with that...'

Belle dried her eyes with her sleeve, hoping Maeveen didn't notice they were wet.

'Try to make it up with Fionn, will you?'

Belle turned away.

'Please try. He wants things to be right between you and him before—'

'Before what?'

'Before he leaves.'

He was definitely leaving then. Going down the country, like he said.

'Is he going to Limerick?'

'How...' Maeveen looked startled. 'Not there; we talked about Galway. I could go to—'

'UCG,' Belle finished.

'Are you reading my mind?'

'You got an offer for there, didn't you?' Belle said, opting not to let Maeveen know she'd overheard her parents and Fionn.

'Well, that's what we're planning. You can come and visit us when we're set up, wouldn't you like that?'

The last thing on earth she'd like was to visit Fionn and her sister, to have to see them together in a home of their own, living happily ever after.

Despair weighed on her heavier than a ton of coal. Why couldn't it be her? She loved him more than Maeveen could ever love him. Why couldn't he wait for her to get older? Envy gnawed at her like a desperate rat and all she could see was the joy in Maeveen's face – joy that was Belle's by right and didn't belong to her sister.

'So, you're going to live in sin, then?'

'You're a proper prude,' Maeveen said. 'Nobody gives a shit about that kind of thing anymore. And Mammy and Daddy are just going to have to put up with it.'

Belle folded her arms.

'You understand all this, don't you?' Maeveen smiled and touched her shoulder. 'You're old enough to get it.'

Belle understood; she understood well. She faked a smile.

'That's better,' Maeveen said. 'The three of us can be friends again. In a few years' time, we'll look back on this and laugh.'

Belle widened her smile.

'So, you wanna play some cards with us?'

'Maybe later; I have to tidy the kitchen first.'

'Grand, we'll see you in a while then.'

'Grand.'

After Maeveen left, Belle stood by the sink contemplating their conversation. She'd made Maeveen believe everything was hunky-dory but that couldn't be further from the truth. Belle couldn't – wouldn't – forgive them. They had no clue how deep they'd cut her, and a pat on the shoulder and a few games of cards wasn't going to put it right.

22

DERRY, PRESENT DAY

The Long Tower chapel was packed – there wasn't standing room – for Fionn's funeral. Nearly two whole weeks since his death, he was finally being laid to rest.

Maeveen was by Belle's side in a crowded pew in the gallery, silently staring at her hands, which were folded together in her lap, lost in the world of her thoughts. She'd hardly said two words all morning, not even on the drive to Derry, and Belle decided it was best to let her be. This was a hard day for her; it was a hard day for a lot of people.

The Long Tower wasn't the biggest church in Derry but Belle thought it was the most beautiful. With rows of dark wooden pews on either side of the T-shaped building, it was a riot of vibrant stained-glass windows, spectacular opus sectile panels and Renaissance-style oil paintings. The altar and its surrounds of pillars, floor and altar railings were carved from white marble and decorated with brass candelabra, oil paintings, statues and more stained-glass windows and opus sectile panels.

Just outside the railings, dwarfed by the altar's magnitude, was Fionn's coffin, resting on a black metal stand and draped in an Irish flag.

From her bird's-eye view in the gallery, Belle could see the whole congregation. In the front rows closest to the coffin were the family members, Chrissie and Dermot among them. Elsewhere, she recognised one or two other faces.

The mass drew to a close and the priest recited the prayer after communion. Stillness fell across the congregation like an invisible mist. For a few moments, the priest sat in a chair by the side of the altar, his head bowed in prayer. The people waited, an intermittent cough or sniff echoing through the hush. With the stealth of a prowling cat, dread rose from Belle's stomach. She knew what was coming next. Memories of every funeral she'd ever attended gatecrashed her mind.

The priest stood up and, along with the altar boys, began preparing for the final commendation. Belle wished with her entire being that she could avert her eyes, the way she might if she was witness to a terrible car crash. But she couldn't. If anything, she was transfixed. The priest circled the coffin with a holy water pot and sprinkler, splashing it with water as he went and, for a single haunted second, Belle imagined Fionn, sealed in the box, underneath that flag.

One of the altar boys took the pot and sprinkler from the priest's hand and a second boy gave him a silver thurible, which spewed clouds of smoke from the smouldering frankincense hidden inside. He circled the coffin again, gently swinging the thurible back and forth, clanking the chain off the metal. The smell of the incense crept through the church, filling every corner, reaching all the way to the panelled ceiling. The spicy, woody aroma cloying and overpowering, yet reassuringly familiar. Belle found it impossible to say whether she liked it or loathed it. Her stomach tightened into a hard knot. The memory of one specific funeral emerged supreme out of all the others.

The priest turned to face the congregation. 'Saints of God,' he began, 'come to his aid. Hasten to meet him, angels of the Lord!'

Every voice in the church responded as one voice like a low rumble of thunder, 'Receive his soul and present him to God the Most High.'

Once those closing words were uttered, there was no going back. Tears pushed behind Belle's eyes and her chest swelled with pain. She heard a muffled sob and, without having to look, knew it was Maeveen. She could feel her sister's body tremble, convulsed with grief. She should wrap Maeveen in her arms and rock her to take away some of her pain. She should. She wanted to. She couldn't.

'May Christ, who called you, take you to himself; may angels lead you to the bosom of Abraham.'

'Receive his soul and present him to God the Most High.'

Belle had the most consuming urge to run away, imposter that she was. She had no right to be there among these good people who'd come to pay their last respects to Fionn.

Tears dripped in a steady flow from her eyelashes and onto her face. She swept them away with a tissue but they just kept coming.

'Eternal rest grant unto him, O Lord, and let perpetual light shine upon him.'

'Receive his soul and present him to God the Most High.'

The undertaker and the pallbearers appeared as though from thin air, and surrounded the coffin. The pallbearers raised it onto their shoulders assisted by the undertaker, who adjusted the position so that they carried the weight evenly between them.

The pipe organ, located at the far end of the gallery, boomed to life like a sleeping bear, rattling the blood in Belle's veins. She recognised the hymn before the solo singer opened her lips: 'Nearer, My God, to Thee'. Everybody stood.

'No,' Maeveen moaned, softly.

The priest advanced down the aisle, followed by the pallbearers, and row after row, starting with the family members, the people filed out of their pews to join the procession, the lingering cloud of incense hovering above their heads. Chrissie walked slowly, like a broken reed, leaning on another woman equally broken. Dermot was behind them. He looked up at the gallery and locked eyes with Belle. He gave her a half-hearted smile and she did likewise.

The mourners in the gallery would be the last in line to exit the church and Belle and Maeveen were on the inside of their pew, which meant they'd be the last to leave the row. Maeveen pulled on Belle's sleeve.

'I can't.' Her eyes were bloodshot and swollen, her cheeks dotted with fiery red blotches. 'I can't go to the cemetery.'

'We have to.'

'You go on your own then.' Her voice was thick with crying. 'The idea of him being put in the ground… it's too much.'

'Okay, okay, we won't go. I don't think I can do it either.'

Maeveen sniffed and touched her nose with a tissue. 'The funeral bought it all back, like it happened yesterday. Fionn and the cubbyhole and the Campbells and Daddy… it's a horror story, isn't it, Belle?'

Belle nodded. It was a horror story, worse even than Maeveen knew.

'I could murder a drink,' Maeveen said.

'Me, too. Do you want to get one?'

'No, not during the day. Golden rule. No matter what the situation.'

'What about a coffee instead?'

'That'd be nice.' Maeveen gave a weak smile that was more pitiful than her tears.

*

They were among the last out of the Long Tower, in time to see the tail end of the funeral procession snaking to the right towards the Folly. It would go on to the city cemetery, which was close enough for the funeral to walk all the way. Instead of falling into line, Belle and Maeveen took a left, unnoticed by the mourners, in the direction of Bishop Street.

'There's a place near the Diamond where we can go,' Maeveen said, blowing her nose.

As they turned onto Bishop Street, Belle glanced across the road. Her eyes fell on two men dressed in black suits appropriate for a funeral. She recognised one of them as Butthead; the other had to be Beavis – he was similar in size and build to Butthead, but had a full head of light brown hair. They were watching her. She was tempted to capture a photo with her phone but decided against it. Too insensitive, given the state Maeveen was in.

Saying nothing, Belle linked arms with her sister and they walked onwards. Every few yards, she checked behind and, sure enough, Beavis and Butthead were never far away. Were they following her or did they happen to be coincidentally walking along the same street?

They arrived at the café and went inside. Maeveen dropped onto a seat at a table near the window. She looked wretched, with her eyelids swollen and her cheeks sunken.

Belle rubbed her shoulder. 'What can I get for you?'

'An Americano's grand, drop of milk.'

Belle grabbed her wallet. She threw a look at the doorway expecting it to be clear. Instead, Beavis and Butthead were standing there, talking to each other but with their eyes on her table. She felt her stomach bubble and twist with resentment that they were intruding on her grief. And she hadn't forgotten the damage to her car. She was convinced this pair of knuckleheads was responsible. Her gut instinct was to march right over to them and… and what? What would she do or say exactly? Tell them to leave her alone or else? Threaten them with the police? When she had nothing but suspicions against them? None of that was a good idea.

Instead, she stared right at them, wishing for the ability to do real, physical harm with her eyes alone, like she had a superpower.

One of the men smirked before they both turned on their heels and left. She let out a breath and swallowed hard.

Belle ordered an Americano and a green tea and brought them to the table. Maeveen gazed into her coffee with the intensity of a fortune-teller peering into a cup of tea leaves. Belle allowed her the silence, happy enough not to talk.

'It's the weirdest feeling,' Maeveen eventually said, 'him gone. As bad as Mammy or Daddy being gone.'

Belle nodded.

'I saw a fair bit of him after h-he... you know.'

'Uh-huh.'

'It was good, getting to know him when I was a proper adult. He was a great person; he had such a big heart... but then, you know that.' Maeveen traced her index finger over the rim of the coffee cup. 'He always put other people first. That was his downfall – why he had nothing, why all that shit happened to him.'

Droplets fell from Maeveen's face onto the back of her hand and she took out a tissue. Belle tensed her lips and her throat and her chest, in an effort to stop the flow of her own tears.

'Life was so cruel to him,' Maeveen said. 'Oh fuck, it wasn't right what he went through. He was never bitter. I never once heard him say an angry word, not even about the Campbells.'

Belle willed Maeveen not to talk about the Campbells.

'Treacherous fuckers.' Maeveen tightened her fists and they went red, then white.

'Don't upset yourself.'

'I'm already upset, no point holding it in now.' She lifted the cup to her lips, spilling the contents as she did and making a little brown pool in the saucer. 'He talked to me about it all – what it was like for him after the summer he stayed with us. Took him time to open up, but once he did, he told me everything. It was hard hearing it, really hard. Even so, I was glad he confided in me.'

Belle felt the swell in her chest. She wasn't going to cry; she was going to wail. Oh God, her heart was being cut out of her.

'He still loved me,' Maeveen said. 'That's something I never told you.'

'No,' Belle uttered the word like she'd been lashed with a whip. She couldn't bear the pain of her sister's lost chance.

'After all those years and all he went through, he still loved me. We nearly got together again, you didn't know that.'

Belle shook her head. She didn't bother to say that Dermot had already told her.

'Yup, one night, not long after he was released from prison, he came to the house for a visit. We had a few drinks and talked and laughed and, well, we ended up sleeping together. Our first time. Our last time. It was like picking up from 1986. And I found I was as mad about him as ever and I wanted to be with him. But he said he couldn't. He wasn't always in the best of health, was the way he put it. Up here.' Maeveen tapped her temple. 'Said he'd only make me miserable and I'd end up hating him.'

Maeveen gulped a mouthful of air and began to weep. 'He was wrong to decide for me,' she mumbled. 'He should've given me the chance to make up my own mind.'

Looking at her sister, Belle couldn't hold in her own pain any longer and she finally gave way to the tears.

'If I hadn't let him make that choice,' Maeveen said, 'if I'd made him be with me, he'd be alive today. He definitely wouldn't have been beaten to death.'

'Don't torture yourself with what-ifs, please, Maeveen. Don't.'

'He didn't deserve to die like that. He didn't—'

'He didn't deserve a lot of things,' Belle said.

Belle let her mind turn over the undeserved things that had happened to Fionn. Everything he could've been or could've done but was denied because of those undeserved things. *It was a tragedy, that's what it was*, she thought. *A Greek tragedy for her Greek god.*

23

Belle was alone in the house the next day. Maeveen had been so upset after the funeral that Cillian decided they should take Friday off and go for a day trip around the Inishowen Peninsula.

Belle showered, pulled on a pair of jeans and a T-shirt, and tied her hair back in a loose ponytail. The funeral had left her in the lowest of spirits and she regretted not going with Maeveen and Cillian just to give her a distraction from the heaviness that pressed down on her heart. She checked her phone as she began to prepare breakfast. Missed call from a Northern landline number that was vaguely familiar. She called it.

'Hello, I'm Belle McGee, I missed a call from you earlier?'

'Oh, thanks for ringing me back,' said a polite, well-spoken voice. 'I'm Rita Wilson, I came back a day early from leave and got your message.'

'Ah, Dr Wilson,' Belle said, perking up. She forced her grief to the side for a while and pushed her way into reporter mode. 'Many thanks for getting in touch. Maybe I should properly explain why I'm calling you.'

Belle paused. Fionn had put 'good info' beside Rita's name. That meant she could be trusted with at least some of the detail.

She ended her brief summary with a question. 'Do you happen to know a man called James Power?'

'No, sorry, I don't.'

'Just checking because James is really the person who switched me onto this story. He found a place where he suspected waste was being dumped. I was hoping you might be able to help me. I need someone who could test soil and water in the area to see if there's been any pollution.'

'I could run the tests you want, but I'd need samples.'

'Thank you so much, Dr Wilson. I'll get whatever samples you need.'

'Please, call me Rita. Have you got a pen and paper?'

'Yes.'

'I'm going to explain the collection process, the materials you'll need to carry it out and so on. And it's important you follow my instructions so we get the most accurate results possible.'

'Just tell me what I need to do; I'll take down every word.'

Belle noted everything Rita told her.

'Once I collect the samples, when can I bring them to you?'

'Right away,' Rita said. 'Just give me a quick call to let me know when you're ready and we'll agree a time.'

*

A couple of hours later, Belle was back at the dumpsite she'd visited with Dermot. For a second, she'd contemplated ringing him to come with her, but decided he was probably in no fit state to do anything so soon after the funeral.

The site looked pretty much as it did first time, but something was a little different. Belle thought for a moment and then got it. There'd been a digger and a bulldozer before and now both were gone.

She stood over the open car boot. Everything she needed for the task at hand was neatly packed inside. The silence of the place was calming and the sunlight drenched it in a golden shimmer, though the air still stank to high heaven. Belle had come prepared. She grabbed a face mask and strapped it across her mouth and nose. She pulled on a plastic windbreaker, which she hoped would protect her clothes, and changed out of her slippers and into a pair of wellies. Next, she reached for a large Tupperware lunchbox and opened the lid to reveal a pair of heavy-duty rubber gloves, a tiny notebook and pen, and several travel bottles that she'd picked up in the chemist on the way. Each lid was numbered.

Belle put on the gloves and did a quick check to make sure she had everything before moving in on the contaminated area. The stench intensified as she drew closer and she was glad of the mask. She hunkered down, leaving the lunchbox by her side. With glove-clad hands, she dug away some soil until she got closer to a layer of waste.

When she was deep enough, she opened bottle number one, scooped a handful of soil into it, sealed it up and returned it to the lunchbox. Removing her left-hand glove, she took the pen and wrote in the notebook "Bottle one – soil sample from dumpsite area." She put the pen and notebook back in the lunchbox.

A rat scurried across the disturbed soil just yards away and stopped. Its black, beady eyes gazed directly at her. Belle shivered. She lifted a small rock and threw it in the general direction of the rat. It landed just a foot from him but the rat didn't flinch.

'What the fuck,' she said. 'I wouldn't want to get into a fight with you.'

She searched around, looking for her next sample. She found a pool of water, or leachate – that was what Brendan Lynch had called it – in a hollow in the soil.

'Perfect.'

She hunkered down for a second time and selected bottle number two. The last thing she wanted to do was go anywhere near that putrid, viscous liquid but she had to. Her stomach lurched, making her gag, and she barely stopped herself from throwing up. She held the bottle down until it filled to the top. Once it was safely in the lunchbox, she made a record in the notebook.

Rita had instructed her to gather some soil and water samples from areas beyond the actual dumpsite, too. She walked away a little , following the gentle gurgle of flowing water. She came to a stream and began the process of collecting the third sample.

A sound in the distance made her stop. She straightened. And listened. A rumbling engine. Coming closer. A lorry? Fionn's notes didn't mention anything about daytime excursions but that didn't mean they didn't happen. The last thing she needed was to get caught again. The rumble grew louder and then it started to ebb. She exhaled heavily. Just a lorry out on the road, not coming to the site.

She worked quickly to gather the remaining samples, six in total. In no time, she was changed out of her protective gear with everything packed away in the boot and on the dirt track taking her to the road. She'd made good progress; it was still early enough with hours to go before her date with Dermot. Maybe she could call in with Martin Higgins.

As she reached the stretch of road leading to Martin's house, she noticed a vehicle parked outside. Her skin went cold in spite of the warm sun beaming through the window and her throat tightened. It was an ambulance. She drove on, slowly, and passed the house just as the paramedics were walking up the drive. Her heart fell. One of them pushed a wheelchair and Belle strained to see the passenger: Seanie, his pitifully small body hunched over.

Belle pressed her foot on the accelerator to get away from the scene as quickly as she could. A tear splashed onto her cheek and then another and soon there was a stream, rolling down her face. She kept on driving.

*

Dermot opened the door, greeting her with a smile, although his eyes were dull and red.

'Belle,' he said, moving in for a kiss, 'you look beautiful.'

Her heart soared. She'd made a big effort for him. Her hair was up in a French roll and she wore a figure-hugging black mini dress, loosely tied in the middle with a silver-buckled belt. All this effort for a relationship she knew could go nowhere – but now wasn't the time to think about that.

Belle pulled back from him. 'You're looking good yourself.'

Seemed like he'd put in an effort, too. He cut a handsome figure in black suit trousers, a white shirt, black waistcoat and polished black boots.

'Want a wee drink before we hit town?'

'Why not?'

He poured them two generous Morgan and cokes.

'Did you buy that for me?'

'Aye, but I'm starting to like it myself. There you go,' he said. 'Slainté.'

'Slainté.'

They got cosy on the sofa.

'I saw you yesterday,' Dermot said. 'You and Maeveen were in the gallery.'

Belle nodded. 'You were in a bad way.'

'It was worst day of my fucking life. The cemetery was the hardest part. Made it very real, you know, that he's gone. It near killed me.' He wiped his eye.

Belle touched his face. 'It's okay.'

'I didn't see you at the graveside,' he said, sniffing. 'I was looking out for you.'

'We didn't go,' Belle said. 'Maeveen was in bits and neither of us thought we could handle it. I'm sorry.'

'Don't be, I can understand.'

'We don't have to go out, you know. We can stay in.'

'After going to all this bother getting dressed up? No chance.' Belle chuckled.

'Anyway, how's the investigation going?' he asked.

'Busy, busy. I've had a few adventures this week.'

She got as far as telling him about the nighttime journey to the dumpsite before he interrupted.

'Jesus, Belle,' he said. He slapped his drink down on the coffee table and sat up. 'I told you to wait for a night I was free. What were you thinking going off on your own? Anything could've happened – and you got caught into the bargain.' He looked agitated.

'It was grand. I know what I'm doing. And I don't need some macho he-man escorting me everywhere I go.' A warm ball of anger grew inside her. She wasn't going to let him, or anyone, tell her what to do.

'Aw, fuck sake,' he said, 'I'd be the last person to try that sexist shit on with you but this isn't about women's rights. These people are dangerous and we don't know how high up the network goes or who's involved. How could you be so fucking stupid?'

'I can handle myself; I do this for a living. And what's it to you what I do, anyway?'

'You have to ask that?' He threw her a disgusted look. 'I… I like you… a lot, I mean, I do.' His cheeks flared red and he looked away.

Belle regretted her careless words, realising he was coming from a place of concern, not control. Her anger fell away. She had intended to tell him about the antics of Beavis and Butthead, but after his reaction to the dumpsite, thought it was better not to.

'I didn't mean to be hurtful,' she said, instead.

He shrugged.

'And I… I like you, too,' she said. The words were alien on her lips; it wasn't often she used them and, in this case, they were an understatement. She more than liked him.

He turned towards her and managed the faintest of smiles.

'I know you're just looking out for me,' she said.

'You need to watch yourself, Belle.'

'I am, honestly. I'm not taking risks. I've done investigations before so I'm not some clueless rookie. Getting caught at the dumpsite was a blip.'

Dermot nodded. 'Okay, but don't let your guard down.'

Belle pecked him on the cheek. 'Why don't we get out of here?'

24

DONEGAL, 1986

'This is pointless, Belle.' Hunter stood shin-deep in the river, his jeans rolled up, his bare feet white like death under the wavering water. 'I haven't seen one yet.'

'I thought I saw one there now,' Belle said, 'but it was just a wee stone moving about at the bottom of the riverbed.'

They were searching for spiddlybacks – the tiny fish that lived in the river – though Belle was never convinced spiddlybacks was their actual name. She and Hunter loved to while away whole afternoons hoping to nab them in cupped hands and hold them for a quick gawk before throwing them back in the water.

'We should give up looking,' Belle said. 'My feet are numb.'

'Mine, too, but we can't stop without seeing a single one. Give it another ten minutes.'

'Okay, another ten minutes, but we're going to have to try the deep.'

They knew the river well. In parts, it ran fast and shallow; in others, it was like a pool, barely moving or making a sound. Those still pools meant one thing: deep water. And they could be treacherous, though only if you weren't extra careful.

Belle set off downstream, Hunter following, towards a deep area that was a few hundred yards away, both of them carrying their slippers high above the water. The pebbles and stones on the riverbed jabbed and scratched the soles of her feet, here and there giving way to a patch of sand that kissed her feet better.

Trees loomed on either side of the banks, their branches meeting in the middle, high overhead, creating a dreamy dance of light and shadows on the water.

The woods were soundless, as though the heat of the sun had put a sleeping spell on every living and growing thing. There wasn't as much as the trill of a bird or a whisper from the leaves. Although Belle thought she heard something in the distance: an echo of what sounded like a giggle. Maeveen. Lost in the thicket with Fionn, she guessed, making the most of her day off work. Sneaking out of the house behind their parents' back. And they were kissing. She could see it in her mind's eye like the day she caught them in the cherry orchard. The very thought of them together made her want to scream and lash out and break things.

'We could be Piggy and Ralph in Lord of the Flies,' Hunter said, trailing behind.

'I hope not,' Belle said, glad he was distracting her from her violent fantasies.

The water was up to her waist now and flowing with less energy. Her shorts and underpants were soaked and the water's coolness pinched her skin.

'You know what I mean. It's so quiet; we're like castaways on a desert island.'

So he noticed it, too. The silence, crushing them with its weight. She wondered if he'd heard Maeveen. Part of her hoped he would. Maeveen and Fionn deserved to get caught.

'We're nearly there,' Belle said. 'I'm going to start looking out for spiddlybacks from here on. Give me your slippers and I'll put them on the bank with mine.'

Hunter handed over his shoes and Belle paddled to the river's edge and swung them onto the bank. Hunter waded onward, moving in slow motion against the heft of the water. His arms were outstretched and he was half-walking, half-bobbing. 'I could nearly start swimming,' he called.

'We should dive,' Belle said, peering into the water. 'Pretend we're diving for pearls.'

'I bet you I can hold my breath long enough to swim to the bottom and back.'

'Bet you can't.'

Belle heard Maeveen again, more laughter, closer this time. Their happiness only increased her misery. This life of hers was unbearable. Damn them.

Hunter stopped. He was full-on immersed in water.

'You're wringing wet,' Belle said. 'Your Daddy's going to know you were in the burn – he'll kill you.'

'I'm going to sneak in my bedroom window.'

'I'll have to sneak in, too. I'll go in our front door and try to get up the stairs without getting caught.'

'Right, time to dive,' Hunter said.

He gasped in a lungful of air and plunged below the surface, leaving circles of ripples in his place. Belle didn't feel so brave. Remaining chest-deep, she took a big breath, plugged her nose with her thumb and index finger, and bent her legs so she could slide under.

Belle opened her eyes and scanned the river from left to right like a searchlight. The water was murky brown, making it impossible to see anything. She'd never spot a spiddlyback, not that she even cared any longer. She stood up, tasting the delicious air, and rubbed her face. She wondered if Maeveen and Fionn were closer now. They could even be walking towards the river, about to arrive at any time. Belle's face twisted with malicious delight. She'd love to see their faces when they'd realise Hunter was here.

Which reminded her, Hunter was nowhere to be seen. The spot where he went under was calm and undisturbed. She watched for him to come to the top. The woods watched, too. She was about to sink below to look for him when the glass surface of the water shattered and Hunter reappeared, breathing deeply, his hair flattened on his head.

'You were down for ages,' Belle said. 'I was starting to get worried.'

'I told you I could do it. I was swimming along the bottom. It was harder than doing it in the swimming pool but I still did it.'

'I'm freezing,' Belle said, her stomach growling like a menacing lion, 'and I'm starving. I wanna go.'

'I'll do one more dive, then we'll go. I saw something shiny down there.'

'Hurry up, then.'

Belle was fed up with the river and fed up with Hunter for the day. These childish games weren't so much fun anymore.

Belle walked towards the bank, pushing hard against the river, and hoisted herself out of the water using a clump of wild grass. She backtracked the few yards to get their things as Hunter disappeared once more. Teeth chattering, she hunkered down on the grassy bank and put her slippers on, letting the sun wrap her in its warmth.

'Hunter,' she called, wiping her face, 'come on.'

Nothing. Where the hell was he? All Belle wanted was to go home.

'Hunter?'

She knew shouting was pointless. He couldn't hear her – underwater, sounds were muffled and faraway – but she preferred shouting instead of sitting like a lump.

Seconds ticked by.

The water remained calm, reflecting golden glints of sun that flashed across her eyes. Water trickled from her hair, down her nose to her lips. She shivered. The woods held their breath.

'Hunter!'

A hard ball deep in Belle's stomach grew bigger and bigger, and her entire body tightened. He shouldn't be gone this long.

'Hunter?' she cried. 'Hunter!'

Over and over, she called his name, like a recording on repeat, over and over.

25

DONEGAL, PRESENT DAY

Splashes of rain dotted the windscreen as Belle drove down the lane from the house. She was on her way to visit Rita Wilson. She'd made a point of asking Dermot if he'd wanted to come along – so he wouldn't be able to accuse her of doing solo runs – but he was back at work and couldn't take any more time off.

Belle reached a straight part of the narrow island road, half-noting she was about to pass the Campbell's, when, without warning, a black-and-white football bounced out in front of the car. Right behind it ran a little boy, oblivious to the car, right into her path. Belle slammed on the brakes, bringing the car to a violent stop, just inches away from the boy.

'Jesus,' she squealed, 'what the fuck?'

She was shaking so badly she couldn't hold the steering wheel and she thought she might throw up. The boy himself was rooted to the spot – why did he seem familiar to her? – his mouth hanging open, his entire face frozen in shock. Thank God he was okay; she'd managed to stop in time. His precious football had escaped harm, too, and had come to rest in a gully at the far side of the road.

Belle wanted to give him a piece of her mind, scold him for being so reckless, but before she could, the boy's father rushed out and swept him into his arms. Belle groaned. The boy's father was Hunter Campbell. The boy was the one she'd seen him with along the road that day.

Hunter fussed over his son, making sure he was okay. The boy started to cry and he buried his head in his father's chest. Belle took a deep breath and opened the door.

'I'm so sorry, Hunter,' she said, emerging from the car on unsteady legs. 'He just ran—'

'You,' Hunter spat, 'you nearly killed my son. Damn you, McGee.'

'No, he—'

A woman arrived on the scene, her face frantic. The boy cried louder and reached over for her to take him. Hunter transferred him to the woman, who was obviously his mother, and she walked away with the boy in her arms. Hunter turned on his heel and followed them without giving Belle a second glance.

'I'm sorry, Hunter,' she called after him.

Even though she understood his snub, it hurt all the same. She got back into the car and, taking a minute to collect herself, cautiously resumed her journey.

*

Dr Rita Wilson had agreed to meet Belle at the reception hall in the main building of the Coleraine campus. The campus was a sprawling affair built on marshland – somewhere in her travels, Belle had heard it was sinking slowly into said marsh. The ruling class of the dysfunctional little state that was the North thought it better to build a new university on a marsh rather than expand the existing college in Derry. Shudder to think they'd give Catholic Derry a break like that.

Belle recognised Rita from the photo on her online university profile as soon as she entered the relatively quiet hall. She looked slightly older than her mugshot and her hair was shorter, in a curly bob with a clip pinning the fringe back from her eyes. She was tall, had an inch or two on Belle, and was built like a rugby player. Belle started walking towards her, conscious she needed to make herself known, for although she recognised Rita, Rita herself had no idea what Belle looked like.

'I'm McGee,' Belle said, reaching out her hand as she neared her destination.

Rita, who'd been looking around like a lost student on the first day of term, took her hand and shook it vigorously. 'Pleased to meet you, McGee. Follow me.'

As they walked through a maze of corridors and staircases to Rita's lab, they chit-chatted about the weather and how Belle had fared on her journey to Coleraine. The unplastered, unpainted walls exposed rough breezeblocks that gave the sense of an unfinished building, and the carpet was the thin industrial kind that felt more like a layer of cardboard underfoot. The air held a faint whiff of chalky dust, probably from the blocks.

'It's quiet on campus,' Belle said.

'It's the summer respite – most of the students are away. Check it out in September; it goes crazy. Oh, here we are.'

Rita opened a heavy fire door and Belle stepped inside.

'There's nobody around today,' Rita said, 'so we have the place to ourselves. Grab a pew.'

The harsh stench of chemicals in the lab cut through Belle's nostrils and into her throat. It wasn't a kick off one of the dumpsites. She coughed.

'You'll acclimatise to the smell after a minute or two,' Rita said. 'It's always a bit much for people not used to it.'

The lab was small with rows of benches partitioned off into individual workstations. Cupboards and equipment – test tube racks, Bunsen burners, flasks – lined the walls in an ordered fashion. A large tank, filled with what was probably formaldehyde, had a half dozen frog corpses floating in it and a load of other grisly things Belle couldn't quite identify.

'My table's just at the end there. Do you have the samples?'

'Everything you asked for.' She lifted the Tupperware box of samples from her bag and left it on the bench.

'These are perfect; well labelled and recorded. Couldn't ask for better if you were one of my students. It'll take me a few days to get these tested but I can give you a ring when I'm done.'

'Thanks, I appreciate that.'

'This is exciting. I've never had to test samples for a journalist before.' Rita smiled, her eyes sparkling. A curl fell over her face, escaping from the clip. She pinned it back, automatically. 'I'm not usually curious to know the story behind the samples I test. This time, obviously… my interest is certainly piqued. Must be more than the usual illegal dumping shenanigans, I'm thinking.'

'It's not anywhere near as exciting as it might sound,' Belle lied. She trusted Rita, but not with everything.

'But you getting involved…?'

'Um, I'm writing a story to highlight the environmental cost of illegal disposal of waste. It's more of an awareness piece, drawing some attention to the issues. Not exciting at all.'

More lies – as if Alma Travers or any editor would let their top reporter spend time on anything so pedestrian as awareness raising.

'Oh, such a pity. Still, it's a very noble job you're doing. It's important to highlight these matters – illegal dumping can be tremendously dangerous.'

'Could you tell me about that?'

'Well, it's common for the soil and water to contain traces of effluents and dioxins, as well as forms of arsenic like arsenite and arsenate. Sometimes there'll be polychlorinated biphenyls – they're man-made compounds used in electrical products, though they're banned in a lot of countries today. And you'll get other toxins, too, like mercury and lead. They can persist in the environment for years. Mercury comes from equipment like flat-screen TVs.'

Belle's eyes widened.

'I'm sure you smelled sulphur at the dumpsite,' Rita said, 'but tell me, did you also happen to catch a strong bitter stench?'

'I do remember something bitter, cloying.'

'That was very likely cyanide.'

'Jesus!'

'Not everybody can detect it, but, yeah, those are the kind of poisons we're talking about. When these toxins and leachates seep into our soil and water, they bio-accumulate, impacting the entire food chain. They contaminate the crops we grow, including the grass and animal feed that cows and sheep eat, which means the food on our tables – from potatoes to cheese to beefburgers – will be contaminated. Rivers and streams are contaminated, too; groundwater and aquifers where we get our drinking water – all of it, poisoned.'

Belle felt sickened, like she'd eaten something well past its sell-by date. The graveness of what she was dealing with began to slowly dawn on her. Sure, she got it at an intellectual level, could imagine in her head how she was going to write it all up for the paper once she reached the end of her investigation, but this, what Rita had explained, made it real, visceral. It took all her fortitude not to run to the police there and then and demand it be stopped. She thought about Seanie being hauled off to hospital.

'How can we let this happen?' Belle said, with a croak. 'We're destroying everything.'

'I know, it makes me want to weep, which is why your awareness piece is so important. We have to bring these environmental crimes into sharp focus.'

Belle sighed and rubbed her face. 'Yes, so we do.'

'What paper do you work for anyway?'

'I'm with the *National Spectator*.'

Rita's brow knitted. 'The Dublin-based one?'

'Right. I live in Dublin, although I'm from up here originally.'

'I figured that by your accent. It's not often a Southern paper comes this far North.'

'It's not the norm,' Belle said, avoiding any mention of Fionn, her real reason for reporting on a story this far North, 'but suffice to say, I have a *personal interest*.'

'Well, it's a good thing. I'll give you all the support I can.'

'That means a lot, Rita. Can I use your name in my story? An expert opinion adds credibility.'

'Go right ahead. It's time we all started working together, bringing whatever skills and expertise we have, to confront these problems. The world around us is dying and it's our fault. We don't have time, anymore, to be genteel about it all, we have to reach for the jugular.'

26

DONEGAL, 1986

Behind her, in between her screams, Belle heard branches swishing, twigs cracking and then somebody grabbed her and shook her head. She didn't realise her eyes were closed until she had to open them.

Right in front of her, so close she could touch his skin, was Fionn, his blue eyes like an ocean she wanted to dive into. She was still screaming – or, at least, she must've been – because Fionn was asking her to stop screaming and tell him what was wrong. A shadow hovered nearby and Belle knew it was Maeveen without properly seeing.

'Calm down, Belle, it's okay,' he said, the sanity of his voice cutting through her trance and bringing her back to the world. 'It's okay, you're okay.'

'H-H-Hunter, it's Hunter—'

'Where is he?'

She lifted her right hand and pointed at the river.

'Jesus Christ!' Maeveen shouted.

'Show me where,' Fionn said. 'Exactly where.'

'At that sycamore branch there.' She pointed to a low-hanging bough. 'H-halfway across the...'

Fionn was gone. Running to the spot. Diving in. There was a splash as his feet disappeared beneath the water and then the silence returned.

She felt an arm go round her shoulders.

'It's okay,' Maeveen said, 'Hunter's going to be okay. Fionn'll bring him back.'

Belle leaned close to her sister.

'He's b-been in th-there too long,' Belle said, her teeth rattling like a bucket of seashells.

'Fionn'll bring him back.'

'We—'

The water erupted. Fionn gasped for air. Belle sank her head into Maeveen's breast, not able to look.

'Help me.' Fionn's voice. Strained. Afraid.

Belle felt herself pushed to the ground as Maeveen jumped to her feet. She turned to see Fionn forcing a path across the river and Maeveen rushing to meet him. In his arms, limp as a drooping flag, was Hunter.

'His legs were all caught up in reeds or some shit or other,' Fionn was saying.

Belle watched, without feeling or moving, as Maeveen and Fionn frantically tried to save Hunter. The whole scene was as though it was happening somewhere else to some other people, as though she was outside it, eavesdropping. Fionn and her sister worked in such harmony, they could've been the one person divided in two, their speech, their movements, like a dance they'd practised forever.

Belle focused her attention on Hunter, willing his lifeless body to move. His skin was a washed-out blue that made him look like an alien and not a human boy. The more time that passed and he didn't wake up...

Belle heard a gargling cough, then another, then a squeal of relief from Maeveen. Hunter's head moved. Belle gasped. He was alive. Belle thought she was going to vomit. Hunter slowly sat up. Maeveen fussed over him, held his face in her hands, hugged him.

'I'm okay,' Hunter said, his voice low, hoarse.

Maeveen started to cry. Fionn gathered her in his strong arms.

Belle never felt so left out, so utterly alone, in all her life. She should've been jumping for joy that Hunter was safe, but the sole thought in her head was how close, inseparable Maeveen and Fionn were. How perfect they were together. She could never have that with Fionn; she might never have it with anyone. But they had it, right now, right in front of her eyes. Belle knew the sensible thing was to accept the truth and give in to it. But she couldn't.

Instead, she seethed, happier to swim around in her bitter juices and let them soak into her skin and her guts and her heart. Her Greek god would never be hers. Her dreams about them being together forever were as likely as snow in July.

*

'I have to go home,' Hunter said. 'They'll be wondering where I am.'

'I'll walk you,' Maeveen said.

'Naw, they'll know something's wrong if you do.'

'It doesn't matter. I'm not letting you walk back by yourself. What if you took a turn or something?'

Hunter rose, helped by Fionn, and put his hands on his knees.

'How d'you feel?' Maeveen said.

'I'm all right,' he stumbled and Fionn caught him. 'Aye, I'm all right.'

'You're in no fit state to walk,' Maeveen said. 'I'll get Daddy to leave you home?'

'No way, I'll be in so much trouble.'

'You're going to be in trouble anyway. Come on.'

'Okay, a lift home would be handy,' he coughed, his speech slurred. He started walking away, staggering.

'I'll take him to the house,' Maeveen said to Fionn. 'Will you look after Belle? I'll see you when I get back.'

'Here's his slippers,' Belle said, managing to struggle to her feet.

Maeveen took them and she and Hunter disappeared into the trees.

Belle and Fionn were alone.

'I'm going home,' Belle said. 'I'm exhausted... and freezing.'

'Stay a minute,' Fionn said. 'I need to talk to you.'

Belle stepped back. 'You can't tell me what to do.'

'Do you understand what's happened here?'

There was gravity in his voice she'd never noticed before.

'Hunter nearly drowned 'cos we were in the deep?'

Fionn came closer, his shaggy hair starting to dry off in the warm air. His eyes never left her; they matched the hardness in his voice. 'Not just that.'

She knew exactly what he meant. ''Cos Hunter saw you?'

'Aren't you the genius? Hunter saw me and it could be a problem.'

'Hunter didn't know his own name when he came out of that water. He hardly noticed you. There's no problem. And, anyway, you were bound to get seen eventually. You've been sneaking out all the time, you and Maeveen.'

'Kitty and Michael know I've been heading out most evenings for a while, and me and Maeveen have been careful not to get seen.'

'Well, your luck ran out. You were bound to get yourself caught eventually.'

'I had to save that friend of yours from drowning – that's not the same as me getting myself caught.'

'So what? You were seen, big deal.'

'Seriously, Belle, you don't know what you're saying. You really haven't a clue, pet.'

186

'I do, I'm not stupid.'

'I didn't say you were stupid.'

'What're you on about then?'

He shook his head.

'If it was Maeveen, you'd tell her.'

'I don't need to tell Maeveen; she knows the craic.'

'Right she does. You like her far better than me. You think she's prettier.' The words escaped like gas from a busted pipe, betraying her heart.

The expression on Fionn's face spoke volumes. His brow furrowed, his eyes went blank, his mouth fell slightly. 'I... I... I don't know what to say.'

Belle's face burned. She wanted to run away, hide, never see him again.

'Jesus, Belle,' he said, his voice soft and kind again as she was used to – or maybe full of pity? 'Aw, pet, you really did get it wrong.'

He reached out his hand and she recoiled so hard she almost fell over.

'Don't touch me.' Tears lurked behind her eyes and in her voice.

'Don't you get it, Belle? You're only a wean and—'

'Shut up, this is bullshit.' She used Maeveen's word, a grown-up word.

'You need to hear this.'

'Damn you. I don't care what you think of me, anyway. You're nothing but a criminal.'

Fionn turned grey and he wobbled. 'Don't you ever say that. Don't ever call me a criminal. I never did anything criminal in my life.' He looked like he was about to take her head off.

Belle should've been warned, but she didn't care. She wanted to goad him, spite him. 'Why're you scared that anybody sees you then, if you're not a criminal? I know you are.'

'If that was true, what would it say about your parents?'

'It... I... you've threatened them to make them hide you.'

'So I'm a criminal putting the fear of God into your family, but we play Ludo and Snap every evening after I've helped wash the dishes.' He threw her a filthy look. 'Catch yourself on, wee girl, that's shite and you know rightly.'

Belle pursed her lips and met his eyes defiantly. Fionn backed down.

'I don't want to fight with you, Belle.' Fionn sounded more like himself again. 'Your mother and father have been good to me. It's not easy what they've done. I'll be going soon, anyway, so it'd be nice to leave without having caused any trouble.'

A wave of dread washed though Belle's body, weighing heavier than a boulder. She wanted to close her ears as though that would make it not true. But it was true. He was definitely going. With Maeveen. And he'd never see her, silly Baby Belle, as anything other than a 'wee girl' – the words from his own mouth.

It didn't matter that he was the love of her life or that she'd devote herself to him and make him the happiest man on earth if he'd only give him one chance. All was a lost cause.

'Come on, let's go,' she heard him saying, his voice coming from another world.

Like a mechanical toy, she did as he bid and they started for the house.

27

DONEGAL, PRESENT DAY

The house was in darkness when Belle got back home that evening. She wasn't surprised. Maeveen had sent her a text earlier to say she was going with Cillian to see a film in Derry. The dogs were locked up in the barn for the night so there was only Snowball to greet her, and the second Belle switched on the kitchen light, the cat trotted over, meowing.

'You must be lonely,' Belle said, 'when you're giving me all this attention.' She leaned down to stroke her soft fur and Snowball purred.

Belle made some cheese on toast with a cup of green tea and got comfy on one of the big armchairs in the sitting room. With just the table lamps lit and one of Maeveen's lavender candles burning, the sitting room felt very cosy. Exactly what she needed. She clicked on the TV, more for company than anything else, keeping the volume low.

As much as she wanted to simply switch off, the details of the investigation rattled around in her head anyway. The deeper she went, the stronger her case was connecting Evergreen to the illegal dumping. Tomorrow she'd contact Patricia Healy and Sammy

Alexander to set up meetings. Who knows what useful information they might have to share? And once the results came back from Rita, Belle would be ready to take her findings to the police. But she wondered if any of that would prove Evergreen was responsible for Fionn's murder. So far, the evidence was circumstantial with the most promising lead being Ed's possible sighting of Beavis and Butthead. If she could get Ed to confirm he saw them, it might just be enough to have the police consider Evergreen a suspect in their investigation.

Belle hopped around the channels, sighing at everything until she came to a rerun of Family Guy.

She thought about Dermot, his anger at the danger she'd put herself in. She didn't need wrapping in cotton wool, but it showed he cared and she had to admit that made her feel good. Truth be told, spending time with him made her feel good. That was what made it so awful. She couldn't have a relationship with him, common sense told her that. If he knew everything about the real Belle McGee, he might never want to see her again. So, yes, common sense said it was doomed and had to end, but the heart didn't have a lot of room for common sense. Instead of ending it, she was keeping it alive.

Talking of doomed relationships, it was high time she did the decent thing and called it quits with Shane. It wouldn't be like a break-up exactly, since they hadn't made any hard-and-fast commitment – they were just messing around. Best to kill it and stop the silliness. And there was no time like the present. Fuck it, why not? She found his name on her phone and pressed the call button. After two rings, he picked up.

'Belle?' he said. 'Finally. I thought you'd dropped off the face of the earth.'

'Hi, Shane,' she said, her voice flat. She didn't relish what she was going to do.

'How are things? Any sign of you coming back to Dublin? I'm missing you something terrible.'

'Shane, look—'

'I'd love to visit you this weekend. What do you think?'

'I'm not ringing to say hello and shoot the breeze—'

'I could take Friday off—'

'Listen a minute, will you?'

Belle could hear him inhale sharply.

'Shane,' she started, 'I've had the space to think while I've been home and, well, the time away from Dublin has given me a different perspective. You're a great guy but—'

'Aw, fuck, I don't believe this. You're giving me a "Dear John". And over the phone, too. Not even to my face.'

'I'm sorry—'

'Don't bother. I don't want pity.'

'We can—'

'You know what, Belle,' he said and she could hear his voice beginning to crack, 'you could always be cavalier with my feelings, cold even. But I liked you so I put up with your shit—'

'Aw, Shane—'

'Let me finish. I kept thinking it'd get better and that you might even grow to love me. The more shit I put up with, the more you piled on. I knew it but I hoped against hope… and now, I have to suffer the final indignity of getting dumped. Over the fucking phone. It's low.'

Belle listened without interrupting.

'I don't know what's wrong with you,' Shane went on. 'You treat people like they're objects for you to use and throw away when you don't want them anymore. You're such a bitch. Do me a favour. When you come back to work, pretend you don't know me from Adam.'

The phone went dead. Belle slumped back in the chair. She felt horrible. She'd done her best to be sensitive to his feelings, but all the same, it hadn't gone well. He'd said some harsh things – that she was cavalier and cold and piled on shit. Ouch! But okay, there was truth in it. The past, it had a lot to answer for. She was damaged, she could admit that, and after what happened, maybe she could be nothing else but damaged. Still, that didn't give her a licence to damage others.

'Fuck,' she said, 'it was never going to be pretty. I'm just glad it's over.'

Belle heard the kitchen door open. Maeveen and Cillian were back.

'Down here,' she shouted, relieved to have company.

The pair came into the sitting room, Cillian holding a reusable carrier bag that clinked with every step.

'Did you enjoy the cinema?' Belle asked.

'I fell asleep,' Cillian said.

'Don't mind him,' Maeveen said, 'he always falls asleep. I thought the film was great.'

'We bought a couple bottles of wine and a few beers,' Cillian said, unloading the carrier bag, 'if you feel like a wee drink.'

Belle smirked. 'You know, that sounds perfect.'

Maeveen fetched glasses from the kitchen.

'Say when,' Cillian said, first filling Belle's glass with wine and then Maeveen's.

'Thanks, Cillian,' Belle said.

'Thanks, love,' Maeveen said.

Cillian snapped open a bottle of beer and took a spot beside Maeveen on the sofa. She stretched her legs out, putting them across his lap. He rubbed her thigh. Belle's thoughts strayed into the past and she remembered the last time Maeveen had shared the sofa in this house with a member of the opposite sex. A different sofa, sure, but the location was the same. The night of the storm when the lights went out and they saw their Granda; poor Fionn nearly passed out with fear.

Maeveen giggled as Cillian tickled her side. It was nice to see her happy, to see her with somebody she loved and that loved her. Belle could never have that with Shane, and she could never dare have it with Dermot.

For a while, the three of them chatted about nothing in particular until the first drink was gone, and then they poured another and then another. Little spots burned on Belle's cheeks that she knew made her look like an Aunt Sally, but she didn't care.

'I was trying to remember,' Maeveen said, 'the name of the dog we had in my last year at school.'

'Which one?' Belle said. 'We had so many down the years, you'll have to give me a clue.'

'You know the one that bit the postman and Sergeant Buckley, and chased our cousin, Declan, down the lane.'

'Hang on, was he a black sheepdog... with, um, tan-coloured patches around his eyes?'

'That's him. Daddy gave him to Uncle Aidan.'

'Oh, because Uncle Aidan fancied himself as a bit of a dog whisperer.'

Belle and Maeveen laughed at the same time.

'What was his name?' Maeveen asked.

Belle rubbed her chin. 'Aw, what the hell was he called, something starting with S... Stagger... no, Sniper.'

'Sniper, you got it. Was he still about when Fionn was here?'

'No, definitely not. Funny, that summer Fionn was here was the only time we never had a dog.'

'That summer,' Maeveen said, 'was the happiest of times. Innocent times, the last of the innocent times.' She looked down at her glass. 'When we were young with not a care in the world.'

Cillian touched her shoulder and she leaned her head on his hand.

'But they're all gone now,' she went on. 'Fionn. And Mammy. And Daddy. We're the only ones who remember that summer, Belle.'

Maeveen's voice cracked the tiniest bit. Belle groaned inside. Maeveen was on one of her trips down memory lane, a trip that only remembered bad memories. She willed her to stop.

'Everything that went on,' Maeveen continued, 'the way things were, the people we were, none of it exists now except in my head and yours, Belle. Up here.' Maeveen tapped her temple. 'Once me and you are gone, it won't exist at all.'

Belle bit her lip. She didn't want to hear anymore.

'The whole of life's the same,' Maeveen said. 'Might as well have never happened.' Maeveen's brow furrowed and she finished in one go what was left in her glass.

'Don't let yourself get maudlin,' Cillian said, as though he was used to her going down that rabbit hole.

'Naw, I won't,' she said, pulling herself back. She kissed him on the cheek and smiled.

Belle exhaled, glad of Cillian's intervention.

'I'm getting a refill,' Cillian said, getting up and going to the kitchen.

'I forgot to tell you,' Maeveen said, 'somebody told me yesterday that Alfie Campbell had a stroke.'

'Aw, shit,' Belle said. 'How bad is he?'

'They don't think he'll make it. Not that I give a rat's fucking ass.'

'Hadn't he Alzheimer's, too?'

'Aye, for the last few years, but it wasn't that advanced and Hunter and his wife were able to look after him at home.'

'I saw Hunter the other day.'

'No avoiding him on an island this size. I see him all the time and I just ignore the fucker. He does likewise.'

Belle could see Maeveen was getting worked up. She found it impossible to talk about the Campbells without going into a rant.

'Can we not talk about the Campbells?' Belle said. 'Not when you've had a few drinks.'

'Do I upset your urbane sensibilities?'

'No, I don't want a whole bitching session about them, that's all.'

'God forbid we'd have a bitching session about the Campbells. I mean, it's not like they destroyed our family or anything.'

194

Belle felt a knot of nausea in her stomach. She hated where Maeveen would take the conversation if allowed, digging up the past and, with it, that putrefying corpse of guilt Belle worked so hard at keeping buried.

'I don't see the point in going on about them,' Belle said. 'The past is the past. We should leave it alone.'

Cillian came back from the kitchen.

'Easy for you to say,' Maeveen said, sitting forward to fill her glass. 'You're away in Dublin. I'm here, surrounded by it. The past's in my face every fucking day.'

'Easy for me to say? The past doesn't care where you live. It comes with you no matter where you go. I'm surrounded by it, too, same as you.'

Belle's eyes locked with Maeveen's and they stared at each other for a moment, silent and still as though they were on pause. For the briefest of moments, Belle considered telling her about the past, a nugget of history that Maeveen had no clue about. She could tell her right now and have it done with.

She opened her mouth, the words lining up, ready to pour out. All she had to do was let the first one out and the rest would just follow.

No, she couldn't do it. Instead, she stood up, putting her half-full glass on the coffee table.

'I think I'll go to bed.'

Cillian nodded. Maeveen looked down. Belle pursed her lips. Seemed like they both agreed. Staggering slightly, she made her way to the door, not looking round, and left the room. As she closed the door behind her, she caught Maeveen's muffled voice say something about 'another one of Belle's huffs'.

Belle let it go unchecked and carried on up to bed. She'd heard it all before. Another of Maeveen's rants – nearly as famous as Belle's huffs. Only Maeveen had every right to rant.

28

Belle waited at reception in the Water Service offices for Noel Kerrigan. Her appointment with him was for four fifteen and it was five minutes shy of that. She expected this to be a strained meeting. Kerrigan wasn't friendly fire according to Fionn's notes. She fidgeted with the handle on her bag as she waited.

'Gina Mullan?' a man's voice said.

She jumped. 'Yes, that's me.'

The man hovering over her was easily six foot. He looked like an outdoors type, sun-kissed skin, muscular with a square frame and jaw to match. His dark hair was cut into a neat short back and sides and a five o'clock shadow threatened an appearance.

'Noel Kerrigan,' he said, putting out his hand, 'pleasure to meet you.'

Belle took his hand in a firm, no-nonsense grip. 'The pleasure's mine; thanks for seeing me.'

'This way,' he said, taking them through double-doors. 'My office is along here.' He held the door open. 'After you.'

'So, you're doing a piece on waste,' he said, when they settled in the cubbyhole that passed for his office.

Belle flashed her reporter's card, which he barely took under his notice. 'Yes, I'm doing an extensive investigation across the whole island. With the environmental implications and so much focus on global warming these days, it's a newsworthy topic.'

'That's for sure,' he smiled. 'I have to say, I'm not sure how I'm going to be able to help you. I'm a senior science officer at the Water Service. We don't deal with waste.'

'But you deal directly with the consequences of pollution from waste. That would be a concern for you, right?'

He raised his eyebrows. 'Um, of course, but we don't have any problem with waste pollution... is that what your piece is going to be about?'

'For some part – can't write about waste and not mention all the dangers involved.'

'Sure. Although there aren't dangers, not really, when it's disposed of correctly.'

'*When* it happens.'

'Are you suggesting we have waste not being disposed of in the way it should?' He was suddenly very stern. The polite demeanour slipped ever so slightly to reveal an interior that wasn't as friendly, like noticing dirty fingernails on an otherwise pristine person.

'I'm not suggesting that for a second. I'm saying that to write a rounded piece I have to cover all angles.'

'We don't have a pollution problem here... with waste.' He almost spat the words.

As though he knew he had betrayed himself, he smiled a brimming, wide smile. Belle played the game and gave him an equally brimming, wide smile.

'Have you any reason to think we do have a problem?' he asked.

'Oh, God, no.' She deliberately didn't elaborate. She hoped it would put the pressure on him to keep talking.

He started to wring his hands. Belle could see he was hiding something – and badly at that.

'What're you on about then?'

She gave him a look.

'I'm sorry if that sounded rude,' he said. 'It came out wrong. What I mean is that the purity of the water is the Water Service's responsibility and we take it very, very seriously. Everything we do has that one objective at its heart. Nothing else matters. For there to be alleged illegal dumping would be the worst news we could hear – the absolute worst.'

Illegal dumping. He'd mentioned it all on his own. He might as well put a sign round his neck. Belle didn't draw attention to his slip-up. Best to cut him a bit of slack, calm him down. She could reel him in again later, if necessary.

'I suppose what I'm most interested in talking about,' she said, 'are the safeguards you put in place to maintain that purity you mentioned.'

'Our safeguards,' he said. 'We have a stringent set of safeguards and I'm more than happy to talk through those.' He was back in safe territory and Belle could see his shoulders and hands relax. 'Our scientists take water samples every day – thousands, in fact – to make sure the water supply is clean and safe. We take samples from hundreds of locations at reservoirs, treatment works and even the taps in domestic properties, all according to the letter of the law.

'The tests we do comply exactly with the regulations. They're designed to detect any problem with water quality. And the testing is strict; we look for the presence of chemical and microbiological parameters like bacteria, nitrates, pesticides, metals like lead, how the water looks and tastes. We ensure compliance with the drinking water standards by analysing the samples against PVC – that's Prescribed Concentrations or Values.'

He sounded like a lecturer from one of those old Open University study programmes, stiff and robotic and reading from an autocue.

'The water testing system we have in place,' he carried on, 'means that if there's anything wrong, anything contaminating our water, at any point, it could never slip past our treatment centres. It would get picked up, without a doubt. I can tell you now: we stand over our processes and can assure the safety of the drinking water from all the sources we use. And we're completely transparent. All our tests are on public record, freely available to anybody who wants to see them.'

'I'd be interested in having a look. I could cite them in my feature.'

'I'll get you a copy of our latest report before you leave. You'll see that all the results meet the highest water quality standards.'

'It sounds extremely regimented.'

'It is – has to be to meet the regulations.'

'With no room for pollutants to go undetected, for error, for any other problems?'

'Not a chance.'

'That's very reassuring.'

'So it should be. And we give regular presentations to council, too. I've presented our reports in the council chamber many times. Councillor Alan O'Dee, you know, the Mayor, he's chair of the environmental committee, too, and I have regular contact with him.'

O'Dee. Another one of Fionn's bad guys and Kerrigan had just admitted they had regular contact. Fionn hadn't mentioned anything about him being the mayor.

'I've heard of O'Dee,' Belle said, 'but didn't realise he was mayor.'

'He's only just taken office.'

'I see. I guess with all those checks and balances, it must ensure a high level of scrutiny,' she said.

'Exactly right.

Kerrigan breathed out a long, satisfied sigh and folded his hands on the desk in front of him. The conversation dried up. Belle recognised her cue to end the meeting.

She cleared her throat. 'I want to thank you, Noel,' she said, reaching out her hand to shake his, 'for your time and your openness. It's a big help.'

'You're more than welcome, glad to be of help.' He shook her hand vigorously and stood up. 'I'll get you that report on our way out.'

'Wonderful.'

As they left the office, he made some wisecrack about the weather, which he immediately followed with a deep chuckle. Belle eyed him carefully. His joviality was real but it seemed exaggerated, like a man who thought he was going to get bad news from his doctor but didn't and the relief was going to his head. Did he think he'd put her off the scent? If that was the case, he was gravely mistaken. All he'd managed to do was confirm her suspicions.

*

Belle was so deep in thought after the Kerrigan meeting, she didn't even notice Beavis and Butthead until she was right beside her car. There they were, leaning casually against the driver's side of the car, blocking her from getting in.

Her heart rate quickened. 'Do you mind getting out of the way?' she said, hoping she didn't sound afraid.

'Nice car,' Butthead said.

'Not so nice after someone scratched the side of it. You wouldn't happen to know who did that?'

The pair looked at each other with mock puzzlement.

'Don't know what you're talking about,' Beavis said.

'No? And I suppose you wouldn't know anything about the text I got either?'

They shrugged.

'I still have that text. Should be an interesting one to show the police.'

200

'Only if you have the sender,' Butthead said, snugly.

Belle stiffened. They knew the text was useless without the sender. They had the upper hand and she could do nothing about it.

'Why don't you two piss off and let me get about my business?'

'Your business?' Butthead said. 'Not so much your business as other people's business. You've been a busy girl lately with other people's business.'

'And you would know, you seem to be following me around everywhere. Have you nothing better to do?'

'We have a message for you,' Beavis said.

'And who would that be from?'

'From interested parties,' Butthead said. 'Important interested parties. You're making a real nuisance out of yourself, annoying a lot of people.'

'You'd be best to get yourself back to Dublin,' Beavis said. 'For your own good, you know.'

'We're asking you nicely,' Butthead said, 'but others might not be as nice as us.'

A shudder rippled through Belle's body, from the soles of her feet right up to the top of her head. Her bag slipped off her shoulder and dropped to the ground with a crunch, spilling some of the contents: Dictaphone, lipstick, wallet, pen, a pack of tissues. She hunkered down and scrambled with trembling hands to retrieve them, doing her best to restrain the panic that wanted to escape.

'We better make tracks,' Butthead said.

'Aye, we've got places to be,' Beavis answered.

'You take care of yourself now,' Butthead said, as they both stepped away from the car and started walking away. 'You take good care.'

As soon as they were gone, Belle slumped to the ground. Sinking her head into her hands, she took a long, deep breath, and then another, and then another. Slowly, her hands steadied, her heart slowed, calm returned. This pair of Neanderthals was getting on her fucking nerves. But their day was coming; once she cracked this investigation, they were going to get their comeuppance. And when they did, she would savour that moment.

29

DONEGAL, 1986

Belle stayed behind Fionn, literally following in his footsteps. Not another word passed between them and apart from the snapping of twigs and the rustle of undergrowth against their legs as they walked onwards, all was quiet. In the shade of the woods, her clothes felt damp against her skin, but she ignored the cold. She stayed mostly in her head, going over and over the things Fionn had said, her eyes trained on the ground.

Without any warning, Fionn stopped dead, and Belle, only half-conscious of what she was doing, walked right into him.

'Shush,' he whispered, 'get down.'

He dropped to his knees. Belle did likewise.

'What's wrong?' Belle whispered.

'Look.' Fionn pointed through the trees.

They were within sight of the house. Parked in the cobbled courtyard was a dark-blue Ford Sierra, the white lettering on the driver's door and the too-big siren stuck on the roof making no secret of what it was: a Garda car.

'Jesus Christ, I'm fucked,' Fionn said, in a trembling voice. 'Hunter must've grassed me up already.'

'He'll barely be back home by this time. There's no way he's had a chance to say anything.' Would be good enough for Fionn if he had.

'So how come the peelers are here?'

'The who?'

'The police.'

'I dunno,' Belle said. 'Will I go in and see what's going on?'

'Naw, stay here.'

Fionn grabbed her arm and although his grip didn't hurt, it was firm enough to hold her. She wondered how forceful he'd get if she tried to free herself and go into the house anyway.

They waited in silence, not moving, crouched close enough for Belle to feel the heat from his body. His forehead was dotted with beads of sweat that slowly crawled downwards. She longed to touch his smooth dark skin.

'How long—' Belle started.

'Shush,' Fionn said.

The yard was so still it might've been a photograph. A round fat bee landed on a nearby flower, buzzing like a faraway lawnmower.

Belle caught a faint sound. 'Hear that? It's Mammy. She's talking to somebody.'

Her voice grew louder, then there was another voice, a man's, and a figure stepped into full view in the courtyard.

'It's a peeler,' Fionn said.

Belle stifled a giggle. 'That's only Sergeant Buckley.'

'Be quiet; what's so funny?'

'Look at his hands.'

'What about them?'

'Can you see what he's holding?'

'Aye, a canvas bag or something.'

'Spuds, do you not remember Daddy telling you Sergeant Buckley bought spuds off us sometimes? Our spuds are always ready before most other farms, so we have the first of the year's crop. That's what the sergeant's here for.'

Fionn didn't take his eyes off the courtyard, but she could see his shoulders relax and he let go of her arm.

'I wish he'd hurry up and piss off,' Fionn said. 'He's standing there chatting like a pair of pink knickers.'

'He'll be gone soon,' Belle said. 'Everything's all right.'

'Listen to me,' Fionn said, turning his gaze directly on Belle, 'nothing's all right. We have to talk about what happened at the burn, me, you, the whole family.'

She saw the disgust in his eyes. It was like a wound – it was her doing and it was never going to leave him.

'I'm going back to the woods,' Belle said. 'I'm fed up waiting and my legs are getting cramped.'

'Wait until he goes; he'll not be much longer.'

'I'm not waiting another second.'

Fionn tried to grab her but she darted out of his reach.

'Fuck it, Belle. Stay put.'

She took off, backtracking the way they came.

*

The sun slipped lower in the sky, casting Belle a shadow ten feet tall. She absently strolled along the lane having come out of the woods at a clearing halfway down, heading to nowhere in particular and chewing on a stalk of grass. The twisting bumpy track was topped with fine white sand, pieces of dried seaweed and fragments of shell that their father brought in a tractor and trailer from the shore. She kicked a pebble, stirring up a cloud of dust.

Her clothes were almost dry but her stomach was empty. She was tired and hungry and wanted to go home. She daren't. Not yet. She had to wait for things to settle; after Fionn and Maeveen told their version of events and her parents had time to calm down. She kicked another pebble.

Thoughts ebbed and flowed as she tried to make sense of it all. Damn Fionn, anyway, but nothing that happened today was her fault. She spit out the chewed grass stalk and reached for a second. And what nobody knew – 'cos they never bothered to ask – was that she'd wanted to go home, only it was Hunter who wanted another dive. Now she was getting all the blame. It wasn't fair. Everybody was against her.

A tear trickled down the side of her nose. She let it reach her lips, tasting its saltiness. More tears followed. Belle wallowed in them; they proved she was hurt, proved she was wronged.

More thoughts festered. She stayed hot with anger, at Fionn, at Maeveen, even at her parents. Every one of them was a selfish pig that didn't care one bit about how she felt. Fionn, most of all. He'd said the most terrible things; he'd been so awful and cruel. How could he when she'd loved him more than anybody in the whole world loved him?

Well, not anymore. He might have saved Hunter's life, but Belle hated him now. She hated his gorgeous face, his funny stories, his origami lotus flowers. She hated him. Because he could only see her as a "wee girl". Because he loved Maeveen and not her. Because he was up to no good, too.

She spit out her second grass stalk and her stomach gurgled. She should stop chewing. Her stomach was going to think she was eating and it would release acid to digest food that wasn't there. She learned that in science, when the teacher told them why it was bad to chew gum all day long.

On a straight part of the lane, Belle came to a rusty iron gate leading into one of the fields. She climbed to the top and sat on the thin bar, keeping her balance by holding on with a hand on either side and placing her feet firmly on the second bar. The metal was rough to the touch and Belle picked at flecks of rust, snapping them off and letting them fall into the grass below.

That was the mystery at the heart of this, wasn't it? Fionn. He was the problem, not her. If this was an Agatha Christie story, he'd be a murderer and she'd have to find clues to prove his guilt. He probably wasn't a murderer – she hoped not, in spite of hating him now – but he was up to something dodgy, she was sure. Why else would he be afraid of the Gards the way he was?

The puzzling thing was why her parents were covering for him. He'd denied he threatened them into helping him, but of course he'd deny that and of course her parents would play along if they were afraid of him, even as far as letting him play Ludo and Snap with their daughters. It would explain why they'd made up that rubbish about him being their cousin. She let out a long breath.

She heard the rumble of what she thought was an engine and looked up to see a car approaching. Sergeant Buckley's dark-blue Ford Sierra. Finished yapping at last.

The car crawled closer, bouncing over the dips and bumps of the lane, until it reached the gate. The sergeant stopped.

'How's it going there, Belle?' He waved though the open passenger's window.

She raised her hand to wave back, careful not to knock off her balance. 'Hello, Sergeant Buckley,' she said.

'Are you enjoying your summer holidays?'

'Aye.'

'Hope you young ones aren't sneaking off to the shore. The tide's dangerous.'

'Not this year.' He was never going to let it go about catching her and Maeveen five summers ago down at the beach on their own. Every year since, he had mentioned it.

'That's good, well, I'm away now.'

Belle watched absently as the car moved off ever so slowly, the tyres crunching into the sand and the shells. It moved so slowly she guessed she wouldn't even have to run to catch it up. If she wanted to catch it up.

The tail of Sergeant Buckley's car vanished round a corner.

30

DERRY, PRESENT DAY

The coffee shop on the quay overlooked the River Foyle and the pedestrian embankment. The sky was overcast, reflecting a blanket of grey-white in the water, but it was humid and the riverside was bustling with walkers and cyclists.

Belle had a table at the back of the shop, facing the door. She was waiting for Patricia Healy, who she had managed to get on the phone that morning and who had agreed to meet her after work when, according to the good doctor, she had a small window of time.

Belle was early. She sipped on a green tea. The row – or, rather, the choice words – with Maeveen the night before was still playing on her mind. Stupid drink talk.

Her phone pinged. She had a new email. She frowned as she read it. An e-invite from the mayor's office, no less, requesting the pleasure of her company at a drinks reception and concert in the Millennium Forum. Alan O'Dee was having his mayoral office invite her to events now. No need to chase him for a meeting. Somebody had been running off at the mouth. Kerrigan, maybe, or Lynch, panicked by her enquiries, the waste company finally sick of her snooping or somebody else entirely who she'd rattled unbeknownst to herself. She was more than a little disturbed by the fact he knew her real name and email address when she'd been using her alias.

The bell above the shop entrance tinkled and Belle lifted her eyes to see a woman in her fifties, long wispy hair tied up untidily in a red headband, scanning the room as though in search of someone. Belle took a chance it was Healy and waved. The woman came over.

'Are you McGee?'

'Dr Healy, I presume?'

They shook hands and Healy took a seat, hanging her bag and coat on the back of the chair and putting her phone on the table. Her cheeks were blotched and ruddy. Belle had to remind herself that the dishevelled woman was a doctor – an oncologist, no less – who worked at the local hospital.

'Pleased to meet you,' Belle said. 'Can I get you something? Tea, coffee?'

Healy put up her hand to indicate in the negative. 'I don't have much time,' she said. 'I'm meeting my husband in a few minutes for dinner in the restaurant next door.'

'I won't keep you long,' Belle said, smiling. Belle's Dictaphone was beside her teacup. 'Do you mind if I record?'

'Go ahead,' Healy said, 'though I want to okay anything you write that makes a reference to me.'

Belle nodded. 'Of course, you've got it.'

Healy seemed content. 'So you're a journalist in Dublin?' She gave Belle a gaze so intense it seemed she was reaching right into her brain and checking it out.

'I am. I'm an investigative journalist with the *National Spectator*. I've won a number of awards for my work in the past.' Belle didn't normally brag, but with Healy she somehow felt compelled.

'Really? What for?'

'My last award was for a series of features about a care home scandal—'

'Interesting.'

Healy stared and this time it was as though she'd momentarily drifted off somewhere else.

'As I told you on the phone,' Belle said, 'I listened to a recording of your interview on Radio Ulster about the rising cancer rates in the northwest and was very taken with what you said.'

'Are you going to write about my findings?'

'Not directly. The focus of my feature is on waste.'

Healy pouted. 'Waste? And how do you see that related to my cancer interview? Be more specific.'

Her statement was more of a demand than a request. Belle could see that the usual vagueness she deployed with most of the people she interviewed wasn't going to wash with Healy. She'd have to be as upfront as she was able.

'I'm going to write about the impact of waste on the environment. I hope to raise awareness about the need to reduce, reuse and recycle.'

Healy turned up her nose. 'Hasn't that been done to death? And by environmentalists, too, with proper expertise – not just a journalist.'

Belle twitched, feeling tempted to challenge the 'just a journalist' remark. She wondered if Healy was as blunt with her patients or was even aware of her insensitivity.

'I agree,' Belle said, 'it has been done to death and yes, by people more knowledgeable than me, but I think you'll agree it's a message that still needs some work. We're not exactly zero-waste standard, are we?'

'Zero waste? Not yet.'

'Zero waste doesn't mean no actual—'

'I know what it means.'

Belle bit her tongue. If this were a social encounter and not a professional one, Belle would be telling this woman to fuck off right about now. Of course, it wasn't, so she didn't. 'My paper has a wide readership, right across Ireland, and my features are popular. If I give the issue some attention, I think it would do a lot of good.'

'I'll take your word for that.'

Belle ignored the put-down and thought about how best to proceed. She wasn't prepared to let Healy in on what was happening, but she had to tell her enough to get her talking about the cancer rates. Maybe she should've lied outright and said the feature was going to be on her cancer findings. Or maybe not. Healy was the type who'd follow her to Dublin to find out when the feature was going to print.

Healy's phone vibrated on the tabletop. She grabbed it and checked the screen. 'Shit, I've got to go. My husband's already at the restaurant.' She began gathering her things.

Belle was about to lose this lead before extracting a single scrap of information. 'There's a link,' she said quickly, 'between waste and public health.'

Healy stood up.

Belle continued, blurting out a pitch like she was on Dragon's Den, 'Waste is full of harmful substances – metals and chemicals, for example – and then there's decomposition of organic waste that releases toxic leachates and so on. If these materials aren't disposed of safely – if they're, say, thrown into unofficial landfills and left to fester—'

'Wait a minute; are you saying that's going on?' Healy sat down again and gave Belle another intense stare.

'I'm not making that claim but it can and does happen – and in those cases, it can cause cancers. I want to make people aware of those sorts of dangers, really drive home the—'

Healy's eyes went wide. She looked like she'd taken a few lines of coke. 'Hang on, if you're talking to me about this, then you must believe that's what we've got going on here, that waste isn't being disposed of safely.'

'Um, well...'

'Oh, come on, I've added two and two and got four. Fess up, tell me the truth.'

Belle tried to smile. Healy was hard work and now she'd latched onto this theory – never mind that it was right – Belle guessed that getting her off her notion would be next to impossible. She had to throw a bone, enough to satisfy her. She thought quickly.

'Okay,' she said, 'I don't have much more than a mist of suspicion, but there might be illegal dumping going on, not much and not all the time, and maybe none at all if my leads don't pan out.' She played down the facts.

'How long?'

'What?'

'How long do you reckon it's been going on? Months, years?'

'If it's going on at all—'

'Assume it is going on and take a guess; how long?'

'Years?'

A shadow fell across Healy's eyes, subduing them. Her shoulders drooped. 'That would... explain a lot.'

'How so?'

Healy leaned her chin on her hands. 'Look,' she said, 'my arms. I've got goosebumps.'

Belle saw that she did.

'God have mercy on us,' she whispered.

'What is it?'

Healy leaned in. 'Over the last ten years, I've noticed trends with my patients here in Derry. Trends that worry me, but trends I'm not seeing for the rest of Northern Ireland when I compare the stats in the northwest against the stats in the Belfast clinic, which handles patients from everywhere else. That's what I went on the radio to talk about and I've raised it formally within the

Department of Health. But we've been scratching our heads about why we're seeing these trends; they're way beyond the general causes of cancer. All we can be sure of is that it's environmental and it's specific to this place, to the northwest. When you mentioned illegal dumping, that fitted perfectly, like a turkey dinner at Christmas – or a nut roast, now that I'm vegan.' Healy rubbed her chin. 'In my research, I came across a journal paper that discussed a lot of the same characteristics I was noticing and guess what?'

Belle raised her eyebrows.

'It was written by a doctor in southern Italy,' Healy went on, 'who linked the cancer rates to large-scale illegal dumping that everybody knew was happening.'

'The author actually made an explicit link between the two?'

'She did, loud and clear. It's widely accepted that being exposed to highly toxic environmental pollutants causes a raft of diseases, including cancer, and it's widely accepted that illegal dumping puts those toxic pollutants right into our water and soil and air. She joined the dots between the two and pointed to medical research that has found a correlation between pollution from waste and disease.'

'And did she mention how the authorities closed it down?'

'She gave that a quick mention – the paper was in a medical journal, after all. She said… this is going to sound like something from a film… but she said the whole operation was being run by the mafia, it had been going on for years and officials were either too afraid to speak out or were getting backhanders to keep quiet. It was outrageous.'

Belle nodded thoughtfully. She mightn't be dealing with the mafia in her investigation, but the level of criminality and corruption wasn't a kick in the arse away.

'If there's illegal dumping going on here,' Healy said, 'and it's been going on for a number of years, it could help explain some of the pathology I'm seeing.'

'So tell me about that, what you've been seeing.'

Healy's phone went again.

'Let me get this.' She answered it quickly. 'Yes, yes, I'm round the corner. I'll be there in a minute. Order us a bottle of white.' She inhaled and put the phone back on the table. 'Back to your question, right, let me organise my thoughts. The really obvious one is the higher-than-normal incidences of cancers in general, across the board. Drilling down, we're talking about abnormally high numbers of children and young people presenting with cancer – it's like my patients are getting younger and younger. I've encountered rising incidents of cancers in any part of the body you can think of: stomach, blood, brain, liver, bone, bladder, central nervous system. I'm also seeing more occurrences of very rare forms of cancers. And a case crops up practically every month of a child, including babies, with cancer.'

'Babies?'

'One of my patients is a young woman who's never smoked but who has lung cancer – now, that's almost unheard of in normal circumstances. I've got increasing numbers of women under forty with breast cancer. I had a farmer who came to me with an extremely aggressive type of bone cancer and he was dead within a month.'

A cold shadow passed over Belle's heart. She thought of Seanie Higgins, the ambulance taking him from the house in a wheelchair.

'The mortality rates are over ten per cent higher when compared with the rest of Ireland and Britain. That's off-the-scale, make no mistake.'

'You believe this could be the result of illegal dumping.'

'Not all of it, of course, cancer is prevalent everywhere, but for the levels we've got here, I'd be willing to put my career on the line by saying, yes, it's a major factor. Especially if there're dumpsites near a river like the Faughan, because that's where the city gets most of its drinking water.' Healy stood up. 'And now, I really have to go.'

'Thanks for talking to me,' Belle said. 'It's been an education.'

'Think nothing of it and you have my full permission to quote me in your feature.'

'I'll take you up on that.'

'Just let me review anything you're going to include.'

'Naturally.'

'And if you do find out about any illegal dumping, let me know. I'd want to be part of whatever it takes to stop it.'

With that said, Healy dashed for the door and was gone.

31

After two hours of frantic typing, Belle finally had her Dictaphone recordings transcribed into a Word document on her laptop. She rubbed her neck and drained the last of the tea from her cup. She had one final paragraph to construct: a summary of the investigation so far. She thought for a second before resuming typing:

Fionn and Dermot see Evergreen security men on night of murder.

Ed Ramsey (possible witness) sees two strangers hanging about in corridor outside Fionn's flat that night; need to confirm by going back to Ed but they are probably the security men.

Confirmed lorries are making trips in wee hours to remote illegal dumpsites.

Gathered samples from one such site; waiting on results from Rita Wilson (friend).

She paused, her fingers hovering over the keyboard, before typing more:

Meetings done with Tom Sweet, Brendan Lynch, Noel Kerrigan (foes) – frosty, cagey SOBs.

Followed by security men several times; threatened by them on two occasions and possibly responsible for damage to car.

Sammy Alexander at Environmental Agency; Fionn's notes say 'good friend'; will ring him today.

Talk to Cllr O'Dee – made easy with invite to his mayoral event; assume to be foe.

As soon as Rita's results come through, take all evidence to police. This will be enough to blow lid on illegal dumping racket; will also show that Evergreen had motive to murder Fionn.

If can get Ed to confirm security men sighting, that will be strong evidence of Evergreen's involvement in Fionn's murder.

Reading her summary to check she had the main points, Belle thought about everything Fionn had worked on to start the investigation; how he'd done a lot of the heavy lifting and left it ready for her to take on the baton. Had he paid for that with his life? She was determined to do right by him.

Belle closed her laptop and yawned. She'd covered enough for one night and she could resume tomorrow. And talking of tomorrow, she had her special mayoral do at the Guildhall. She reached for her phone to ring Dermot. Some company at the occasion would be nice.

'Hey,' she said, when he answered, 'how you doing?'

'Okay,' he said, but she could hear he sounded flat and not his usual upbeat self.

'You don't sound okay.'

'Ah, it's nothing to worry about. I'll deal with it.'

'Did something happen?'

'It doesn't matter, McGee,' he said, impatiently.

'Well, it does matter, so tell me what's going on.'

Dermot sighed. She imagined his face wearing an exasperated expression. 'I was taken aside at work today by my supervisor. He said he'd been watching me this last while and wasn't happy with my output.'

'Shit.'

'He said if I wasn't careful, I wouldn't have a job much longer.'

'Oh, Dermot, I'm sorry. This is my fault.'

'Wise up, how is it?'

'Of course it is. They know what I'm up to and they know you're in my company a lot.'

'Or maybe I'm just a lazy so-and-so at work.'

Belle tutted. He couldn't help making light of it. 'It's no laughing matter, you could end up unemployed.'

'That'd be a pain in the arse but I'd live. I've been through worse.'

'I'm worried about you,' she said, deciding not to bother mentioning the event in the Millennium Forum. The last thing he needed was to be seen with her at something like that with O'Dee and God knows who else watching on.

'I like that you're worried about me,' she heard him say, 'but listen, I'm okay.'

She wasn't convinced but she knew it was pointless going on about it any longer.

'If you want to cheer me up,' he said, 'there is one thing you could do?'

'What?'

'Call round, soon.'

'What about the night after tomorrow?'

'Can't wait.'

They signed off, leaving Belle with her thoughts. These people were ramping up the intimidation. She needed to move faster and bring her investigation to a close, because if her suspicions were right, these people weren't going to stop at a few idle threats.

32

Belle found herself standing alone in the Millennium Forum. The invite hadn't said anything about formal dress so she'd opted for a casual but tasteful outfit that would be, above all, comfortable: satin silk harem pants with flat lace-up espadrilles and a boat neck blouse. She stood next to a tall pedestal table, sipping on a glass of red wine. Her eyes scanned the room.

The drinks reception was going on in the forum's marble-floored piazza, with the bar at one end, the curved staircase to the upper floor at the other end, a dining enclave on the right and the entrance to the auditorium on the left. Light from the still-bright evening radiated through the tall windows near the staircase and delicate aromas from the buffet table floated gently through the air.

The space was crowded and noisy, and clusters of well-dressed people stood around drinking and eating and talking and laughing. Of course, Beavis and Butthead were there, too, loitering by the entrance to the auditorium, their watchful eyes trained on her and looking as out of place as a couple of cats in a dogs' home. Belle grinned, enjoying their discomfort. She lifted her glass in a salute and they simply turned away.

She continued searching the room, hoping to finally catch sight of Alan O'Dee. She'd looked him up on the council website as she had no clue what he was like. His mugshot, when she found it, was no Michelangelo, with his wispy white hair, ruddy skin, overgrown eyebrows and a smile that more closely resembled a leer.

Belle checked her watch. A half an hour before the concert was to begin. She really needed to find him. She was about to start wandering when she heard a voice behind her. She jumped, almost spilling her wine.

'McGee,' the voice said, 'the famous Belle McGee. I finally have the honour of meeting you.'

Belle spun round and was face-to-face with Alan O'Dee.

'Councillor – or should I say, Mayor – O'Dee. Thanks for the invite.'

He was taller than she'd imagined and bulkier, like a rugby player, and he stood too close. She was uncomfortable – probably exactly how he meant her to feel.

'I wasn't sure you'd come,' he said, giving her a glimpse of his creepy smile. 'So, you're the hotshot reporter come here all the way from Dublin.'

Belle hoped she was giving off an air of cool. 'I wouldn't say hotshot exactly. And I do work in Dublin, but I'm from this part of the world originally.'

'I know where you're from, I know all about where you're from. And I know about your connection to Fionn Power.'

She sensed the menace in his voice, stalking her and waiting to pounce like a cat hunting a sparrow.

'You say that like it's a crime,' she said.

'It was a crime at one point, though, wasn't it? You and your family got your comeuppance.'

Anger, hot and trembling, rose from Belle's gut and she wanted was to grab his throat.

'How dare you mention that, you—'

'I haven't the time to listen to you get all indignant. You can rage to somebody else. I'm busy tonight, in my official capacity, and I want to make my conversation with you a quick one.'

'If that's the case, you should've come straight to the point instead of beating about the bush and insulting people.'

'Quite right, that's exactly what I should've done – although Fionn Power is relevant to the point.'

'Hurry up and say whatever it is you want to say. I'd like our conversation to be quick, too.'

'Here's the thing, McGee – that's what you like to be called, isn't it? Not Miss or Ms or Belle or even Mullan – you're making a nuisance of yourself. And worse still, you're following a lot of breadcrumbs down a rabbit hole.'

'What the hell does that mean? You might be better laying off the metaphors.'

'A smart mouth like that is going to get you in trouble. Let me take the gloves off, if you can live with that metaphor. I know you've been prying into the fascinating world of waste, asking a pile of questions, pretending you're doing some news story on waste management. Like anybody would buy the Sunday paper to read that. I also happen to know what got you involved in the first place. Our mutual friend, Fionn Power. Poor Fionn. A troubled man, very troubled and very disturbed. Paranoid, too... oh, his paranoia was off-the-scale.'

'That's not the Fionn I knew, so why don't you have some respect for the dead?'

'Not the Fionn you knew? I'd contend you didn't know him at all.'

Belle breathed in sharply. He had her on the back foot and she could tell he sensed it.

'As I said, paranoid. He was full of notions, too – conspiracy theories of all sorts. God help him, he was more to be pitied than anything else.'

'He doesn't need your pity. He had more humanity and integrity than anybody I know.'

'I've touched a nerve and understandably so. You met him at a very impressionable age and I'd say he made quite a first impression. It's impossible to be rational. I get that.'

'Don't tell me how I feel about Fionn, you've no id—'

'McGee, pack your emotions into a box for a minute and listen carefully.' His voice became stern all of a sudden, his smile gone. 'You're poking your nose into something you know nothing about. The local council appoints contractors to carry out waste disposal for the council area. As a councillor, it's my job to make council and the contractors accountable and ensure waste's being disposed of safely and according to regulations. I take that job seriously. I work hard at it. I'm elected by the people, which I'm very proud of. For some amateur like you to come along and suggest there's corruption and criminality—'

'Excuse me, Mayor, but I never said any such thing, I'm working on a general piece about waste management.'

'Don't take me for a fool. It's obvious what you're at.'

'Making assumptions—'

'Enough. Now, take note: there's no criminality, no corruption. Elected reps and officials in this city can stand over the process, and we have evidence to demonstrate that everything is as it should be. You'll find all actions by council bear up to scrutiny. I'll provide you with the stats, the annual reports.'

'Please do.'

'Please what?'

'Provide me with these stats and reports.'

'Oh, right, well… of course, I'll make sure that happens.'

'And can I quote you on what you've talked about today?'

'I wouldn't recommend that – no, wouldn't recommend it at all.' He paused. 'There's something else,' he said, his voice calming. 'If you think you have evidence that suggests anything contrary to my position, if you're about to make allegations, you have an obligation to bring it first to the attention of council. We need to know so we can investigate it for ourselves and take it through the proper channels. Carrying on like Miss Marple isn't how things are done.'

'I'll think about that.' Belle felt she was getting the upper hand.

'You need to do more than think about it – this is council business. We have to get the chance to investigate it first.'

Belle stared. He stared back.

'So, do you have any?' he asked.

'Any what?'

'Evidence.'

'Of corruption or criminality? No,' she lied.

He gave a grunt. 'I hope, for your sake, that's true.' His gaze drifted past her and his face lit up with that smile again. 'Ah, Mickey, how are ye?' he said, to somebody in the crowd.

And with that taste of a threat as the final word, O'Dee was gone.

Belle left her glass on the table. Only then did she notice that she was shaking and her heart was beating a hole through her ribcage. She took a moment to settle down.

O'Dee was one nasty piece of shit. He sounded like a man used to dishing out threats. He was also incredibly informed – where did he get his intel? He didn't just know what she'd been getting up to, he knew about her past and her connection with Fionn as well. She wasn't comfortable with that. And saying those nasty things about Fionn and her family; well, it was as low as a person could stoop. On top of that, he'd made an outright threat against her. Not that it was the first time she'd been threatened in an investigation, but still, it was one of those things you never got used to.

Getting the samples from Rita and going to the police with her evidence couldn't happen soon enough.

33

After the unnerving ding-dong with O'Dee, Belle wanted to move quickly, so instead of wasting time arranging to meet Sammy Alexander, she decided a chat on the phone would do the trick. She got the number for the Environmental Agency from an Internet search.

'Good afternoon,' Belle said, to the man who answered the phone. 'Can you put me through to Sammy Alexander, please?'

'May I ask who's calling and what it's in connection with?'

'Belle McGee; I'm calling to report some fly-tipping.' A little porky – from their website, fly-tipping was the most common reason for calls from the public. Best to keep her powder dry until she talked to Sammy.

'We have a specialised team for fly-tipping; it's not Sammy you need to talk to.'

Belle thought on her feet. 'Ah, he... he's helped me with this particular problem in the past and told me if it happened again, I should contact him directly.'

'Right, I see.' The man paused. 'Connecting you now.'

The call went on hold and Belle doodled nervously in her

notebook. A tinny-sounding pop song from the eighties came across the wires, one that Belle knew but couldn't place.

'Hello,' someone interrupted the chorus, 'Sammy Alexander speaking.' He had a deep voice like a bullfrog croaking from the bottom of an empty barrel. 'David said I dealt with you before but I don't—'

'Mr Alexander—'

'Sammy's grand,' he said, 'Mr Alexander's what my bank manager calls me.'

'Sammy, it is. Sammy, my name's Belle McGee. I'm an investigative journalist. People call me McGee.'

'All right, Mrs McGee—'

'It's not Mrs, just McGee on its own.'

'Uh, grand, but I'm sorry, I still don't recognise the name.'

'I'm a friend of Fionn Power's. Do you recognise that name?'

Silence filled the space between them. Belle bit her lip.

'Give me your number. I'll ring you back from my mobile.'

Belle recited her number and a minute later, they picked up where they left off.

'I knew Fionn,' Sammy said.

'Did he mention his suspicions to you, about Evergreen Waste?' Belle asked.

'He did. So, you must be *the* journalist.'

'What?'

'Fionn said he had a journalist friend he was going to contact.'

'I guess that would be me. I was hoping we could have a chat.'

'More than happy to – in fact, I'm relieved I'm finally getting the chance to talk to you. It's good we're doing it this way, over our personal phones and not in person. Less chance of the wrong people twigging anything.'

'What makes you say that, Sammy?' She already knew but she wanted his spin.

'There's folk involved in this who're very powerful. What Fionn stumbled on is a big deal, massive implications. It's important it's exposed… hang on a second,' he said, 'just going to lock my office here. I don't want interruptions.'

Belle heard a metal click.

'Do you want me to tell you what I know or do you want to ask me questions?' he asked.

'Why don't you tell your story and I'll jump in whenever I have anything I want to ask?'

'That'll do.' He cleared his throat again before his big voice began, 'I met Fionn at a training event. I was giving a presentation on fly-tipping and, well, let's say he was a keen student. We got talking after and he was asking me all sorts of odd questions – I realised after that he was sounding me out, checking if I could be trusted. At one point, he said, "Do you want me to show you a spot where there's been fly-tipping?" and I said, "I do, of course. Where's it at?" and he said, "I'll take you." And so he did. The next day we went to an old, abandoned sand and gravel pit, miles away in a remote part of Co. Tyrone.'

Sammy paused. It sounded like he was taking a drink of something. 'Sorry about that,' he said, 'mouth's as dry as a stone in a drought. So, I was expecting the usual kind of thing – a car boot of rubbish dumped off, a load of tyres, a pile of construction rubbish – but boy was I in for a surprise. There was this massive area of fresh, overturned earth but not much else. "Do you get that smell?" Fionn asked. "Could you miss it?" I replied. I was familiar with that smell – waste decomposition, without a doubt. Fionn was all prepared; he had a shovel with him and he started digging. After a while, he said, "Have a deck at this." And what I saw…' Sammy whistled. 'It was only a patch of what was underneath, but I could tell just by looking that it wasn't a case of fly-tipping. It was full-on industrial, hazardous, the lot.'

Belle was about to respond but Sammy went on talking. No need to interview this guy; he was a one man show.

'Fionn told me how it all worked. Evergreen had the waste they were getting through their own public sector contracts with

226

councils, hospitals and such. But more waste was coming in illegally from corporations, developers and operators who had public sector contracts elsewhere. That was being hauled in by unmarked lorries from all over: right across the province, other parts of the UK, from the Republic. The lorries would be unloaded and the waste mingled with the Evergreen waste. But bringing the waste as far as Evergreen was only the first stage. The next stage was disposing of it.

'Close to home time most days, Fionn noticed a crew of six or so men arriving. They weren't Evergreen employees that he knew of and they'd still be there when everybody else was leaving. He decided to stay late after work one evening, kept out of sight and waited to see what would happen. He sat in his car for hours. "I have the patience for it," he said to me, "when I'm onto something." It got dark and he was starting to doubt himself when the first lorry appeared. Then three or four more. He followed them for miles, up into the hills, to a real out-of-the-way spot. Night after night, he did that, and soon enough he had a whole list of different sites. He marked them out on a map and took down all sorts of details like lorry reg plates, numbers of lorries, estimates of tonnage – up to three hundred tonnes a night was his estimate, six or seven nights a week, every damned week. He basically wrote down anything he thought was important.'

'I've seen the lists he made.'

'Damning, isn't it? And let me tell you this: I never saw anything on that scale before, ever. These operators have dumpsites everywhere and anywhere possible – old quarries and mines, caves, secluded bogs, wells. All of that would be with the knowledge of the landowner, too, you know.'

'It must involve a lot of people and have a big reach.'

'Big? That's one word for it. I reckon it's as big as any illegal dumping in the whole of Western Europe. We're talking hundreds of thousands of tonnes.'

Belle caught her breath. 'Are you serious? It's really that much?'

'I'm always serious when it comes to the environment. I took extensive water and soil samples from the site me and Fionn went to, and wrote up the results and my recommendations in a report. I didn't hide behind the door either. I was explicit about just how bad the pollution was—'

'And how bad was it?'

'Shocking, the worst I'd come across. I found toxins I couldn't even explain; didn't know how they could've got into the soil and the water. The kind of stuff that burns shortcuts through steel tanks. There were heavy metals, solvents, chlorinated compounds, asbestos all in the ground, festering, seeping into the land, leaching into the water and the aquifers beneath the surface. Anybody who'd put this shit in the ground has respect for nothing, not even themselves.'

Sammy breathed out, his distress audible. 'Waste like that,' he went on, 'a lot of it's coming from big companies that don't want to pay for disposing of their waste safely. It's cheaper to dump it all illegally. No doubt about it. We're supposed to be fighting global warming, cutting back, reusing and recycling, whatever it takes to saves ourselves. And what's happening here? We've got this crowd turning a profit and to hell with the damage.'

'Which is why it has to be exposed. What happened to your report?'

'I marked it urgent and submitted it directly to my manager, telling him this was an exceptional case. He said, "Sammy, you're right, this is no normal situation." I said, "I'm glad you agree." I thought he'd take it up the line and the powers-that-be would do an intrusive survey. I even thought I might be assigned to the survey team.'

'Don't tell me,' Belle said, 'there never was an investigation and your manager never mentioned it again.'

'Exactly right. I waited a couple of weeks and when I heard nothing, I asked for a meeting with him. "Where's things at?" I said to him and he said, "I'm sorting it out, Sammy, don't you worry." I waited another few weeks. I asked him again. He just dead-handed it again. That happened two or three more times 'til one day I got a call from my manager's manager and he gave me a very strong heads-up. He said, "The problem's being handled by a team in Belfast and you've no reason to concern yourself further." It was very loud and clear. He said, "If you keep pursuing this thing, Sammy, you might want to reconsider your career in the agency." Can you believe even my report disappeared? I had it stored on the server and it vanished. I hadn't made a copy – we're not supposed to, data protection and all – so I lost all the evidence.'

'So that was that.'

'Not quite. I tried giving it one last go. I decided to go to a few of the councillors – they're elected reps, after all, so this is right up their street. They listened, they said they'd look into it and then they never mentioned it again, bar one who told me he'd made an inquiry and that everything was being taken care of. Then, one day, I got a call from Councillor Alan O'Dee, an auld hand.'

Belle nearly choked. Seemed like he was the Rottweiler they sent out to put the squeeze on problem people.

'He invited me to meet him in the wee coffee place round the back of the council offices. He even bought me a coffee and a slice of carrot cake and we had a friendly chat, talked about all sorts: the maritime festival, the Halloween carnival, the upgrade to the road to Belfast, the new Brandywell stadium – just about any subject you want to mention. The whole encounter was very friendly... until he got up to go. He put his hand on my shoulder – a good, hard squeeze that dug into the muscle – and leaned down so he was close enough to give me a kiss. I'll never forget what he said, "If you want to keep your job, stay the fuck out of that report" and then he left.'

'I'm not surprised he actually threatened you. Did you tell your manager?'

'Are you joking? He was probably the one that got O'Dee to meet me. This corruption, it's all sown up between Evergreen, landowners, officials, politicians – all of them working together, and they're all being paid-off or intimidated to keep a lid on it.'

'Were you concerned at all? For your safety, your career?'

'I was. I told Fionn the craic and he was raging. He was determined we wouldn't let them stop us and that's when he told me about his journalist friend and said it was time to contact you.'

'Only he didn't live long enough to do that,' Belle said, slowly. Was it a coincidence he was murdered just as he was on the verge of exposing Evergreen? She didn't think so, and if anything, Sammy's account only made her more convinced Evergreen was responsible.

'Right. And that left me not knowing what to do next. He never told me who you were so I had no way of contacting you. But truth be told, I haven't been in the form for anything since his death. I've been sick to my stomach about what happened him. It was shocking. Just shocking.'

Sammy went quiet for a moment.

'Fionn hated the corruption of these people,' Sammy went on. 'He hated the damage they were doing to the environment. It really mattered to him that he could put it right. Fionn had a rare sense of justice. Fionn was... he...' Sammy cleared his throat. 'He was a good man.'

Sammy's high praise for Fionn warmed Belle. 'I appreciate how open you've been with me,' she said, 'in spite of the risks.'

'I wish you luck with breaking this thing open. You should be careful, though, McGee, these folks play dirty.'

Belle remembered the conversation with O'Dee. Sammy wasn't wrong.

34

'I'm starting to make a habit of this,' Belle said.

'What?' Dermot said.

'Waking up in your bed.'

'Um,' he snuggled closer, 'good habit or bad habit?'

It was a bad habit, a bad habit she couldn't stop. Despite trying to keep a distance, she couldn't remember liking anybody as much as Dermot. 'Haven't decided yet,' she said.

'You're a cold one,' Dermot laughed, tickling her.

Belle squealed and writhed out of the way. 'Don't you dare! Tickling turns me to jelly.'

'Ah-ha, Belle McGee's kryptonite!'

'Stop or I'll kill you,' Belle managed to say through the laughter.

He eased up, a smug look on his face of having got the better of her. She felt a sudden yearning inside, a pang of desire that took her by surprise.

'But I do… I like you,' she said.

His face turned serious and he looked directly at her. 'I like you, too. I think I lo—'

Bang! Bang!

Dermot shot up in bed. 'What the fuck was that?'

'Sounds like somebody trying to ram your door in.'

He jumped onto the floor. 'I'm going to make them sorry.'

He pulled on a pair of tracksuit bottoms and, with chest and feet bare, he disappeared.

The banging continued, louder. Belle sat up and scanned the room for her clothes. The front door opened at the same time as she located her underwear. Then she heard what sounded like a scuffle with shouting from Dermot and stern retorts from several unknown voices. She wasted no time pulling on her blouse, jeans and slippers, and raced downstairs.

Belle stopped dead when she reached the sitting room. Four uniformed policemen surrounded Dermot. He was handcuffed, face pressed against the wall, hands behind his back.

'Stay back, madam,' one of the officers said.

Another officer approached. 'Do you live at this address, madam?'

'I, no, I, um…' She was caught on the hop.

'Madam, do you reside here?'

'No, just visiting,' she said, deciding 'visiting' sounded better than 'dirty stop-out'.

She took a moment to gather her senses. She was no stranger to police arrests in her work as a journalist and wasn't fazed by them ordinarily. But the arrest of somebody close, a family member, a friend – in this case, a person she was maybe falling for – that was a whole different thing. She was no stranger to arrests like that either, only, the thing was, arrests like that fazed her very much.

The past came rushing at her with such force, she nearly lost her balance. She felt weak, unable to stand, unable to ask why exactly the police were there – although she could take a guess. Tightness in her chest made it hard to breathe.

'I have rights,' she heard Dermot shouting, his voice distorted with being pinned to the wall.

'And we're just about to read them to you,' one of his restraining officers said, 'though it's hardly a first for you, Dermie boy?'

A third officer went to the far side of the living room and spoke into the walkie-talkie clipped to his stab vest. 'Have forensics been dispatched?'

A burst of static crackled in an answer Belle couldn't make out.

'Dermot McDermott, you are under arrest,' another officer began, 'on suspicion of the murder of James Power.'

Dermot wailed. 'You must be mad. Belle, go on, tell them, I didn't do it. You know I didn't kill Fionn.'

'Go easy on him,' Belle said, raising her voice and feeling a ball of fire grow in her chest. 'There's no need for this.'

She made a move towards Dermot but felt a strong grip on her arm from one of the officers.

'Stay back, madam,' he said.

'Belle, tell them what happened.'

'He's innocent,' she said. 'He had nothing to do with Fionn's murder. You're arresting the wrong person.'

Two officers grabbed Dermot and marched him out the door. Dermot didn't go quietly or without resistance; he struggled and protested.

Belle stood watching as Dermot was manhandled out of the doorway. She seethed, powerless to do anything. Powerless like a time long ago. But this time didn't have to be the same as back then. This time, she was all grown up. She was going to prove the police were wrong.

'You've got this so wrong,' she said, the ball of fire now in her throat, making breathing difficult.

'Take it easy,' a remaining officer said, putting his hand on her shoulder.

She shrugged him off. 'Don't fucking touch me.'

Belle fell back against the sofa. Her head was dizzy. She took some deep breaths to help get her emotions in check. Losing control wasn't going to help matters.

The officer who'd told her to take it easy took a seat by her side on the sofa. Belle glanced at his name badge. Inspector Fairley. He was six foot tall, she guessed, and had a shiny bald skull and handlebar moustache, trimmed enough to make it acceptable for police dress code. A black stab vest sat over his white uniform shirt and a Glock snugly fitted into his gun belt.

'I'm going outside to wait for forensics, sir,' the officer on the walkie-talkie said, and left.

Fairley nodded.

The room was suddenly deathly still in the aftermath of the previous mayhem. Only Fairley and Belle remained.

'I'd like to ask you a few questions, madam,' he said, 'and then we'll need you to leave.'

'Ask whatever you want,' Belle said. 'It's not like I can stop you.' She pushed her hair back from her face. 'I want to gather my stuff; that's my bag on the coffee table.'

She felt more stable, but still didn't think she could stand up.

'Forensics will have to see that first,' Fairley said. 'Are you okay?'

'I'm fine, not that it's any of your business,' Belle said, disgusted at this fake concern. 'I'll need my car key – the very least you can do is give me my car key.'

Fairley took the bag, his hands clad in a pair of blue Nitrile gloves, and searched. 'Here you go,' reaching her the key.

'Right, thanks,' she said.

'Can you tell me your name?' Fairley said. 'And your connection to Mr McDermott?'

'I'm Isabelle McGee; I'm a reporter with the *National Spectator* in Dublin. I knew Fionn Power from childhood. When I heard what happened to him, I took some leave and came home to

Donegal. I met up with Dermot shortly after I arrived back and, ah, well, we've met up a couple of times since.'

'And when you say home, where is that exactly, Ms McGee?' Fairley scribbled in his notebook.

Belle told him. 'And it's McGee, by the way, I just go by McGee.'

'If you wish. You work for the *National Spectator*?'

'Yes,' she said, snapping, 'I live in Dublin but my family home's in Donegal. If I have to tell that to another person, I'm, going to scream.'

'And you say you knew Mr Power from childhood. What was your relationship to him at that time?'

Now this nosey PC Plod was asking about 1986. The last thing she wanted was to answer questions about 1986.

'My parents knew him,' Belle began, determined to make her answer technically truthful without revealing crucial details. The police would hunt out the facts, anyway – that was their job, after all – so they didn't really need every jot and dot from her. 'He came to work on our farm for a while.'

'Unusual, a city boy doing that?'

'Is it?'

'When was this exactly?' Fairley gave his moustache a twirl.

'In the eighties.'

'Specifically.'

'Mid-eighties, as far as I remember. I wasn't that old.'

'I'd like to take a number we can contact you on, if you don't mind.'

'Sure, I've got business cards in my wallet. Help yourself. You're going to, anyway.'

He rummaged in her bag again and came upon the wallet. He took out a card and read it aloud. 'Investigative reporter? Your name's familiar; have you been involved in high-profile stories?'

'Yeah.'

'You probably have a lot of dealings with police in your line of work.'

235

Belle sniffed. 'Some.'

'And do you treat them with contempt, too, like you're doing with me?'

She sneered. 'Not unless they haul away somebody I care about, especially when he's innocent.'

'You seem very sure about that.'

'I didn't need to come out of the womb with him to know he wouldn't brutally beat a human being to death – least of all, Fionn. And I must say, his behaviour isn't consistent with a person who's committed such an awful crime.'

'Thanks for your opinion,' Fairley said, 'which I wasn't asking for. But that's all I need from you; you can go on.'

Belle got up and limped to the door. 'When will I get my bag back?'

'We'll have to determine if it's part of the investigation first. If it is, you may never get it back. I assume it's not, however, which means you'll probably get it back in a day or two.'

She swore inwardly. All her cards, her ID, including her fake ID, were in the bag, along with a load of other crap she couldn't live without. At least her phone was in her back pocket, so that was some consolation.

'Will you call me to let me know when I can collect it?'

Fairley raised one eyebrow and gave his moustache another twist. 'What do you think?'

'No, thought not. I'll ring myself.'

'Now you're talking. And it's the Strand Road station you should call.'

Belle left in a daze and full of anxious nerves. Outside, Dermot and all the officers were gone, bar the one who told Fairley he was going to wait for the forensics team. He nodded and bid her goodbye, but she snubbed him. She felt a surge of resentment well up from her stomach and fought the desire to tell him to go fuck himself.

She jumped into her car and drove away, meeting what was probably the forensics team on her way out of the close. Once out on William Street, she took a left. Her hands barely had the strength to steer the wheel. She indicated left and parked up by the kerb.

Belle covered her mouth with her hands. She inhaled, forcing herself to relax. It would be easy now to panic. An image floated to the forefront of her mind, the one that summed up the pain of the past for Belle: her mother sliding to the kitchen floor, a wooden spoon in her hand, dripping stew gravy onto her blouse.

Tears pressed against her eyes, demanding release. And now Dermot was arrested. Those stupid police; those stupid, stupid fucks. They were completely wrong.

35

DONEGAL, 1986

The sky was aglow with purple-pink as the sun lingered on the horizon. Several hours had elapsed since Hunter's rescue from the river and Belle had spent the time wandering, away from the house, away from the lane. Heavy with guilt, she decided it was time to go back. Once the sun fell under the horizon, it'd be late and they'd start to worry. She imagined them already worrying, her mother getting worked up and her father trying to keep her calm. But if it got dark and she still wasn't home, her father would get worked up, too.

Reaching the bottom of the lane, she picked up her pace, not slowing until she reached the last bend. As soon as the house came into view, she knew immediately things were off-kilter.

She heard the voices first, strangers' voices, interrupted by her mother's voice and Maeveen's, high-pitched.

Every inch of her turned sickly cold, the way you do when you know something bad is about to happen, something catastrophic, an end-of-the-world kind of bad. All she wanted was to run back down the lane, run away and not watch. But hearing Maeveen's screams, she forced herself to press on.

The courtyard at the back of the house was jumping with activity; four, no, five vehicles were parked at odd angles – three Garda cars and two army jeeps. A cluster of soldiers blocked the back door and a Gard held a writhing Maeveen in one place with a heavy hand.

'Let go of my daughter,' Belle's mother stood facing the Gard defiantly. 'There's no need for this.'

The Gard holding Maeveen didn't answer. He stared straight ahead, not even noticing who was talking.

'If she promises to behave herself,' said one of the soldiers, 'we'll let her go.' He was wearing a fancy uniform and had more stripes than the others.

'This is bullshit,' Maeveen said. 'I've done nothing wrong.'

The striped soldier turned away and marched to one of the jeeps.

'I'll be making a complaint,' their mother said, 'about the way you people have manhandled my daughter.'

'We've acted appropriately,' the striped soldier called from the jeep. 'We have to restrain anybody impeding us in the line of duty.'

'Line of duty, my arse,' said Maeveen. 'You're victimising innocent people.'

'Be careful we don't arrest you.'

'I dare you,' Maeveen squealed. 'Go on, arrest me.' Her face was the colour of a ripe strawberry.

'Mammy,' Belle whimpered.

Her mother shot around. She ran to Belle and hugged her. 'Jesus, where've you been? Stay beside me.'

'Wuh... what's going on?' Belle asked, even though she was pretty sure of the answer.

Her mother looked her in the eye. Belle saw she was on the verge of tears. She'd never seen her mother like this before. It frightened her.

'Stay beside me,' her mother repeated.

Belle took position behind her mother. 'Can I go into the house?'

'Shush, do you see that row of soldiers? Nobody's getting in that isn't already in.'

'Is Daddy—'

'Yes, he's in there.'

'And—'

'Hold your tongue, daughter. The army and the Gards are in there, searching.'

'They won't find anything,' Belle said.

But Belle had spoken too soon. The soldiers guarding the door stepped back. Someone was coming out. Belle knew what was next, she knew it as surely as she knew her name. And she wished she'd drowned in the river.

Two soldiers emerged and stuck between them was Fionn. Straight after them came a Gard and another soldier. Belle blinked in disbelief. Held between them was her father.

Maeveen's screams were hoarse but loud, echoing off the walls of the house and the outhouses and the courtyard's cobblestones, screeching wails that went on and on and on as the men took Fionn and their father towards the Garda cars.

'You bastards! Jesus, no! You fucking bastards!' She flayed against the Gard's grip and dropped to the ground, screaming and howling like she was being burned alive. The Gard dragged her to her feet, pulling her upright as though she was a floppy ragdoll. She gave no resistance, everything she had was going into her anguish.

'Stop them, Mammy,' Belle croaked. What was unfolding in front of her eyes didn't seem like reality, more like a film, a make-believe celluloid film that she was passively watching. She couldn't feel anything, not the way she should've. In her head, she knew it was so, so terrible, but she couldn't feel it.

'We're caught,' her mother whispered, 'no way round it.' Tears dropped from her eyelashes and Belle watched them soak into the sleeve of her cardigan. She had a strange look on her face. Steely and determined. But proud, too. 'We're caught.'

'Aw, Jesus, no,' Maeveen squirmed to get away from the Gard's grip, all the while yelping. 'Fionn, Daddy…'

It was then she seemed to notice Belle for the first time.

'This is your fucking fault,' she shrieked.

Belle froze. Maeveen was accusing her.

'If you hadn't been messing about in the river with that Hunter Campbell,' Maeveen's voice was muffled with tears, 'if you hadn't called Fionn to come and save his useless fucking life, he never would've seen Fionn, he never would've told. He never would've told. Aw, God, he never would've told.' Maeveen wailed and the Gard finally let her go. She dropped to the ground, hitting her knees hard on the cobblestones.

Fionn and their father were piled into two different cars. The soldiers and Gards boarded their respective vehicles, quickly and precisely like a well-rehearsed dance troupe. Engines roared to a start. One by one, in an orderly fashion, they drove away, leaving the women of the family in a vast, empty silence.

*

They might've stayed that way for five minutes or fifty, Belle couldn't tell, without moving, without speaking. Not a whimper was uttered by Maeveen. She stared straight ahead, her mouth slightly hanging. Shadows and darkness filled the courtyard, creeping up the walls and along the cobbles.

'Let's go inside, daughters,' their mother said. 'Come on now.'

She went over to Maeveen and helped her to stand up the way you might help a very old person.

'Come on, pet,' she said. 'That's it, you're all right.'

Maeveen was led into the house. Belle followed.

'You know what, Maeveen,' Belle's mother finally said, 'why don't I make up a bed for you in the sitting room and get you some hot milk? A wee sleep is what you need.'

'Do you want me to help, Mammy?'

'Would you, love? Go upstairs and get me some blankets from the hot press and a pillow off Maeveen's bed, and when you've done that put a pan of milk on the range for your sister.'

Belle jumped into action, glad to be useful, and it wasn't long before Maeveen was wrapped up in the makeshift bed and falling into an exhausted sleep.

'I need to talk to you, Belle,' her mother whispered. 'We'll go to the kitchen.'

Belle's chest tightened and she felt the tiniest tingle of worry at the back of her brain. Her mother sat at the table and pulled out a chair for Belle.

'Are you okay?' she said. 'Belle?'

Belle searched for words to answer. 'I don't know, I mean, I don't even know what that was about. Is Fionn a criminal?' The moment of truth, she'd find out now if her suspicions were right all along.

Her mother shook her head slowly.

'But why would the Gards arrest him if he—'

'They arrested your father, too; does that mean he's a criminal?'

'No.'

'Neither is Fionn.'

'None of this makes sense.'

'No wonder, we deliberately kept the truth from you and your sister... though we did tell her more than we told you, and I've a suspicion Fionn went and told her everything.'

The tiny tingle of worry got bigger. Not a criminal. So, what the hell was going on?

'Remember us telling you that Fionn was my cousin's son?'

'Me and Maeveen didn't believe that.'

242

'Naw, so we noticed, with Maeveen at least. We weren't a bit happy her and Fionn started up their wee romance. But you can't stop a thing like that with young people. They think it's forever, that nothing will separate them, that nobody's ever had what they have. Love in a bucket. Until the bucket starts to feel too small and you don't know this person who's attached to your hip.' She sighed.

Belle squirmed. Her mother wasn't in the habit of talking this way. The subject was very grown up, difficult to grasp really, and she was uncomfortable hearing it.

'We hoped it'd fizzle out in its own time,' her mother went on, 'but the opposite seemed to be happening. See, we wanted Fionn to get out of the house a bit, stretch his legs and take in some fresh air. But he couldn't go on his own and we didn't want to put that responsibility on you, so Maeveen was the obvious choice. She was to be his chaperone and make sure he wasn't seen.'

Belle thought about the day she caught them kissing. She felt so stupid… childish.

'I suppose the mystery is,' her mother continued, 'if Fionn wasn't related to us, why did we say he was? Why were we letting him stay and keeping him hidden?'

The steady thud of Belle's heart throbbed in her ears. She'd wanted to know the answer to that mystery since the first day Fionn had arrived, but now that she was about to find out, she was afraid. She didn't know why but she was.

'Do you know what a safe house is, Belle?'

Belle shook her head.

'It's a place that's used to hide somebody running away from the law.'

Belle bit her lip. 'But wouldn't somebody running away from the law be a criminal then?'

'Not always.' Her mother put her hand on Belle's shoulder. 'This is confusing, pet, so I'll do my best to help you understand. You know what's going on in the North, don't you?'

243

'The Troubles. The IRA's fighting to get the British out of the six counties.' Belle knew her history and her present. 'A lot of countries round the world say the IRA are terrorists and criminals, but that's lies – the lies colonisers tell against the people they've colonised.'

Belle understood this well.

'And we don't believe those lies,' her mother said, 'and plenty others don't either – and well, Fionn…'

Slowly, the lights were going on for Belle; slowly, the things she didn't understand were falling into place. Her mouth began to salivate. She closed her eyes and breathed deeply, hoping she wouldn't be sick. 'Is he fighting the British?' Belle stopped short of asking if he was an IRA man.

'He is.'

Belle's stomach heaved and she breathed in deeply again. 'Why was he hiding in our house?'

'He's on the run. Do you know what that means?'

Belle nodded. 'What did he do?'

'Three IRA men were ambushed by the army when they were going to an arms' dump. The army shot one of the men dead, they arrested the second and the third got away.'

'Fionn?'

Her mother tilted her head to the side. 'The RUC interrogated the man they arrested and beat him so badly that he gave Fionn's name as the third man.'

Belle held her stomach. She had everything so wrong; she had it all so, so terribly wrong. What a stupid cow. Now she knew the truth, the whole thing seemed so obvious. But she'd been so eager to think the worst of Fionn that she'd ignored the obvious.

'Before the RUC could arrest him, the Republican movement got Fionn out of the North and brought him to us. He was to stay here a short while, long enough for them to arrange a permanent place for him in Limerick.'

'That's why...' It made sense now, his plans to go away to Galway with Maeveen. Galway, Limerick, the same thing really; they were places far enough away for him to live without being suspected, if he kept his head down. The room began spinning and with her sick stomach, it was as if she was on an out-of-control fairground waltzer. Belle grabbed the table to keep steady.

'We were to keep him safe, out of sight,' her mother went on, 'until his place in Limerick was ready. But we were careless. We got so used to him being here and everything was going so well, we let our guard down, lost sight of the danger.'

'Why did Daddy get arrested?' Belle said.

'For knowingly harbouring a terrorist. Before you got here, they told him if he didn't cooperate, they'd come back for me.'

Belle whimpered.

'Don't cry, love,' her mother came closer and hugged her. 'It's going to be all right.'

They rocked back and forth in silence as guilty thoughts spread across Belle's mind like mildew.

'The thing I don't get,' her mother said, as she stroked Belle's hair, 'is how they knew about the cubbyhole.'

Belle hugged her mother closer, wishing she could fall deaf and not hear anymore.

'The head soldier told them to look for a hidden door upstairs.' She paused. 'Did you ever tell Hunter about the cubbyhole?'

'Muh... me, I mean, Hunter, what's he got to do with this?'

Her mother pulled back and held Belle's shoulders. 'You heard Maeveen, didn't you? She didn't mean what she said to you, you know, she's just destroyed.'

'I know.'

'Who else could've informed on us? Maeveen left Hunter home and when she was away, Fionn told us what happened at the burn, how the boy nearly drowned. We knew there and then Hunter was going to tell them at home – he's a wee mouth. Once he did, it wasn't going to be hard for Alfie and Joy to put the story together.'

'But Fionn could really have been our cousin, for all they knew.'

'Maybe, but our Protestant neighbours are mistrustful. Since Fionn's been with us, a couple of safe houses were uncovered in Buncrana and a Protestant farmer phoned the Gards on some fishermen who turned out to be a group of IRA men hiding weapons on the Southern side of the Foyle. Any stranger at all raises the alarm. I just know the Campbells. If Hunter told them some man he didn't know was staying with us and we hadn't made any mention of him, that Alfie Campbell wouldn't take five minutes to get over to Sergeant Buckley – and, Jesus, when I think of it now, Buckley was only after leaving before Fionn appeared.'

The grip on Belle's shoulders tightened. Her mother had an angry look in her eyes, but not the kind of angry Belle was used to seeing in Kitty McGee. This was a cold, vengeful anger, the kind where if her mother could get her hands on Hunter, she'd throttle him without raising her pulse.

'Are you sure it was the Campbells, though?' Belle said.

'I'd bet the house on it. Not that we were going to take any chances. As soon as Fionn told us the story, we jumped into action, arranging to get him moved on. We nearly had him away, too, poor Fionn. He was packing his bits and your father was on the phone to our contact in Derry when the Gards and the army arrived. We couldn't believe they'd be that fast, that's what fucked it up.' Her voice began to crack.

Belle wanted to escape. If her mother started to cry, it would be Belle's undoing.

'Aye, they were so fast,' her mother went on, 'and now Fionn's gone and your father... I'm worried about your father. He could get a prison sentence, he likely will... he has that thing with his heart.' Her eyes glazed.

'Please don't cry, Mammy.' The mildew was spreading to every part of Belle's body, contaminating her with guilt. Her father was going to jail, too.

'I'm not going to cry, daughter. I'm too far gone to cry. All I can think of is them Campbells. For as long as I live, they better not cross my path for I won't be responsible for what I'll do.' Her mother banged her fist on the table. 'They better not.'

36

DONEGAL, PRESENT DAY

A crack in the curtains let in a ray of sharp sunlight that blazed a glowing strip right across Belle's face, nearly blinding her. She rolled over on her side as she emerged from sleep and her brain began to kick into action.

Dermot's arrest had only been yesterday and the priority task for today was to go to the Strand Road barracks to try to get a visit with him. Once she did – and she didn't see why she wouldn't – she'd call with Ed Ramsey. He knew something, that was for sure, and she was determined to eke it out of him. She should've paid him a visit before this point, but she'd got caught up in following the leads from Fionn's notes. Now she'd put that right.

Belle sat up in bed. She felt exhausted in spite of a night's sleep and the pressure in her brain pushed at the walls of her skull. Reaching over the side of the bed, she grabbed her bag and rummaged around for the painkillers she always carried with her. She washed two of them down with a drink of water and slid over to the edge of the bed.

She'd needed to make a start on drafting an article for Alma, too. Belle envisaged a series of features, not just one, but that could wait until later, until she talked to Dermot and Ed, tonight.

Her phoned pinged, a text message. She glanced at it. Speak of the devil; it was Alma Travers looking to have a quick chat. Belle groaned. She didn't have the inclination for a chat with Alma, quick or otherwise. She'd ring her later when she had the first draft knocked out. Right now, she had to get going.

The phone buzzed. A call this time. Please not Alma. No, it wasn't Alma, it was Rita Wilson. Belle did have the inclination to talk to her.

'Rita?'

'I need to meet you.' Rita's words came out staccato-like. Something was off.

'Rita? What's wrong?'

'I… it's, I can't, look, I just need to fucking meet you.'

Belle did a double-take. She didn't know Rita hardly at all but she had a fair idea that f-bombing wasn't a major habit.

'Are you at work? I can be with you in two hours.'

'No need, I'm coming to Derry. I'm getting into my car right this minute and-and I'm coming straight there.'

'I'm worried about you driving,' Belle said. 'I hope you don't mind me saying so but you seem… um, distracted.' What Belle actually thought was that she sounded scared – terrified, in fact.

Rita snorted. 'Distracted is one way to put it. Oh God, I don't know what to think. I… I really don't. I did the tests yesterday and the results… I thought I messed them up. There was no other explanation.'

'The tests on the samples I gave you?'

'Do you know exactly where you got them?'

'Of course I do. Rita—'

'We'll have to get more samples, from a wider radius,' Rita rambled, like she was thinking aloud rather than having a conversation. 'It'll be belt and braces stuff, no room for doubt. They'll expect that… but we can give them that, right? Can't we?'

'If you mean—'

249

'I didn't sleep a wink last night,' Rita's voice cracked slightly.

Belle had a sinking, queasy sensation in her stomach.

'The samples were pure, weren't they?' Rita was saying. 'Were they pure?'

'I don't know what you're asking me?'

'You didn't mix them with anything else... you got them on that site you went to, out in the open air. That's what I mean by pure.' Rita sniffed.

'They were exactly what I gathered at the site.'

'Shit, fuck. I ran the tests again, exactly the same, I came in early because I couldn't stand waiting... did you ever want to be wrong? Like, want it so badly you'd rather your reputation was destroyed than be right.'

'N—'

'I wished I could be wrong—'

'Rita, please, calm down. I don't understand what you're talking about.'

'It's the extent of it, that's what we have to ascertain now. How far does it reach? We're all exposed, all in danger.' Rita gasped. 'I mean, we live with it, don't we?' she said.

Belle knew the question was rhetorical. She knew, too, it was pointless trying to converse and she let Rita continue.

'And what I can't understand is where it came from? Whoever put it in the ground, where the hell did they get it from? Oh, I'm sorry, McGee,' Rita said, as if only realising she was talking to somebody else, 'you must think I'm sniffing glue. I sound mad. It's just the shock, you know. But I'm a scientist, a rational being, I have to pull myself together.'

'That's good, Rita, that's good,' Belle said, soothing her like she would a baby. 'It can't be as bad as you think.'

'Of course, yes, I have to see the positive. It might be possible to contain it.'

'That's it, the positives.'

'They came out the other end in the Soviet Union, didn't they, and that was catastrophic, right?'

Belle frowned. *Soviet Union?*

'We're nowhere near that level of calamity.'

'Rita, I'm sort of losing track of where you're going now.'

'The samples, McGee, the water, the soil, all of it,' Rita said, 'what I found was traces of… the samples were radioactive. Do you understand me now?'

The phone slipped from Belle's hand. Yes, she understood at last. Those reckless bastards. They were dumping nuclear waste.

She remembered her encounter with O'Dee and how it had rattled her. And suddenly a wave of realisation washed over her – cold, paralysing. These people were bad people. If they had such disregard for human life as to poison everybody around them, then it wouldn't cost them a thought to murder Fionn. And possibly anyone else who got in the way.

*

Belle and Rita found themselves in a large meeting room in the Strand Road barracks. Rita had just finished telling the police about her devastating findings, only this time, unlike her phone call with Belle, she'd cut to the chase and was calm to the point of being comatose. This was her third telling of the story, too: the first to the duty sergeant at the front desk, the second to an inspector who was alarmed enough to push it up the ranks, and now to the district commander, Superintendent Carruthers.

Carruthers went to speak but nothing came out. His mouth flapped up and down like a fish drowning in air. His subordinates looked equally stunned and the one taking notes was visibly trembling.

'You must be mistaken,' he said, after some effort. 'That's simply not possible.'

'I wish it were so,' Rita said. 'There's a chance that the samples are invalid; perhaps when an investigating team goes out there, they'll collect samples that won't show any uranium.'

'Could that be the case?' Belle asked, clinging to the glimmer of another outcome.

'It's unlikely in the extreme,' Rita eyed her directly, a sober expression on her face, which was now the colour of a bleached stone, 'but you never know.'

'You're very blasé about this, Dr Wilson,' Carruthers said, 'if you don't mind me saying. Is it really as serious as you're telling us?'

'I'm blasé, as you put it, because I took two diazepam before I drove down here. I could fall asleep on that floor at the click of a finger. I didn't know how else to stop becoming hysterical.'

'Okay,' Carruthers looked seasick, 'I've no reason to disbelieve an academic from the university.'

He turned to his subordinates. Belle could see they were all trying to maintain stony indifference but with little success.

'Let's go back a step or two,' Carruthers said, dabbing his forehead with a handkerchief he'd taken from his breast pocket. 'Tell me how you two came to discover these samples in the first place?'

All eyes turned to Belle and Rita, and Rita's eyes turned to Belle. Belle took a deep breath.

'Here's the information you need,' she said.

She slid a buff document wallet across the table towards Carruthers. It contained a copy of her investigation notes.

'This, you can keep.' Inhaling deeply, she began. 'You'll see for yourself, but I've been investigating a highly organised illegal dumping operation involving hundreds of thousands of tonnes of every kind of waste you can imagine. A friend of mine works – worked – for Evergreen Waste. He noticed suspicious behaviour and tipped me off.'

'Who was this friend of yours?' Carruthers asked.

'Fionn – James Power.'

Carruther's eyes widened. 'The recent murder victim?'

'The same. Using his evidence as a starting point, I went about compiling my own. I followed a convoy of lorries one night, in the early hours of the morning to be precise, to one of their many dumpsites and witnessed them, with my own eyes, as they disposed of tonnes of waste. After talking to Rita, I went back to that same site and took samples of soil and water – those were the samples Rita tested. I also talked to a number of people: the manager at Evergreen, an official from the council, the Environmental Agency, Water Service and so on. I can say with certainty that within these structures, key personnel know what's going on, but are covering it up.'

'There's official corruption?' Carruthers said.

'Without a doubt.'

'That's a serious allegation.'

'I know, which is why I wouldn't make it unless I was absolutely sure. One of the people I talked to told me he was closed down, from the top, when he submitted a report showing evidence of illegal dumping. I, myself, was issued with multiple veiled threats. Facts aside, from my extensive experience in investigative journalism, it's always the case that rackets at this scale thrive on systemic corruption. They simply couldn't go on without key officials either being complicit or being threatened to keep quiet.'

Carruthers rubbed his forehead. 'We'll have to scrutinise this,' he tapped on the document wallet, 'and draw our own conclusions—'

'You can scrutinise my test results,' Rita said, 'but unfortunately, you'll find the same outcomes as I did. I'd be willing to swear by them in a court of law.'

'We're not doubting your results, Dr Wilson,' Carruthers said, 'but we have procedures to follow. We must show due diligence.'

Rita pursed her mouth. 'And how long is all that going to take?'

'In this case, not long.'

'In this case, a day's too long,' Rita said. 'We've got nuclear waste seeping into our water. For all we know, it's already reached aquifer level and contaminated every drop we drink. The damage it can do, I can't bear to think about; spent nuclear fuel can be radioactive for thousands, millions, of years. The levels of radioactivity I discovered are too high for it to be the kind of waste from hospitals or general industrial activity. At these levels, it can only be from the nuclear industry.' She started breathing rapidly. 'I might need another diazepam.'

'It's okay, Rita,' Belle said. 'The police'll act quickly, but they have to be certain before they take any action.'

'That's right,' Carruthers said. 'Making a mistake at this stage could have serious consequences at any future trial – it could mean the guilty walk. We don't want to take a risk like that.'

Rita nodded her head vigorously. 'Any help you need from me, you only have to ask. I'll make myself available.'

'Thank you, Dr Wilson.'

'Likewise, anything you need from me, just ask,' Belle said and she meant it. She was able to put aside her prejudices against the police when it came to her job – she did it all the time. 'And the file I've given you there is just the evidence I gathered. If you want to see more, I've got a box file full of Fionn's evidence.'

'We'd like access to that, too,' Carruthers said.

'I'll make sure you get it.'

'The thing I don't understand is where this nuclear waste's coming from,' he said. 'Northern Ireland doesn't have any nuclear plants or operations; the Republic doesn't either.'

'Good point,' Belle said. 'The fact is, the waste's coming from outside Ireland, from Britain and maybe even Europe.'

'But it wouldn't be allowed through our ports.'

'Not knowingly. If the nuclear waste was being comingled

with municipal and industrial waste, which seems to be the case, it would remain concealed. Unless you were specifically looking for it, it could easily get through.'

Carruthers stopped. 'They're concealing it? If they're concealing it, then the people handling it, even the men dumping it illegally, don't realise they're handling deadly materials. Dr Wilson, what do you think?'

'If they're handling the waste frequently,' Rita said, 'without wearing any protection, they're at risk of radiation exposure – not necessarily fatal, but certainly harmful.'

A sickening dread passed over Belle's heart like an ill wind. Rita saw the look on her face and second-guessed what she was thinking.

'The small amount of samples we examined won't affect us.'

Belle tried to smile.

'We're launching an investigation as of now,' Carruthers said.

'I'm relieved to hear that,' Belle said.

'And me,' Rita said.

'Sergeant Graham here will take you back to reception. We'll be in contact if and when we need to talk to you further. And McGee, bring us that box file right away.'

The group stood up and began moving towards the door.

'Would it be possible to get a word with Inspector Fairley?' Belle asked. 'I want to talk to him about Fionn Power.'

'Inspector Fairley? I should think so.' Carruthers turned to the officer taking notes. 'Sergeant Dunn, will you locate Inspector Fairley and tell him that Ms Isabelle McGee would like to speak to him?'

'Yes, sir,' Dunn said.

'She'll be waiting for him at reception,' Carruthers called, as Dunn disappeared out the door. 'And let him know it's in connection with the murder of James Power.'

Carruthers hung back, letting the others go out first. He gave Belle a wry look. 'Do you think there's some connection between the illegal dumping and his murder?'

'I'm convinced of it.'

'Be careful not to draw conclusions where there are none. Just because Mr Power rumbled this operation prior to his death, the argument doesn't necessarily go in the other direction and doesn't prove his death had anything to do with the operation.'

Belle sneered. 'It's a very big coincidence.'

'And not out of the question. You'd be surprised at the coincidences that occur – we're especially careful about that kind of thing. We follow the evidence every time and that usually keeps us right. Do you have evidence?'

'Of course I have evidence,' Belle said, faking self-assurance. She had nothing yet that the police would be happy with, but any fool could join the dots to make a picture.

37

Sergeant Graham brought Belle and Rita as far as reception.

'I've got to wait here, Rita,' Belle said. 'I need to talk to one of the inspectors about another matter that... well, I think is connected with the illegal dumping.'

Rita looked at her with dull eyes. 'Oh sure, go ahead. I'm going home. I think I need to lie down a while.'

'Are you going to be okay driving, you know, with the way you're feeling?'

'I'll be all right, don't worry. I'll drink a vat of coffee before I get in the car.'

They said their goodbyes and Rita left. About ten minutes later, Inspector Fairley appeared.

'McGee, we meet again. You wanted to speak to me?'

'If you have a window.'

'We can go to my office. I've a meeting in twenty minutes so you've got until then.'

'More than enough time. I don't want to be in this place or around you people any longer than necessary.'

If Fairley heard her, he didn't respond and they headed to his office. Once there, he offered Belle a seat before settling himself behind his desk. Straightaway, she noticed her bag sitting on his desk wrapped in plastic.

Fairley noticed her noticing. 'Yes, that's yours,' he said, 'you can take it with you. It's clear so I had them bring it up when I heard you wanted to see me.'

'Thank God for that,' she said, pulling the bag near.

'Now, over to you,' he said, lifting a biro and writing in his notebook.

'Are you aware of what's been uncovered regarding the illegal dumping racket?' she asked.

'Superintendent Carruthers briefly updated me so, yes, I'm aware.'

'I believe it's connected to what happened to Fionn Power.'

'And I assume you're making this connection because he worked for the same company involved in this waste scandal. That's flimsy and we wouldn't take that as proof of a link.'

'Hear me out. I deserve that.'

He sighed and twisted his moustache.

'It was Fionn who discovered the illegal dumping. He had a load of evidence about the location of dumpsites, about secret convoys transporting illicit caches; he had times, dates, vehicles registration plates.'

'Are you saying you were in possession of this evidence and didn't bring it to us immediately?'

'I didn't know it was evidence.'

Fairley raised his eyebrows and gave her that 'as if' look.

'I had to make sure it checked out.'

Fairley tutted. 'Not your place to do so.'

'I think that was a legitimate approach,' Belle said. 'And, anyway, it's not like your lot can be relied on.'

'You have a real problem with the PSNI,' he narrowed his eyes, 'and maybe police in general. Unhealthy, I'd say.'

'I don't have a problem with people doing their job right. I do have a problem with injustice, but I don't want to get into that now.'

Belle noticed Fairley's stony-faced expression. She was hardly going to open his mind about her theories if she kept up this attitude. She made a mental note to hold back on the contemptuous remarks and to get the conversation back on track.

'Look, I apologise,' she said, 'I'm out of order.'

Fairley nodded. 'Going back to the point I was making, you should've reported anything you thought was evidence.'

'Point accepted, but I wanted belt and braces so there was no chance of it being dismissed. Do you realise that several reports of illegal dumping had already been made to the correct authorities – not by me and not to the PSNI, right enough – but to the council, the Environmental Agency. Those reports were buried and in one case, the employee involved was told, in no uncertain terms, to take it no further. The people telling him were at the highest levels of their organisation, even public representatives.'

Fairley twirled again on his moustache. 'The super said something to that effect. Well, at least you finally did the right thing.'

'So, Fionn was being followed,' she continued. 'He was out with Dermot on the night of his murder and they were both followed.'

Belle got another 'as if' look from Fairley. 'By?'

Belle resisted commenting on his scepticism. 'By two men; one of them is this man.' Belle brought up a photo on her phone and handed it to Fairley. 'The one on the left in that photo; he's an Evergreen security man. This photo was taken on one of the times I visited Evergreen.'

Fairley examined the photo. 'Who's the other man here?' He returned the phone.

'Tom Sweet, CEO of Evergreen. But the two security men, Dermot and Fionn saw them that night in a few of the bars. And that wasn't the first time they saw them on a night out.'

'If we lived in a city the size of London,' Fairley said, 'I might be suspicious, but we don't. We live in Derry and you can't go out to get a sandwich for lunch without bumping into somebody you know. Seeing the security men doesn't prove anything. They could've been in the same bar as Fionn and Dermot by pure coincidence.'

'One bar, maybe, but more than one? Fionn and Dermot were in several bars in Waterloo Street and they saw the security men every time. That's too much of a coincidence, even for Derry.'

'Not necessarily,' Fairley said. 'From what I've heard, it's a common occurrence to visit more than one of the bars in Waterloo Street on a given night out.'

Belle pursed her lips. She remembered her first night with Dermot.

Fairley went on. 'Is this your proof? Because it's not proof we could take seriously. Sorry, McGee, you'll need to give me more.'

'They've been following me, too,' she said, 'more than once. They made threats. And they scratched my car and left me an intimidating text. I've got it here.' She began searching her phone. 'Here it is; read it. I got this right after my car was scratched.'

Fairley took the phone and read the text. 'It's a threat but it's from a withheld number, so you can't prove who it's from.'

'You're deliberately dismissing me,' Belle said.

'No, I'm following the logic of what you're telling me. Did you see them damage your car?'

'For God's sake, they're not complete morons – of course I didn't see them.' Belle was struggling to keep her annoyance in check. 'Who else could it be? Who else would vandalise my car?'

'I have no idea. You should formally report that as an incident.'

'Yeah, right.' Belle raised her eyes to heaven.

'You have nothing linking these security men to what happened to your car.'

Belle inhaled and counted to ten. She was getting nowhere, but she had to keep her cool and she had to keep trying. 'What if I could place them at Fionn's on the night of the murder?'

Fairley shot her a glance. 'That might be significant. Can you do that?'

Belle faltered. 'Um, well, not quite yet, but—'

'So the answer's no.' Fairley reached for a folder on his desk. 'I think we're done here.'

'Dermot isn't your man,' Belle said.

Fairley smiled. 'I can tell you want that to be the case, but it simply isn't. Maybe it's time for me to enlighten you. I can share some facts with you now that I couldn't when we arrested him. What I'm going to tell you is being released to the press today, anyway.' Fairly looked her squarely in the eye. 'We have strong physical evidence tying him to this murder. There's CCTV footage putting him in the vicinity at the crucial time. That made him a person of interest from the beginning. But our forensics team also found his fingerprints in several places in Mr Power's flat, most significantly on the lager cans in the living room. And his fingerprints were on a carrier bag we found lying in the blood.'

Belle guessed it was the bag of cigarettes and the teacakes Dermot had bought in the shop.

Fairley continued, 'We know the two men were in each other's company earlier in the evening in some of the town centre bars, and that they were both in the flat drinking later in the night. Eyewitnesses can verify all of these movements.'

'Who's the eyewitness for the flat?'

'Come on, you know better than to ask me that.'

She did, too. Though it didn't matter if he told her for she had her own suspicions about who that particular eyewitness might be; in fact, she was nearly certain.

'None of that proves Dermot's guilty,' she said, 'only that he was with Fionn.'

'Correct, however – and this is probably the most conclusive evidence – we also found boot prints in the pool of blood beside Mr Power's body. We've verified that they match boots belonging to Mr McDermott, boots that have since been tested and found to have Mr Power's blood on them.'

Belle gasped like she'd been winded with a kick to the gut. That certainly fucked it. Dermot looked guilty as hell. 'It still doesn't mean he's guilty,' she said, feebly.

'Another set of prints were found,' Fairley said, giving his moustache a satisfied twist. 'Shoe prints, but we've yet to identify whose.'

'I hope you're going to keep looking for the owner of those prints. What I mean is, I hope you're not going to stop now because you've got your number one suspect. You know, the way you people nearly always do.'

'McGee, we're going to conduct this investigation to the highest standards and I take exception to any suggestion to the contrary.'

'I don't have much faith in your standards,' she said. Now that it was clear he wasn't taking what she said seriously, Belle was less careful about being diplomatic.

'Another thing you might be interested to know,' he went on, 'is that we've identified what we think was the murder weapon.'

The blood drained from Belle's face.

'Based on the injuries sustained by Mr Power, it was a ball-peen hammer.'

'Jesus. Fionn was beaten to death with a hammer.' Her hand went to her mouth. Her Greek god… she held back tears, refusing to cry in front of Fairley. 'Dermot never could've done that.'

'Have you any idea how many times Mr McDermott's been in this station for questioning? How many times he's been arrested? Convicted? We have his fingerprints on record, which is why we were able to match the prints we found in the flat. His rap sheet's longer than Santa's list. Granted, he's been quiet for about twenty years, but there was a time he was a regular visitor to us… and the courts. Some of our older officers still remember him.'

Belle tightened her fist. 'Never for anything criminal, always political. And besides, what he's done in the past can't be compared to this.'

'All the same.' Fairley had the slightest smirk on his lips, barely visible underneath his moustache.

He checked his watch, a signal the meeting was drawing to a close.

'You're so wrong about him,' she said, 'but you don't give a shit as long as you get your arrest. I want to see him. Today. Can you arrange that?'

'In spite of your less than courteous manner, McGee, I will indeed arrange that. We're holding him here while we wait to charge him. After that, he'll be remanded in Magilligan.'

Magilligan was a prison just a few miles away. 'You're definitely going to charge him then.'

'Absolutely. I shouldn't have to tell you that most murders are committed by someone the victim knows. They're less likely to be the random act of a stranger. And in this case, for us not to recognise it was Mr McDermott would require a serious suspension of incredulity. We'd be expected to believe that Mr McDermott and Mr Power were together all night, that Mr McDermott left the flat for a short time – he went out to buy cigarettes and the CCTV footage confirms that – and during that brief period of time, someone else entered the flat, murdered Mr Power and disappeared without trace. Does that sound likely?'

'It's possible, and maybe more likely than Dermott beating his cousin and lifelong friend to death with a hammer.'

'You'd think, wouldn't you? But it's not uncommon. After drinking, people can carry out any manner of uncharacteristic and unexpected acts. We've seen it all.'

'Jesus Christ, but that's what you think this is?' Belle said. Her frustration wanted to erupt, like a kettle on the verge of boiling point. 'A drunken row got out of hand?'

'Not what you want to hear, I know.'

'It's not what I want to hear,' she said, 'nor is it true.'

And she was going to prove it. She certainly wasn't going to stand back like a helpless victim. She'd done that once, when she

263

was young and powerless and didn't understand the world. She'd done that once, but never again.

Fairley stood up. 'I'll have one of the constables take you to see Mr McDermott.'

Belle stood, too, feeling strengthened by her resolve.

'By the way, McGee, we're now aware of your connection with Mr Power. Seemed to slip your mind yesterday when we arrested Mr McDermott.'

Belle saw the smirk dance across his mouth again. So, he thought what happened in 1986 was amusing. Bile rose from her stomach and she came close to spitting on him.

'It didn't slip my mind,' she said, with restraint. 'I just didn't bother to tell you because I knew you nosey so-and-sos would make the connection all by yourselves.'

The smirk dropped off Fairley's face. She'd finally managed to touch a nerve, if only a little one and if only for a second.

38

Dermot faced her from the other side of a beaten-out wooden table. The interview room was impossibly stuffy and stank like the inside of a crowded bus on a rainy day. A constable stood to attention by the door.

'You have five minutes,' the constable said.

'How've you been keeping?' Belle asked Dermot.

'All the better for seeing you,' he said. He managed a smile though his eyes told a different story.

'You look tired,' she said.

'Didn't sleep a wink last night. They're going to charge me. The peelers matched my boots with the footprints in the blood. They have me on CCTV – must've been when I went to the shop for the cigs. And that Ed Ramsey, rat bastard, he's their eyewitness. I'm totally fucked.'

So it was Ramsey, as she suspected. 'You are not,' Belle said, sternly, 'and don't even entertain that notion. We know you're innocent and we're going to prove it.'

'You can see now why I didn't fess up to being in the flat that night.' He looked down at his hands.

'Yeah, but I think you made yourself look guilty.'

'Shit, no point crying over that spilled milk now.' Dermot sighed like he was carrying the weight of the world and her mother. 'I'm being sent to Magilligan.'

'I heard.'

'Not a good sign.'

'Have you got a solicitor?'

'Aye, he's shite. I met him this morning. His starting point is: I'm guilty. He was talking about a manslaughter plea and cooperating with the court to get the lowest possible sentence. I'd sack the ballbag only he's the best I'm going to get on legal aid.'

'Piss on that,' Belle said, 'I'm not having you represented by a second-rater. I can get you hooked up with somebody better. I've got loads of contacts.'

'But—'

'And don't worry about the cost, we'll sort something out. Right now, the focus is on getting you off.' Belle slid her hands across the table and took his hands.

Dermot squeezed tight. 'I wouldn't know what I'd do without you.'

'I've got your back.'

'You said we were going to prove my innocence. What's your plan? 'Cos I don't have one.'

'Well, there's been a big breakthrough in the illegal dumping thing. I'm just after making a formal report so it's being investigated as we speak.'

The blue in Dermot's eyes came alive. 'That's fucking brilliant, I mean it.'

'I talked to Fairley about the connection between the dumping and Fionn's murder, and how you'd seen Beavis and Butthead that night.'

'And what did he say?'

Belle couldn't hold eye contact.

'They're not buying it.' Dermot guessed right.

'Not yet, but we must stay positive. The police have hardly started investigating and I'm convinced somebody's going to get spooked or want to save their own skin and they'll let the truth slip. I've seen it before.'

Dermot didn't look hopeful.

'There's also Ed,' Belle said. 'He knows something, though he doesn't know he knows.'

'Aw, he's a dead loss. Don't you think he's done enough harm?'

'He said he saw two heavies that night, not just you. I'm going to pay him another visit; see if I can get his addled brain to identify one of those heavies.'

'I don't see that being enough to take the peelers off my scent.'

'It will, when they take into consideration that Fionn was going to expose the illegal dumping.'

'Time's up, Ms McGee,' the constable said.

Belle nodded. 'Be with you now.' She turned back to Dermot. 'There's another thing you might not know. The cops found shoe prints in the flat and they don't know who made them. I'm guessing they'll match either Beavis or Butthead. If that's the case, it's going to really put them in the frame.'

Dermot straightened in his seat. He looked alert; he even smiled. 'Jesus, McGee, that could be the ticket.'

'I know. You could be out of here in a few days.'

She stood up to go. 'Look, Dermot,' she said, 'I want to give you a heads-up. I'll probably be heading back to Dublin soon.'

He shot her a wounded glance. 'You've cracked the dumping racket and you have your story,' Dermot said, a tremble in his voice. 'I suppose there's nothing else to hang about for.'

'I never made promises that I was going to live here permanently. Surely you always knew I'd be leaving at some stage. But I'm not going anywhere until I get you out of here, I promise you that.'

'Me and you,' he said, 'we could've had something.'

A lump stuck in her throat.

'Maybe we can still have something,' he said, 'once I get out. I could visit you in Dublin; you could come up to visit me.'

'It'd be hard to make it work.'

'We'd figure it out.'

Tears trickled onto Belle's cheeks. 'Relationships and me, they don't mix very well.'

'I don't exactly have the best track record either, but it doesn't mean we can't get it right once in our lives. We have a spark, us, something different. Tell me you feel it, too?'

'I do.'

She wasn't pretending, wasn't blowing smoke up his ass to keep his spirits high. She meant it. From the first time she saw him, from their first night together, she was drawn to him, she wanted him. Being with him made up for never getting the chance to be with Fionn. And yet, Dermot was more than that. He had a way of being that all on his own and she found herself attracted to him for his own sake, nothing to do with Fionn.

She could love him; she could let him in. She didn't have to keep him at arm's length or shut off her feelings. Just because she'd always done it that way with Shane and a whole string of others like him didn't mean she couldn't change. It was possible she could be happy with Dermot.

Her heart swelled with the joyous possibilities of what could be. And then her heart dropped, like a child in the water, swimming along until they realise the adult isn't holding them up any longer.

Who was she kidding? She could never be with Dermot. She didn't deserve to be with him. If he knew the truth, he wouldn't want anything to do with her. And he'd be right to.

Belle could see his mouth moving as he talked to her from across the table, but she couldn't hear a word. She couldn't dare let herself.

'I'll get you out of here,' she said, going towards the door.

Dermot got up to follow her.

The constable put his hand up. 'Stay seated, Mr McDermott.'

'Don't forget me, McGee.'

'I won't,' she called as she left, not able to look back.

*

'I'm floored,' Alma Travers was on the other end of the phone.

She wasn't a woman who was often floored. Belle had phoned her after coming out of the police barracks and had just finished updating her on the investigation.

'Nuclear waste,' Alma said. 'It's… it's insane.'

'I know,' Belle said, 'I haven't properly processed it yet.'

'What kind of people would do that?'

'That's capitalism for you. When the rest of us see disaster and misery, they see pound signs.'

'How're you planning to run with this one?' Belle asked. 'An overview of the headline issues in the first one, followed by a few detailed pieces that would include progress on the criminal case. I want to promote this as not just a corruption piece but as an environmental scandal as well. I want people to be outraged.'

'Sounds good, I'll clear all the space you need. When can you have the first piece ready?'

'I've already written up rough notes so I reckon I can have a draft ready for tomorrow. But I'll sync with the police so I don't jeopardise anything they're doing.'

'Goes without saying.'

'I'll be coming back to Dublin soon, too – maybe in the next day or two.' Dublin, where her life was waiting for her. Her life. The one where her favourite pastimes were binge drinking at the weekends and avoiding meaningful relationships with the opposite sex. She shouldn't forget her awards, of course. They made a fantastic mantelpiece display, though they were lousy company.

'Looking forward to having you back,' Alma said. 'You'll make it for Carrie's birthday bash.'

'Next weekend, right? Yeah, reckon I will.'

Belle ended the call just as she reached Fionn's apartment block. No time like the present to have that chat with Ed. The outside door was open and in she went. She climbed the stairs and walked along the gloomy corridor until she got to number thirty-six. Before she knocked, she straightened herself, mentally preparing for what she was going to say.

She rapped on the door and waited. Inside was silent. No wild barking from Spanner or angry muttering and shuffling from Ed. She knocked again. Still nothing. Fuck it, he wasn't in. And God knows where he was. She contemplated waiting for him but thought against it. Best to get home and make a start on her article. She could come back tomorrow.

Belle walked to where her car was parked, her head down, deep in thought. She felt good about the investigation. She'd accepted the baton from Fionn and had run with it to the finish line. Fionn would've been so proud.

A tiny flame of anger ignited deep inside her. Fionn shouldn't be dead – worse still, dead at the hands of those contemptible fuckers. Her job here wouldn't be done until she found the final piece of evidence that would link them to his murder and free Dermot.

If she did that, it might, just might, make up for not putting things right when Fionn was alive. And it might, just might, help rid her of the guilt that she carried with her everywhere. The thing was she didn't just owe Fionn. She had to make things right with a couple of other people, too.

Belle arrived at the car and stopped. She took a deep breath. The hardest part was yet to come.

39

DONEGAL, 1986

Belle didn't have the words to describe how she felt during those weeks and months after the arrests. Sure, she knew she was sad and scared and stunned and full of guilt, but she didn't have the words to say out loud how deeply, how completely, those feelings had become part of every minute of every day. There was no getting away from them, no more than she could get away from her own skin. How could she properly explain that to anyone so they'd understand when she could barely understand it herself?

Her mother went into meltdown. Not in a noticeable way, though. On the surface, when it came to functioning and getting things done, she was a sergeant major, running the house like a military camp, following the usual routines of mealtimes and chores, making sure Belle went to school, visiting their father when possible, managing the farm. She was remarkable. Everybody said so, relatives and friends who came to visit and lend help and support; all had a comment to make about how strong Kitty was and how well she was coping.

The problem was, none of those people had to live with her and none of them saw what she was like when it was just her and her children in the house. Belle's mother had pulled down the shutters to her heart, so much so that for Belle it was like she'd lost two parents, not just one. She wasn't gone like Belle's father, but she wasn't really there either. Was it too harsh to say she didn't show her and Maeveen any love? She loved them – Belle was never in any doubt about that – but she didn't show it anymore. Belle felt no kindness from her. Sure, she didn't show any cruelty or neglect, but she didn't hug them, didn't chit-chat over meals, didn't give a word of encouragement, didn't inquire about school.

Maybe all her energy was going into keeping things afloat and she had nothing left to give the girls. Or maybe she deliberately closed herself off because otherwise life would get too painful.

Belle didn't know what the truth of it was and, at some level, she was glad her mother was the way she was. Better that she was a zombie than somebody who wanted to talk about her feelings and wanted her daughters to do the same. Because for Belle, she'd sort of closed down, too, and the last thing she wanted was to talk about her feelings. She crawled into herself, hiding from the world around her, and her mother didn't take a blind bit of notice.

As time moved on, Belle became more and more disconnected from her mother and sister, more isolated in her confused understanding of events. And she wasn't hurt by that. Far from it. She decided she very much deserved it that way. After how she'd behaved, she was getting her just deserts.

Maeveen was a different story. If Belle and her mother were blank pages on the outside, Maeveen was a novel from one of the Romantic writers that Belle learned about at school, thrown wide open, busting with outpourings of high drama, tragedy, pain and suffering.

She made the decision to postpone her university studies for a year and stay at home. She held onto her part-time job and spent all her money and time on her newfound hobby: drinking alcohol. When she wasn't working, she was either sleeping off a hangover or getting ready to go out to find herself another hangover. No one stopped her, not even when Uncle Paddy came round with the story that his sons had found Maeveen four sheets to the wind lying in the street in Buncrana outside a dance hall – he still couldn't get his head round the fact that it was discos young people went to now and not dances. Again, their mother didn't take a blind bit of notice of that shocking news either.

The next September, Maeveen went to UCG. By Easter, Auntie Siobhan was able to tell them that she was living in Derry and had been kicked out of her course. Belle's mother had no reaction other than to say, "At least she's still alive". It wouldn't be until years later, when Maeveen was in her late twenties, after she'd lived a drink-fuelled existence in London, Dublin and a remote island off the Scottish coast, that the prodigal would return, her young life and its potential pretty much squandered.

By then, Belle had already left home and embarked on her own independent life in Dublin, coming home religiously for a week in the summer and a few days every Christmas – making sure to be back in Dublin for New Year's Eve. She accepted the arrangement for what it was. It was a form of exile, in reality, self-imposed for sure, but still an exile that denied her the comfort and love of her family's company.

*

Even in the middle of all the awfulness that her broken family endured, some days were worse than others and some moments stood out as particularly dark. For Belle, one of those moments was the altercation with Hunter and his father, Alfie. If she could've removed herself from the face of the earth that day, she would gladly have done so.

Hunter called round to visit; it was early September, just weeks after the arrests. Belle was upstairs in her room, reading

273

and listening to records when she heard the shouts. Maeveen was screaming swear words and abuse; their mother was shouting at her to be quiet.

Belle ran down to the kitchen to discover Hunter Campbell at the back door, a frozen stupid look on his face, and her mother holding Maeveen, who was trying to claw at him. "Go," her mother was saying, "leave our house and never come back." Tears sprayed from Maeveen's face as she screamed, "You've some nerve coming to this door, you treacherous wee bastard". Belle met Hunter's gaze for less than a second before he turned on his heels. In his eyes, she saw confusion, a lot of confusion, and a bit of fear. "I'm sorry" he said, running off.

Later that night, when the sisters were in bed, a knocking at the door woke Belle. Her mother was still up and Belle heard her answer. She went to the landing to hear what was being said. It was Alfie Campbell. In a calm but distressed tone, he told Kitty McGee he was disappointed at the way they'd treated Hunter and he wanted to know why.

Belle's mother didn't waste any time in telling him why: the Campbells had betrayed the McGees. Alfie insisted he didn't know what she was talking about but Belle's mother was having none of it. Alfie raised his voice, his distress growing, and said, "If I'd known you were keeping a murdering terrorist here, I'd have informed on you in a second. But I didn't know and nor did anybody in my house." Belle's mother didn't relent. "This is a shocking, uncalled-for display," Alfie said and he left, though not before vowing never again to step foot inside their door.

Of course, there were more dark moments, far more traumatic: the fate of her father and of Fionn. Fionn was extradited to the North and his trial was heard close to two years later. He was given a devastating sentence of twenty-five years in the H-Blocks – the prison where most Republicans were sent, where the Dirty Protest had happened, where ten men had died on hunger strike. He would end up serving fourteen years before his release under the Good Friday Agreement.

Belle's father remained in the Southern judicial system as that's where his 'crime' took place. Just over a year from his arrest, Michael McGee was sentenced to five years and went to Portlaoise Prison near Dublin. The time he spent on remand was taken into consideration, so they were told he'd get out in four years, maybe less.

Belle cried for a solid week after his sentencing. The idea that her father was to be locked up for four years was unbearable. Every day she cried until she had no tears left, and every day her mother pretended not to hear. She went about her business and only took notice of Belle when she called her for meals. Eventually, she told Belle she'd have to pull herself together and get back to school. Maeveen was in Galway at that point, going off the rails most likely. Belle never knew how her sister felt about their father's fate because they never talked about it.

Each month, without fail, their mother made the trip to Portlaoise for her visit. Sometimes Belle would go with her, sometimes her mother would go alone. The visits were glum, depressing affairs and often his health wasn't the best. As time went on, the visits got steadily worse and after a while Belle noticed that hardly a word passed between her parents. They seemed to crawl into themselves, neither of them able to say what they were feeling, both beyond putting on a brave face. Belle could see the toll the visits were taking on her mother. It was as though a little bit of her died and was left in the prison, visit after visit. Of course, the worst hadn't happened yet.

*

Belle was lazing in the armchair beside the range, reading and daydreaming, her mother stirring a pot of stew, when the phone rang. The shrill 'Brrring!' was loud and jarring and unexpected.

275

'Who the hell's that?' her mother said. 'Every damned time when I'm in the middle of something. Will you get it, Belle?'

Three years had now passed since the arrests and time hadn't softened Kitty McGee's attitude. If anything, Belle thought she was harder and colder and more distant.

Belle went out to the hall where the phone had its own little table. She lifted the receiver, silencing the intrusive ringing.

'Hello,' she said.

'Hello, this is Portlaoise Prison,' a strong Southern accent came over the line. 'Can I speak to Mrs Kathleen McGee?'

Belle pursed her lips. It was unusual for the prison to ring. In fact, she couldn't remember them ever doing so before. 'Hold on, I'll get her.'

She went back to the kitchen. 'Mammy, it's the prison... they're looking for you.'

The wooden spoon dropped from her mother's hand into the stew. She tried to keep stony-faced but Belle saw a flicker of worry in her eyes. She rushed out to the hall. Belle stood in the jar of the door, close enough to hear what her mother said, far enough so her mother wouldn't notice her ear-wigging.

'Kathleen McGee speaking.'

Her mother listened as the voice on the other end of the phone talked. Belle thought it sounded like the phone voice in a cartoon, squeaky and miniature and speedy. The voice stopped.

'I don't understand,' Belle's mother said. 'He's only served three years and—'

More squeaking.

'You must be wrong, I... I... it doesn't make sense. He would've told me.'

More squeaking.

'You're right it's come as a shock. What's going on in that place? Aren't you supposed to be keeping an eye on them, making sure they're okay?'

276

More squeaking. Belle could see her mother's hand shaking, her whole body was shaking, and she was leaning so hard on the telephone table that the knuckles on her free hand were white. A slow, sickly wave undulated in Belle's stomach.

'I can be there tomorrow,' her mother said. 'I'll leave here first thing. But let me tell you this, you are very mistaken.'

Her mother returned the receiver to its home and walked past Belle into the kitchen as though she didn't see her.

'What did they say, Mammy?'

Her mother stirred the stew.

'Mammy?' Belle's voice cracked.

For the first time since the arrests, her mother finally broke. The tears came with intensity so violent, it frightened Belle. Her mother took a step back. She slid to the floor, the wooden spoon in her hand and dripping with thick drops of stew that plopped onto her blouse. She cried in choking whoops, almost suffocating with the force of her grief, her entire body going up and down in rhythm with every wail.

'Yuh… your father,' she sobbed, the wooden spoon lolling on her lap. 'H… he's coming home.'

'For good?' Belle was confused. This was the best news ever and yet her mother was broken on the floor.

'Aye, for good.'

'But why're you crying? I don't—'

'He's coming home to die, my love. He's coming home to die.'

*

Three days later, Michael McGee was home. Belle's parents' bedroom became his hospital room, her mother became his nurse. She tended him hand and foot, from morning 'til night. The doctor visited every week, hospice nurses came round every day. The house took on the smell of a hospital and the usual aromas of meals being cooked, a bunch of flowers in the hall, the fresh outdoors coming in through an open window, just-washed laundry, a whiff of perfume, all of them were gone. In their place was the clinical smell of the handwash the nurses used and the very particular stench of disease and death – not quite something rotted, but something that was about to rot.

For the next two months, Belle felt she was living an endless funeral. There was no hope for her father, so all they were doing was making him comfortable until he passed. That's what Belle overheard the hospice nurses telling her mother, 'We'll make him comfortable, Kitty. He won't be in any distress.' Belle also overheard her mother on the phone talking about what was wrong with him. She had no one to ask and no one bothered to tell her, so overhearing was her only means of finding out.

'I knew he wasn't keeping well,' her mother was saying on the phone to Auntie Maria. 'For the last four or five visits, he had a cough or a flu and he didn't seem to be shaking it.' Her mother's voice faltered. 'I kept on at him to get it seen to and he swore blind he was grand and the prison doctor was looking after him.'

Belle leaned her head on the banister at the top of the stairs and silently listened to the unfolding horror.

'They couldn't have been looking after him at all. No able-bodied man should die from pneumonia these days, not if things are taken care of. They neglected him, Maria, I know it. They neglected him for so long he went past the point of being able to recover. He's so weak now, he can't fight back. I thought if anything was going to give him trouble, it would've been his heart, but this...' Her mother sobbed softly. 'I hate them. I can't wish them enough bad luck.'

She went quiet for a minute – Auntie Maria was probably saying something – before starting again. 'Do you know what one of them screws said to me when I went to Portlaoise to bring him home? He said if he'd hadn't been a terrorist, this never would've happened.' A deep sigh drifted all the way to the top of the stairs like rising smoke. 'I'll be making a formal complaint about that, once I get the time. I'll make a formal complaint. I'm not letting them call him a terrorist or what he did terrorism, for it's fucking not.'

Maeveen, still living in Derry and getting by on a part-time job as a shop assistant, spent Sundays to Tuesdays at home and Wednesdays to Saturdays in Derry. She was a terrible nuisance to have around. She was so upset most of the time and would burst out crying at the mere mention of her father's name, or at the sight of her mother taking him his medication, or at the sound of the nurses coming in the door, at pretty much everything. 'I hate to leave you,' she'd say each time she returned to Derry, 'and not stay to help.' Their mother always replied, 'Best to keep your job – keep your mind occupied with things outside of this house.' Maeveen would nod and say, 'You're right, Daddy would want that.' Then she'd go. And every time their mother would come back from dropping her at the bus stop, she'd sit down at the table with a cup of tea and say, 'Thank Christ she's gone for another while.' Their mother couldn't cope with Maeveen and all her manic behaviour, on top of looking after their father.

Then one night, Belle woke up in a sweat and a panic. As she sat up in bed, disorientated, she saw him. Her grandfather. He was standing at the end of her bed, a smile on his gentle face, looking in her direction but not looking at her.

Belle's skin turned cold like she'd been dropped naked into a pool of icy water and she was filled with the most pressing sense of terror. Not because of this vision of her grandfather, but because she knew – as sure as she knew one and one made two – why he was there.

And then a scream shattered the delicate hush. Her mother.

Belle leapt out of bed, thanking God it was one of Maeveen's Derry nights. She ran onto the landing, past the forsaken cubbyhole and straight to her parents' room, the weight of what she knew pressing on her shoulders like a twenty-stone gorilla. She might be wrong, but she knew she wasn't. She knew.

Belle stepped across the threshold, feeling the change in texture under her feet from the hard wood of the landing floor to the spongy carpet of her parents' room. She'd run across this same threshold a thousand times, on Christmas mornings, on birthdays, breakfast in bed on Mother's Day, hide 'n' seek, putting away ironed clothes, and one time when she was very young and her father broke his leg and was laid up for a week and his daughters sat with him for hours, reading him stories, playing board games and drawing across every inch of his plaster cast.

All that happiness was in the past; it had no place in her home anymore.

Belle knew.

Her mother was draped over the bed, wailing her heart to breaking.

Belle knew.

He was gone. He was really gone.

She stopped by the door, surveying the scene before her eyes.

Father.

Mother.

Him, dead.

Her, destroyed.

And life would never be the same again.

40

DERRY, PRESENT DAY

Belle's body bristled with nervous energy. She was at the Evergreen facility. Carruthers had contacted her early that morning to let her know they had search warrants. The car park was never so busy. Belle counted eleven or twelve land rovers, six patrol cars and a few strange looking vans that she identified as forensics. Teams of police, nearly all of them dressed in the white coverall suits so familiar at crime scenes, moved around silently, quickly, with purpose.

'Ah, there you are, McGee,' Superintendent Carruthers said. 'Now, stay back out of the way and don't make me regret telling you we were going to be here today.'

Belle joined him beside an unmarked car with tinted windows. Nearby was a police constable, standing to attention and staring straight ahead.

'I'll be good,' she said and meant it. 'I appreciate the tip-off.'

'I thought it was deserved. The evidence you presented to us yesterday, about the site with the nuclear waste, checked out. We've since assigned a forensic team to the case and they'll be responsible for collecting and examining evidence at every site. We also followed in your footsteps last night and tailed lorries leaving Evergreen and going to a dumpsite. We arrested them as soon as they reached the site and started unloading.'

'But they're only the lackeys, doing what they're told to get a few extra quid. Why haven't you arrested—'

'Steady on. We're conducting a methodical investigation and we must act based on the evidence. We've brought in Tom Sweet and the directors of the Evergreen board for questioning.'

'It's a start, I suppose,' Belle said, struggling to curb her impatience. 'What about the rest of them? Like Councillor O'Dee. The manager in the Environmental Agency. The—'

'McGee, step at a time, methodical investigation, remember? We'll follow the evidence whoever that takes us to. Here's something you'll find interesting: a lot of the dumpsites are owned by three of the directors. One of them is a cousin of a senior council official and another one is the brother of Councillor O'Dee.'

'I knew it.'

'These links are helping us build a picture of the network that's operating here.'

'What about the security men?'

Carruthers' brow knitted. 'What about them?'

'They're aiding and abetting, aren't they, and they're involved in the murder of Fionn Power. Do you realise that?'

'What I realise is that you've been making those allegations – Inspector Fairley filled me in – but we haven't found evidence to connect the security men to Mr Power's death or even evidence connecting them to the illegal dumping.'

'And what about evidence connecting Fionn's death to the illegal dumping, for they are connected?'

Carruthers shook his head.

'I suppose I'm just going to have to get the evidence for that, too,' Belle said.

A crackling, buzzing noise interrupted their conversation and a garbled voice came over the two-way radio attached to the constable's uniform. He pressed a button and answered, before speaking to Carruthers.

'Sir,' he said, opening the back door of the car, 'they're looking for you at the Strand Road.'

Carruthers nodded. 'I have to go, McGee, and unfortunately, so will you. You're only on site because of me and I don't want you around when I'm not here to keep you in check.'

'That's okay, I'm happy enough with what you gave me.'

'Get Mulvanna for me,' Carruthers said to his constable, who hurried off in the direction of one of the men in the white coverall suits.

Soon he was back with a man in tow that Belle assumed was Mulvanna. Carruthers took Mulvanna aside and said a few words that had Mulvanna nodding his head before walking away. Carruthers returned to the car.

'Before you go,' Belle said, 'I wanted to ask when I can publish my feature?'

'We're going public Monday morning at ten so if you have your piece ready you can put it out a minute past ten if you like. It won't compromise us and you'll be guaranteed the scoop.' Carruthers got into the car.

'Very good of you.'

'As I said, it's deserved. Now, get in the back seat and let me take you to your car.'

'It's only parked outside the gates.'

'It's not the distance that has me worried.'

'Come on, I'm going to leave, trust me.'

'I'll trust you when I see you driving away, now get in. And in case you get any bright ideas about sneaking in when I'm gone, Mulvanna is my lead investigator and I warned him to keep you out.'

283

Belle shrugged and did as he instructed. In a few minutes, she was driving away from the Evergreen site, conscious it was under the watchful eye of Carruthers following in the car behind.

*

Buoyed by her meeting with Carruthers, Belle wanted to share the good news. Martin Higgins, she was certain, would appreciate knowing, and Chrissie Power should hear about it too. Granted, it was going to be in the news in a couple of days anyway, but Belle thought it was important they hear it from her first.

As Belle drove in the direction of the dumpsite she'd visited with Dermot, she pulled up Chrissie's number on Bluetooth. After a few rings, she got an answer.

'Hello?' Chrissie sounded tired, sluggish.

'Chrissie? It's Belle McGee.'

'Aw, Belle, love, what's the craic?'

'I'm grand, what about you? How have you been holding up?'

'Grand, doing me best, you know.'

'Me and Maeveen were at the funeral but I'm sorry we didn't get a chance to speak to you.'

'Don't worry about that; I wouldn't have remembered anyway. I was out of it. You should get a run over someday soon – Maeveen, too. I'd love to see the both of you.'

'We'll definitely do that, Chrissie, soon.' Knowing what was ahead, Belle made a promise she knew she couldn't keep. Easier to do that than tell the truth.

'And did you hear they arrested Dermot?' Chrissie said. 'Are they fucking mad? My cousin Dermot's supposed to have killed Fionn? No way. They're clueless.'

'It's totally ridiculous,' Belle said. 'Though I think I might know how to help – which sort of connects with what I'm ringing you about.

'Aye?'

'Fionn's box file, the one I picked up from your house. Fionn found out that the people he worked for were involved in a highly illegal racket. His file had evidence, lots of it. He planned to come to me and have me blow the whole thing open.'

'Jesus, I... I... that's mad. God, I don't know what to say.'

'I took his evidence to the police and they've launched an investigation. You're going to hear about it in the news on Monday.'

'All because of Fionn?'

'All because of Fionn.'

Chrissie began to cry. 'I'm so proud of him.'

'So you should be. I'm going to write a whole series of articles on this scandal and I'll make sure Fionn gets the credit he deserves.'

'He'd be happy about that. Thanks for telling me, Belle.'

'It's the least I can do. I'll be in touch.'

The call ended and Belle continued driving until she got to the Higgins' house. She parked near the gate, in tight to the ditch, and got out. She walked to the entrance and rang the bell. A woman opened the door. She was in her thirties, Belle guessed, maybe the mother of Seanie. Her entire appearance was dishevelled, her face lifeless, her eyes saturated with sadness.

'Can I help you?' the woman said.

'I'm sorry to bother you. I was wondering if I could speak to Martin, if he's in.'

'Martin? I'll get him.'

The woman disappeared and, seconds later, Martin came out, looking slightly bemused.

'I don't think you remember me,' Belle started, 'I'm Belle McGee. I'm a reporter. We met not long ago out at the road there and we talked about the goings-on up at that old quarry.'

Recognition flashed across Martin's face. 'Got ye now.'

She quickly told him what she'd told Chrissie. He nodded his head slowly, the way a wise old man contemplating the woes of the world might do.

'That's good to hear, aye, good to hear.'

Belle was slightly disappointed in his reaction. She'd expected him to be happy, relieved, vindicated, something, anything but this. Silence fell between them as Belle waited for him to say more.

'Well, I thought you'd like to know,' she said, saving herself any further embarrassment. She turned to leave. 'Oh, I meant to ask, how's Seanie doing?'

Martin lifted his head and when he did, Belle stepped back in shock. The look in his eyes was so tortured she knew the image of them would haunt her for the rest of her life. His mouth opened but it was a while before any words came forth.

'He's gone,' Martin said, as though the words had crushed his heart on their way out.

The lump in Belle's throat left her speechless. She looked away, finding it too painful to see him.

'I'm sorry,' she rasped, stepping away from him, from the horror of his world. 'I'm so sorry.'

41

Belle made the return journey to Derry, her heart sick with remembering the little boy whose life had ended before it had properly started. Reaching the city limits, she forced herself to think about her next task: to get a positive ID from Ed Ramsey, no matter what. She parked a street away from Fionn's apartment block and, getting out of the car, breathed in deeply as though it was a prayer.

Two rat-tats on the door of Ed Ramsey's flat had Spanner barking like he was losing his little doggy mind.

'Away now,' Ed scolded, his voice muffled behind the door. 'What've I told you about making a racket.'

The dog carried on oblivious and then Belle heard a scuffle, a yelp and an interior door close with a loud bang.

'You stay in there 'til you learn some manners.'

The door opened a crack and the flat breathed out the same hot sickly air as before. Ed peered through the space.

'Hi, Ed,' Belle put on her best smile and cheery voice, 'remember me?'

His eyes narrowed into tiny slits behind his glasses. 'Um, you're McGee, the journalist from the big-time paper in Dublin. You're doing a story on Fionn Power.'

'That's me,' she was surprised he had the details still in his head.

'Where is it?'

'What?'

'Where's the story, then? I've been checking your paper every day; I've been going down to the library especially. Haven't seen a thing written by you, definitely not any story about what happened here.'

This guy didn't miss a trick. Belle thought on her feet.

'Quite right,' she said, 'it's all written and ready to go, only my editor's been sitting on it. You know what bosses are like. But it should be out within the next week.'

'What's his problem?'

'Who?'

'Your editor. Why won't he print it?'

Belle felt a throb at the base of her neck. Talking to Ed was a struggle. 'Oh, no, my editor is a woman and there's no problem at all, just the norm for the newspaper world.'

He stayed quiet for a while, his face in suspended animation. He must be deciding what to make of it, Belle guessed.

'Okay, okay,' he nodded, 'I'll keep going to the library and checking... another week.'

'Give or take.'

'Give or take, what?'

'What? Look, could I come in, Ed? I have another question to ask. It's important.'

'Is it for the feature?'

'Very much so.'

'I'm heading out soon,' he said, his hoarse voice making Belle's skin crawl like it was being overrun with ants. 'I'm going to the council offices but I could spare you a couple of minutes.'

He opened the door and stood aside to let her go through. Spanner must have sensed her entrance from his captivity and he greeted her with a renewed bout of barking and frenzied scratching on the door that was blocking his way.

'Behave yourself,' Ed banged his fist on the door. Spanner growled but stopped scratching.

They went through to the kitchen, which was tidier than on her previous visit. Belle didn't take a seat this time and neither did Ed. He leaned on the worktop beside the sink and folded his arms.

'I'm going there to make a complaint,' he said.

They were on parallel conversations again and Belle groaned inwardly. Why did nothing ever come easy?

'I've had it up to here with them bin men,' he slapped his forehead, as though saluting. 'They're going through my rubbish, I've seen them. I told them to stop.'

'Of course.'

'They just laughed at me so now I'll have to go to the council and make a complaint. They've given me no choice.'

'Best to make that complaint... but I wanted to ask you a very, very important question.'

'A formal complaint,' he carried on, 'and if that doesn't work, well, I'll have no choice but to take matters into my own hands.' His voice shook slightly and he looked flushed.

Belle thought he seemed more unstable than before, more lost in the world inside his own strange mind, not really in the physical world. The throbbing in her head intensified. She wanted to do the job she came here to do and get away as quickly as possible.

'It would be a huge help to me if you could take a look at this photo.' Belle held out her phone. On the display was Butthead's photo.

'They underestimate me; they think I'm soft in the head, easy to push over.'

'Please, take a look.' Belle came closer.

'Well, they'll underestimate me at their peril, at their fucking peril.'

He said the last words like he had his hands around somebody's neck and was squeezing with all his might, and he began tapping his forehead quite aggressively. She took a backwards step and wondered if she should run. But no, she wouldn't run, she had to get the answer she came for. She stood her ground, the throb now a full-on thumping headache.

'Ed?'

The mention of his name seemed to snap him out of his fugue state.

'What were you saying?' he asked.

Belle breathed out. 'I wanted to ask if you recognised one of the men in this photo, the bald man on the left?'

Ed looked at the phone, as though noticing it for the first time. 'Could I hold it? My eyesight's not great.'

Belle handed over the phone. He took it and held it close to his face, peering into the display like it was a crystal ball. He repeatedly tapped his forehead, not as forcefully this time.

'Um, okay,' he said, 'um, he looks familiar.'

Belle felt a tiny ripple go down her spine. She'd been right. Somewhere in that foggy head of his was the key. She just needed to keep pressing him.

'You've seen him before, right?'

'I seen him somewhere…'

'Try to think. Maybe you saw him in the building here, maybe the night Fionn was murdered. Might he have been one of the men you saw loitering in the corridor?'

She was leading him, breaking the first rule of interviewing. She was past caring, so long as she got a result.

Ed clucked his tongue. 'Shush, you're putting me off.'

Belle did as she was told.

'I definitely seen him; was it in the building?'

Belle nearly screamed.

Ed shook his head. 'Naw, it wasn't the building, it was the… it was the Post Office. I have it now. He works in the Post Office.'

'What?'

'Or maybe it's somebody that looks like him – it might be his brother I saw. That's it, I know his brother. I think he's Doherty.'

Belle snapped. 'Half the fucking town's Doherty.' Belle grabbed the phone out of his hand and put it in her jacket pocket.

He didn't have a clue, after all. She'd been fooling herself. She so badly wanted to believe that his malfunctioning brain had the answer, she'd been willing him to recognise the man in the photo. Her heart was in her shoes and all she could feel was the beginnings of an oppressive headache. She wanted to cry.

'I may as well go,' she said, resigned. 'Let you get on with your complaint at the council.'

Belle turned on her heel and walked up the hallway towards the front door. She could hear him trotting behind her, talking gibberish as he went about how he'd keep an eye out for the feature and was so looking forward to reading it. She tried not to be angry with him – it wasn't his fault – but even so, she was too deflated to be bothered making small talk.

Spanner whined from his prison as Belle reached the exit.

'I'll let you out,' Ed caught up with her. 'With all the bolts and locks, there's a knack to getting the door open.'

Belle waited, holding down her impatience like a spring as he methodically went through his unlocking routine. She didn't have a word for how disappointed she was. Ed was her last hope and now that was gone. How was she going to get Dermot out? And how was she going to link those Evergreen bastards to what they did to Fionn? Oh shit, it was a disaster. She'd been so sure, too, so—

She saw it before she understood what it meant. She stood frozen, just staring, as everything around her faded into the background.

Lying in the darkened corner behind the door was something that hadn't been there last time. Belle's gaze fixed on it at the same time that her brain scrambled to remember why it was significant.

'Got it,' she barely heard Ed say, as he finally unlocked the door.

Belle reached down and lifted the object in the shadows. 'What's this?' she said, holding her find up to the light.'

'That's mine,' Ed said, looking agitated. 'I need it for self-defence. I keep it behind the door, you know, in case—'

'I didn't see it last time I was here.'

'Um, I don't know what you're talking about.'

And then, all at once, she knew. Understood completely. She'd been so blind, so one-track minded, she'd missed what was right under her nose.

Their eyes met. Specks of red flashed in his pupils. What could he see in her eyes? Realisation?

'Let me out, Ed,' she said, her voice loud and on the edge of hysteria.

'Gimme that,' he said.

He made a grab for what was in her hand but she kept it just beyond his reach.

'I'm not going to do that,' she said. 'Get out of my way.'

'That belongs to me and you need to give it back,' he shouted, angry, scared.

Spanner sensed his master was in trouble and started barking and jumping against the door, thumping and scratching to get out. Ed began slapping his forehead with the palm of his hand, over and over until the skin turned red, repeating the same words 'Give it back, give it back' like he was a cyborg with its neural net fried. Belle half expected his pores to start leaking white fluid any minute.

Without thinking, she pushed him against the wall, the object still in her clutches. Spanner doubled his efforts to come to the rescue. Ed stumbled as she got past him and out to the corridor. But before she could make a run for it, he grabbed her by the hair and tugged it hard. She squealed, dropping to her knees.

Ed stood over her, still entangled in her hair, his face contorted with rage. 'He deserved it,' he screamed. 'He was a noisy pig. He said nasty things about me. He fucking deserved it; he deserved it!'

The clamour brought people from the other flats to their doors.

Belle wailed. She tried to loosen his hold on her hair and the object fell out of her hands, hitting the floor with a loud clang. Ed let go of Belle and darted towards the object. Belle was too dazed to stop him. He clasped it and lifted it up, up over her head.

'He deserved it. And you deserve it, too,' he roared, spittle flying out of his mouth.

To Belle, he looked a hundred feet tall and terrifying. He was unrecognisable.

He was about to bring the object down on her skull when the hand of one of the onlookers came from nowhere and stopped him.

Ed screamed with rage. 'Let go, let me go!'

The man kept his grip on Ed, shouting, 'Somebody help me, for fuck's sake!'

Two others appeared, restraining Ed and arm-locking him to the ground. The object fell just a foot away from Belle and the wrestling men. She seized it, and through teary vision and trembling hands and a shrieking Ed, retrieved her phone.

'I f-found it,' she cried into the phone. 'F-Fairley, I found it, you have to come right now.'

'Who is this?'

'Belle McGee, I've got it in my hand. There's stains... brown.'

'What's in your hand?'

'A ball-peen hammer.'

42

Belle stumbled out of the building, leaving Ed behind with his captors. She slid to the pavement in a broken heap, her back leaning against the wall of the apartment block. Minutes passed like hours before the police roared into the street in a squad car, an unmarked car and two armoured Tangis. If Belle had any doubts whether or not Fairley took her call seriously, this was surely proof positive. She tingled with nervous energy, every part of her body charged.

Fairley hopped out of the unmarked car as it came to a stop and he made a beeline for Belle. Police in riot gear disembarked from the vehicles and stormed the building.

'Let me see it,' Fairley said.

Belle held up her hand. The hammer was gripped so tightly it could've been an extension of her arm, fused with her fingers, part of her as surely as the nose on her face.

'Evidence bag here, right now,' he ordered.

One of his team rushed to Fairley, who pointed to the hammer. Using blue Nitrile gloves, the cop reached out to take the hammer. Belle wouldn't let go.

'Give it to him, McGee,' Fairley said.

'Evidence,' she whispered, 'it's evidence. I can't lose it.'

'Go on,' Fairley encouraged her, 'it'll be in safe hands.'

Belle carefully relaxed her grip, one finger at a time.

'That thing,' she said, referring not to the hammer but to Ed Ramsey, 'that thing killed Fionn. And he nearly killed me, too.'

The realisation was too much to bear. Sobs came forth from the deepest part of her, wracking her body.

Fionn was dead. Gone. Her Greek God, once full of vitality and beauty, cut down in the vilest, ugliest act. Everything was taken away so entirely and so finally. And why? Because somewhere in the grey mass of Ed Ramsey's brain, with its neurons and nerve impulses, was a perfectly rational explanation that made sense of it all.

Belle felt someone kneeling beside her and an arm went round her shoulder. It was Fairley.

Belle cried herself hollow until the tears subsided.

'Are you able to talk?' Fairley asked.

She dried her face with a tissue. 'I think so,' the words came out like a croak. 'What's happening now? Are you going to arrest Ramsey?'

'Already done,' Fairley said. 'He's been taken to the Strand Road.'

Belle breathed out heavily. 'I didn't even notice him being taken away.'

'You had other things on your mind.'

'Will this mean Dermot'll go free?'

'I can't say that for certain—'

'Fuck's sake, I'm on the floor here… literally.'

'Off the record, and because you're on the floor, if the hammer checks out, Mr McDermott will be released.'

Belle put her head in her hands. 'He could've been sent down for life, blamed for killing a man he loved. The criminal justice system had him condemned. If I hadn't gone back for one last desperate try, if I hadn't noticed the hammer, if—'

'Stop, you're torturing yourself when there's no need. Ramsey's in custody.'

'No thanks to you fuckers.'

'We don't always get it right, I accept that.'

'I told you it wasn't him, but you didn't listen.'

'I don't want to nit-pick when you're so upset, however, if you recall, you suspected the security men at Evergreen.'

Belle was about to answer and then stopped. He was right and it wasn't often she found herself agreeing with the PSNI. She'd been as wrongheaded as they'd been. 'I suppose we should call it quits,' she said.

'You did good work,' Fairley said. 'I want to commend you for that.'

Belle leaned her head on the wall, welcoming the coolness of the concrete. 'I was convinced Ed saw the security men that night when probably they were just two random people visiting one of the other flats. I thought it was a matter of asking the right questions to cajole the answers out... Jesus, I had no idea.'

'Let's get you up,' Fairley said. He signalled to two policemen standing nearby and they came over and helped Belle to her feet. 'We'll take you back to the Strand Road and get a statement off you, if you're feeling up to it.'

'I'm up to it, though I don't know if I can drive.'

'Don't worry about that; we'll take you in one of the squad cars.'

'Something occurred to me,' Belle said, pushing her hair back from her face with a shaky hand. 'That print you found in Fionn's blood, the one you couldn't identify... what's the chances it'll match a shoe belonging to Ed.'

'We're taking care of that,' Fairley said.

'He was shouting at me,' Belle said, the memory of Ed's repulsive voice echoing in her head. 'He said he deserved it, he said Fionn deserved it.'

She imagined Fionn lying on the carpet in his flat, his face and head smashed into a bloody mass of flesh. Her body turned cold – somebody stepping on her grave, the old folks would say.

*

The reception area of the Strand Road barracks was empty apart from the duty officer who was behind the security screen. The constable who'd driven Belle from the apartment block directed her towards a chair.

'Wait here,' the constable said. 'I'll find us an interview room. We'll get this done quickly so you can get home.'

Belle closed her eyes and yawned, the stillness of the room filling her with calm. She wished she could lie down somewhere, anywhere, and sleep.

The sound of an electronic buzzer came out of nowhere, jolting her from her drowsy state. The reception door opened and two officers entered. Belle's eyes widened when she saw who they had with them: a handcuffed Butthead, his face like a busted slipper. He spotted her as he was led through the door into the barracks.

Belle wanted to squeal with delight but constrained herself to a smirk. 'You take care of yourself now,' she said, repeating his words to her last time she had seen him. 'You take good care.'

Minutes later, her constable returned and escorted her to an interview room.

'I have a message for you from Superintendent Carruthers,' the constable said, once they were seated. 'He wanted you to know a number of arrests have been made in the illegal dumping case and they've been released on bail.'

'Really?' Belle perked up.

The constable pushed a sheet of paper across the table. 'There you go.'

Belle scanned the paper and managed a second smirk. Tom Sweet's name jumped out at her. She didn't recognise the other names, although she didn't need to know who they were to understand why they were listed: eight Evergreen board members; the chief executive at the Environmental Agency; three of the top brass at the Water Service; five high-ranking officials in council and six councillors; not to mention a dozen or so local businessmen and landowners, including one Eddy O'Dee, who was undoubtedly the mayor's brother.

'I don't see Alan O'Dee on here,' Belle said.

'No, he was released without being charged.'

'Fuck,' she said, 'he's probably the worst of them and he's just going to walk away.'

The constable's expression was blank. 'Whenever you're ready,' he said, 'we can start taking down your statement.'

43

That evening, after giving her statement, Belle drove to Dermot's house. It was empty, as she knew it would be. Staying in the car, she got out her notebook and pen and began writing. Writing and writing without ceasing until half an hour or more had passed. When she was done, she wrapped a clean sheet of paper around the pages to create a makeshift envelope and wrote on the blank sheet, 'To Dermot, I hope you'll understand'. She pushed the correspondence through his letterbox; it would be waiting for him once he came home from jail.

With that done, and exhausted to the point of wanting to fall down dead, she made the journey home. After all that had happened, she deserved to have nothing more to do other than roll into bed. But this eternal, relentless day was not over yet. Her one last task remained before she could return to Dublin, a task that should have been dealt with long, long ago. She spoke a prayer to her soul, willing it to find the strength she needed. Dread, deeper than an ocean, darker than the far side of the moon, rose up from her stomach.

*

Belle stopped the car in the yard. The dogs were tied up for the night and Maeveen's was the only other car there, which meant she was alone in the house. The scene was set.

'You're home,' Maeveen said, as Belle came through to the kitchen.

She was stretched across the armchair beside the range, her legs dangling over the side, holding a mug in one hand and petting the cat with the other as it dozed on her lap. A corner lamp spilled gold against the insipid evening light from the window.

'Any more developments with the investigation?'

'They charged some people, big wigs.'

'I still can't believe they were dumping radioactive shit; I mean, what the actual fuck? It's got me really worried. Are we safe? Will they be able to clean it up? I mean, can they ever properly clean up stuff like that?'

Belle shrugged, lacking the energy to exude any stronger emotion despite having all the same fears as Maeveen. 'They've also arrested Fionn's killer. Just today.'

Maeveen sat up and the cat meowed in protest. 'Oh God, I knew Dermot had to be innocent. Who was it?'

'His neighbour, a man called Ed Ramsey.'

'Ed who?'

'He has mental health problems; he might be psychotic. I think he just snapped and decided Fionn was a threat or a nuisance or some damned thing.'

Maeveen's eyes turned into pools of sorrow. 'That's so horrible – his life cut down because of something so banal, so random. I can't bear to think about it.'

She sobbed for a while. Belle just stared, her dread growing.

'It had nothing to do with the illegal dumping in the end,' Belle said. 'I was way off track.'

'I sort of wish it had been about that, it'd make more sense… better than the truth. Maybe that's stupid.'

'No, I think you're right.'

'And poor Dermot,' Maeveen said. 'At least he's not going to be put away in the wrong.'

'They haven't released him yet but it's only a matter of time.'

Maeveen nodded. 'What about you and him? You seem to be getting close. You going to make a go of it?'

'Dunno,' Belle lied. Of course she knew. After Dermot read her letter, it would put an end to whatever they had together. No more than she deserved.

'I hope you'll give it a chance this time,' Maeveen said, showing Belle a forlorn smile.

Belle inhaled. She forced herself closer and closer to telling Maeveen the truth. It was like teetering on a diving board and she was terrified of jumping. *Do it now*, she urged. *Stop fucking around and do it now*. She thought she might throw up.

'I suppose you'll be heading to Dublin,' Maeveen said, her voice sad, 'with everything you came home for sorted.'

Belle stepped back from the brink. 'I'm going tomorrow, or the day after,' she said, clenching her fists to ride out the turmoil in her gut. *Time to jump*, she thought, *now*.

'Thought you would. I'm sorry about, you know, us having the wee tiff the other night. We always seem to end up doing that, spoiling things.'

There was no mistaking the hurt in Maeveen's voice – sorry, perhaps, to see her little sister leave, in spite of their broken relationship. Belle wanted to cry. It made what she had to do even harder, if that were possible. But do it, she would. Now. Jump.

'Stop, please,' Belle said. 'Don't say sorry, you've done nothing wrong. It's me, it's always me, always my fault.' Her words rushed out, unstoppable.

'That's very harsh, you can't blame your—'

'Maeveen, you don't understand, it really is all my fault. And I made myself pay the price. I deliberately distanced myself, I mean,

I worked at it, staying away, putting up steel walls between you and Mammy. I, you see, I… had to… had to deny myself. I—'

'What're you on about?'

'I sent myself into exile, as soon as I was old enough to leave home, and it was exactly what I deserved.'

'You're scaring me, Belle, I don't understand.'

'How could you?'

Maeveen looked at her with eyes that begged for answers. Tonight she would get them, Belle was determined.

'I need to tell you something… about the day the Gards came for Daddy and Fionn.'

44

DONEGAL, 1986

The still evening air held the warmth of the sinking sun as Belle balanced on the old gate halfway down the lane.

The quiet purr of the blue Sierra interrupted the sour thoughts racing through her mind, the tyres crunching over the shells and sand. She raised her head. Sergeant Buckley stopped at the gate.

'How's it going there, Belle?'

'Hello, Sergeant Buckley.'

'Are you enjoying your summer holidays?'

'Aye, they're great.'

'Hope you young ones aren't sneaking off to the shore. The tide's dangerous.'

'Not this year.'

'That's good, well, I'm away now.'

The car moved off, ever so slowly. So slowly.

Belle returned to her sour thoughts, her only comfort. Where had she left off? Right. Fionn loved Maeveen, she had seen it with her own eyes when they helped Hunter; and he'd said such horrible things to her; and even though she loved him so, so much, he could only see her as a child; and he was up to no good.

The tail of Sergeant Buckley's car vanished round a corner.

Belle hopped off the gate, landing on the grass with a thud. She began walking briskly down the lane. She picked up the pace so she was taking long strides until soon she was running altogether. Turning the bend, she saw the Sierra go round the next corner. She ran faster. Getting to the corner quickly. But not quickly enough. The Sierra was out of sight, only a tell-tale cloud of dust hinting it was ever there.

Belle let go, full pelt, like she was in the hundred-metre sprint at school. The car came into view again. They weren't far from the end of the lane now so she had to hurry.

She went faster, then faster again, until she was up to the passenger door. She knocked on the window, her heart hammering against her chest.

Sergeant Buckley's eyebrows shot up. Belle raised her hand.

He stopped the car. 'What kind of carry-on are you at? You could get hurt chasing after a moving vehicle like that.

'I… I have something to tell you.' The hammering in her chest got louder.

'Take your time, girl.'

She pointed in the direction of home. 'Th… there's… we…' Belle swallowed, her throat dry. 'A man called James Power's staying in our house,' she croaked. 'He's from County Derry somewhere and I… I think he's done something wrong 'cos he's sleeping in the cubbyhole.'

'County Derry?' the sergeant said. 'And he's called James Power?'

Belle noted how grave his face was. He was actually taking her seriously, the way he would an adult. She felt important, but nervous, too.

'That's very interesting, Belle, that's very interesting. I wouldn't mind hearing a bit more.'

*

Belle wandered and wandered and after what felt like an eon, she found herself at the shore, sitting atop a large, flat boulder. She sat with her hands wrapped around her legs, rehearsing in her mind what it was going to be like on the day Sergeant Buckley came back. She smiled as she played and replayed the fantasy of the sergeant finding Fionn and pointing out the error of his ways and warning that if Fionn didn't leave with him now, he'd be a very sorry boy. She saw Fionn's head go down, heard him apologise to the whole family, but most of all to Belle. She forgave him just before the sergeant took him away... and fade. The daydream ended and she started over.

But something was off, the way milk tasted just before it turned bad. Her imaginings always ended with Fionn getting into Sergeant Buckley's car before going back to the beginning. What they left out every time was the next step; what was going to happen to Fionn after the sergeant took him away?

Belle swayed back and forth and as time passed, she realised she didn't feel angry anymore. What she felt was hunger and cold and, worst of all, a nauseating guilt that gnawed at her every nerve-ending.

The daydream ceded into the background and Belle remembered the origami lotus flower Fionn had made 'specially for her. She remembered his card tricks and funny stories and the way he saved Hunter and how he was the most amazing person she'd ever met...

She wanted to take it all back. She wanted to put it right. She had to get home right away and fess up to what she had said to Sergeant Buckley so her mother and father could explain it was all a misunderstanding. It wasn't too late yet.

45

DONEGAL, PRESENT DAY

Belle was done. She had no more to tell. After decades of carrying this disgusting, ugly secret, of never speaking about it even though its stench blighted every part of her – the betrayal of her family, of Fionn, of the IRA, even her country, some would say. She had now, at last, laid it out, not hers to carry any longer, for her sister to see.

Maeveen didn't utter a word when Belle finished. She sat motionless, even when the mug she'd been drinking from dropped out of her hand, falling with a deafening smash on the floor tiles. The tan-coloured liquid inside spilled out, spreading into a shallow pool that drowned every little piece of broken crockery.

Maeveen looked so very small in the armchair, her body shrunken as though she was caving in on herself, her face looking ten years older.

Belle endured the discomfort of the silence.

The kitchen filled with shadows as evening gave way to night, the corner lamp not strong enough to conquer the darkness beyond a few feet.

Belle wished Maeveen would speak.

The rumble of a car engine crashed into the uneasy quiet and the orange beam of car headlights swept across the kitchen ceiling.

Maeveen seemed to snap out of her trance. 'Cillian,' she whispered. 'Thank God, Cillian.'

With the silence broken, Belle dared to say something. 'I want you to know I love you, Maeveen,' she said. 'You're the most precious part of my life. Not a day goes by where I don't think about that moment I went after Buckley, how it might've been so different if I'd just let him drive on. And I've wished a million times I had.'

Maeveen didn't look her way as she went to the back door to greet Cillian.

'Maeveen, I don't expect you to forgive me, I—'

'Belle,' Maeveen slowly turned in Belle's direction; her eyes, narrow slits, 'you said you were going back to Dublin in a day or two, but, you know what?'

Belle held her breath.

'I want you to pack your stuff and leave right now.'

Maeveen's words burned as hot coals in Belle's heart.

'Get out,' Maeveen said, with quiet, suppressed fury. 'Get out of my parents' house before I stab you with something.'

46

DUBLIN, TWO WEEKS LATER

'This is a turning out to be a hell of a story,' Alma Travers poured a generous shot of cognac into two highball glasses. 'Here you go.' She handed Belle one of the glasses.

Belle took it and held it up. 'Slainté.'

'Slainté,' Alma echoed.

Belle should've been on a cloud numbered nine. Alma Travers kept her £133-a-bottle of Rémy Martin XO cognac for very, very special occasions and for very, very special staff reporters. Belle had had this treatment twice before and each time she'd ended up winning an award. No doubt, Alma thought another was on the way.

'You've got the inside track on what's turned out to be the second-biggest waste scandal in Western Europe,' Alma said. 'Corruption right at the heart of politics and the public sector, the environmental devastation, the nuclear hazard – Jesus, that nuclear shit still turns me cold. With all the fear about global warming, the Amazon rainforest, polar ice caps, polluted oceans, disappearing habitats, the public aren't prepared to stand by any longer and let greedy capitalists profiteer at the expense of our planet. Your story's showing them that these people can be stopped.'

Belle threw Alma a half-hearted smile.

'And if that wasn't enough, the man who tipped you off was murdered in an attack so grizzly and banal it gave me nightmares. The suspect the police had in custody wasn't guilty at all and it was you who tracked down the actual killer. You couldn't make it up. All this, when you were supposed to be on leave. Belle McGee, I'm proud of you. Really fucking proud.' She took a swig of brandy and grimaced.

Alma painted her like a surefooted investigator, but the truth was far from that, especially when it came to Ed Ramsey. Giving her credit for tracking him down was a bit of a stretch – stumbling upon him was a better description. Her interest in Ramsey wasn't because she suspected him, but because she thought he held a vital clue. Fairley was able to confirm later that Beavis and Butthead had an alibi for the time of the murder and that his team had discovered two 'heavies' were just visiting one of the other flats. Red herrings. Though not quite, because they were the reason Belle had returned to Ramsey's flat at all. Fairly also told her another interesting nugget: why the hammer was behind the door on her second visit and not her first. Ramsey confessed that he'd kept the hammer hidden out of sight until after the police interviewed him. When he thought the coast was clear, he put it back where it belonged. That made perfect sense in his unfathomable brain.

'It's your exclusive, too,' Alma said. 'Anyone else writing about it will have to write about it second-hand. People will want to read the story from the horse's mouth.'

Belle sipped from her glass, the liquid hot and tingling in her throat and all the way down to her middle. 'There's still guarantee that anybody will be convicted.'

'But boy, isn't there an impressive line-up going to trial?'

'Not Alan O'Dee, the bastard,' Belle said.

'You can't win 'em all.'

'They've hired the best legal representation crooked money can buy. And you know what these cases are like; they can fall on the turn of a penny.' She meant what she said; she wasn't simply being pessimistic. 'The system sucks, Alma. It protects the corrupt, the corporate criminal – it's designed that way. The casualties – ordinary people, society, our environment – none of that matters.'

'Well, write about that, too, show the big picture. Although none of that changes the fact you brought these scumbags and their vile activities into the spotlight. You've got a bestseller here, make no mistake. Every publishing house on this island, maybe farther afield, will be knocking your door down. This is life-changing stuff.'

Belle squirmed, the half-hearted smile still stuck on her face.

Alma took another drink, her eyes trained right at Belle through the distortions of the glass. 'So, why is it you've got a mug on you like a million pounds of debt?'

'I'm just tired, that's all.'

'Aw, come on, who do you think you're kidding? Tired? You'll have to come up with a better excuse than that.'

'It's nothing to do with the story,' Belle said. 'I'm happy enough with how it's working out.'

'So, what is it?'

Belle sighed. 'It's complicated.'

'Most things are.'

'The man who was murdered; he wasn't some randomer. He was very special to me... very special...'

'I know, and you got justice for him, for his family. You made sure an innocent man didn't go down for his murder. Weren't they cousins, too?'

Belle nodded.

'Can you imagine the irreparable hurt for that family to believe one of their own killed Fionn? You're a fucking hero to those people.'

Belle wondered what Alma would think if she knew the truth, that Belle might've saved Dermot from a prison sentence, but she'd been the cause of Fionn – and her father – getting one. That didn't sound so heroic.

'Maybe I had a lot to make up for, Alma.'

'I find that hard to believe.'

'It goes back a long way.'

'Talk to me then.'

Belle swallowed what was left in her glass. How could she talk to Alma about it when she'd barely been able to tell Maeveen? 'Maybe another time,' she said, 'when it's clearer in my head.'

Alma pursed her lips. 'Well, you know where I am if those thoughts do get clearer.'

Belle's phoned vibrated with an incoming text. Might it be from Dermot? Maeveen? She hadn't heard from either of them. Dermot would have seen her tell-all letter by now. She thought he might at least want an explanation or to give her a piece of his mind or something. Anything but this snub. She let her eyes fall on the display. A yearning pang twisted like a piece of glass in her chest. The text was from no one important.

'Alma, do you mind if I nip off early today?'

'Go ahead.' Alma put away her precious brandy. 'But don't forget drinks tonight in O'Sullivan's. And remember, everybody wants you there to congratulate you, so no mopey face and no trying to get out of it.'

'Yes, ma'am,' Belle saluted as she left Alma's office, faking her best smile.

*

Back home, Belle dropped her coat and laptop bag in the hallway and kicked off her shoes. All she wanted was to get into bed, under the covers, and close out the world for a couple of hours.

311

She picked up her post, which was lying on the carpet by the door. One of the letters was junk mail. The other was a white handwritten envelope. Belle was curious. A British stamp was stuck to the top right-hand corner, the Queen's head upside down, and the postmark read '*Londonderry*'. Her breath quickened, her skin turned cold. She ripped the envelope apart to reveal a folded piece of paper, just the one, handwriting on either side. With clammy hands, she opened the paper out and went straight to the sign-off. Her heart soared. Dermot. It was from Dermot:

Dear McGee,

I hope this letter finds you well. I don't often put pen to paper these days but it seemed right this time, so here goes.

I got released, you probably know, and I heard the craic about you and Ed Ramsey. That bin lid nearly killed you. And he did kill Fionn. Fuck. I still can't hardly believe that. You caught him though. You saved me, got justice for Fionn. I'll never forget that, McGee, as long as I live.

I've been buying the Spectator every day and reading your articles on the whole dumping thing. You're seriously doing Fionn proud and thanks for acknowledging him. Chrissie was well pleased, we're all well pleased.

Ah, so what do I say next? I'm not used to this.

I suppose I should just come out with it. I read your letter. The one you pushed through my letterbox.

It hit me as hard as a policeman's boot to the balls. Worse.

You're a good person, McGee, that's for sure, but it was a terrible thing you did, even though you were only a wean, it caused a lot of fucking harm. Though no point me going on about it, I won't be able to tell you anything you haven't thought yourself.

Can you believe it's taken me half an hour to write this far? Fuck sake, glad I don't have your job.

I'm picturing you back in Dublin now, back in your life with your work and your friends and your house, and not giving a second thought to us up North.

I miss you, like I really miss you, and I think every day about the times we had together. It was the happiest I'd been in a long while. But that letter. McGee, fuck it, I just can't get over it.

Maybe someday I will, I hope so.

Look after yourself, Baby Belle, I'll always care about you.

Dermot.

Belle let go of the letter. It fluttered to the floor. He'd been more forgiving than she'd expected and for that she was grateful. But she realised now she wanted more. She wanted to be with him, no matter how irrational or fantastical the notion.

She felt numb except for a gaping, empty pain in her chest. She knew she should cry now, fall down on the floor and scream sobs. But nothing would come, nothing but that empty pain. She couldn't bear to stay awake a minute longer.

She limped to the bedroom, pulled the heavy drapes to block out the light, and curled up into the foetal position on her bed. The cotton sheets were cold against her skin and she shivered until the heat of her body warmed them. Her head was as heavy as a boulder and it sank deep into the pillow, immersing her in the fresh smell of the fabric. Like the air at home... her eyelids closed... the wide, open air at home.

*

Belle sprang up with a gasp. For those seconds after waking, she didn't know where she was or what day it was. Then she remembered. She was in Dublin. Today was Thursday. She'd read Dermot's letter. She reached for her phone on the bedside table and checked the time. After six.

Her head was still heavy and she fell back onto the pillow. The air made a whistling sound as she breathed in and out through her nose, soothing her with its regular rhythm. It reminded her of home and lazy Saturday mornings and the summer of 1986, that endless, beautiful, terrible summer.

Did 1986 jump into her mind because she'd seen him unbeknownst to herself? Over there, in the shifting light and shadows?

He was standing in the stillness.

Looking at her.

She couldn't see his face but she knew he was smiling.

'Fionn? I'm sorry.'

The words stuck in her throat and tears burned like acid.

She heard his voice whisper in her head.

Forgive yourself.

Without warning, the doorbell sounded, its chime exploding like a bomb in the pure silence. Belle's heart jumped.

He was gone.

She was alone.

The bell went again.

Belle considered not answering but something told her she should. She dragged herself from the bed, hoping whoever it was would be easy to get rid of.

She reached the door and slowly pulled it open, and when she did, she thought she would burst.

There, standing on the step, her smile lighting up her beautiful brown eyes, was the person Belle most loved in the world.

Maeveen.